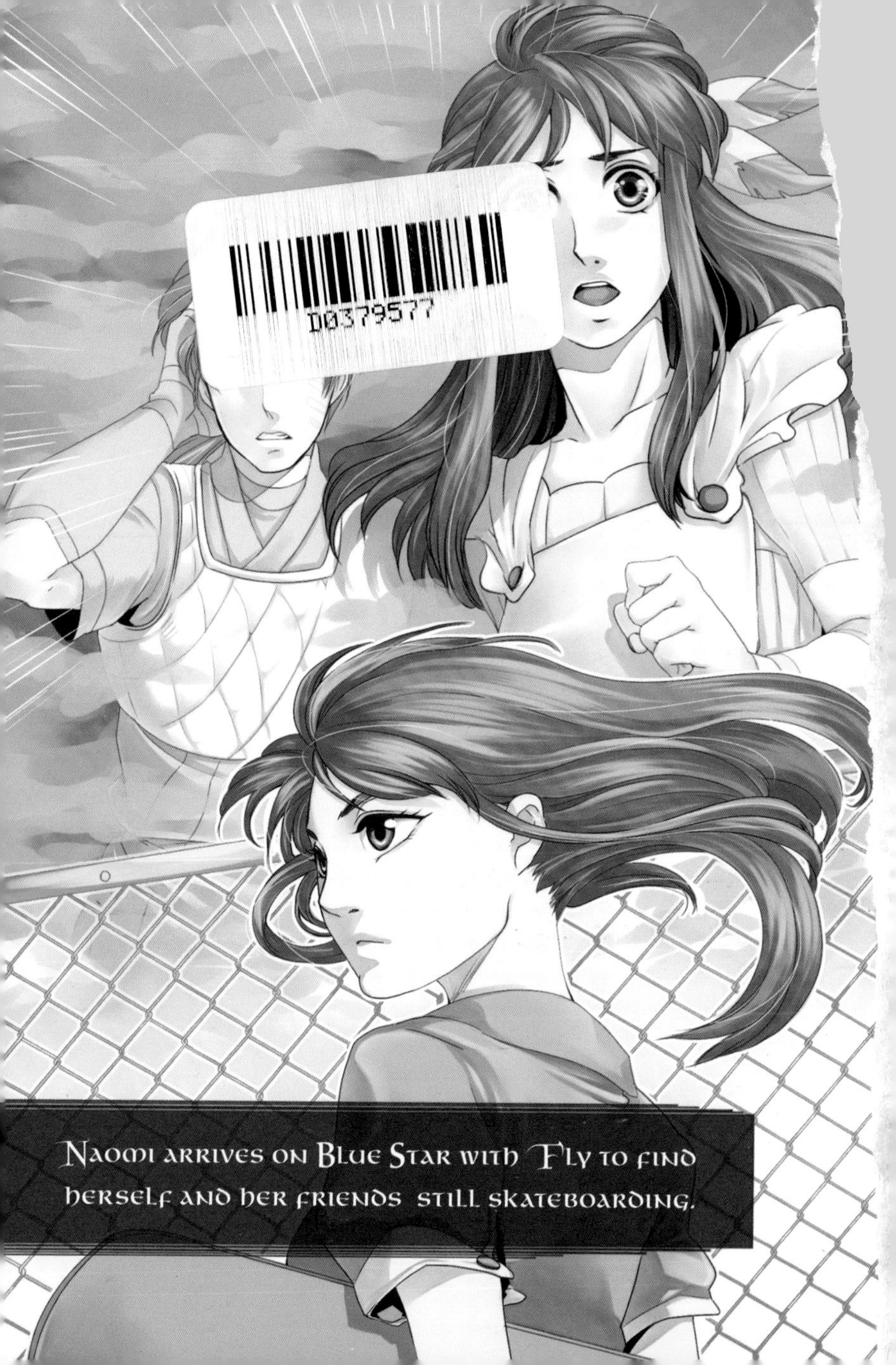
Naomi arrives on Blue Star with Fly to find herself and her friends still skateboarding.

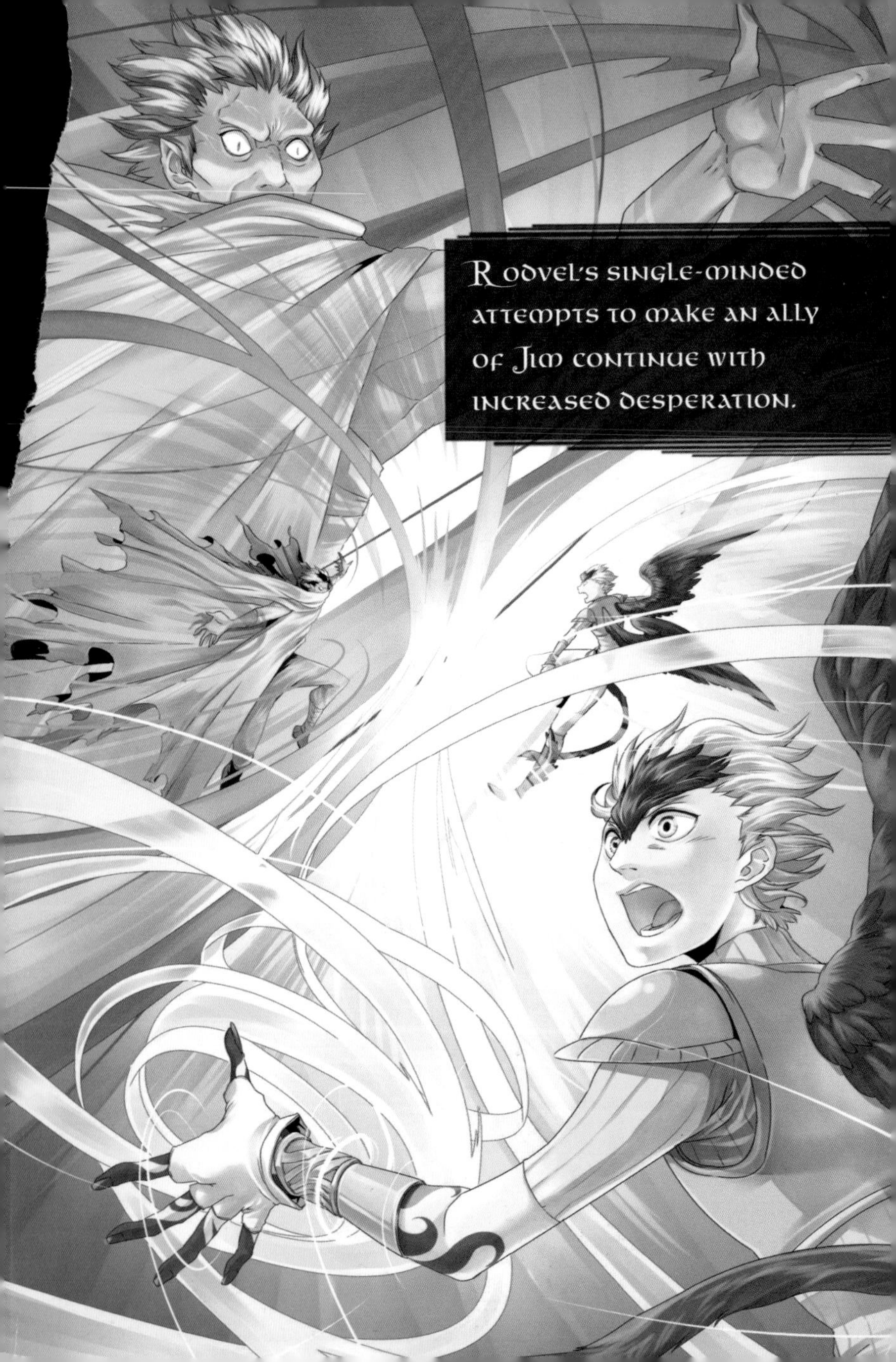
Rodvel's single-minded attempts to make an ally of Jim continue with increased desperation.

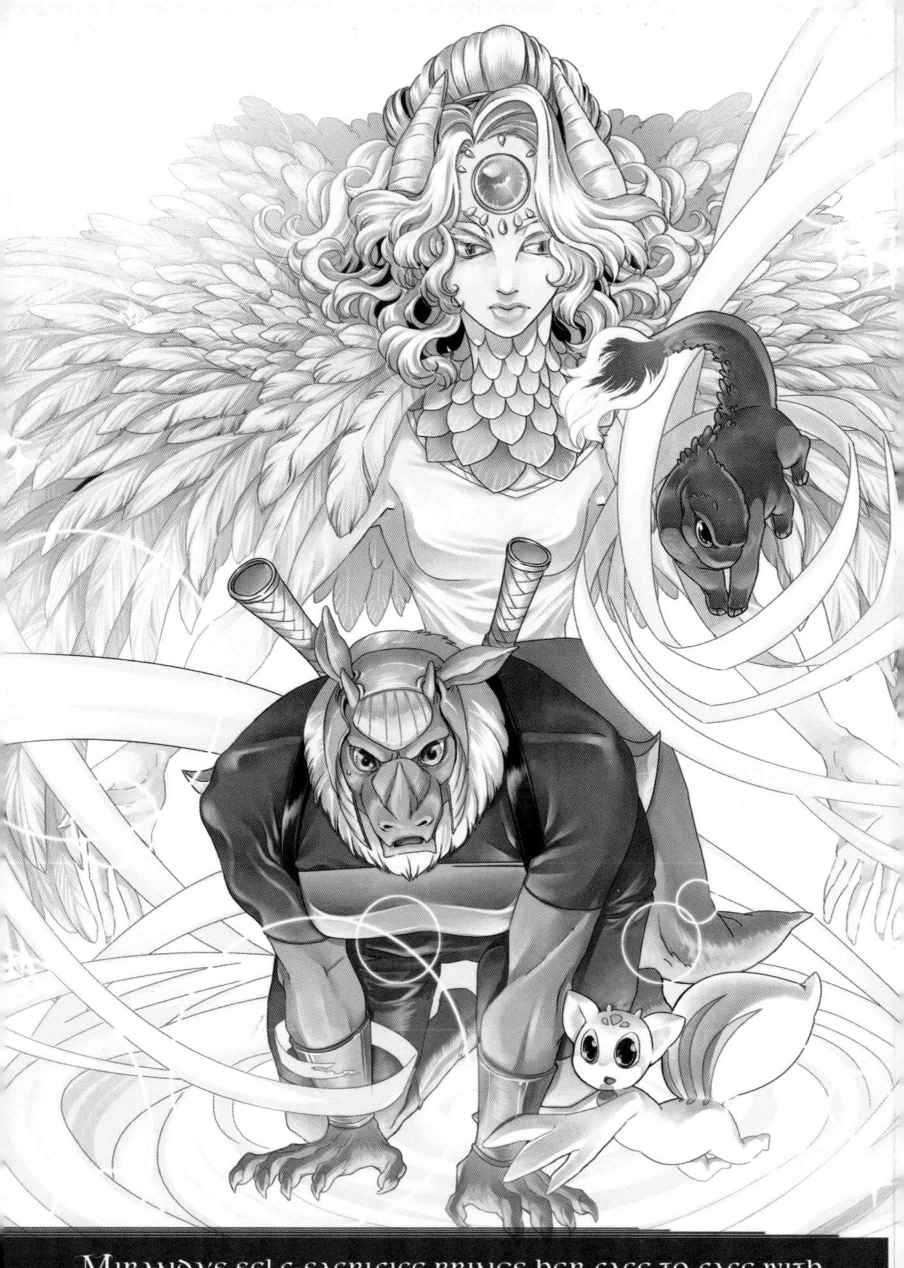

Miranda's self-sacrifice brings her face to face with the Tientiyu. Soleite's destiny finally becomes clear.

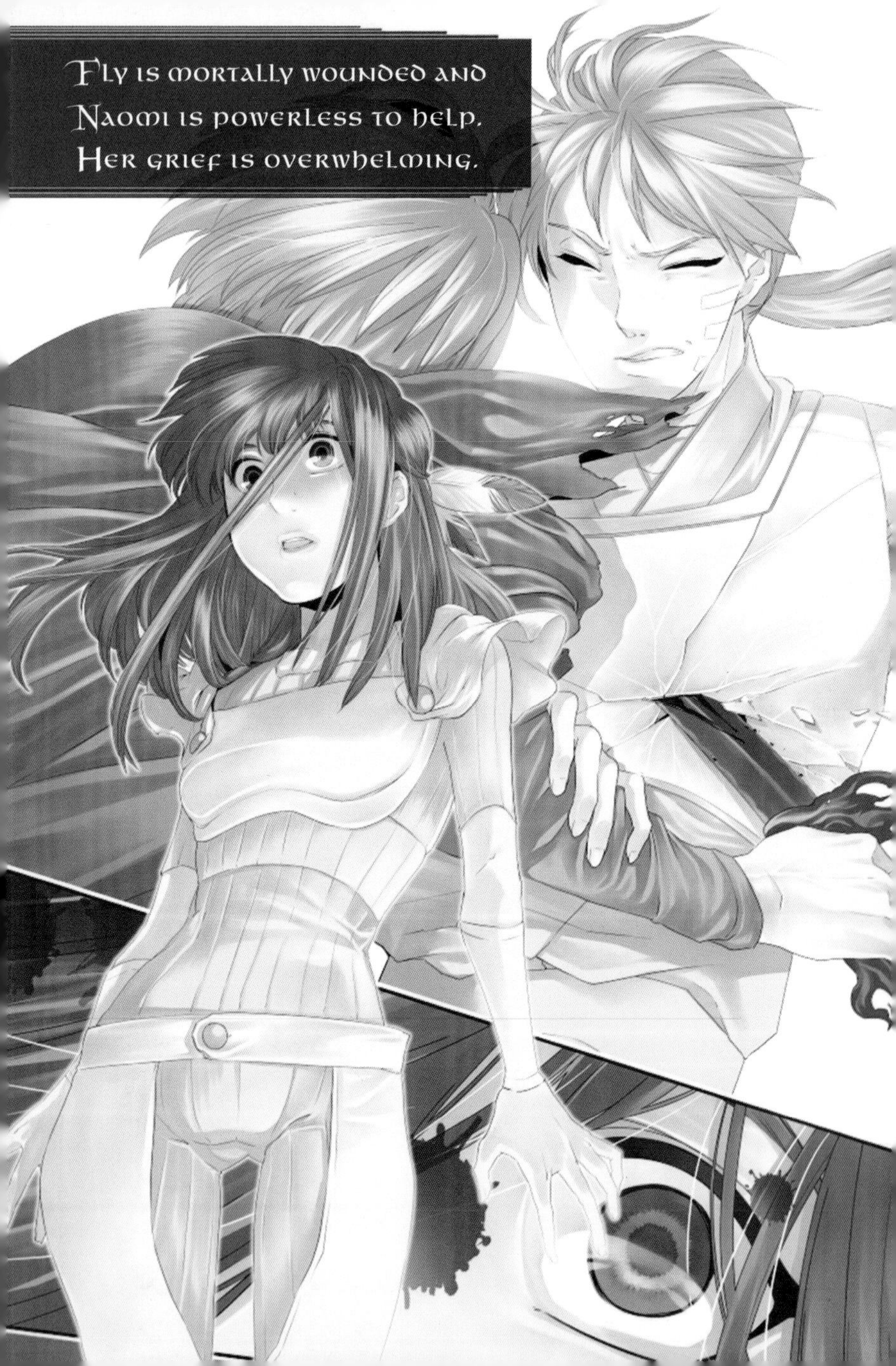
Fly is mortally wounded and
Naomi is powerless to help.
Her grief is overwhelming.

VERMONIA

RETURN OF THE QUEEN

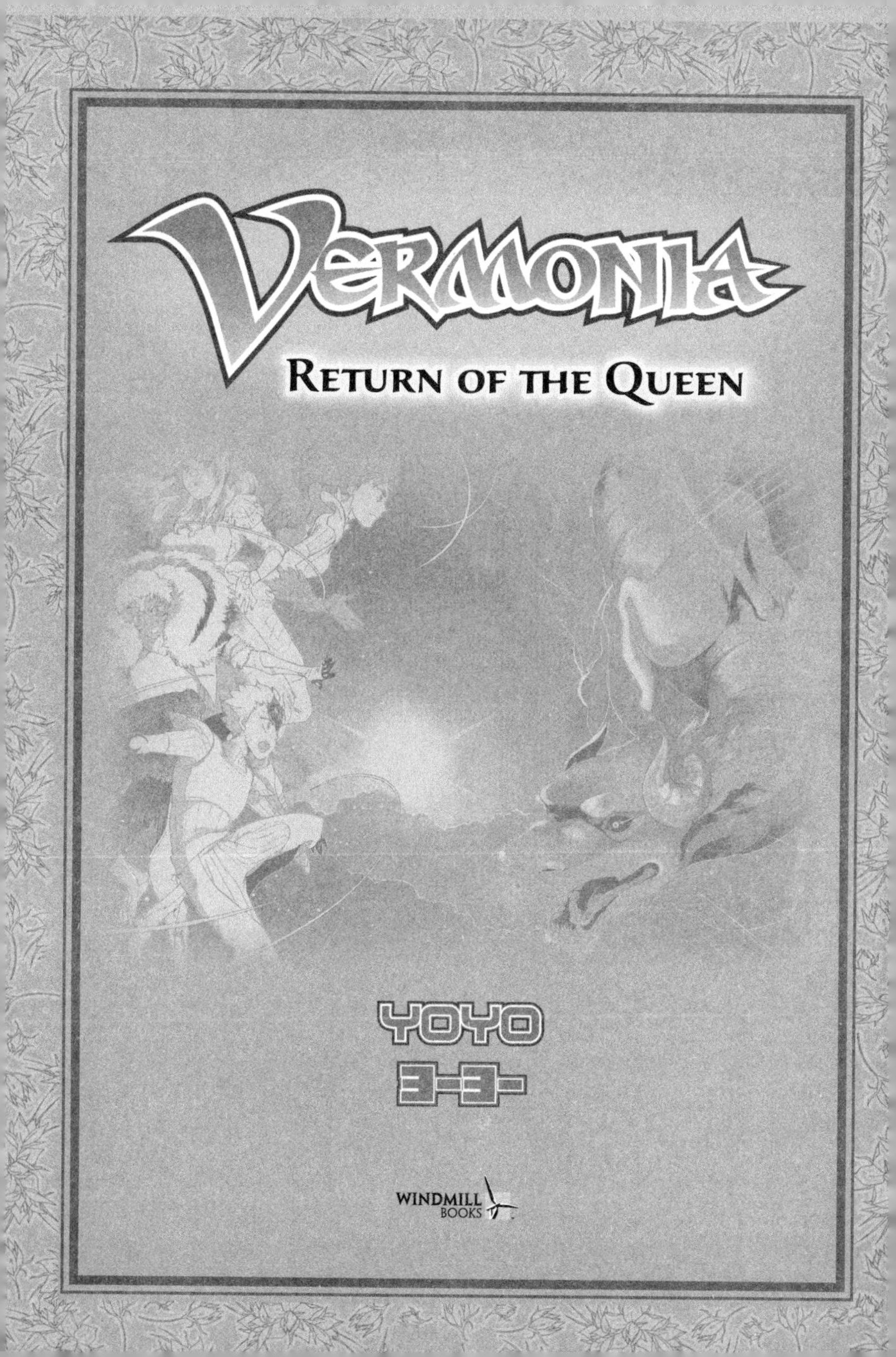

YOYO

ヨーヨー

WINDMILL BOOKS

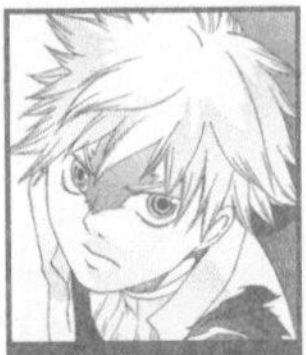

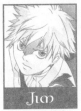

Jim

Bass Player
Blue Star Warrior

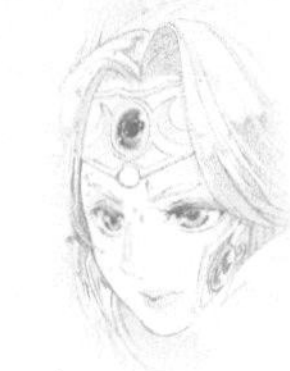

Frasinella

Queen of Vermonia

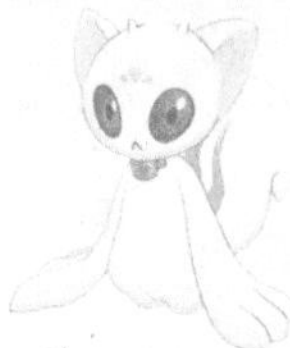

Satorin

Magical Squelp

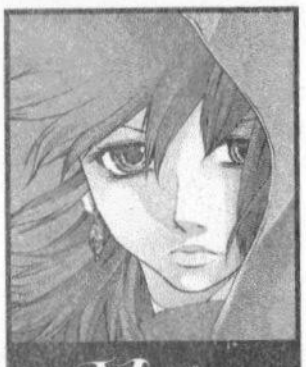

Mel

Lead Vocalist
Blue Star Warrior

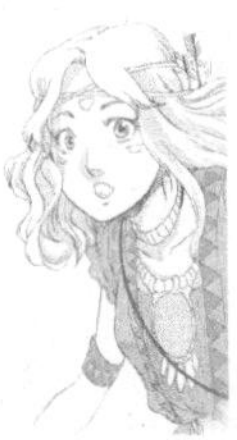

Rainbow

Bard of the Potonawi

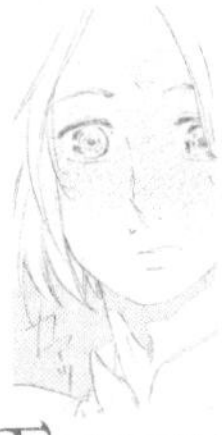

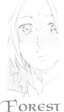

Forest

Bard of the Potonawi

When Jim, Doug, and Naomi, three skateboarders from Union City, left their home in pursuit of their kidnapped friend Mel, they could never have imagined that their journey to the Turtle Realm would thrust them into the forefront of a titanic battle against General Uro, Master of dark Yami magic. Throughout seven action-packed volumes, the kids, supported by their personal power animals from the kingdom of Vermonia, have fought against Uro's soldiers led by Captain Acidulous. They have been welcomed by the tribes of the Turtle Realm and together with their warriors have valiantly defended the four pillars upon which the Turtle Realm rests. But to no avail.

In volume 7, the Pillar of Wind is the only one left standing, creating extreme weather in the Turtle Realm and all the way to Blue Star where Fly and Naomi witness life in Union City. But the two warriors are anxious to get back to the battle because they recognize that all hands are needed against the overwhelming advantage enjoyed by Uro's superior forces. Mel's gift of foresight is futile against destiny but still she tries to prevent the two from returning. Alas, once Fly returns, he joins Miranda among the fallen. Forest walks into his sister's arms through rivulets of blood.

Uro's impatience with victory is increased by his impatience to obtain the Bolirium. In his frustration he visits the Squelp Satorin looking for answers. He gets none and Satoran pays with her life. Suiran emerges to bring Ruka to Mel but their merging does not bring her back to fight with her friends. Will the Blue Star Warriors ultimately fail in their quest to save the Turtle Realm? Will they be submerged in Yami never to return to Union City and their families and friends? All might be set right if the Bolirium should fall into the right hands. But Uro's reach extends farther than anyone's and the prize seems within his grasp.

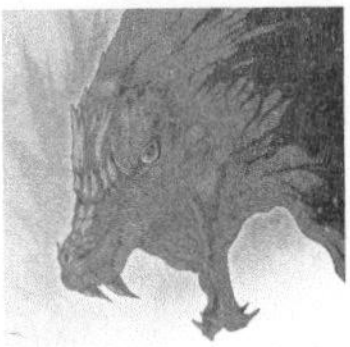

Uro

Master of Dark Yami Magic

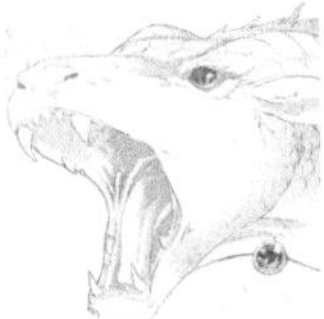

Boros

Master of Hikari, the Bright Light

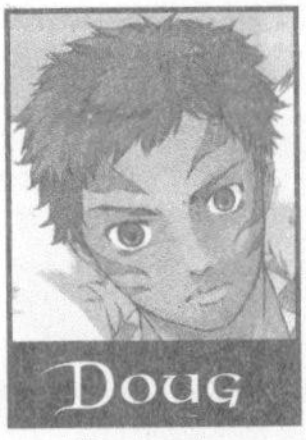

Doug

Drummer
Blue Star Warrior

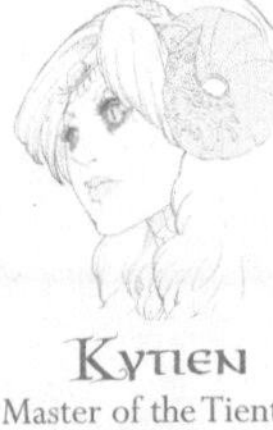

Kytien

Master of the Tientiyu

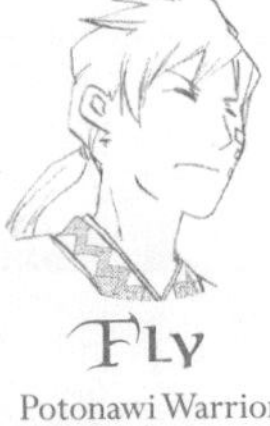

Fly

Potonawi Warrior

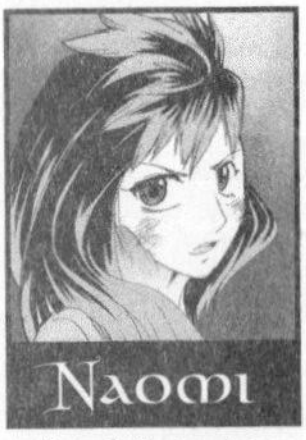

Naomi

Lead Guitarist
Blue Star Warrior

FOR MORE INFORMATION GO TO VERMONIA.COM

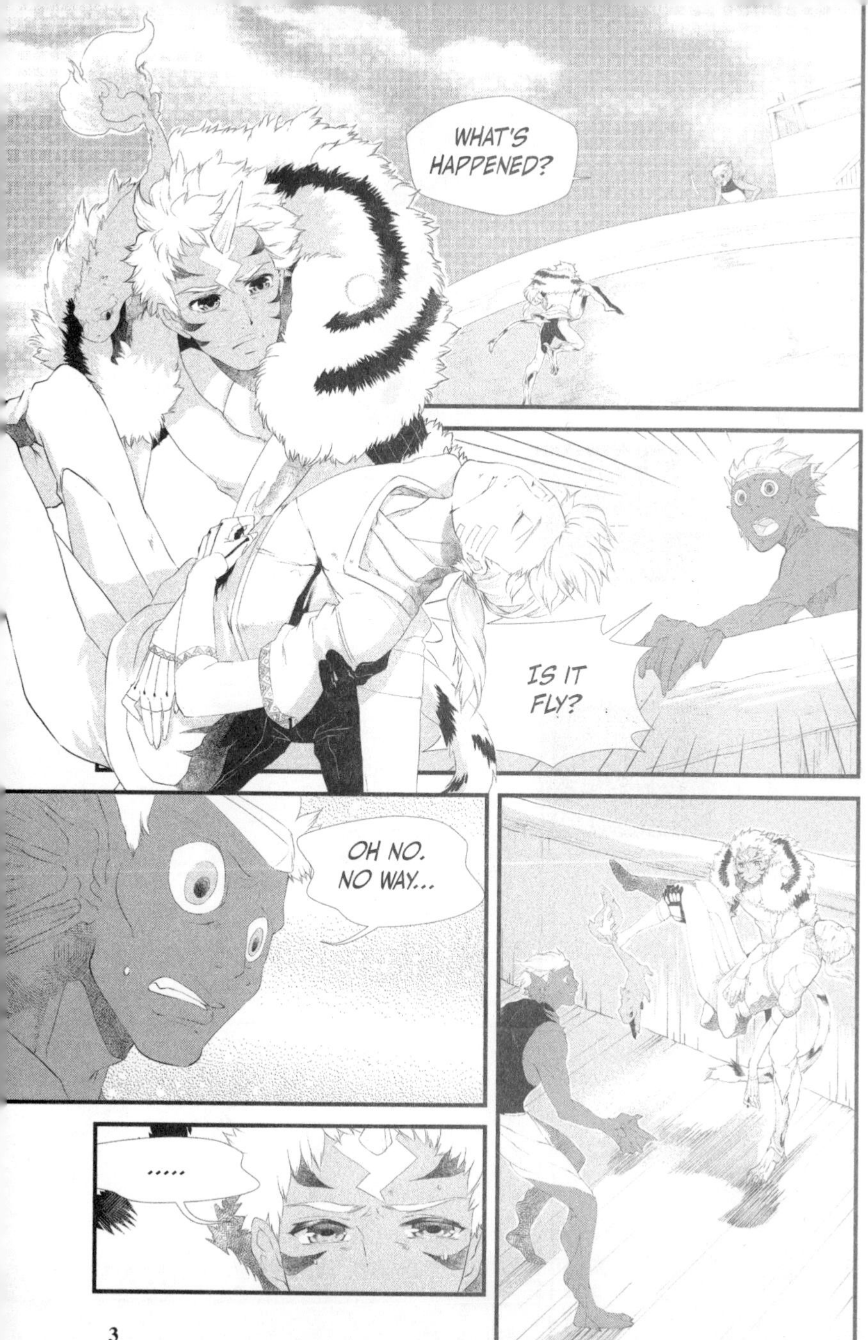
WHAT'S HAPPENED?
IS IT FLY?
OH NO. NO WAY...
.....

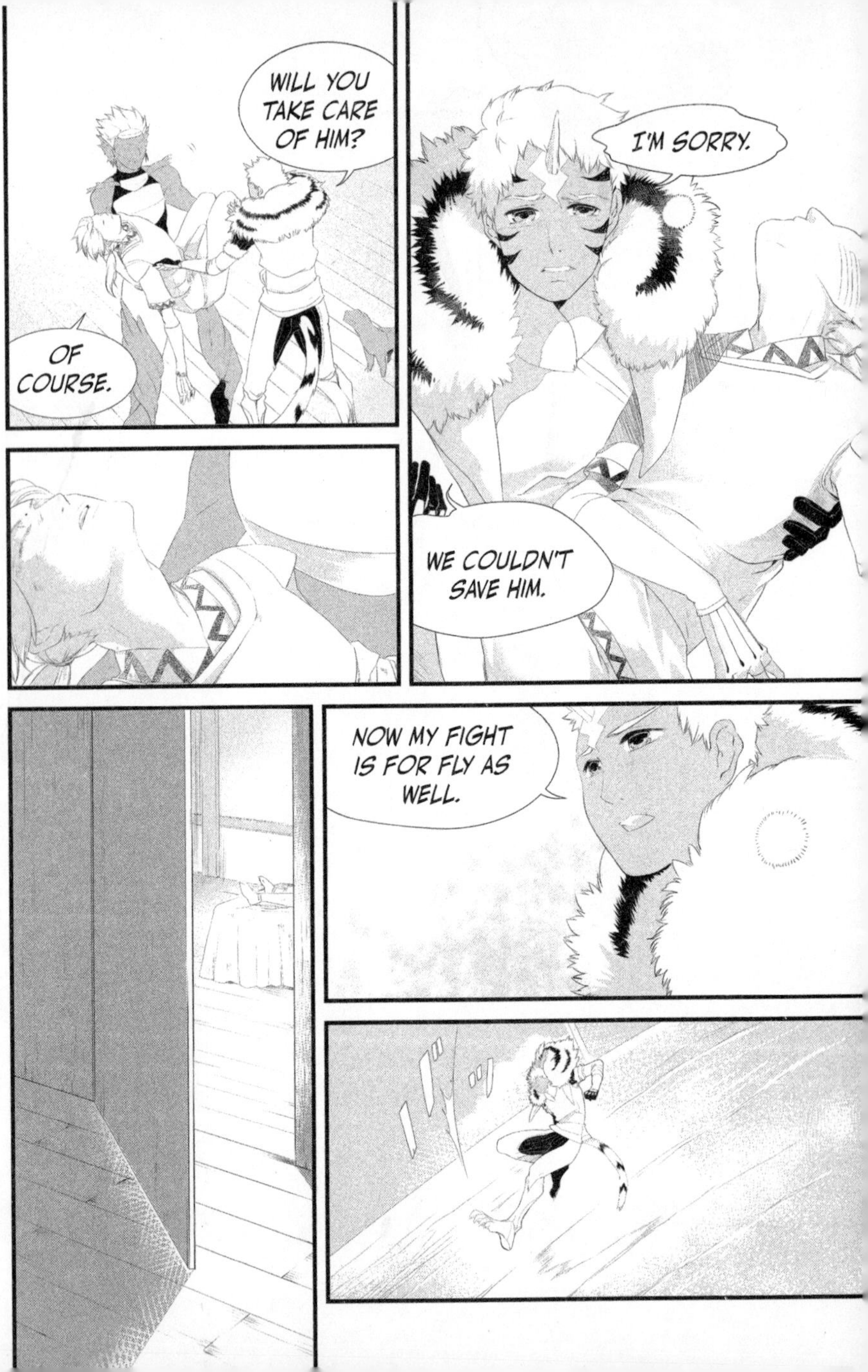
I'M SORRY.
WE COULDN'T SAVE HIM.
WILL YOU TAKE CARE OF HIM?
OF COURSE.
NOW MY FIGHT IS FOR FLY AS WELL.

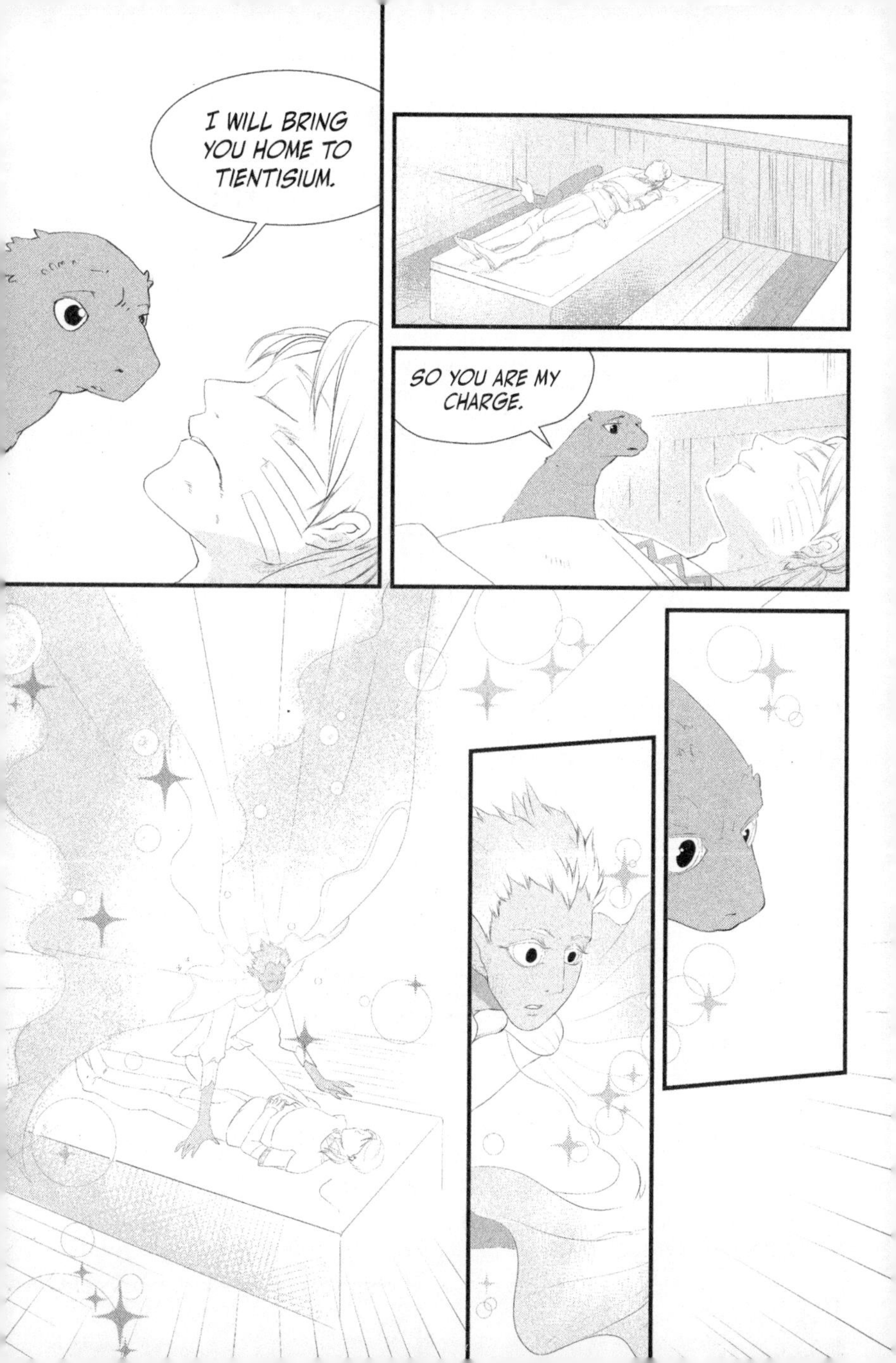
SO YOU ARE MY CHARGE.
I WILL BRING YOU HOME TO TIENTISIUM.

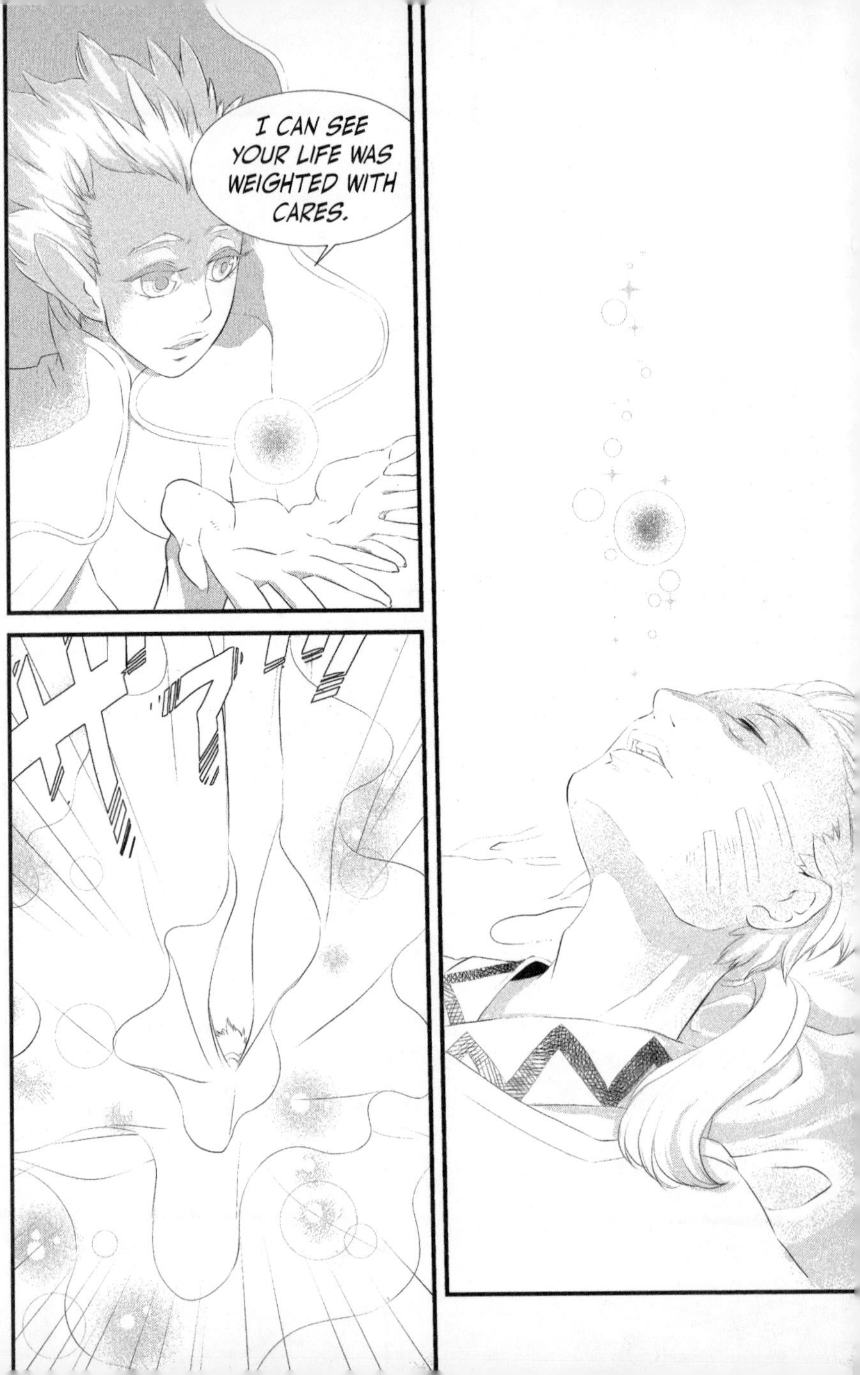
I CAN SEE YOUR LIFE WAS WEIGHTED WITH CARES.

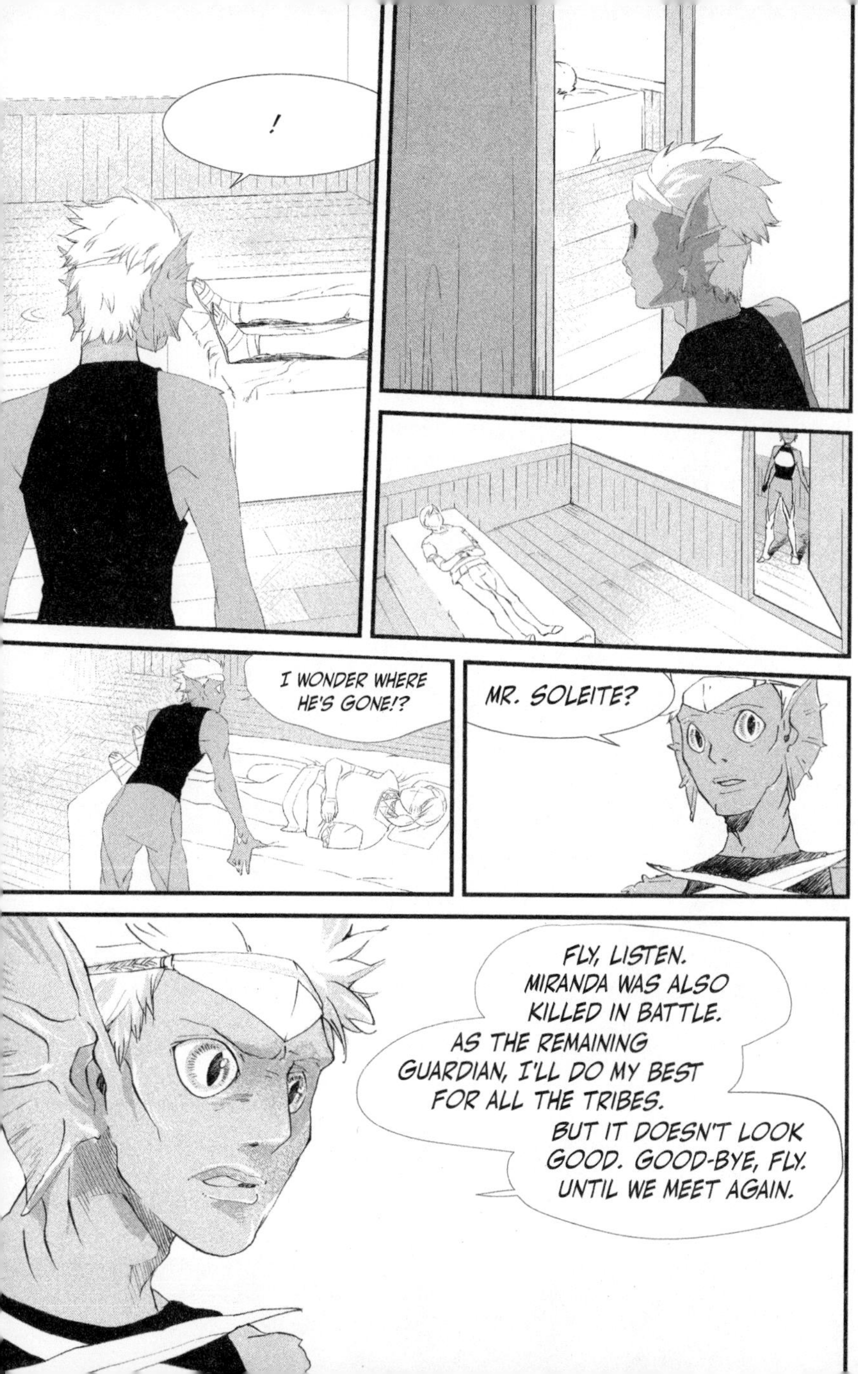
!
MR. SOLEITE?
I WONDER WHERE HE'S GONE!?
FLY, LISTEN. MIRANDA WAS ALSO KILLED IN BATTLE. AS THE REMAINING GUARDIAN, I'LL DO MY BEST FOR ALL THE TRIBES. BUT IT DOESN'T LOOK GOOD. GOOD-BYE, FLY. UNTIL WE MEET AGAIN.

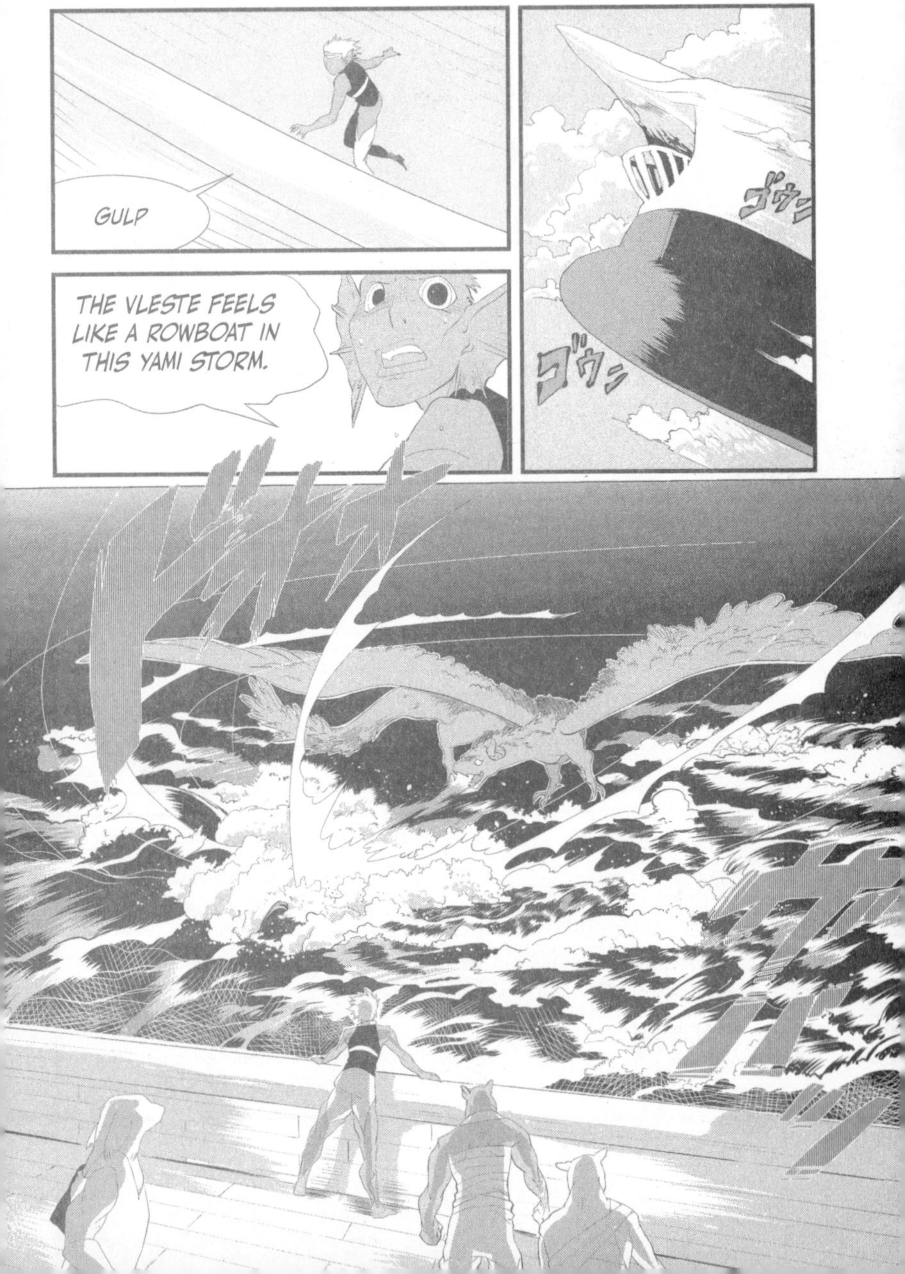

GULP
THE VLESTE FEELS LIKE A ROWBOAT IN THIS YAMI STORM.

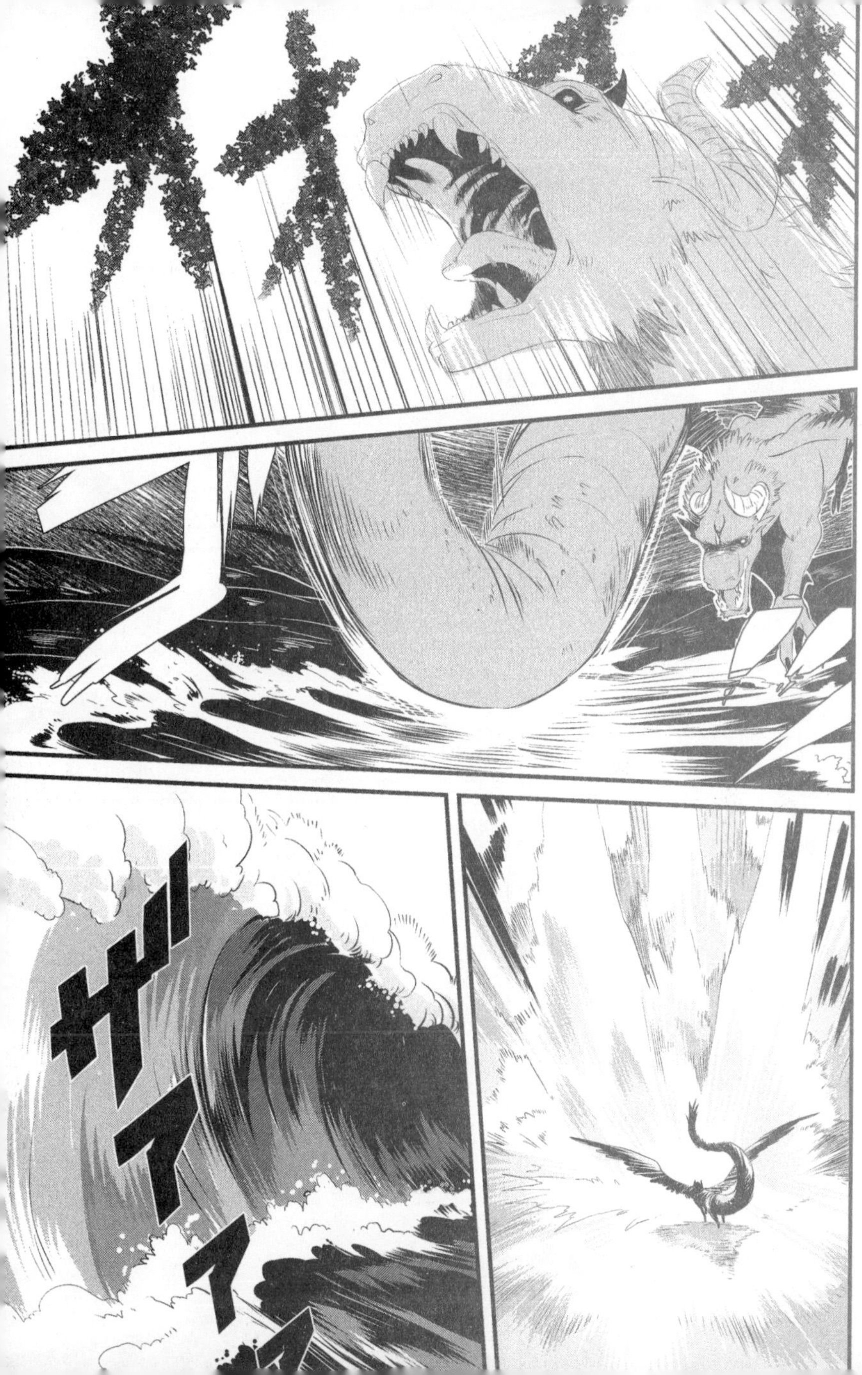
ザァァ

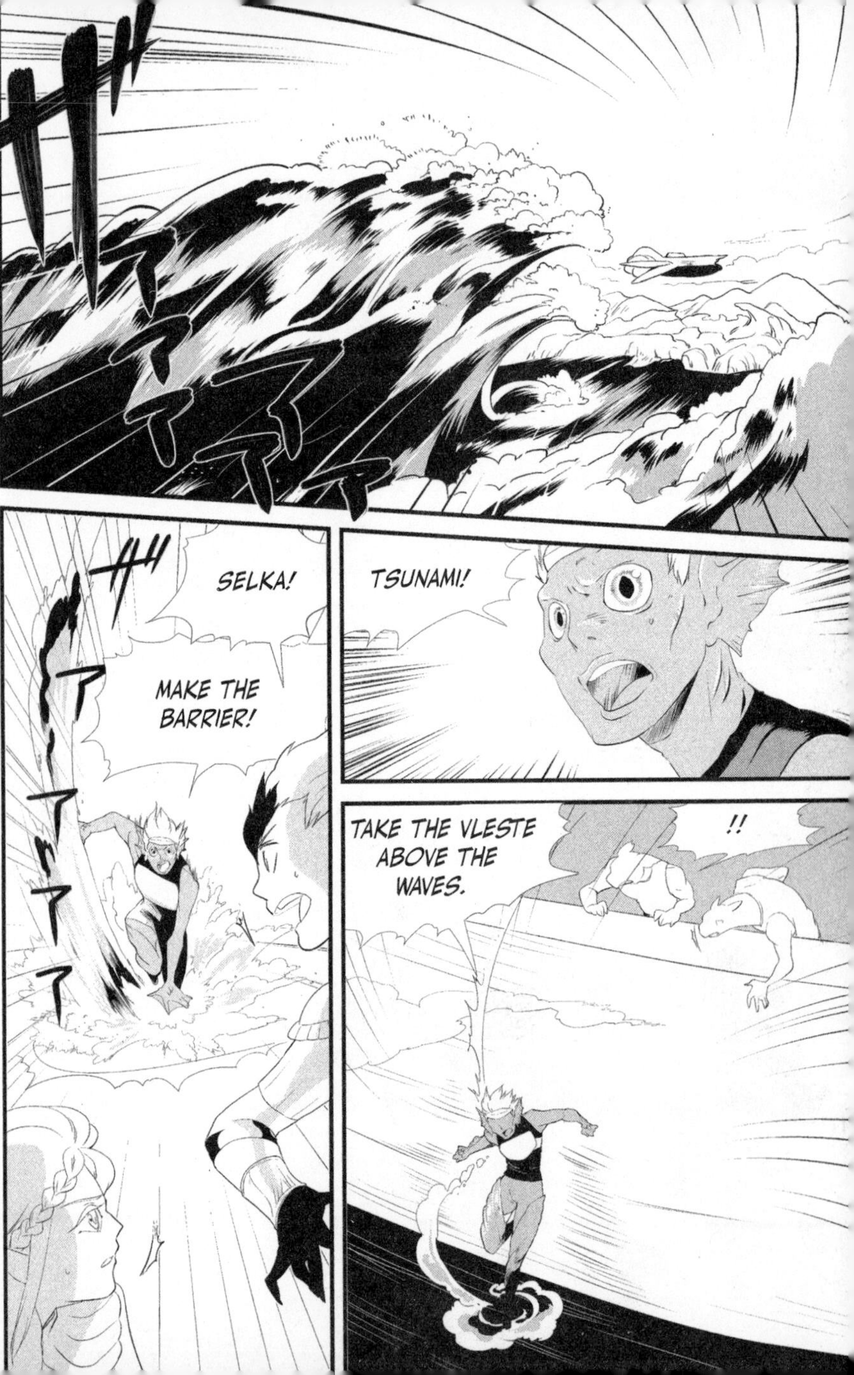
TSUNAMI!
TAKE THE VLESTE ABOVE THE WAVES.
!!
SELKA!
MAKE THE BARRIER!

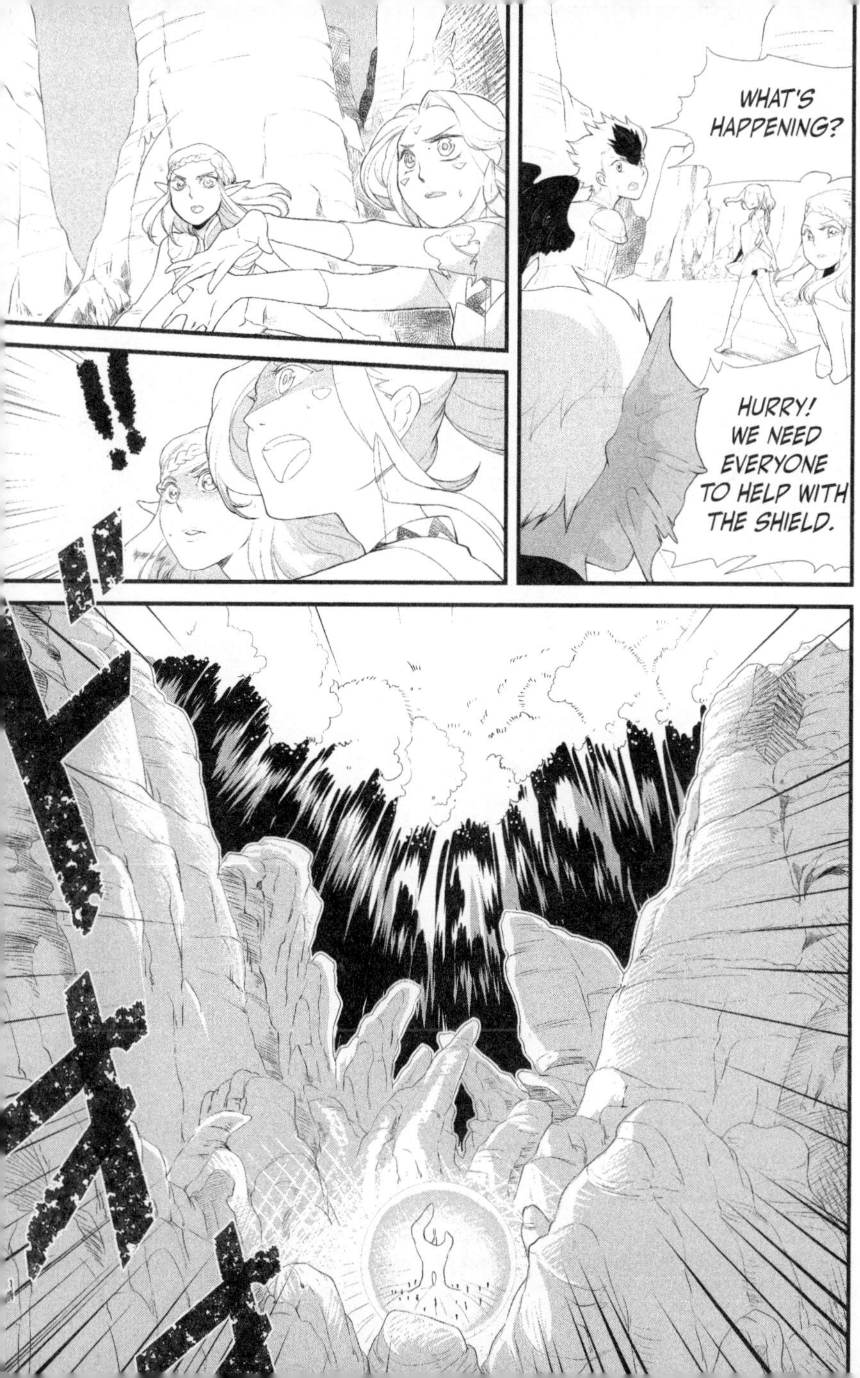
WHAT'S HAPPENING?
HURRY! WE NEED EVERYONE TO HELP WITH THE SHIELD.
!!

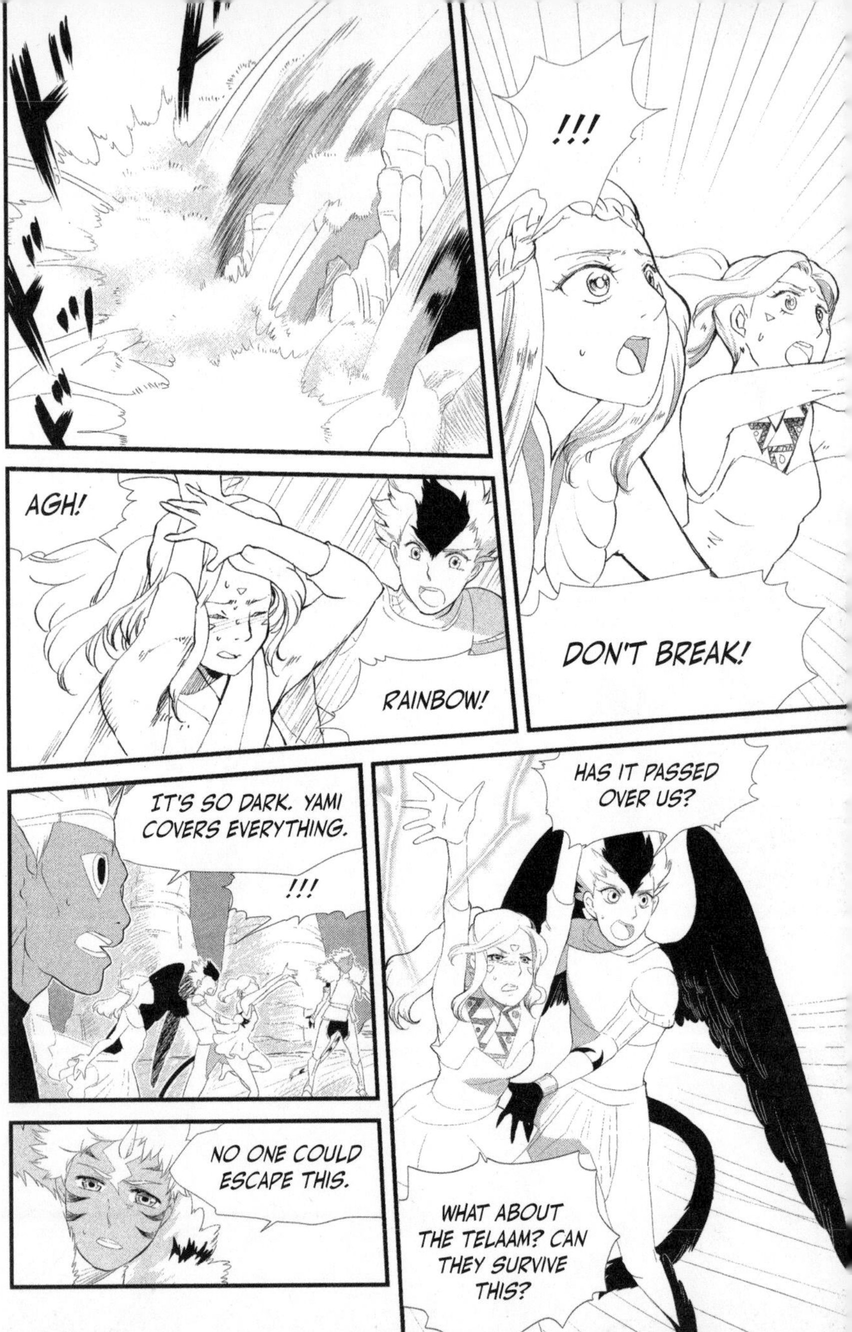
!!!
DON'T BREAK!
AGH!
RAINBOW!
HAS IT PASSED OVER US?
WHAT ABOUT THE TELAAM? CAN THEY SURVIVE THIS?
IT'S SO DARK. YAMI COVERS EVERYTHING.
!!!
NO ONE COULD ESCAPE THIS.

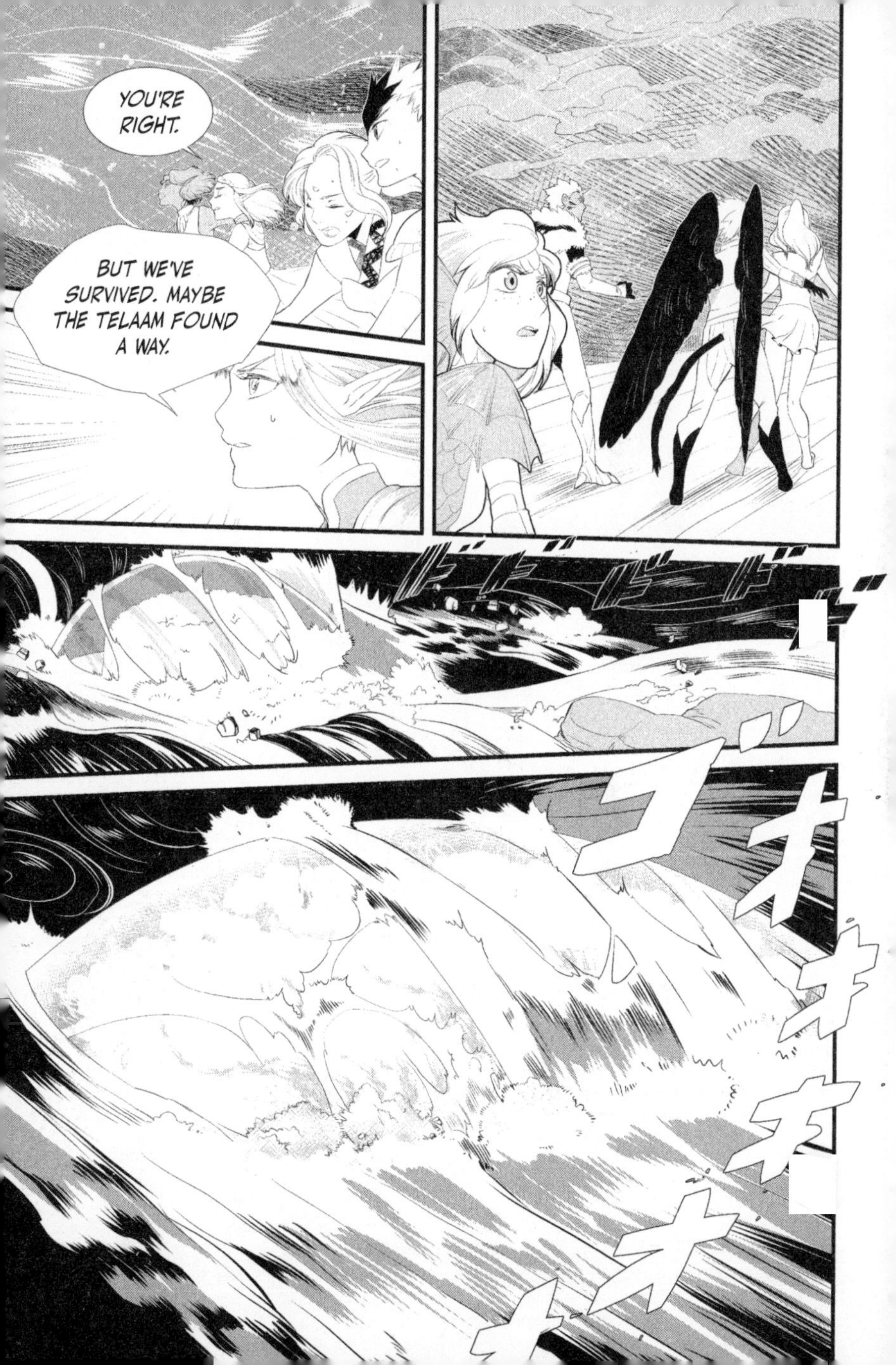
YOU'RE RIGHT.
BUT WE'VE SURVIVED. MAYBE THE TELAAM FOUND A WAY.

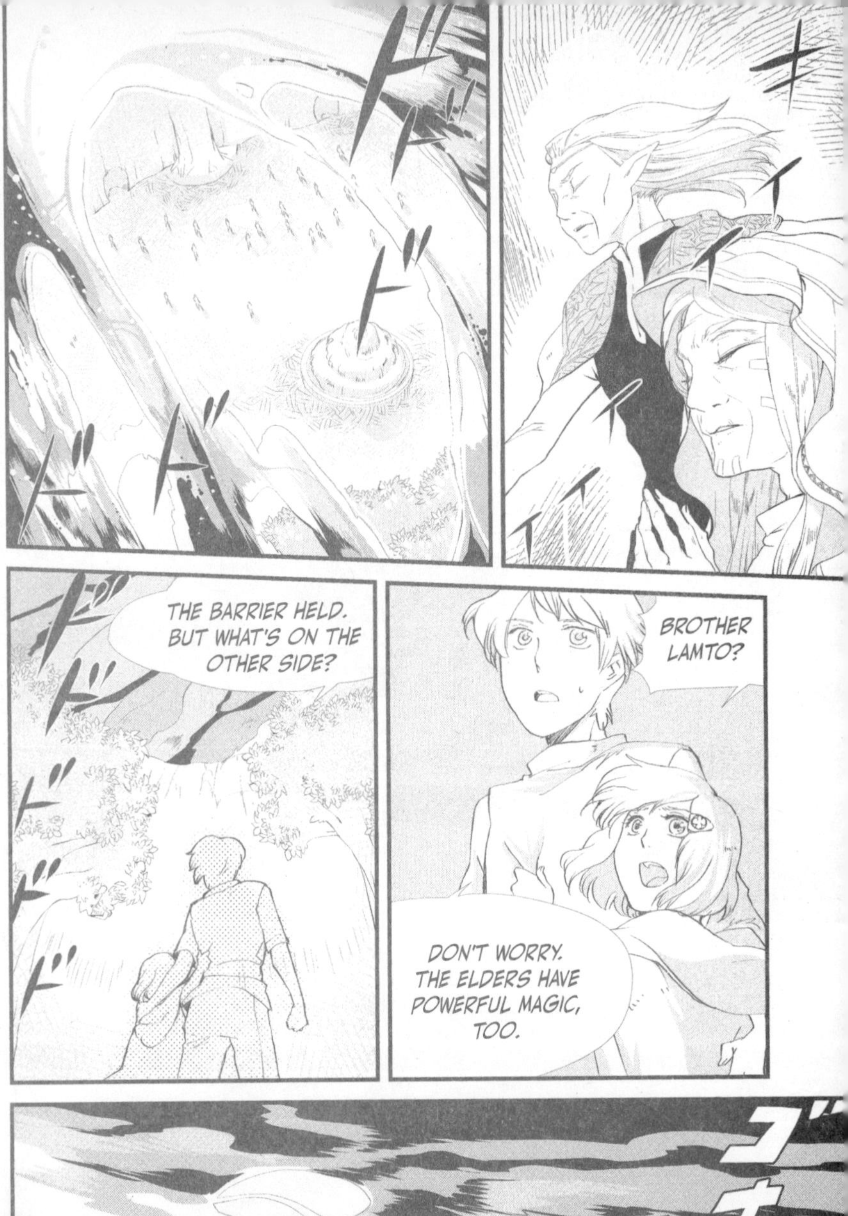
BROTHER LAMTO?
DON'T WORRY. THE ELDERS HAVE POWERFUL MAGIC, TOO.
THE BARRIER HELD. BUT WHAT'S ON THE OTHER SIDE?

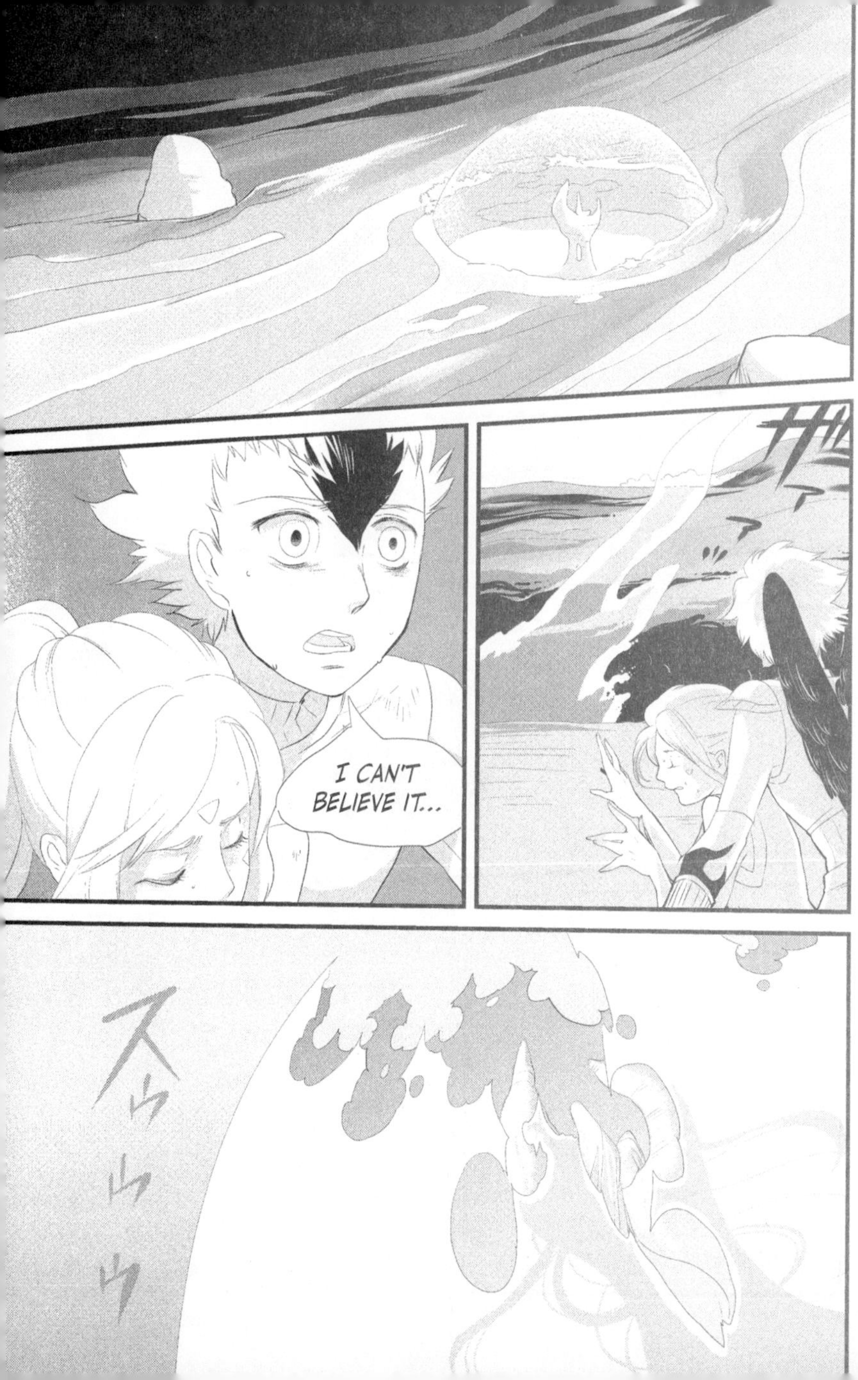
I CAN'T BELIEVE IT...
スゥゥゥ

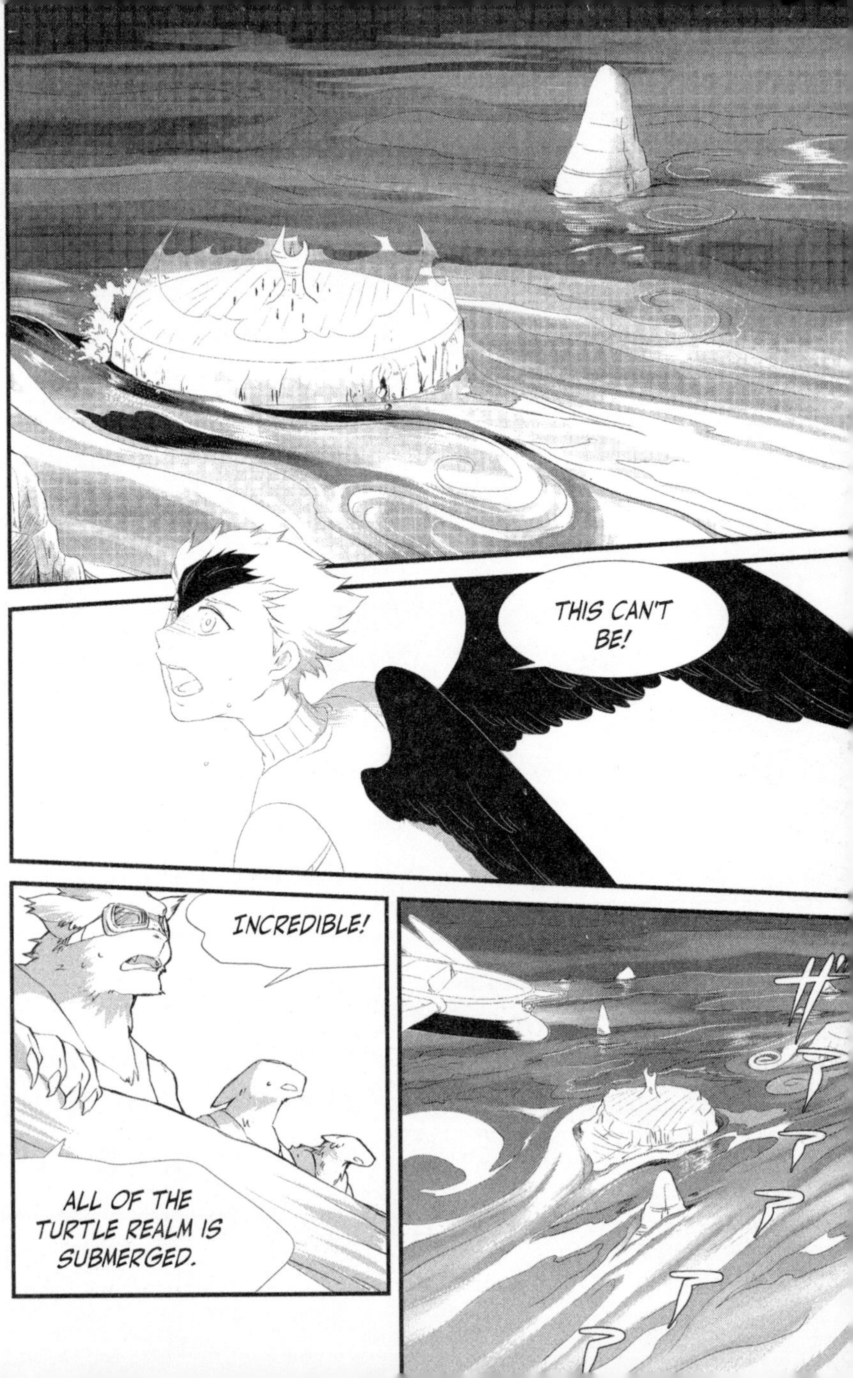
THIS CAN'T BE!
INCREDIBLE!
ALL OF THE TURTLE REALM IS SUBMERGED.

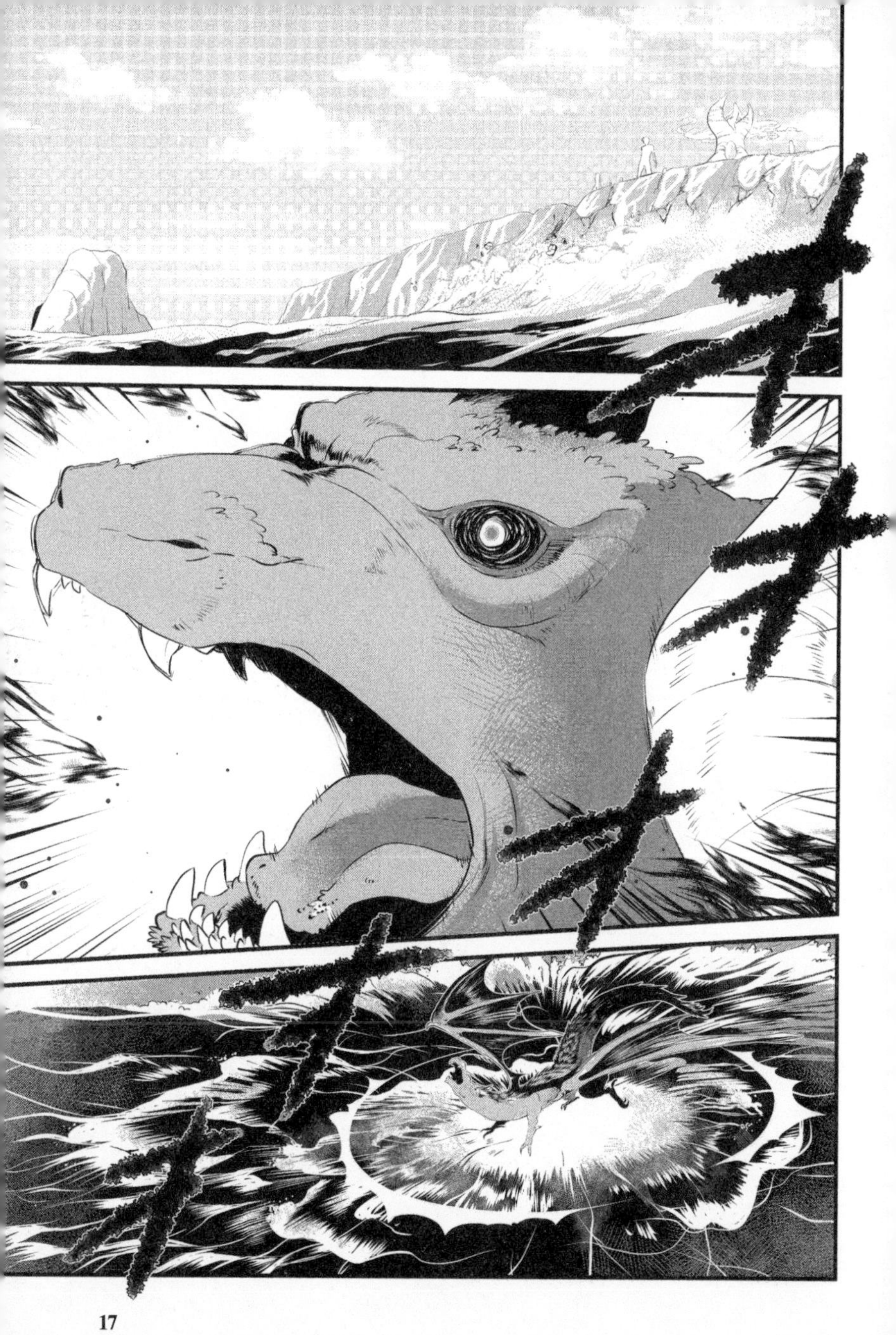
オオオオオ

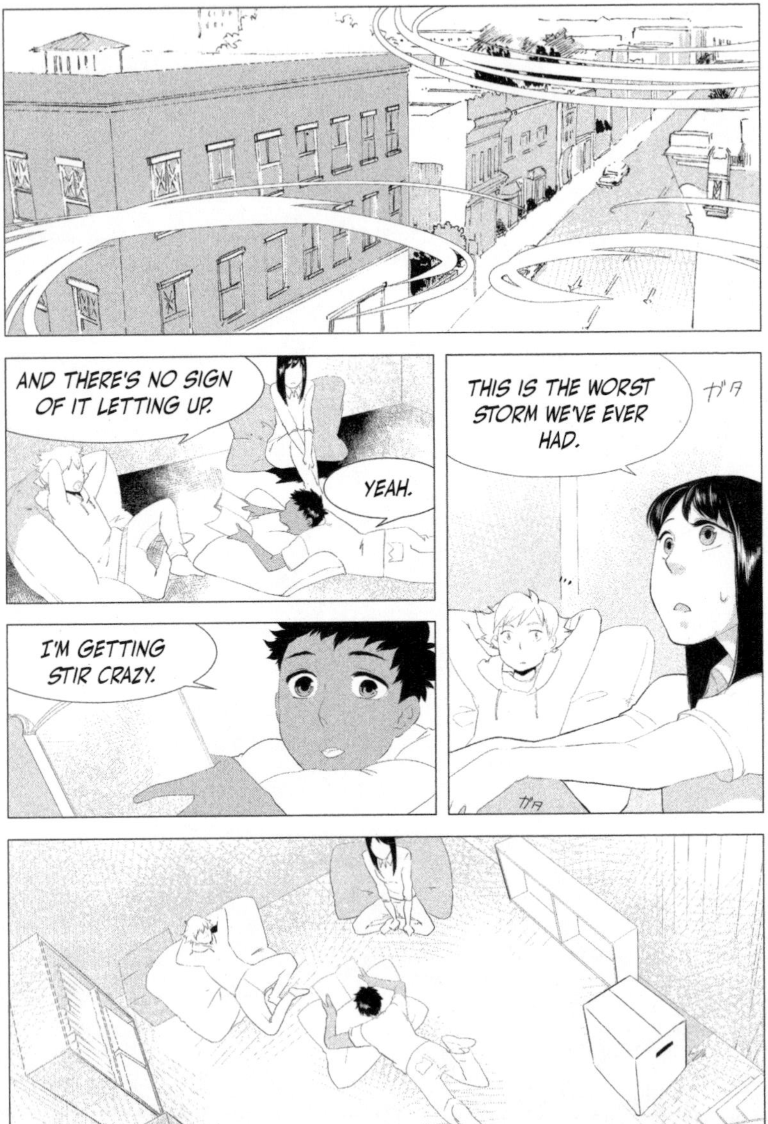
ガタ
THIS IS THE WORST STORM WE'VE EVER HAD.
ガタ
AND THERE'S NO SIGN OF IT LETTING UP.
YEAH.
I'M GETTING STIR CRAZY.

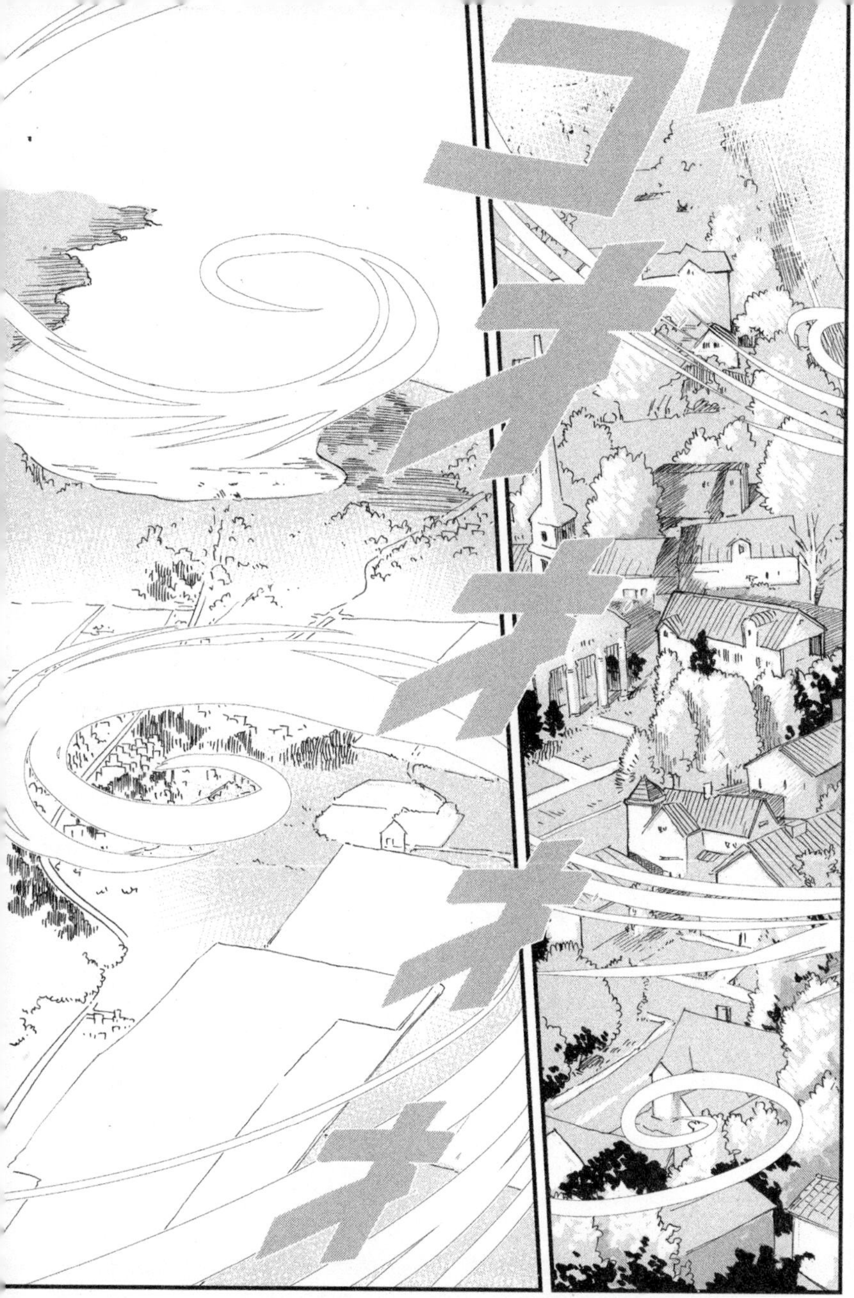
ゴオオオオオオ

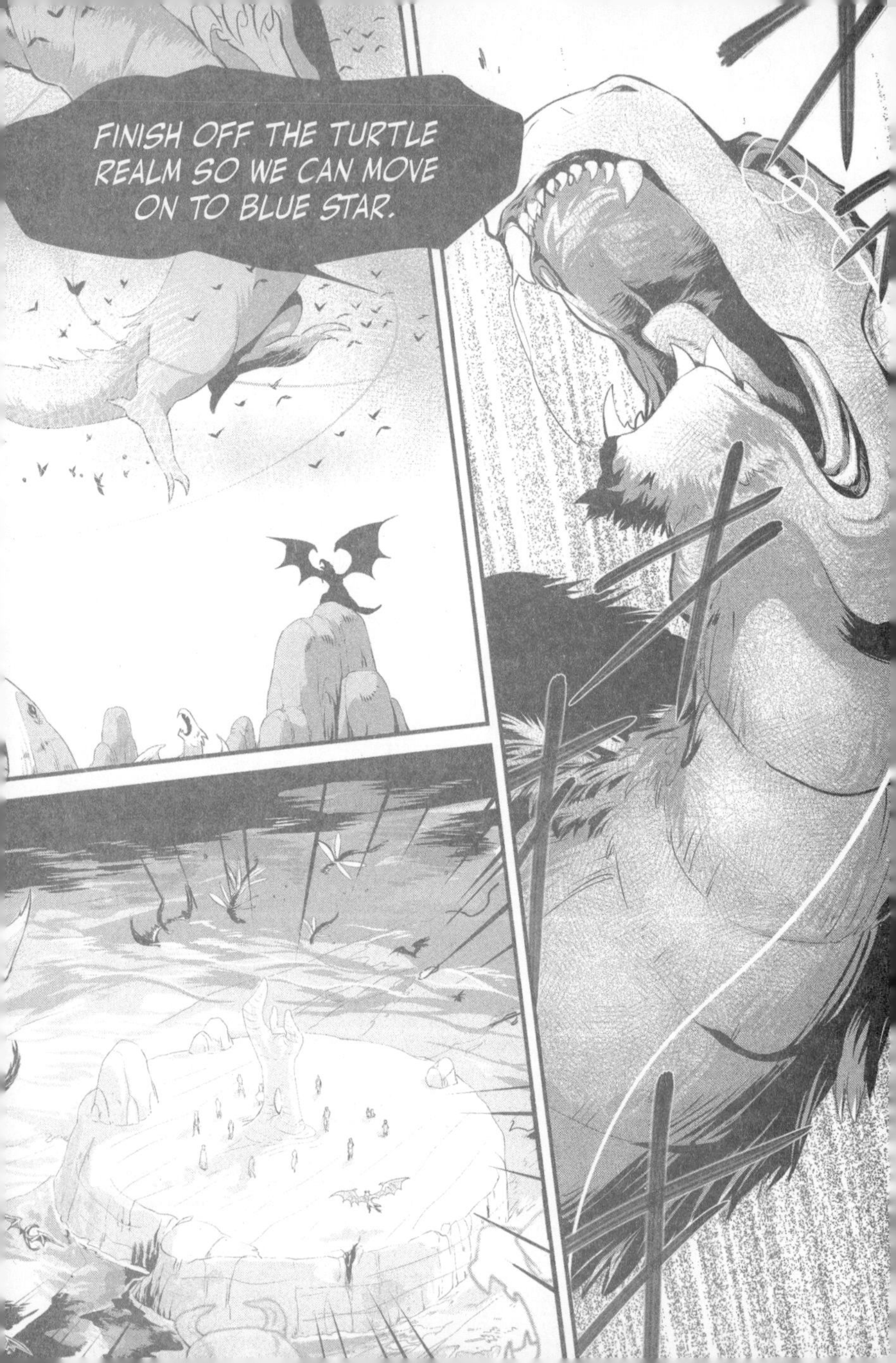
FINISH OFF THE TURTLE REALM SO WE CAN MOVE ON TO BLUE STAR.

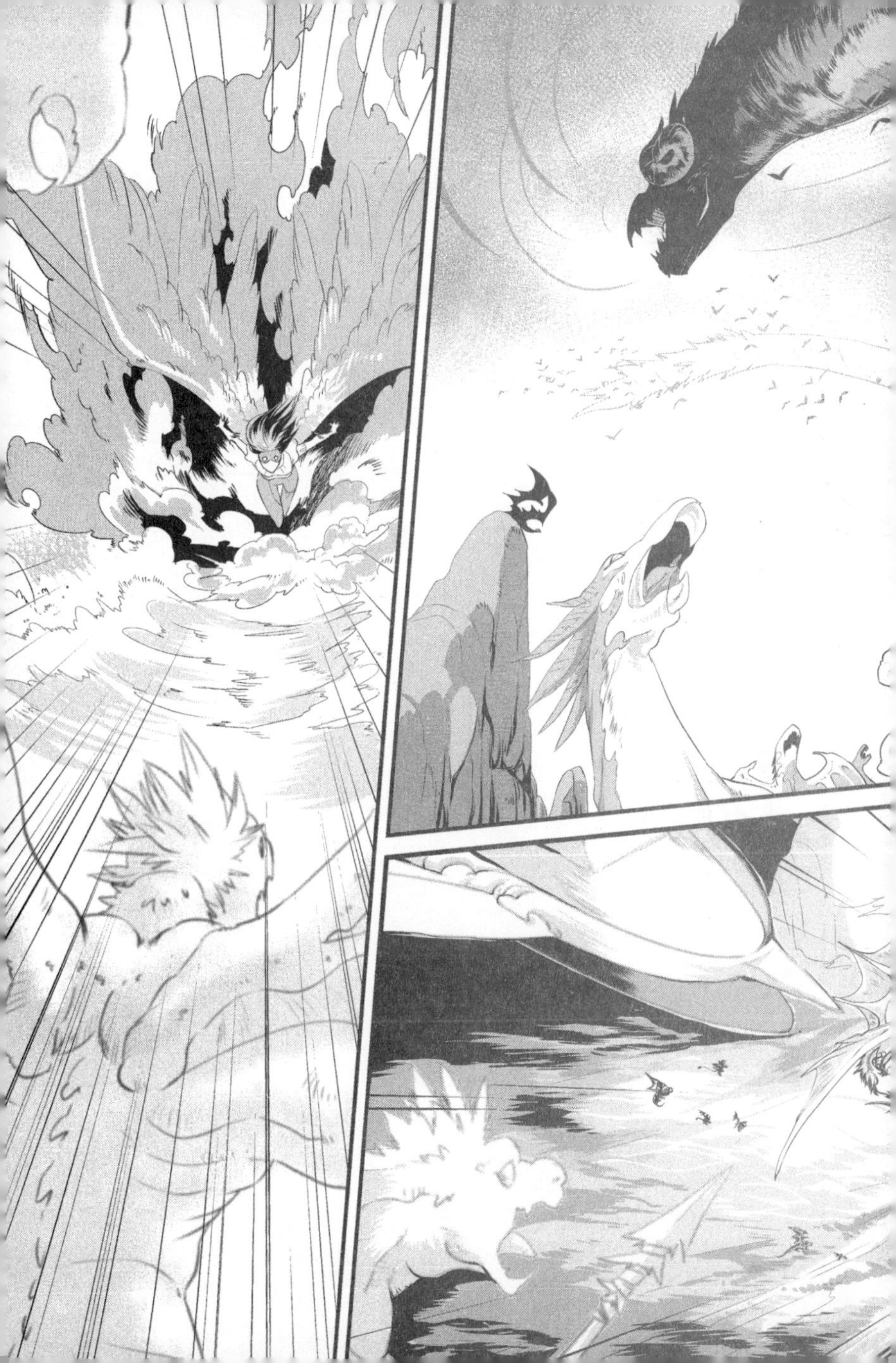

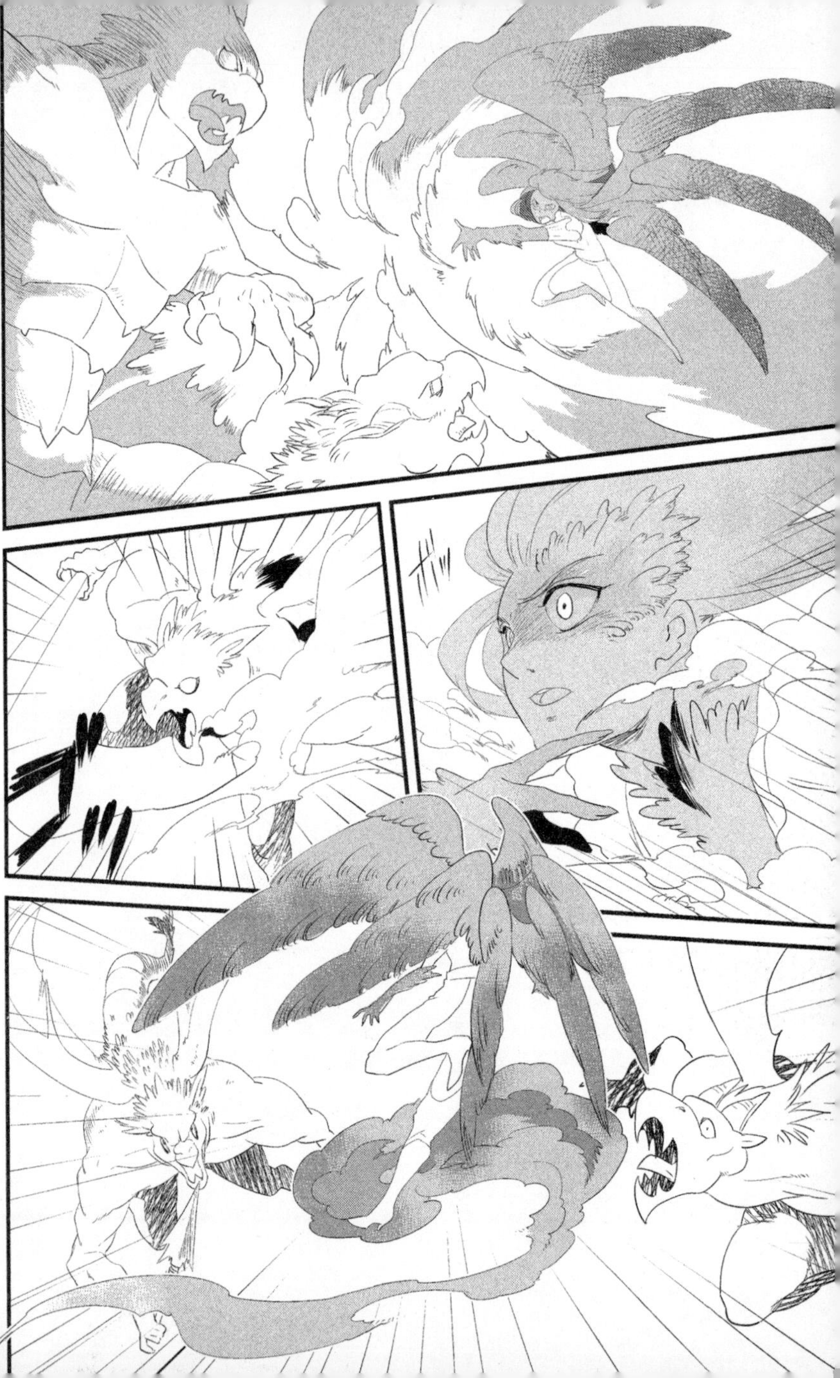
ガッ

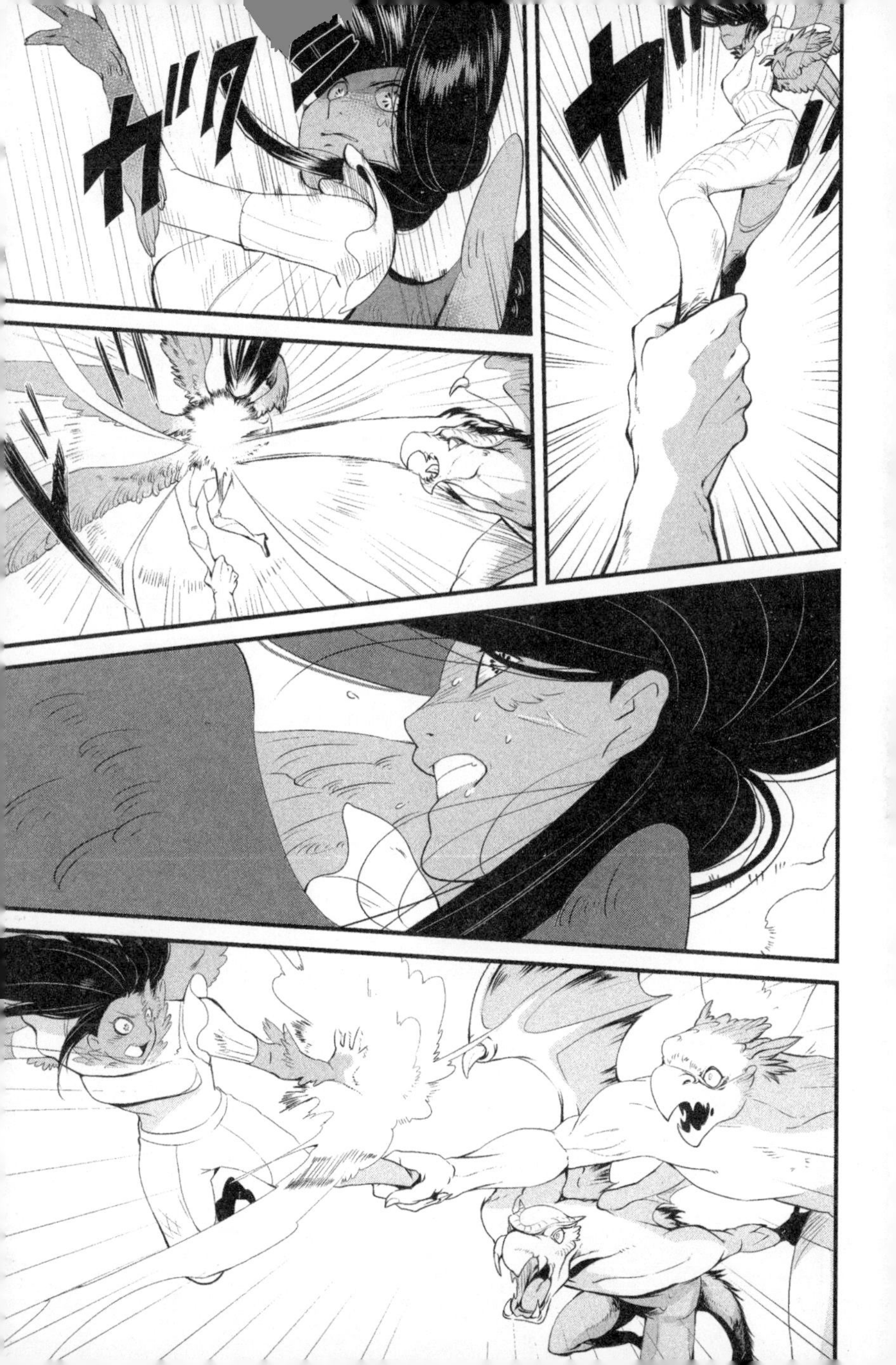
ガ
ガク

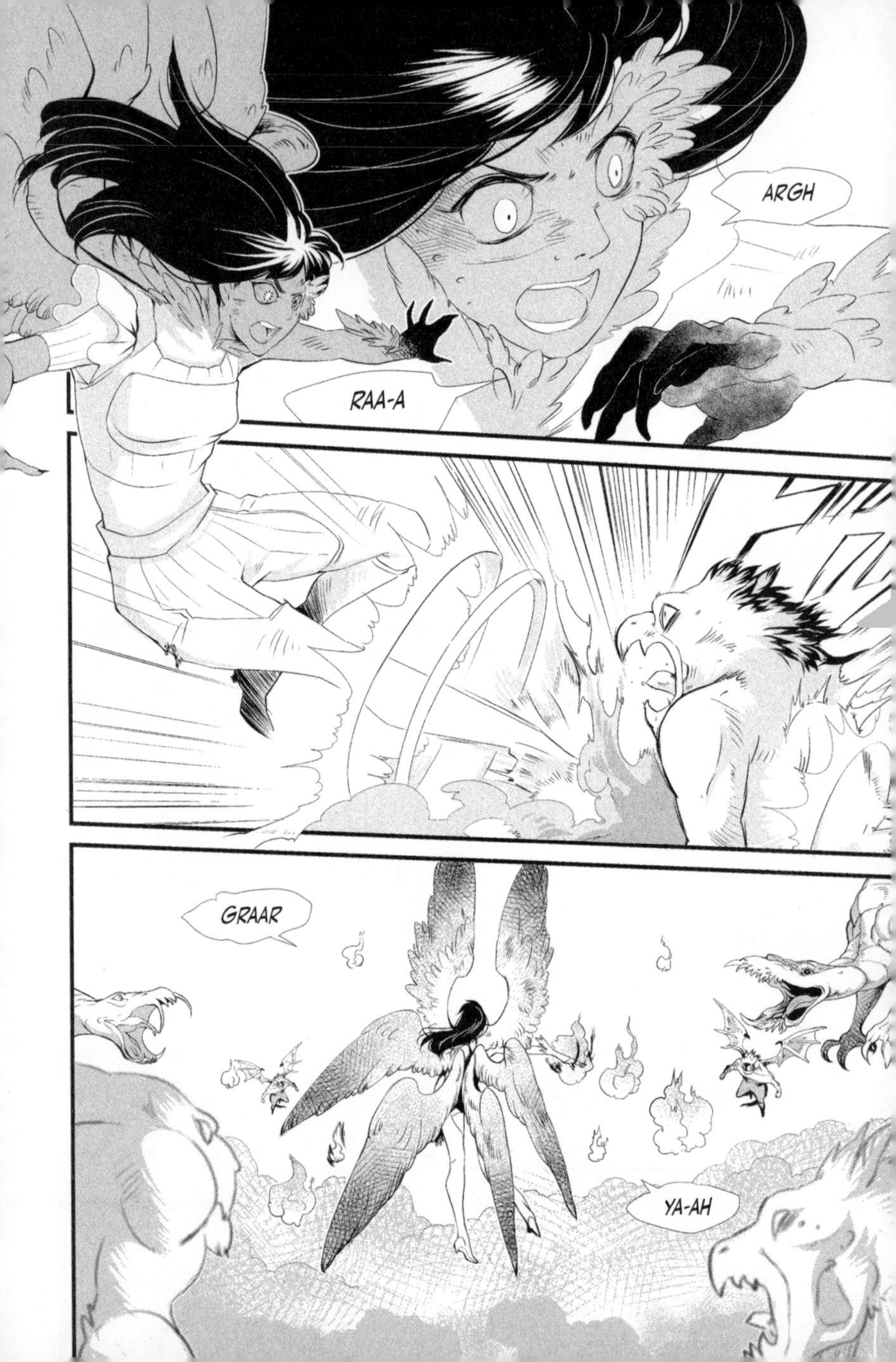
ARGH
RAA-A
GRAAR
YA-AH

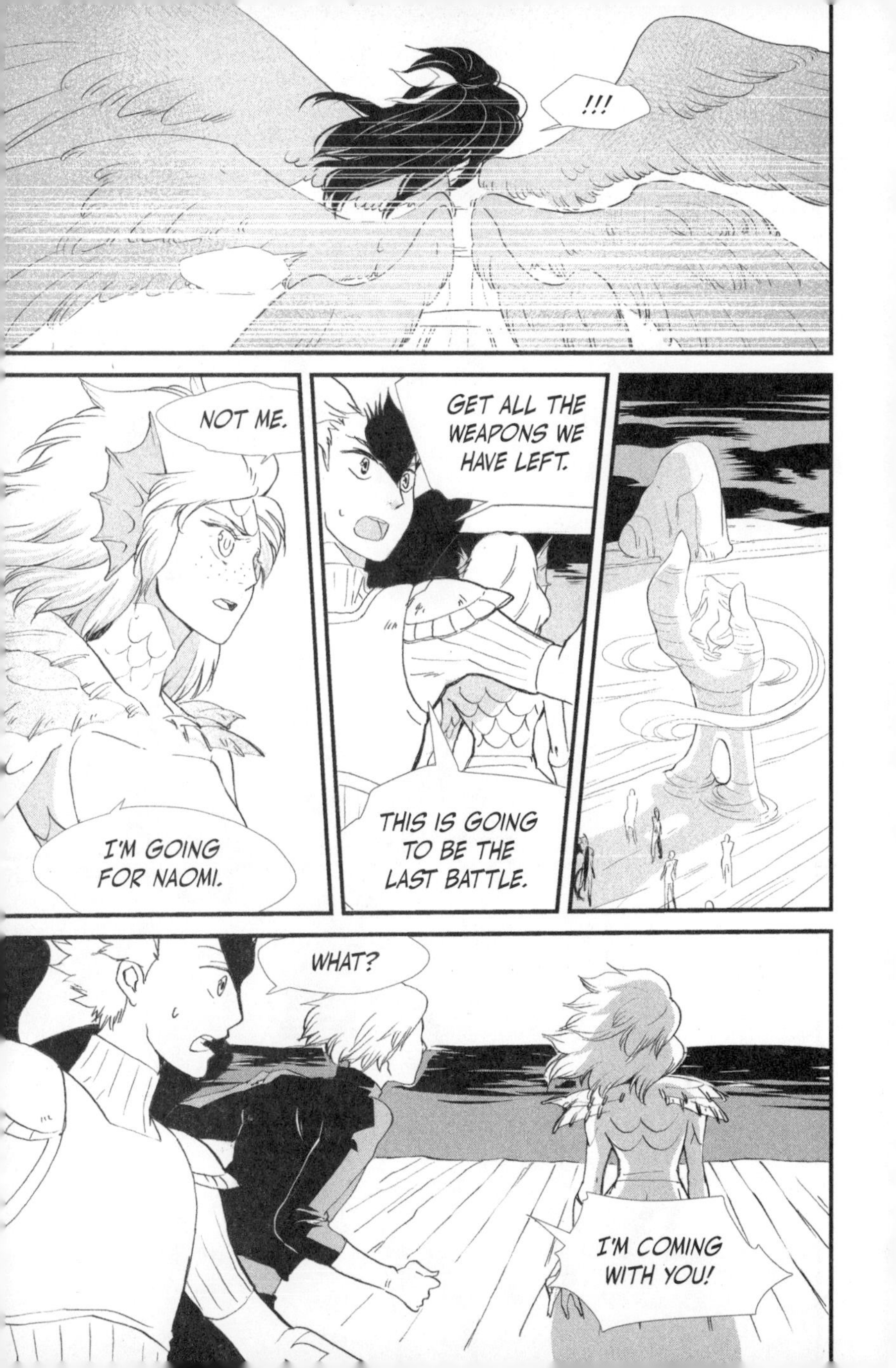
!!!
GET ALL THE WEAPONS WE HAVE LEFT.
THIS IS GOING TO BE THE LAST BATTLE.
NOT ME.
I'M GOING FOR NAOMI.
WHAT?
I'M COMING WITH YOU!

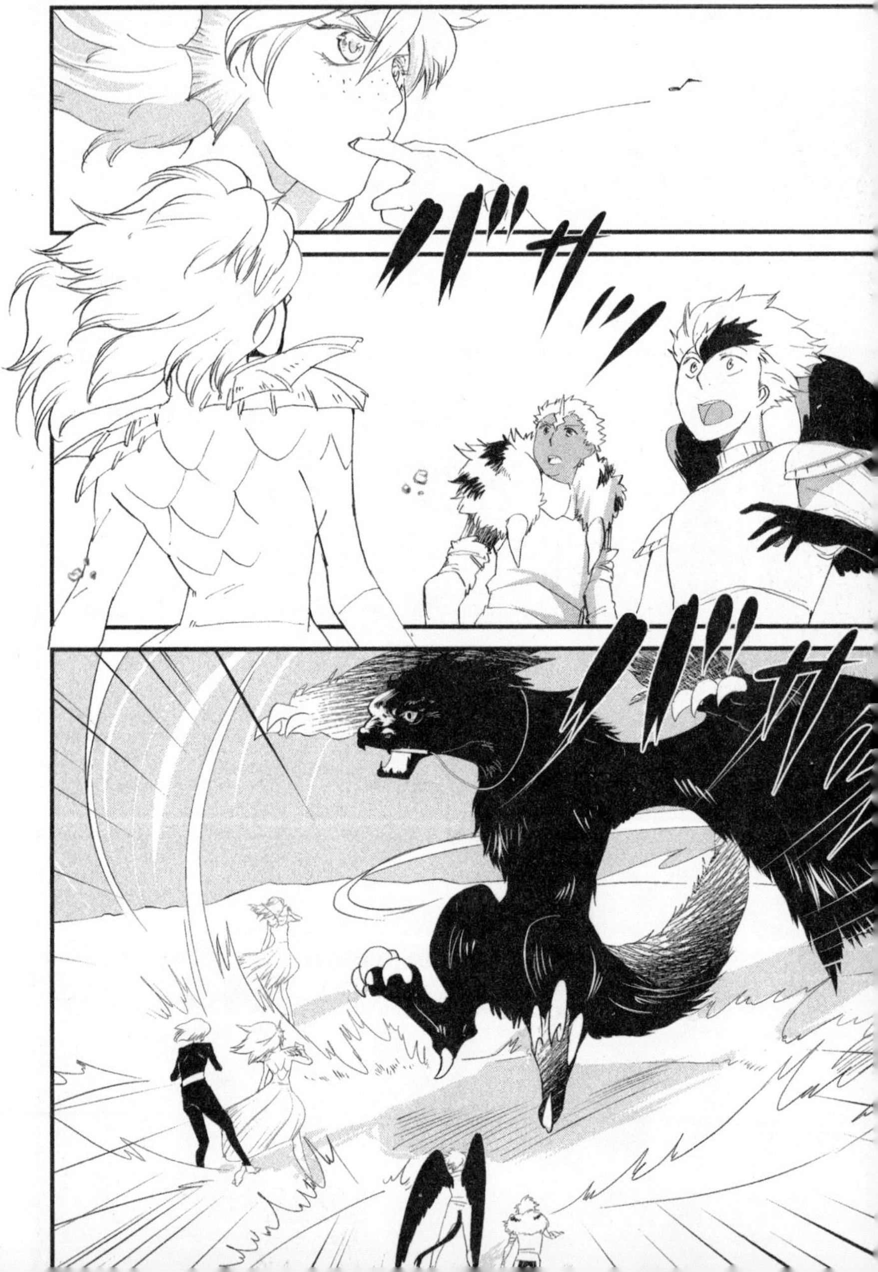
バサッ
バサ

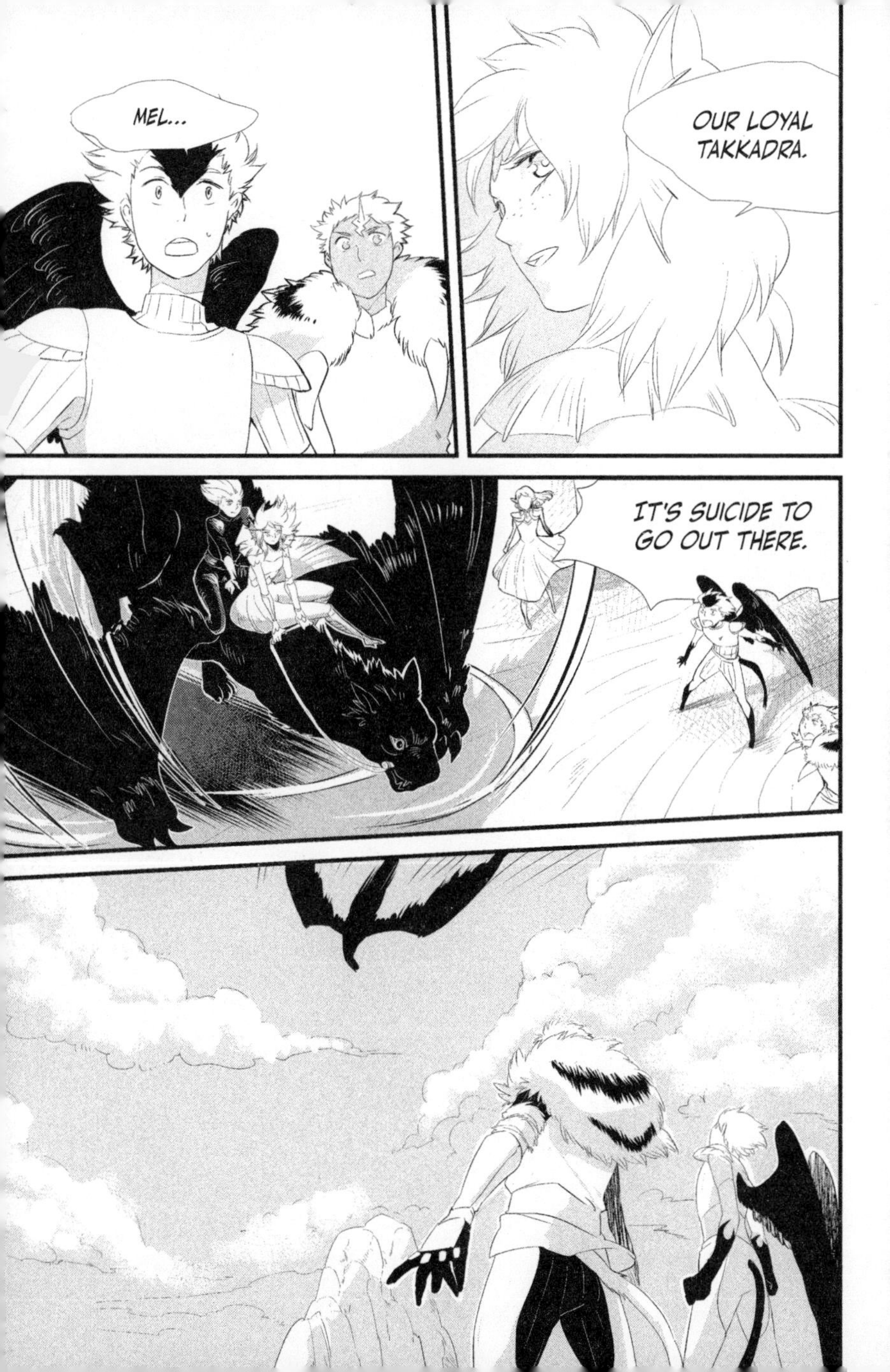
OUR LOYAL TAKKADRA.
MEL...
IT'S SUICIDE TO GO OUT THERE.

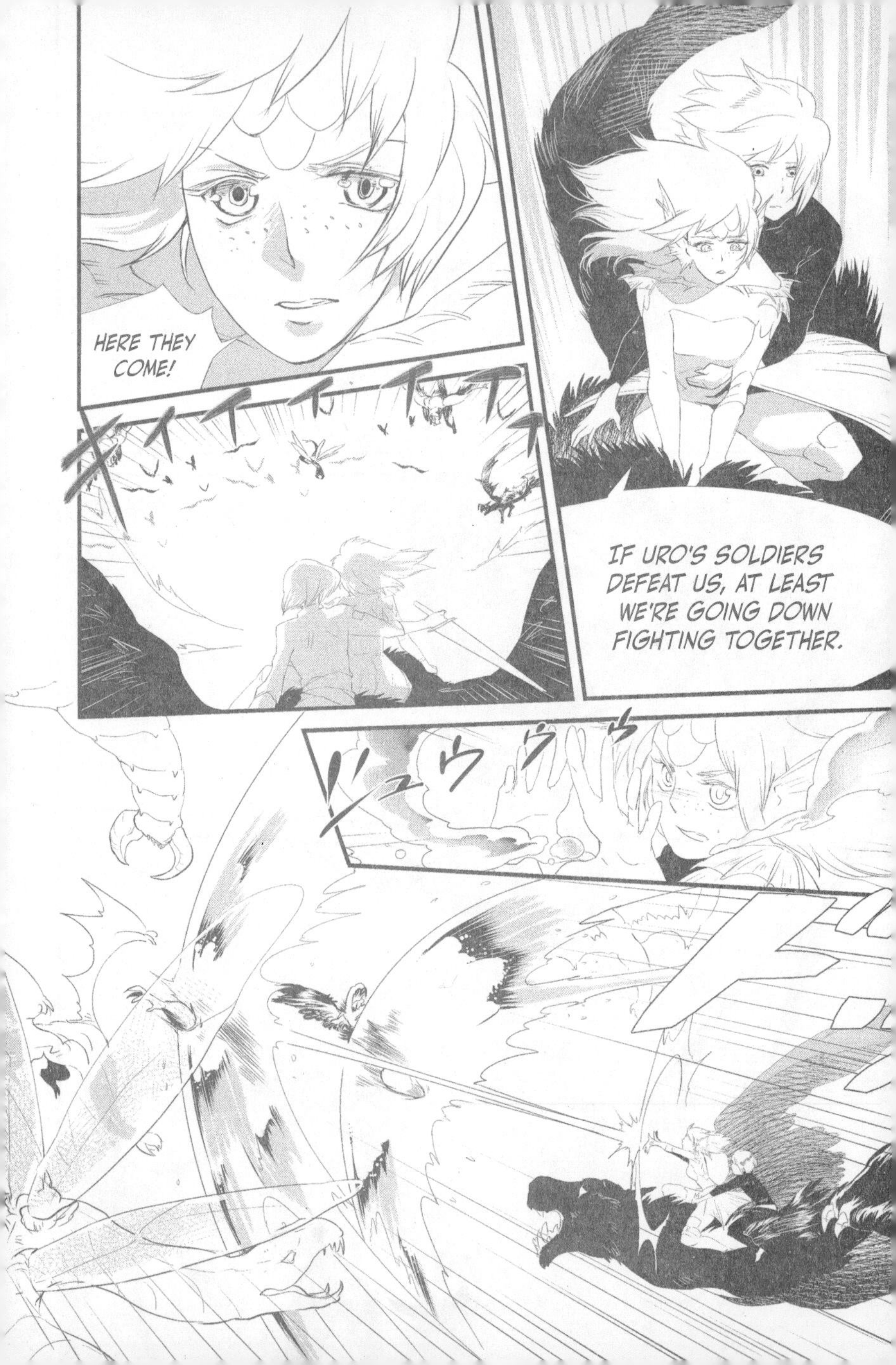
IF URO'S SOLDIERS DEFEAT US, AT LEAST WE'RE GOING DOWN FIGHTING TOGETHER.
HERE THEY COME!

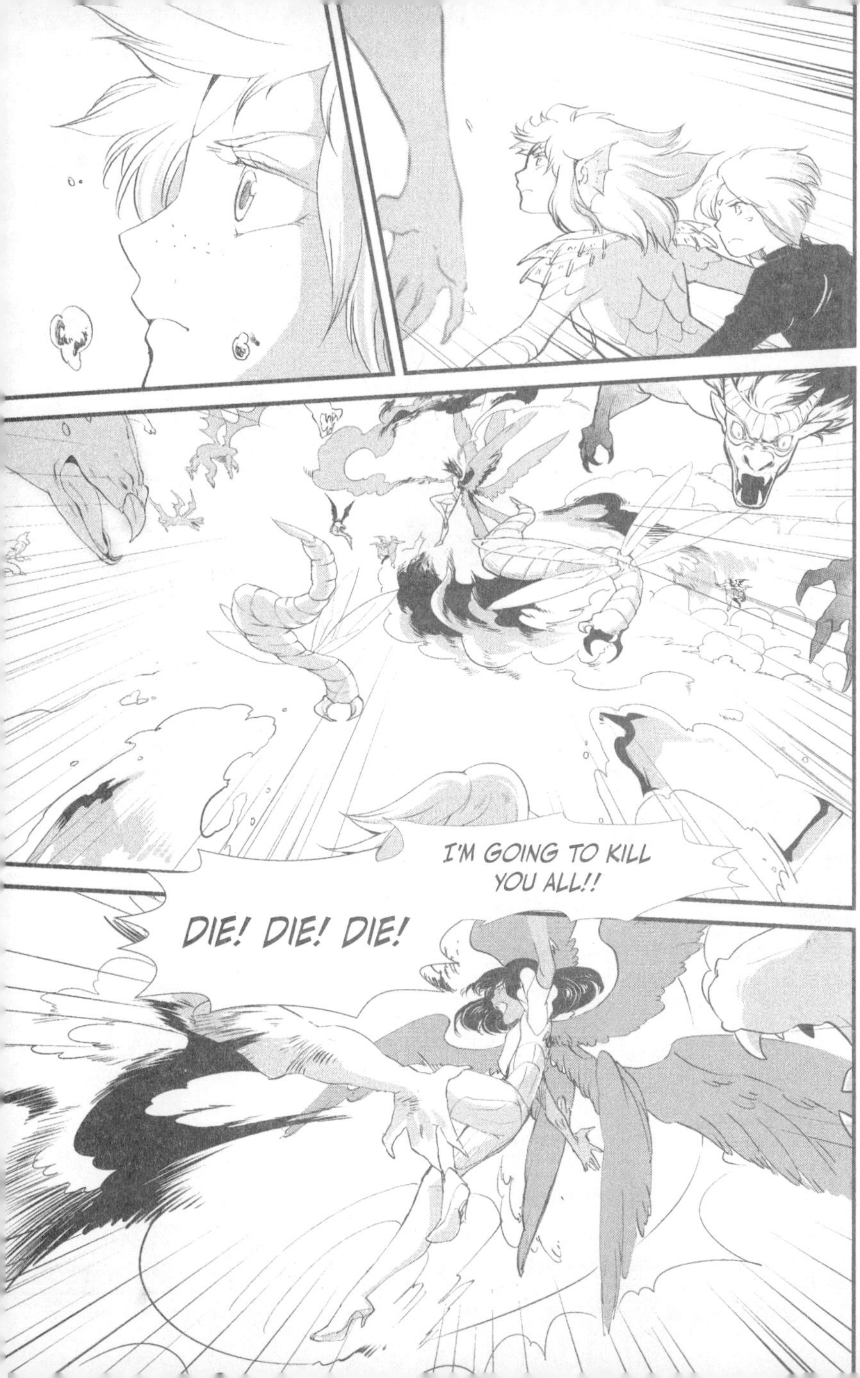
I'M GOING TO KILL YOU ALL!!
DIE! DIE! DIE!

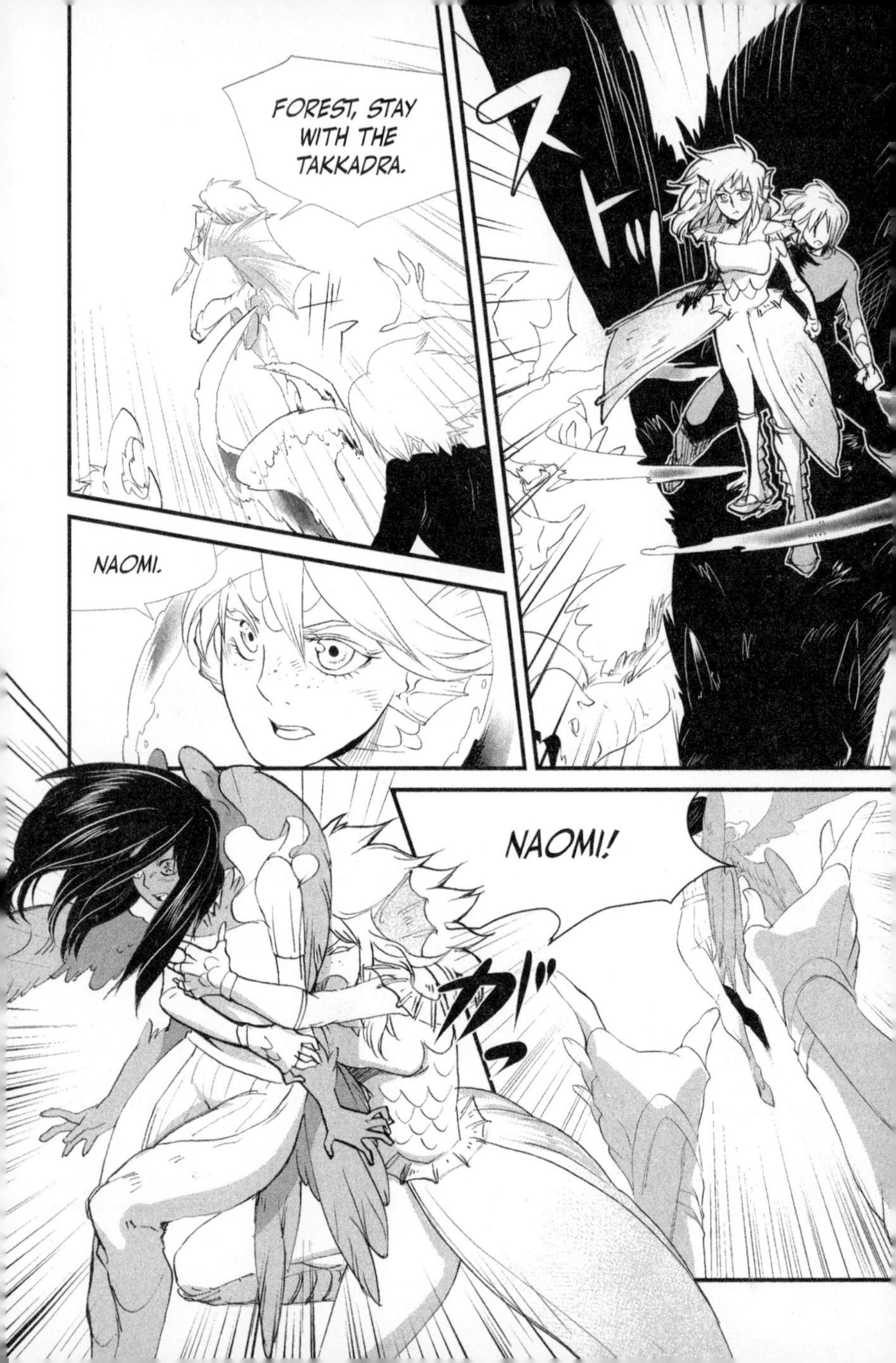
FOREST, STAY WITH THE TAKKADRA.
NAOMI.
NAOMI!

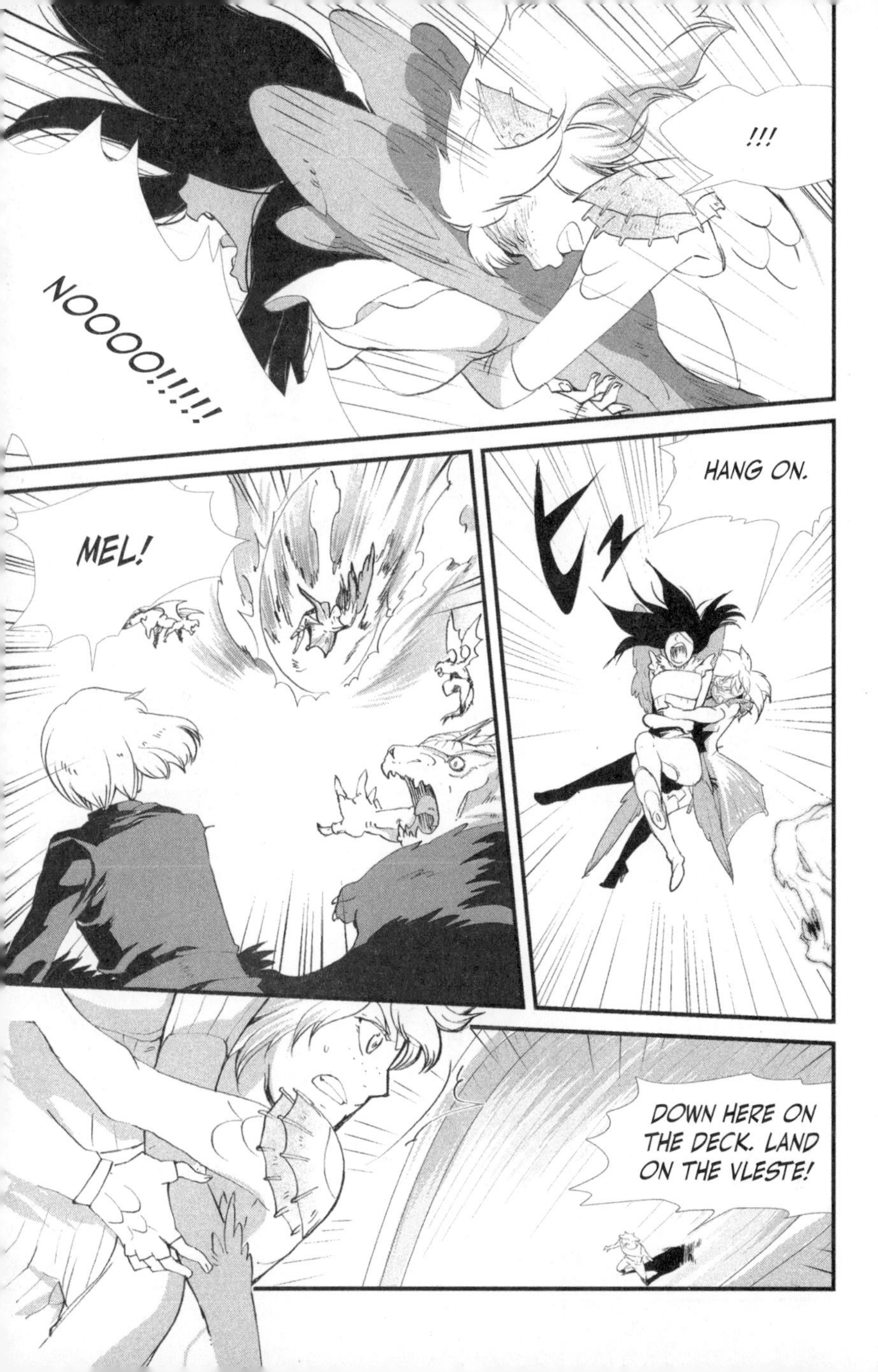
!!!
NOOOO!!!!!!
HANG ON.
MEL!
DOWN HERE ON THE DECK. LAND ON THE VLESTE!

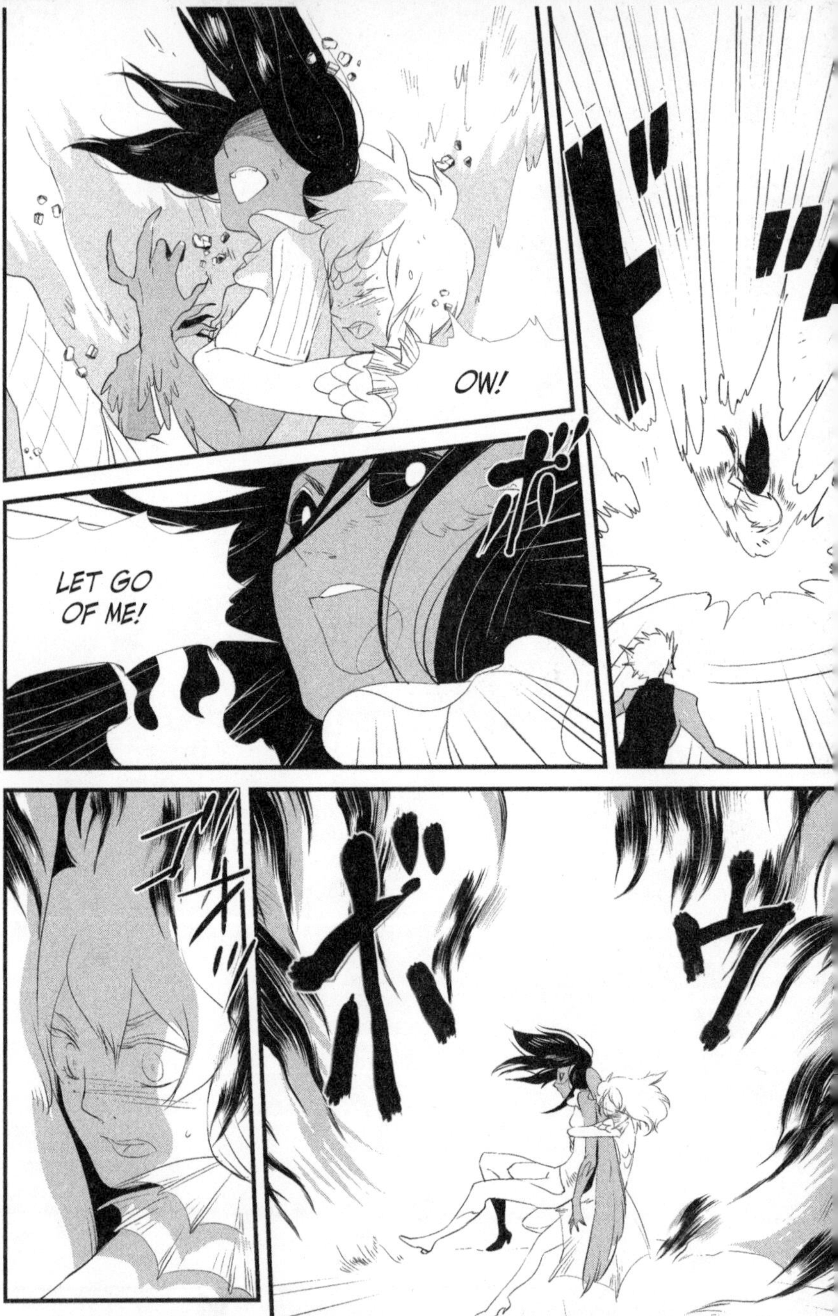
OW!
LET GO OF ME!

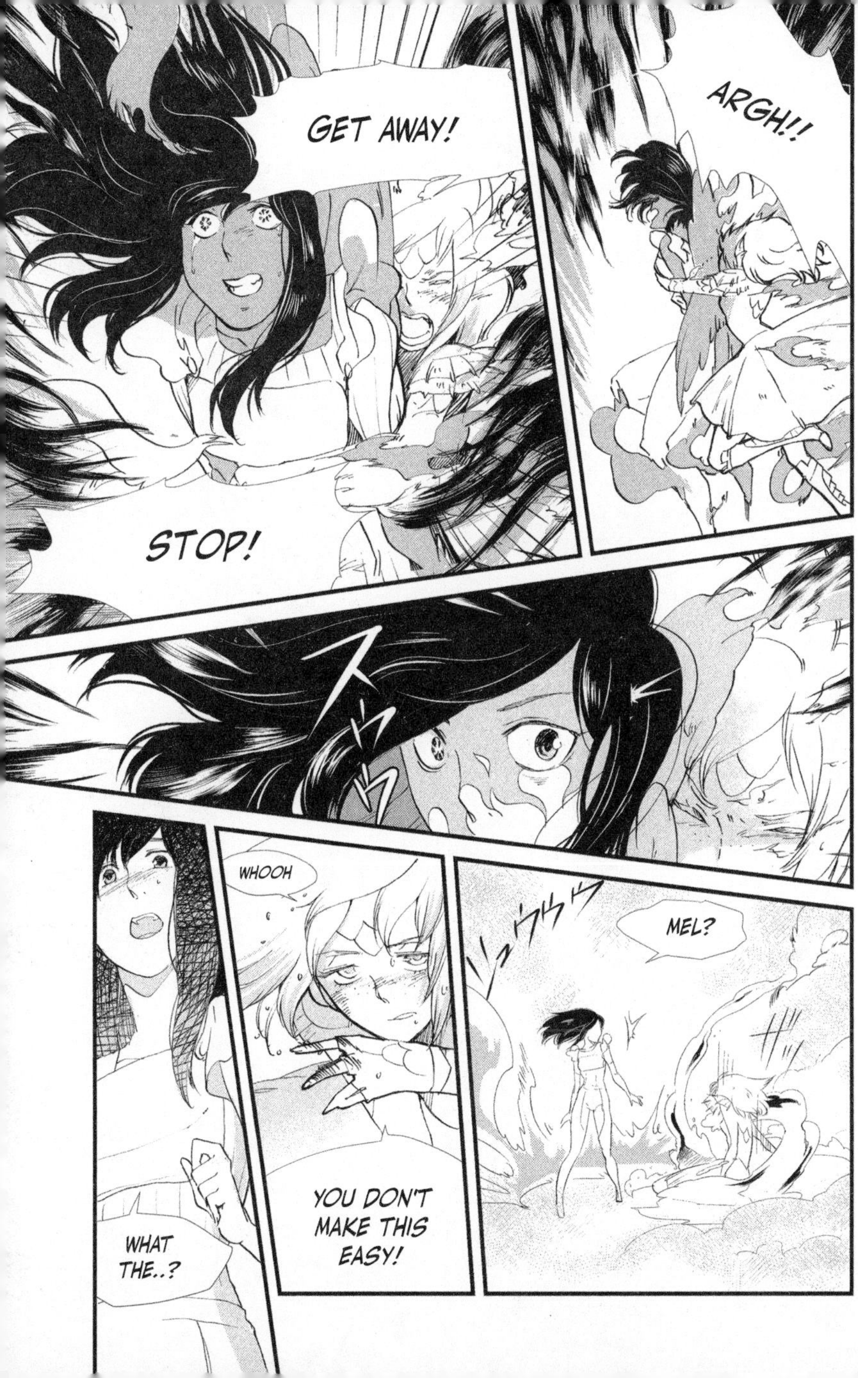
ARGH!!
GET AWAY!
STOP!
MEL?
WHOOH
YOU DON'T MAKE THIS EASY!
WHAT THE..?

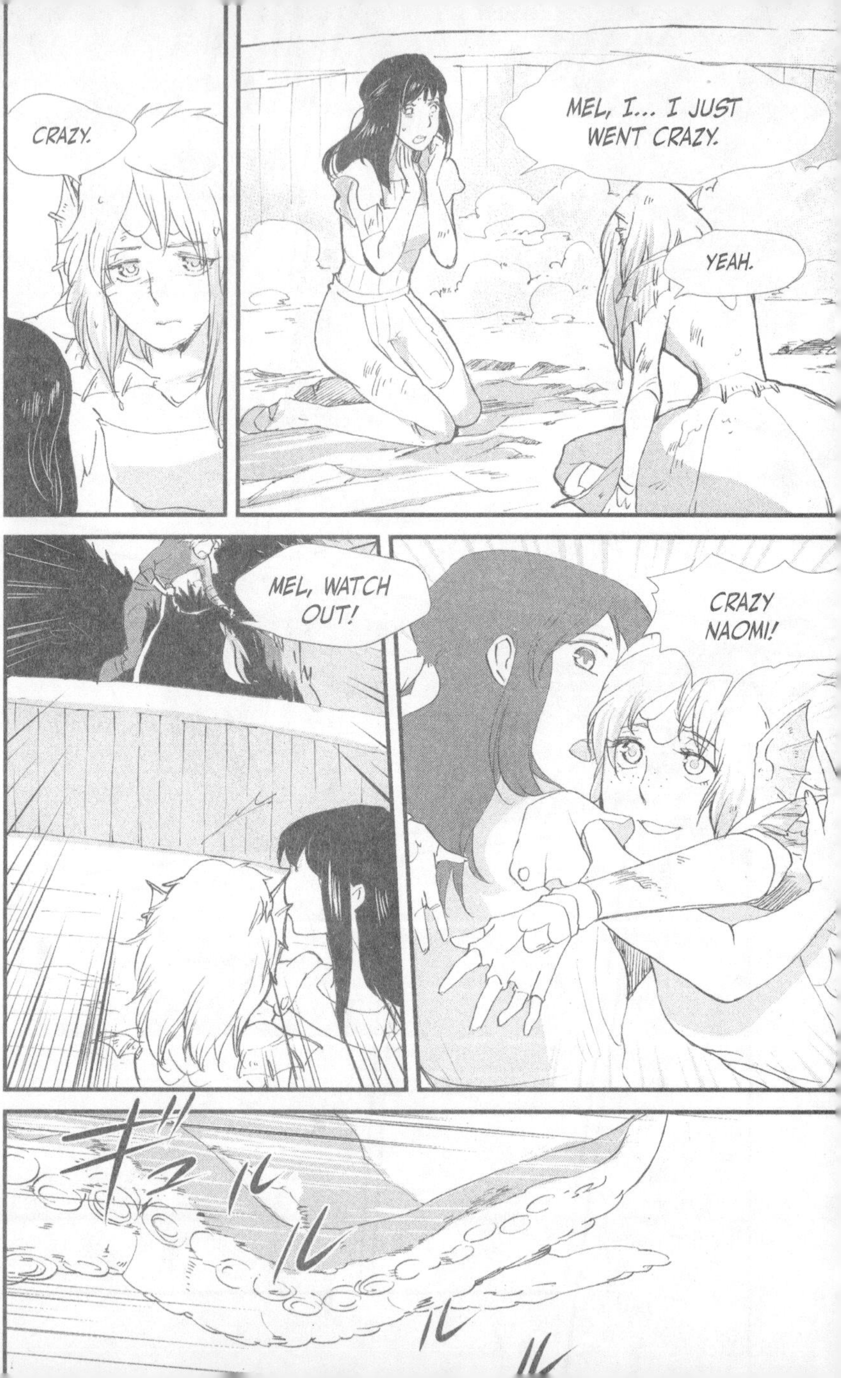
MEL, I... I JUST WENT CRAZY.
YEAH.
CRAZY.
CRAZY NAOMI!
MEL, WATCH OUT!

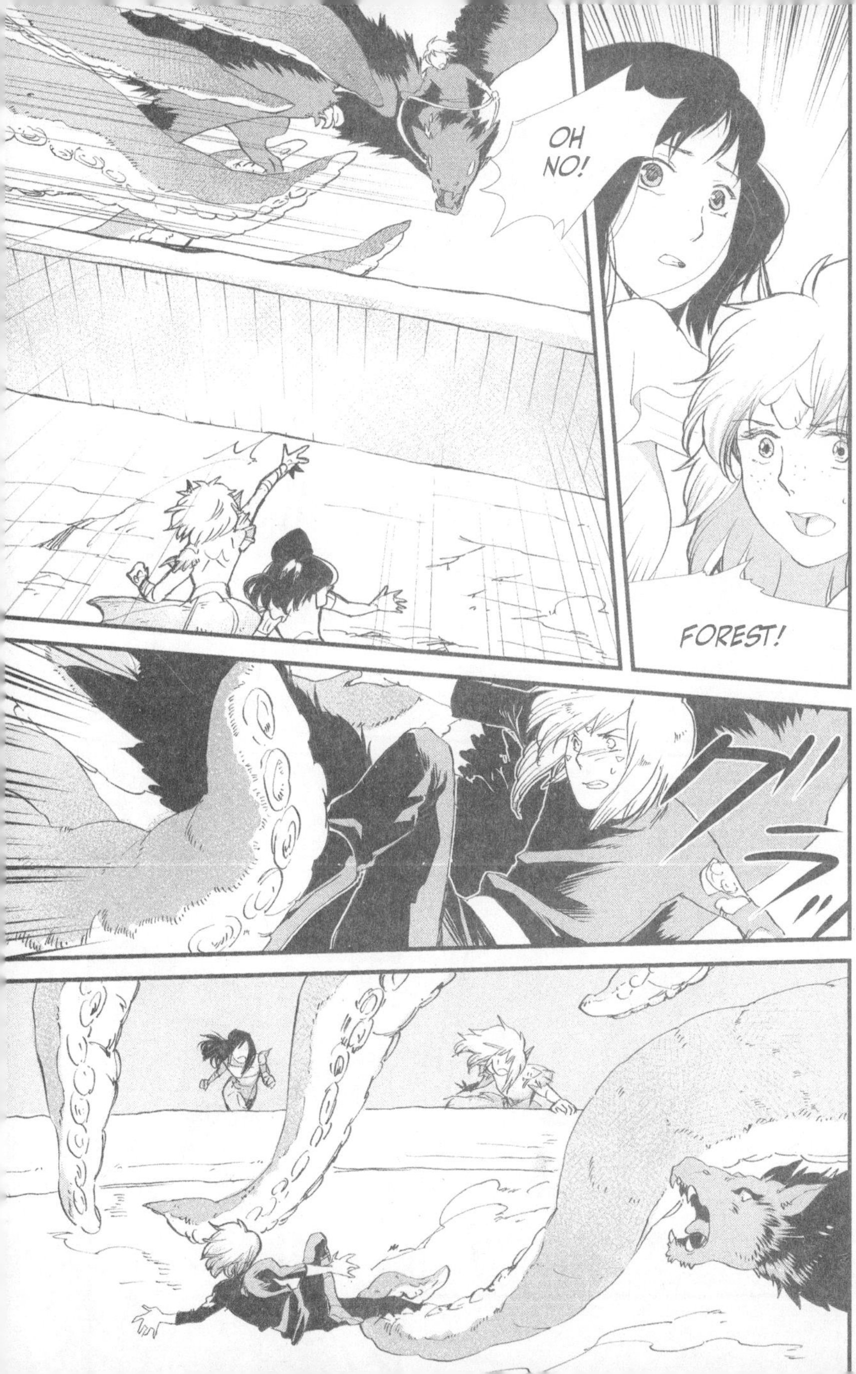
OH NO!
FOREST!

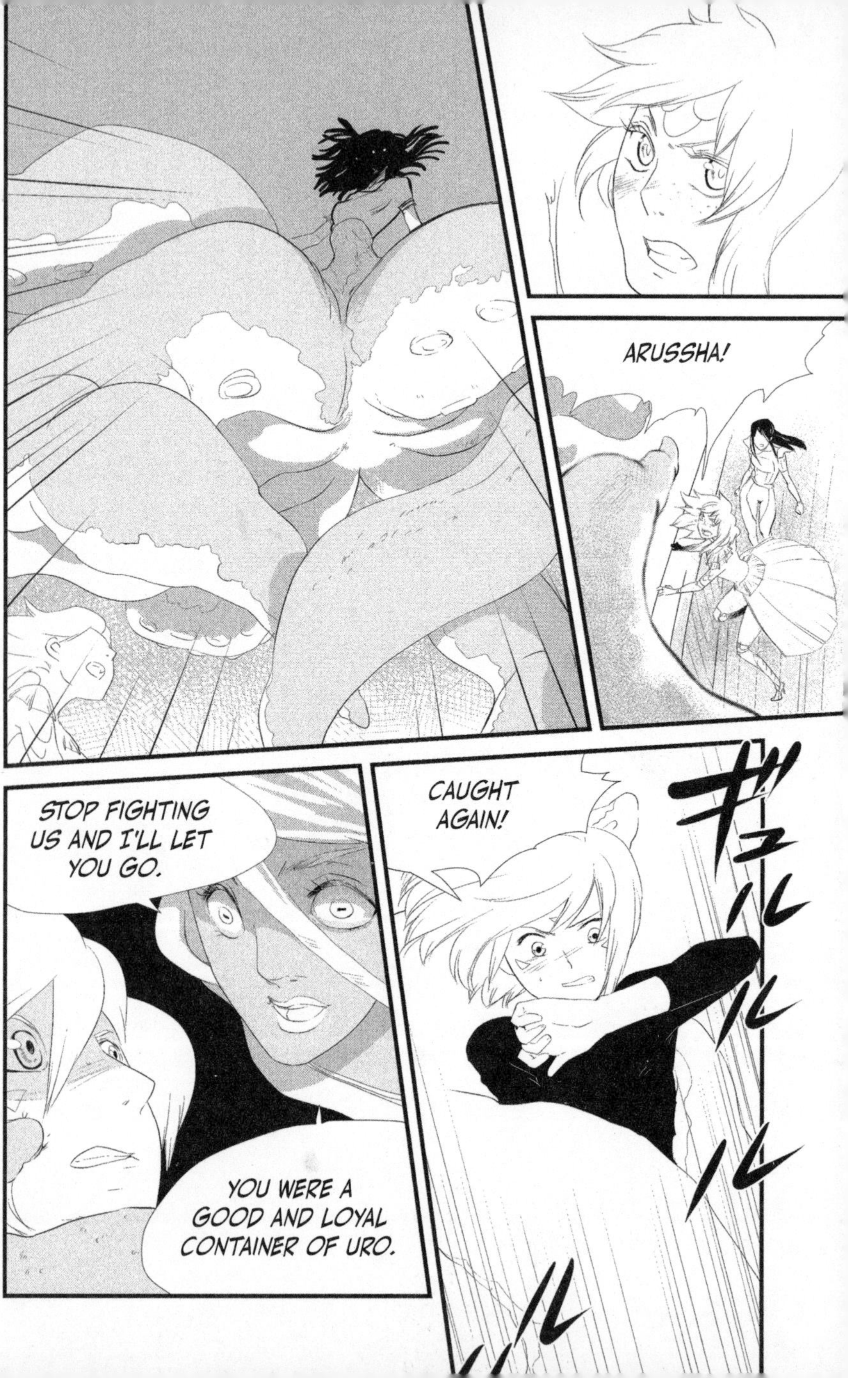
ARUSSHA!
ギュルルル
CAUGHT AGAIN!
STOP FIGHTING US AND I'LL LET YOU GO.
YOU WERE A GOOD AND LOYAL CONTAINER OF URO.

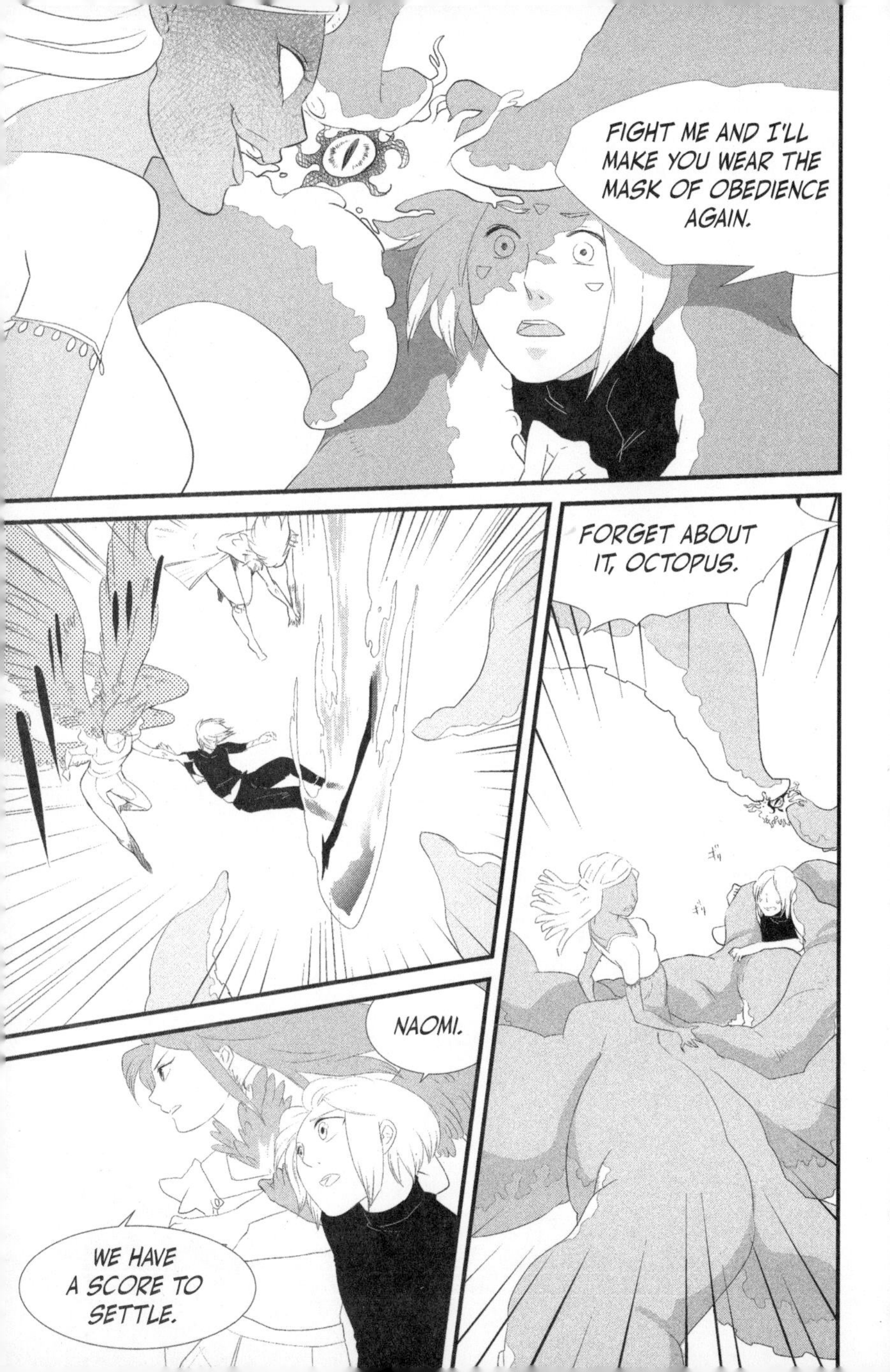
FIGHT ME AND I'LL MAKE YOU WEAR THE MASK OF OBEDIENCE AGAIN.
FORGET ABOUT IT, OCTOPUS.
NAOMI.
WE HAVE A SCORE TO SETTLE.

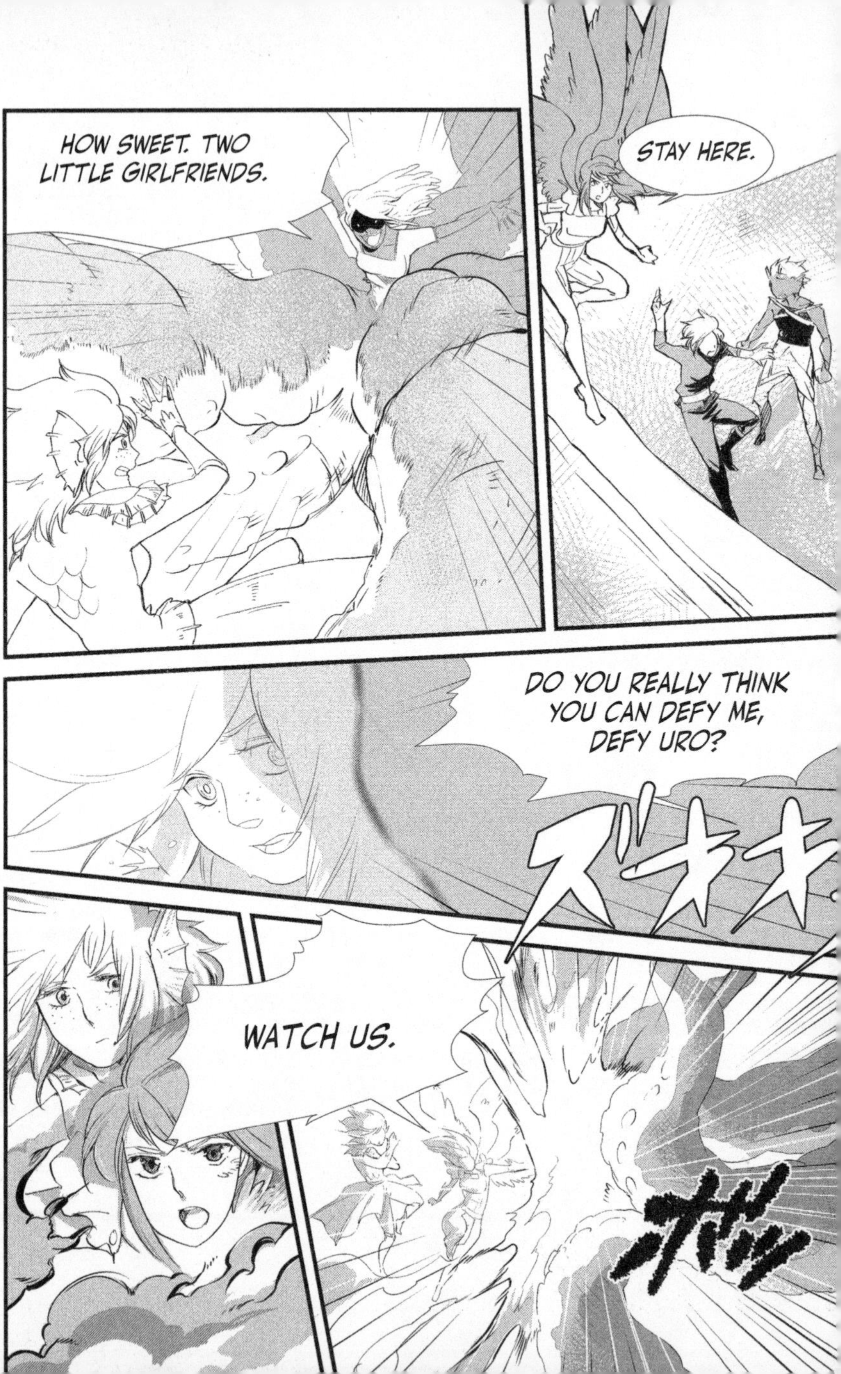
STAY HERE.
HOW SWEET. TWO LITTLE GIRLFRIENDS.
DO YOU REALLY THINK YOU CAN DEFY ME, DEFY URO?
ズオオ
WATCH US.
ザッ

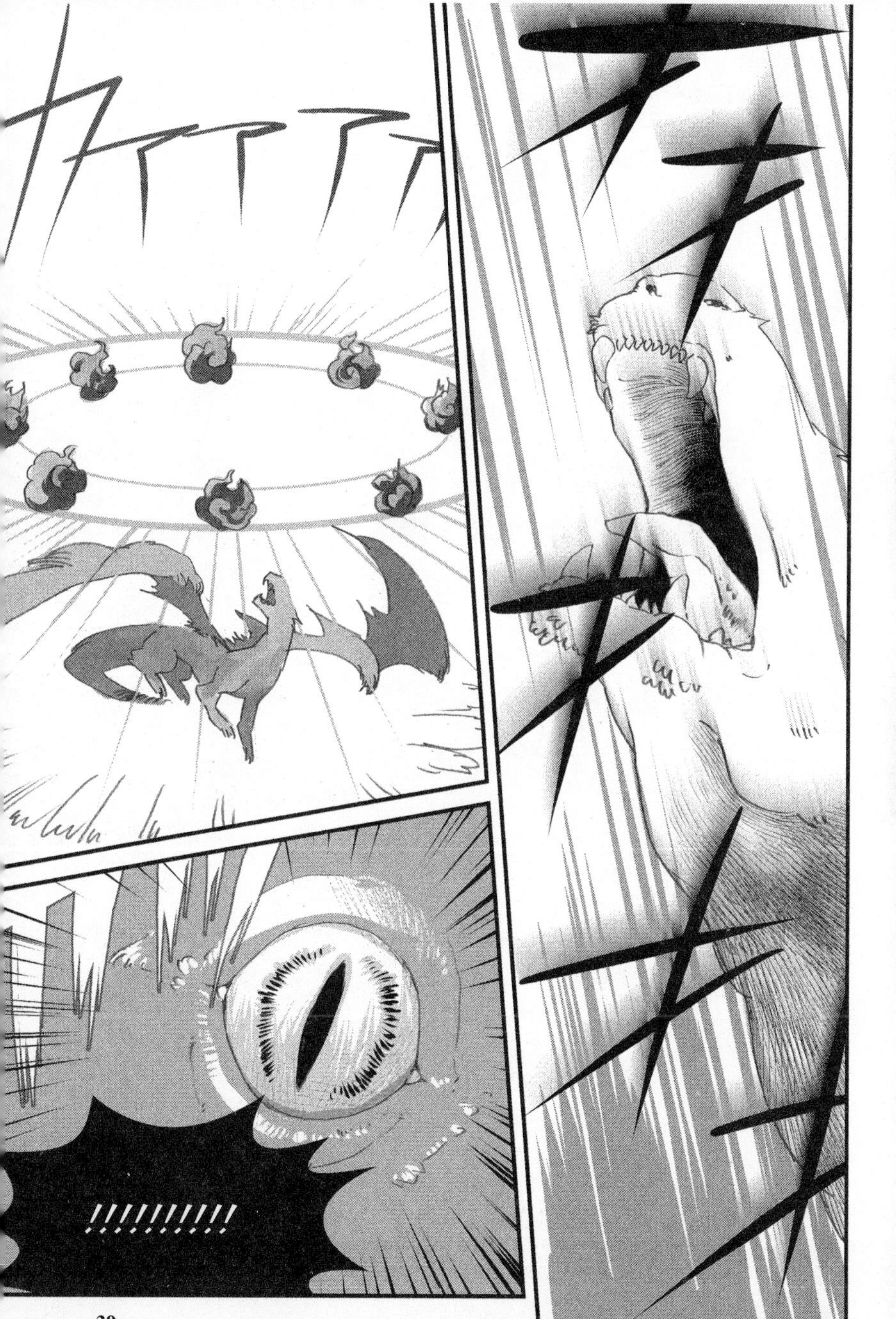
!!!!!!!!!!

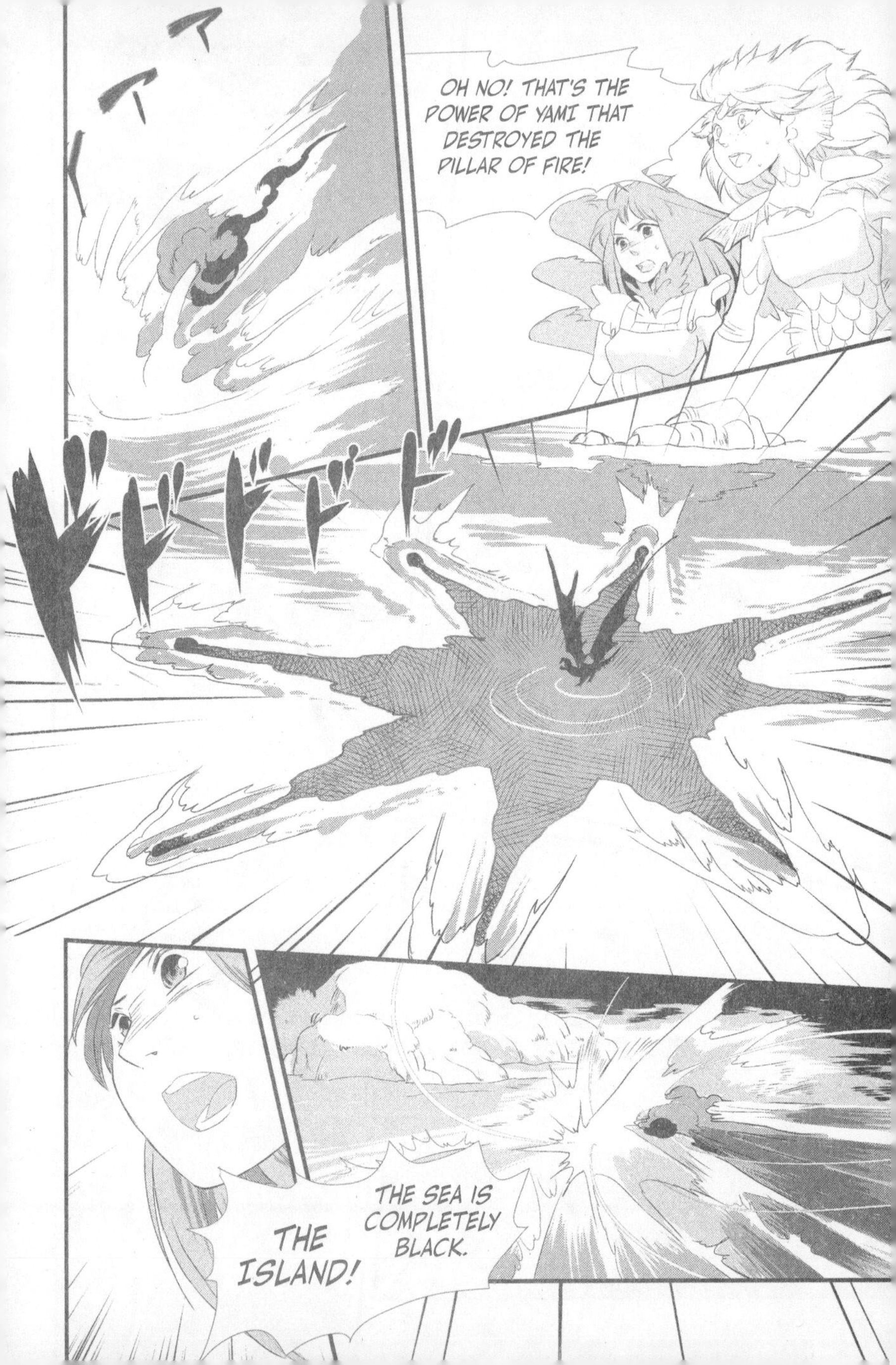
OH NO! THAT'S THE POWER OF YAMI THAT DESTROYED THE PILLAR OF FIRE!
THE SEA IS COMPLETELY BLACK.
THE ISLAND!

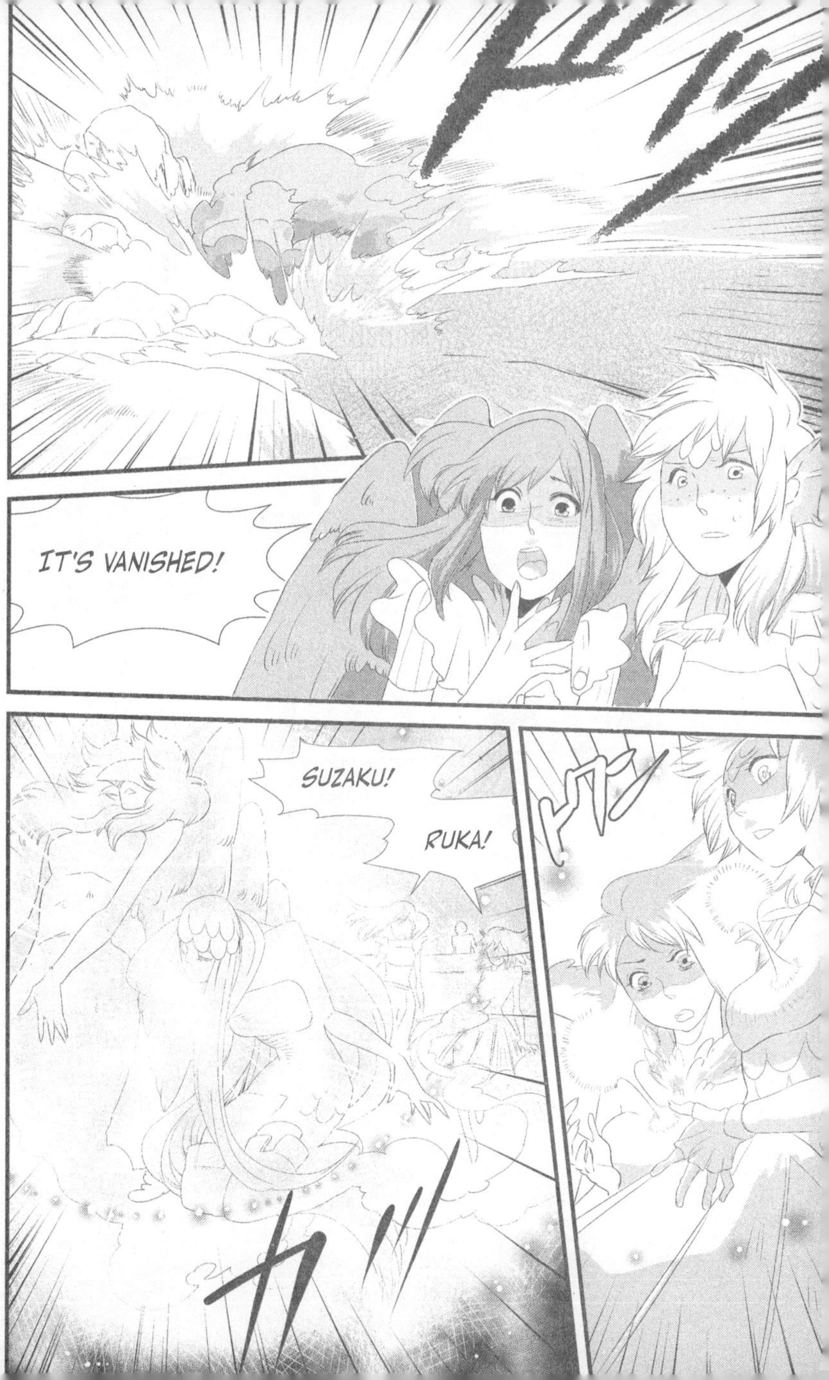
IT'S VANISHED!
SUZAKU!
RUKA!

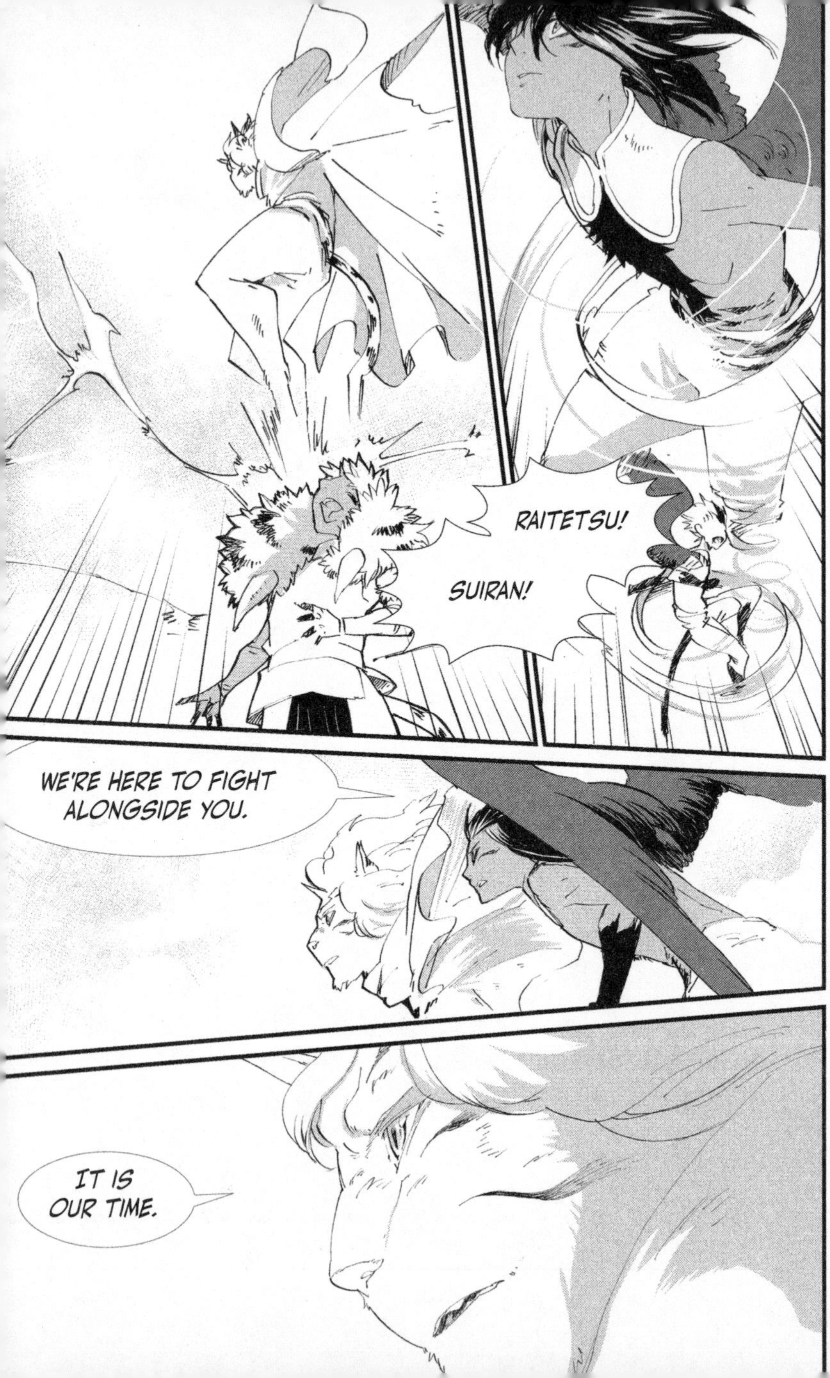
RAITETSU!
SUIRAN!
WE'RE HERE TO FIGHT ALONGSIDE YOU.
IT IS OUR TIME.

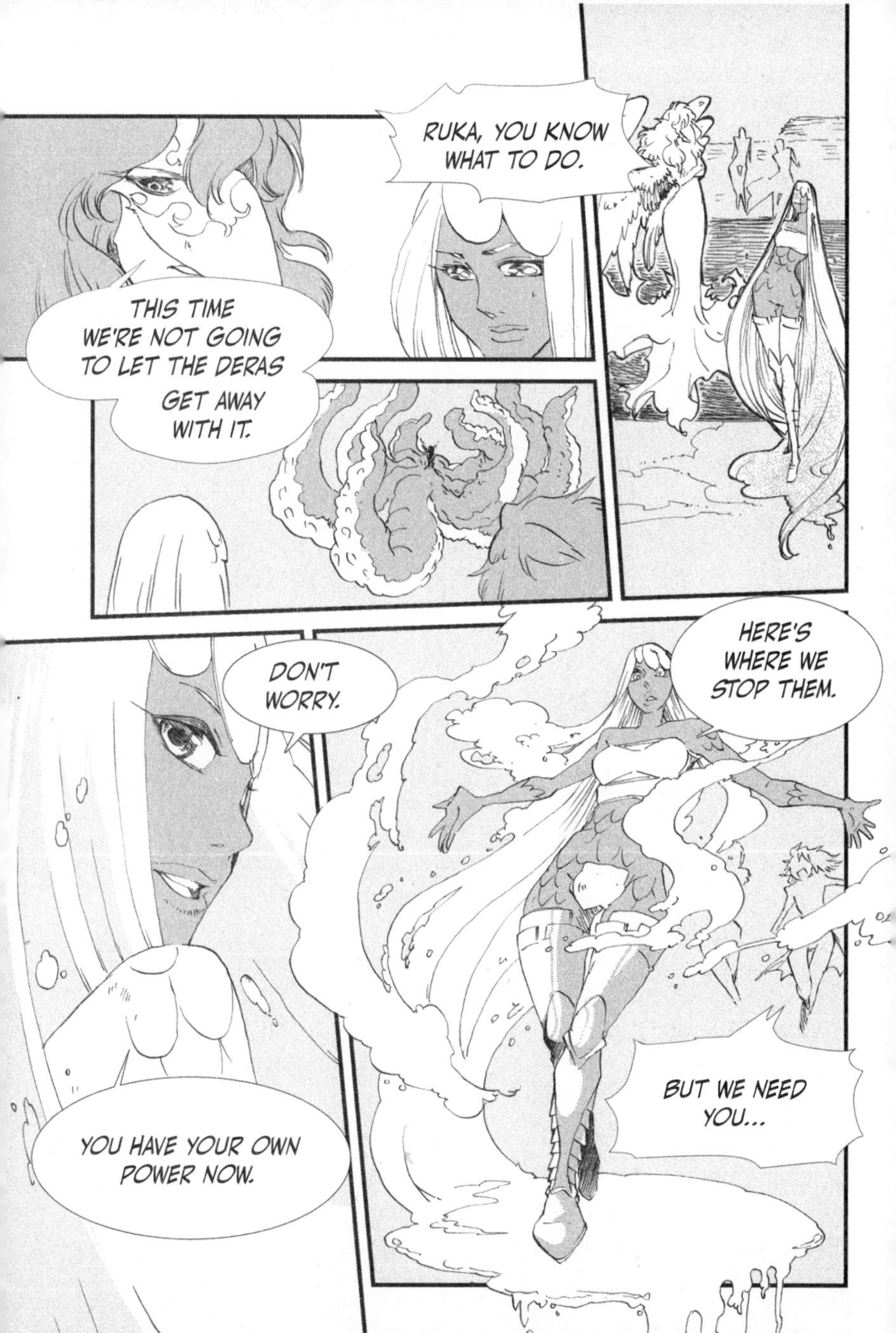
RUKA, YOU KNOW WHAT TO DO.
THIS TIME WE'RE NOT GOING TO LET THE DERAS GET AWAY WITH IT.
HERE'S WHERE WE STOP THEM.
BUT WE NEED YOU...
DON'T WORRY.
YOU HAVE YOUR OWN POWER NOW.

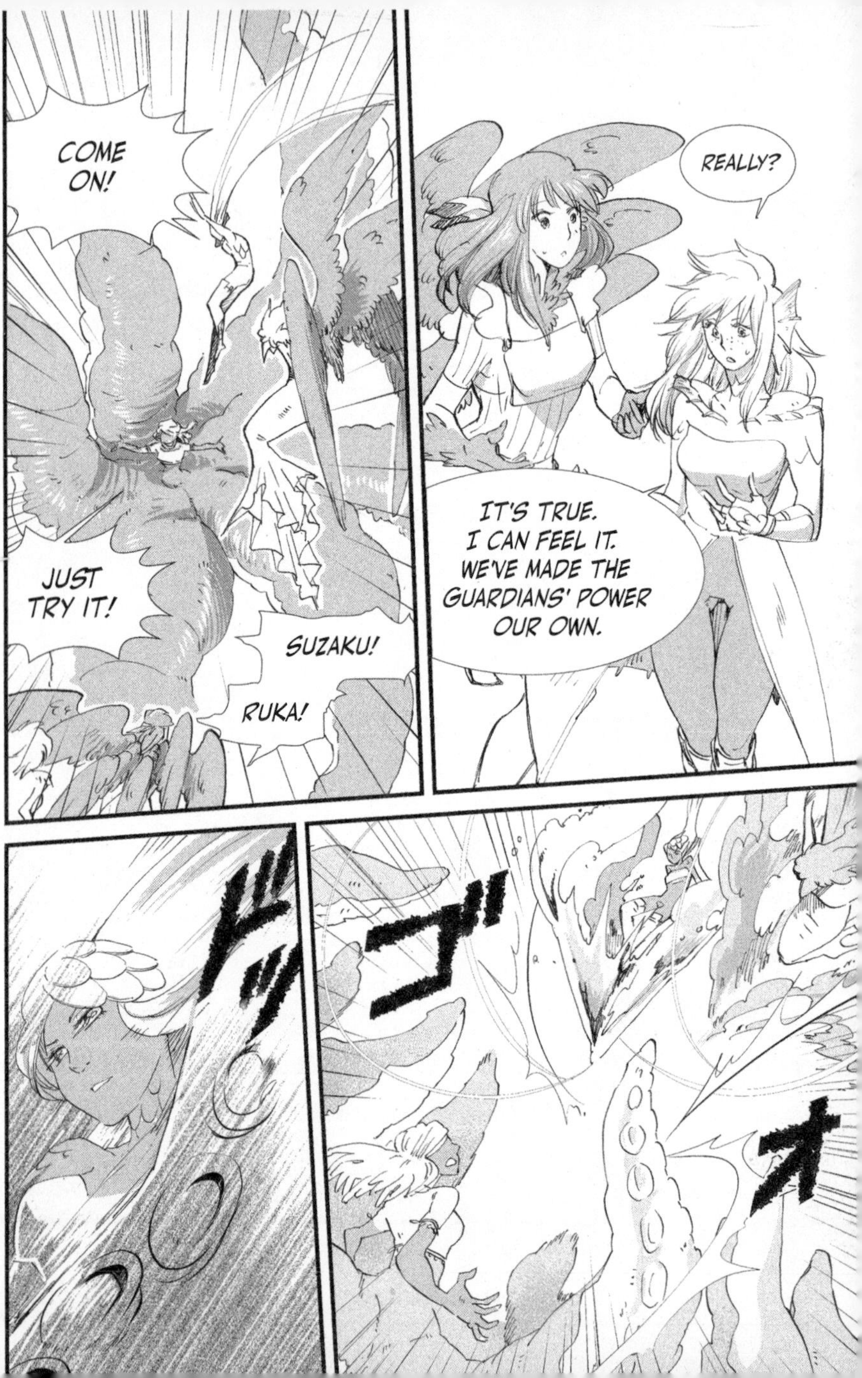
REALLY?
IT'S TRUE. I CAN FEEL IT. WE'VE MADE THE GUARDIANS' POWER OUR OWN.
COME ON!
SUZAKU!
RUKA!
JUST TRY IT!
ゴ
オ
ドッ

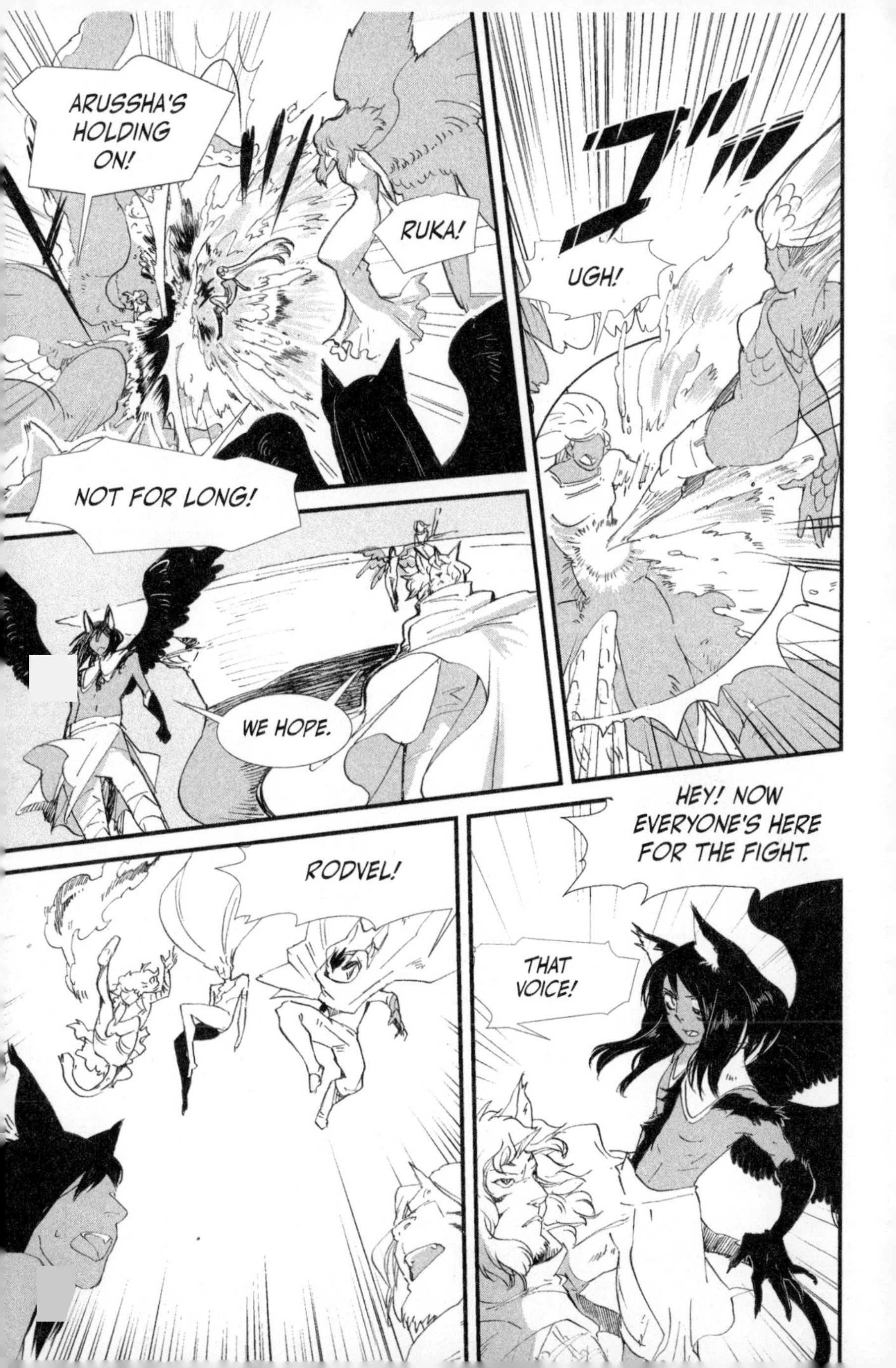
ゴ
UGH!
ARUSSHA'S HOLDING ON!
RUKA!
NOT FOR LONG!
WE HOPE.
HEY! NOW EVERYONE'S HERE FOR THE FIGHT.
THAT VOICE!
RODVEL!

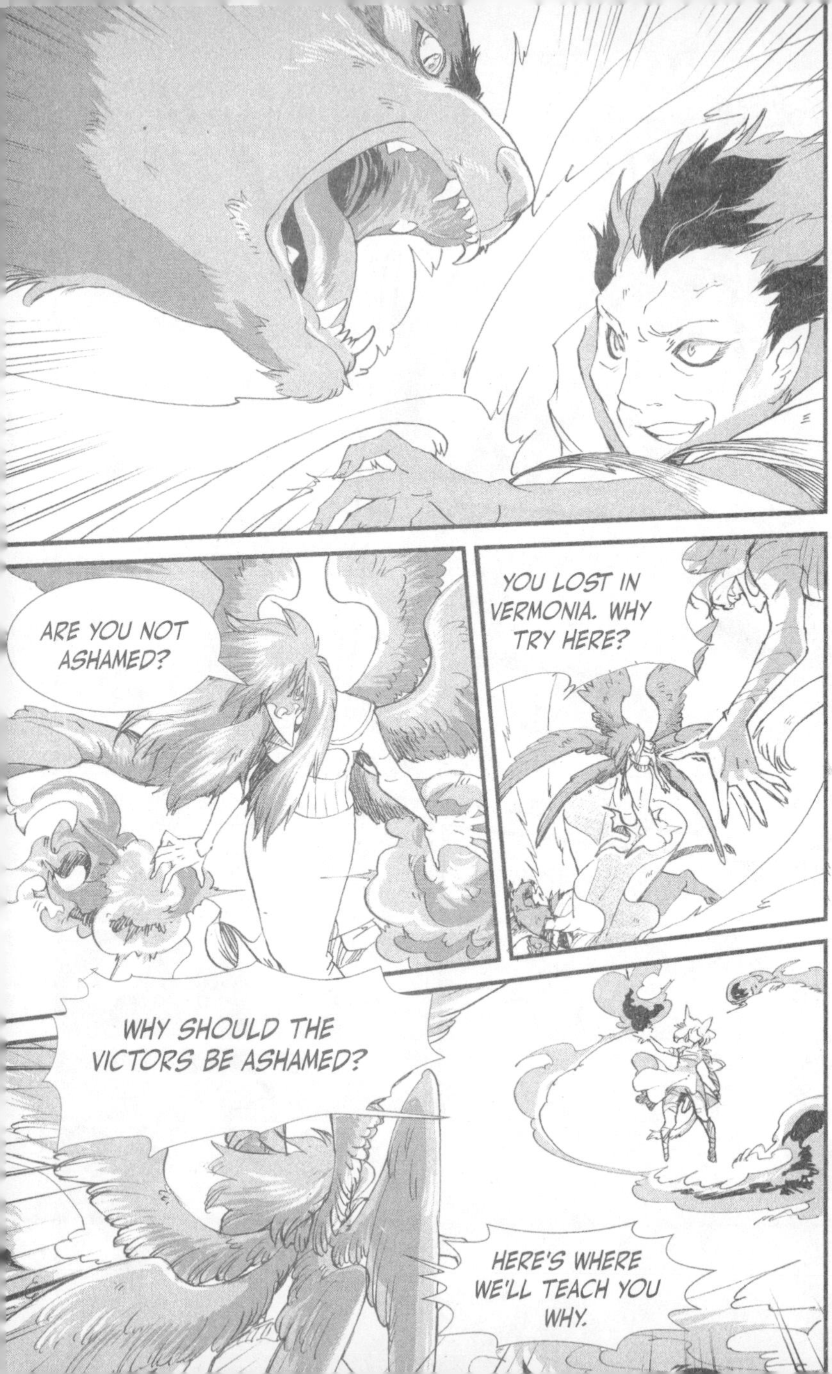
YOU LOST IN VERMONIA. WHY TRY HERE?
ARE YOU NOT ASHAMED?
WHY SHOULD THE VICTORS BE ASHAMED?
HERE'S WHERE WE'LL TEACH YOU WHY.

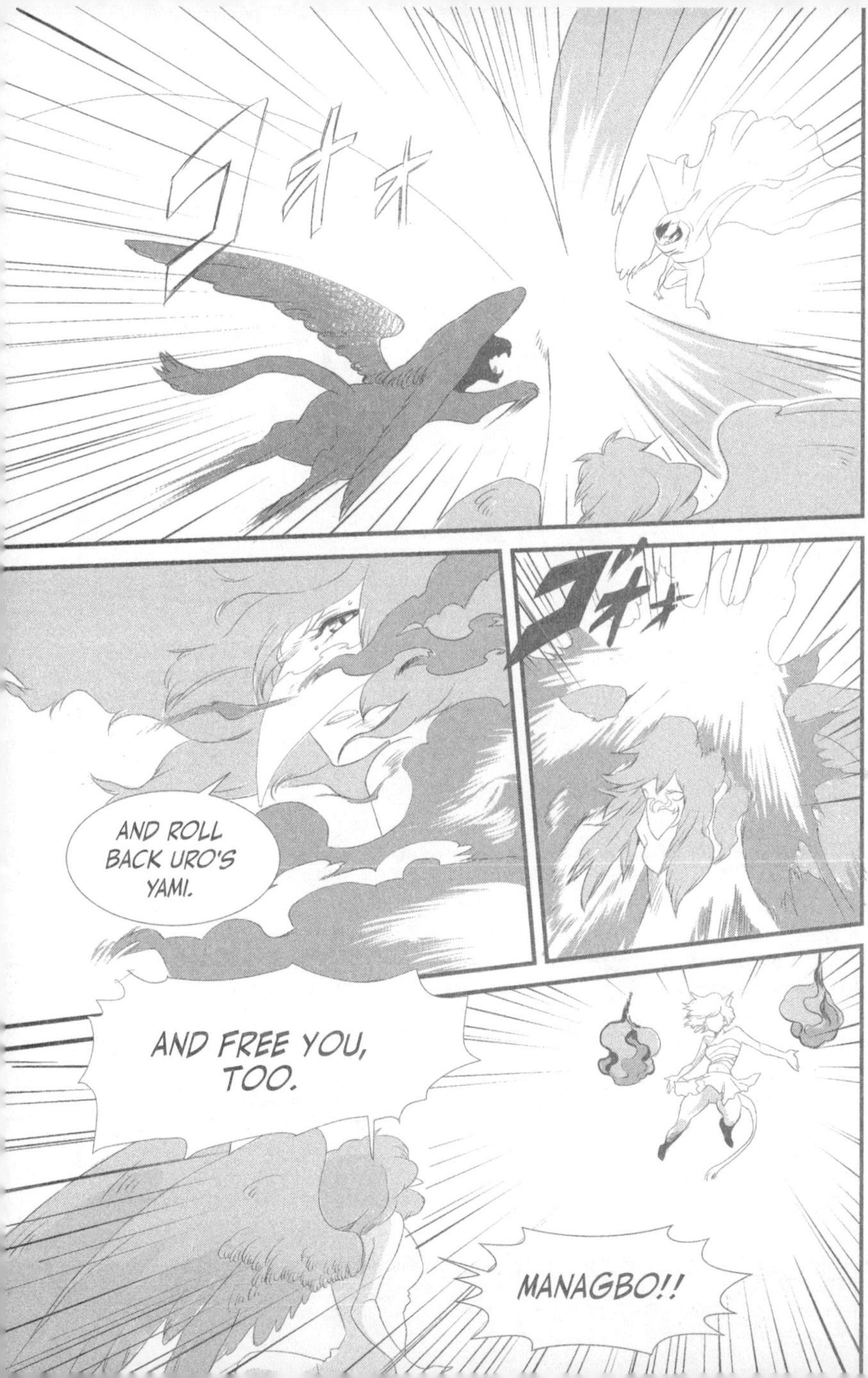
AND ROLL BACK URO'S YAMI.
AND FREE YOU, TOO.
MANAGBO!!

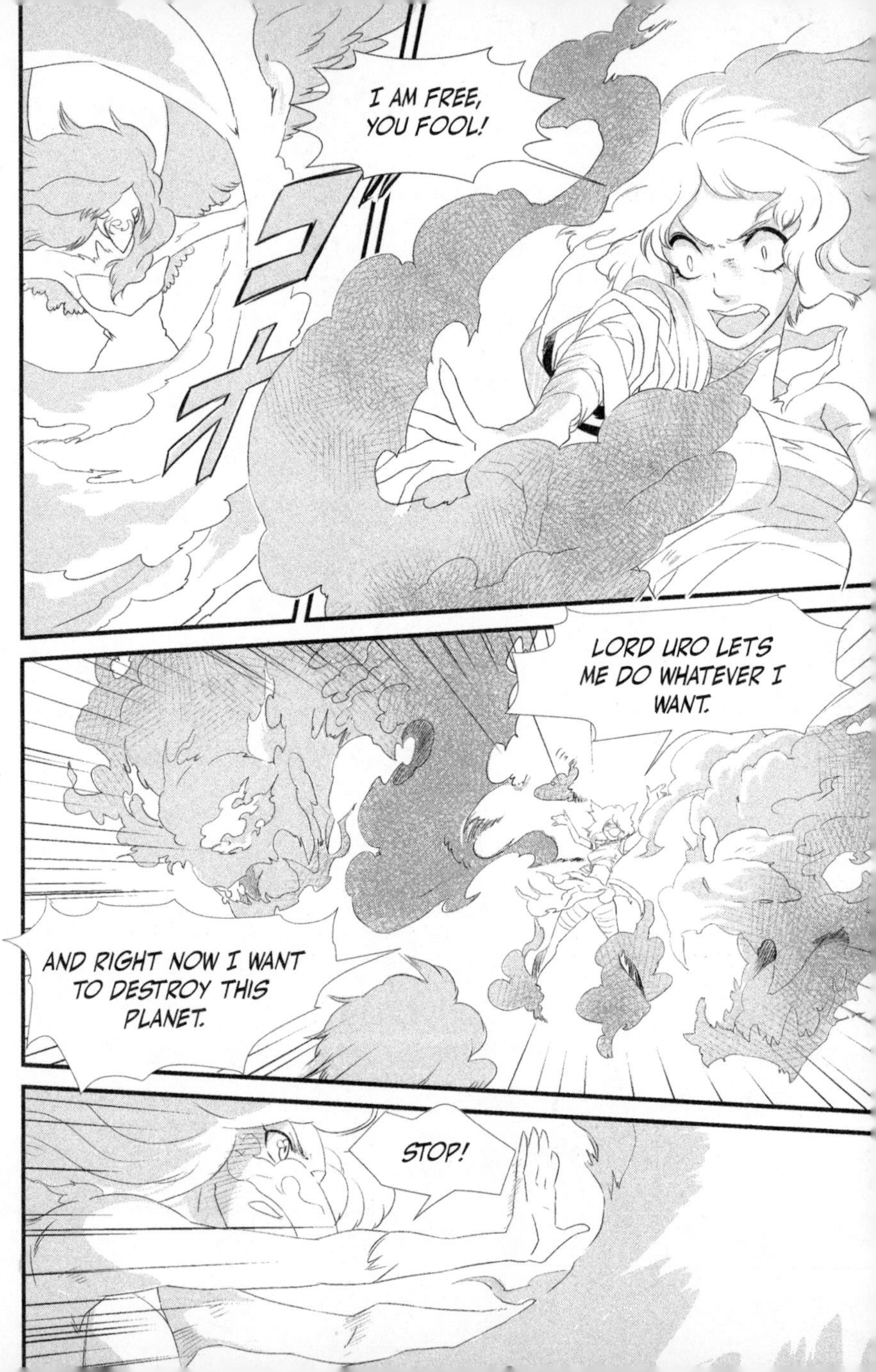
I AM FREE, YOU FOOL!
LORD URO LETS ME DO WHATEVER I WANT.
AND RIGHT NOW I WANT TO DESTROY THIS PLANET.
STOP!

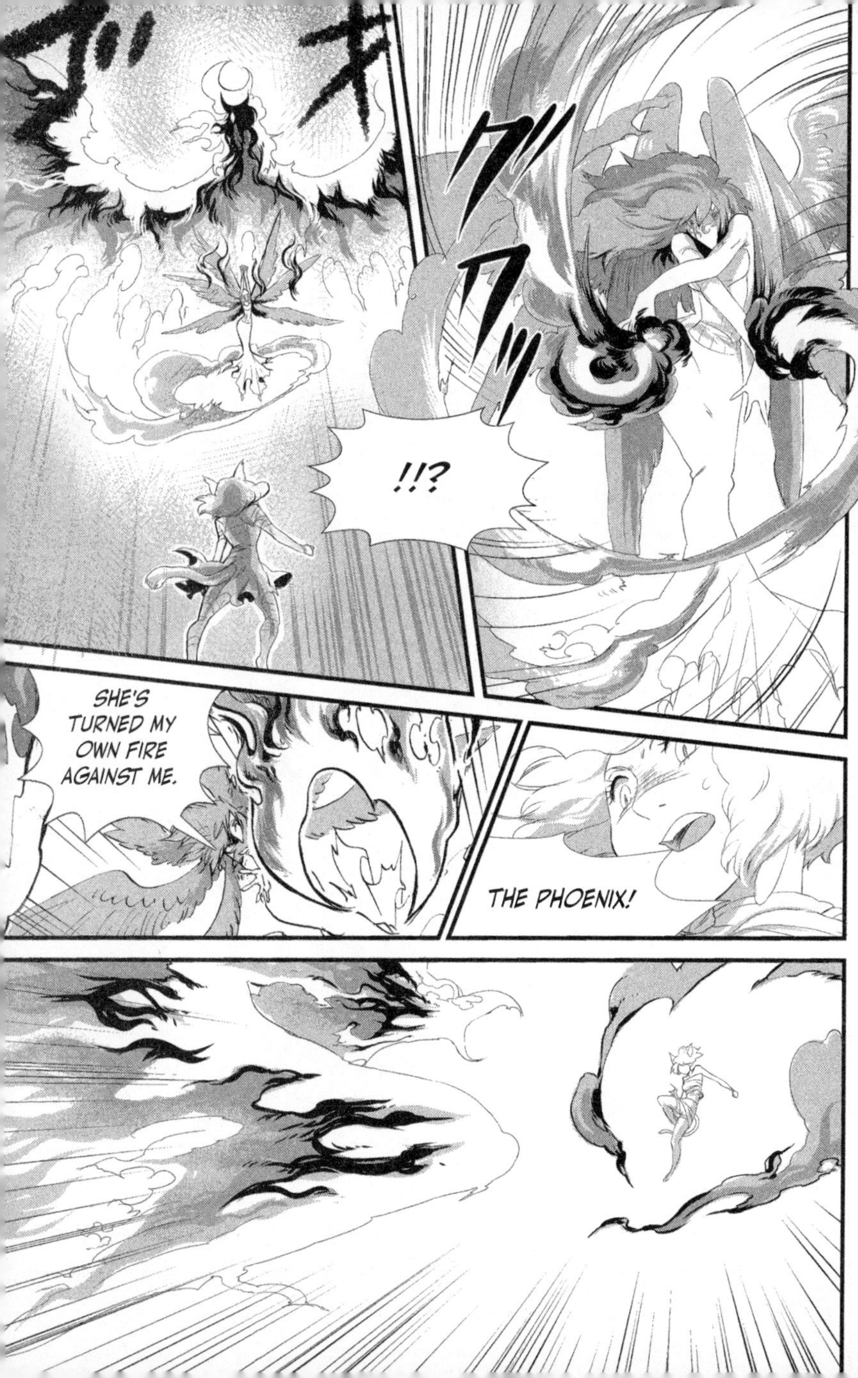
!!?
THE PHOENIX!
SHE'S TURNED MY OWN FIRE AGAINST ME.

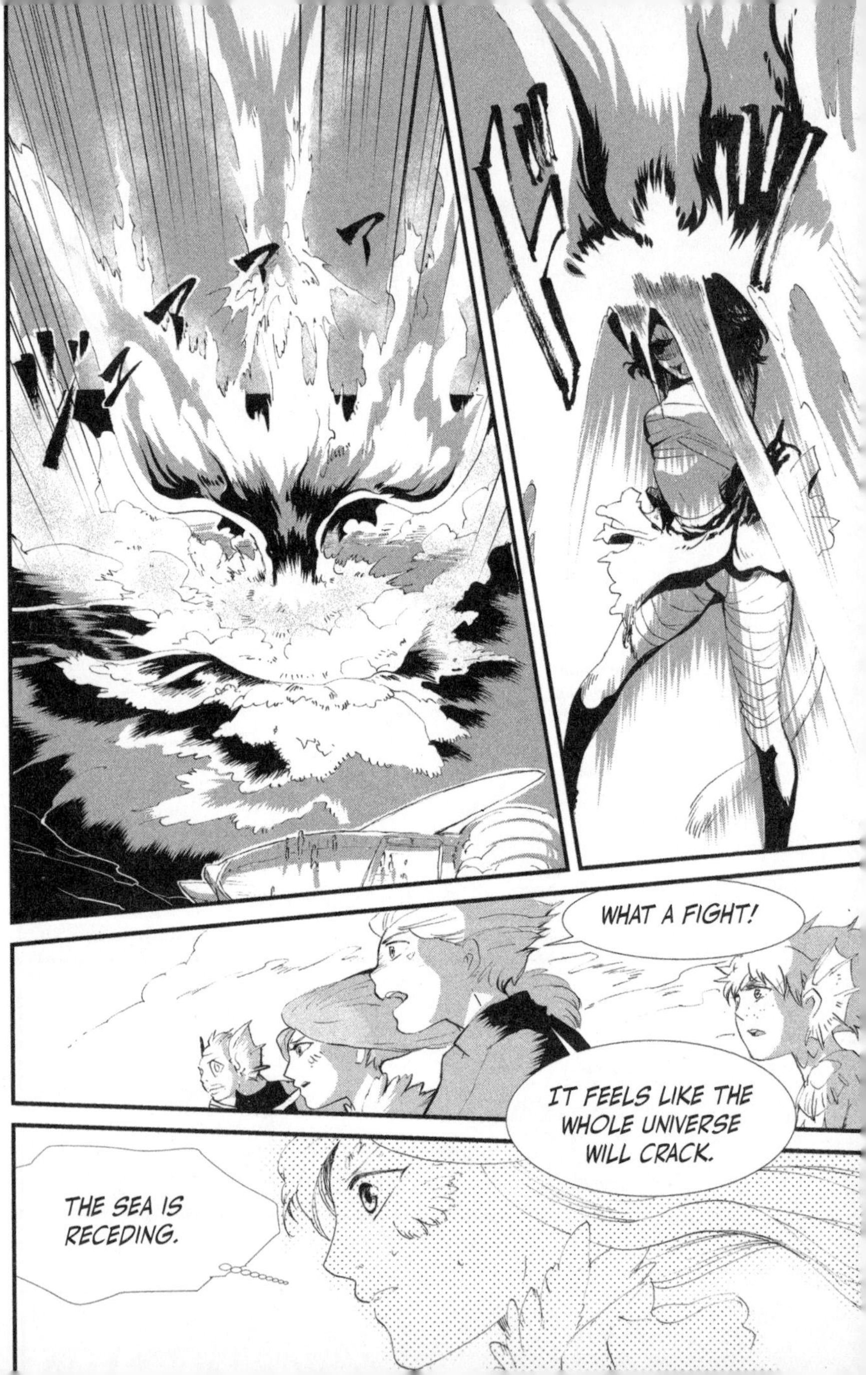
WHAT A FIGHT!
IT FEELS LIKE THE WHOLE UNIVERSE WILL CRACK.
THE SEA IS RECEDING.

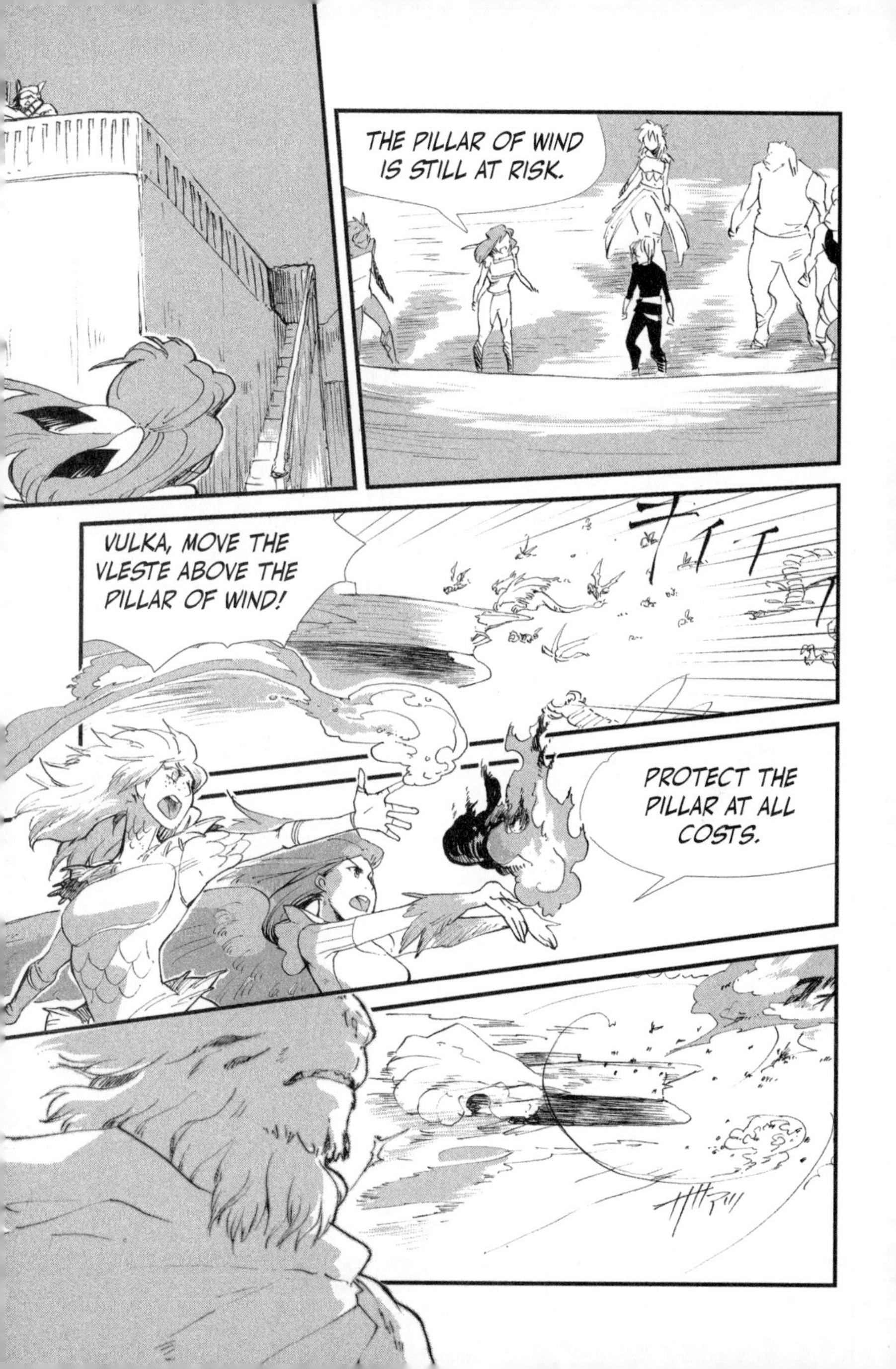
THE PILLAR OF WIND IS STILL AT RISK.
VULKA, MOVE THE VLESTE ABOVE THE PILLAR OF WIND!
PROTECT THE PILLAR AT ALL COSTS.

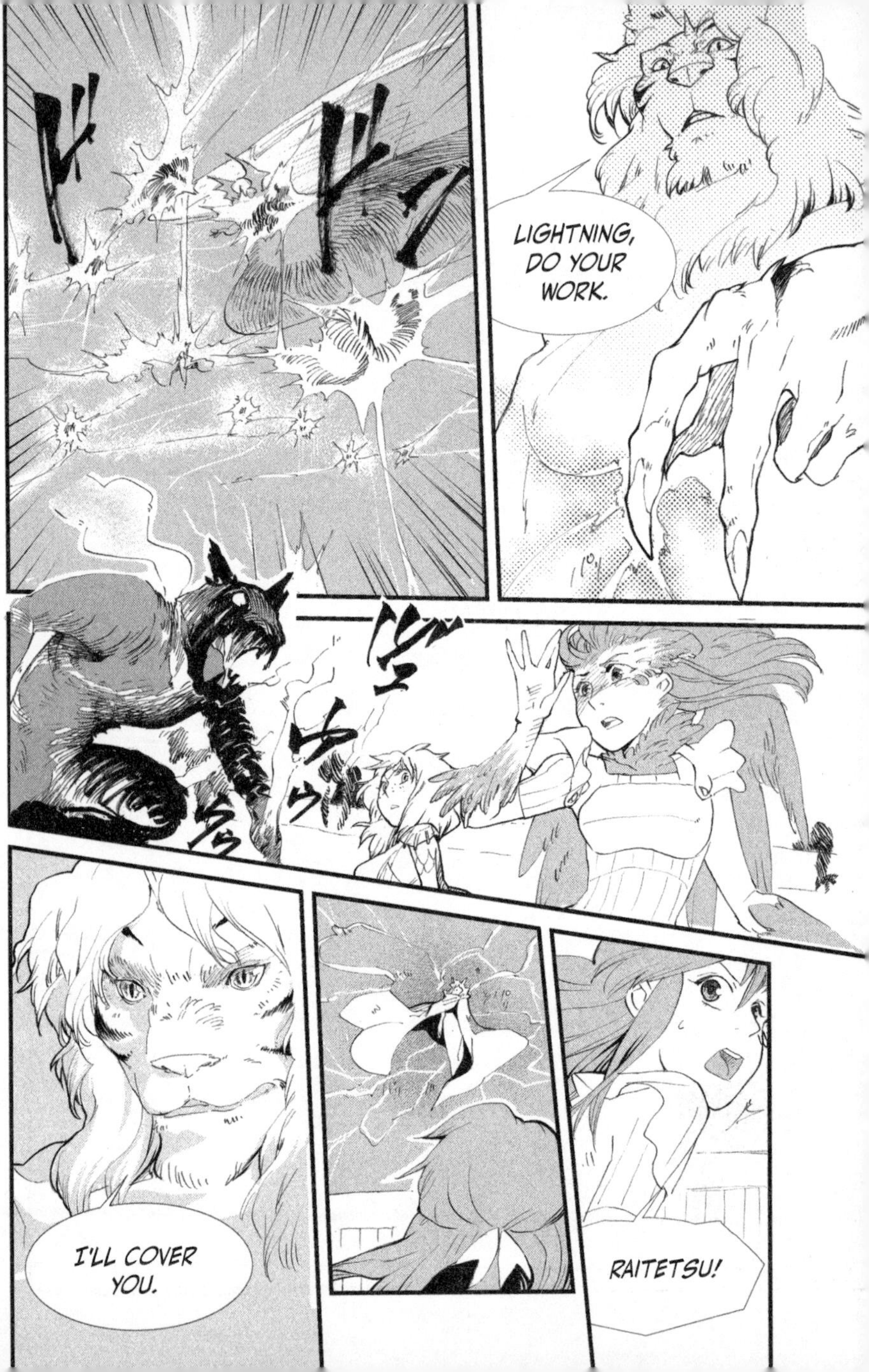
LIGHTNING, DO YOUR WORK.
RAITETSU!
I'LL COVER YOU.

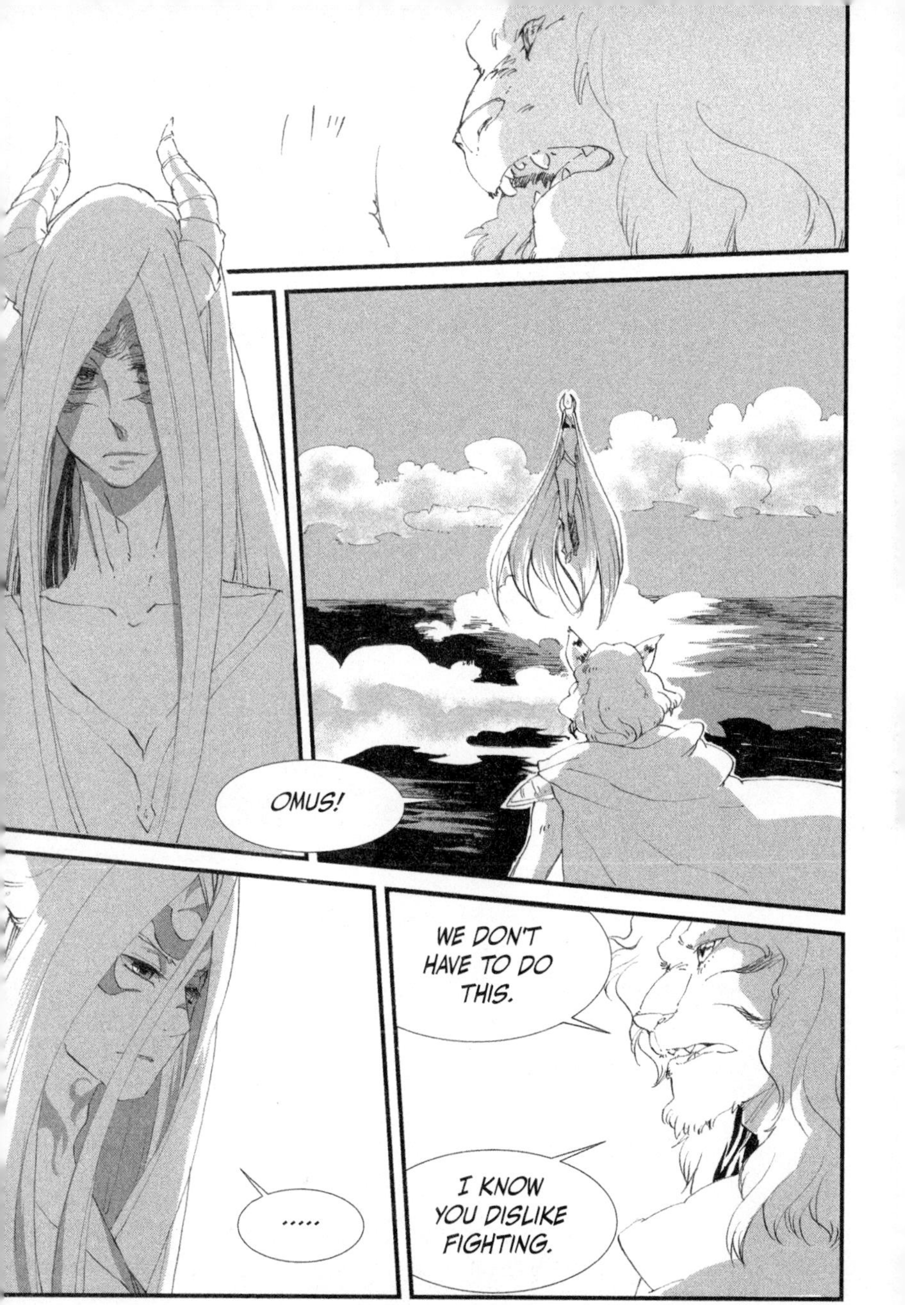
OMUS!
WE DON'T HAVE TO DO THIS.
I KNOW YOU DISLIKE FIGHTING.
.....

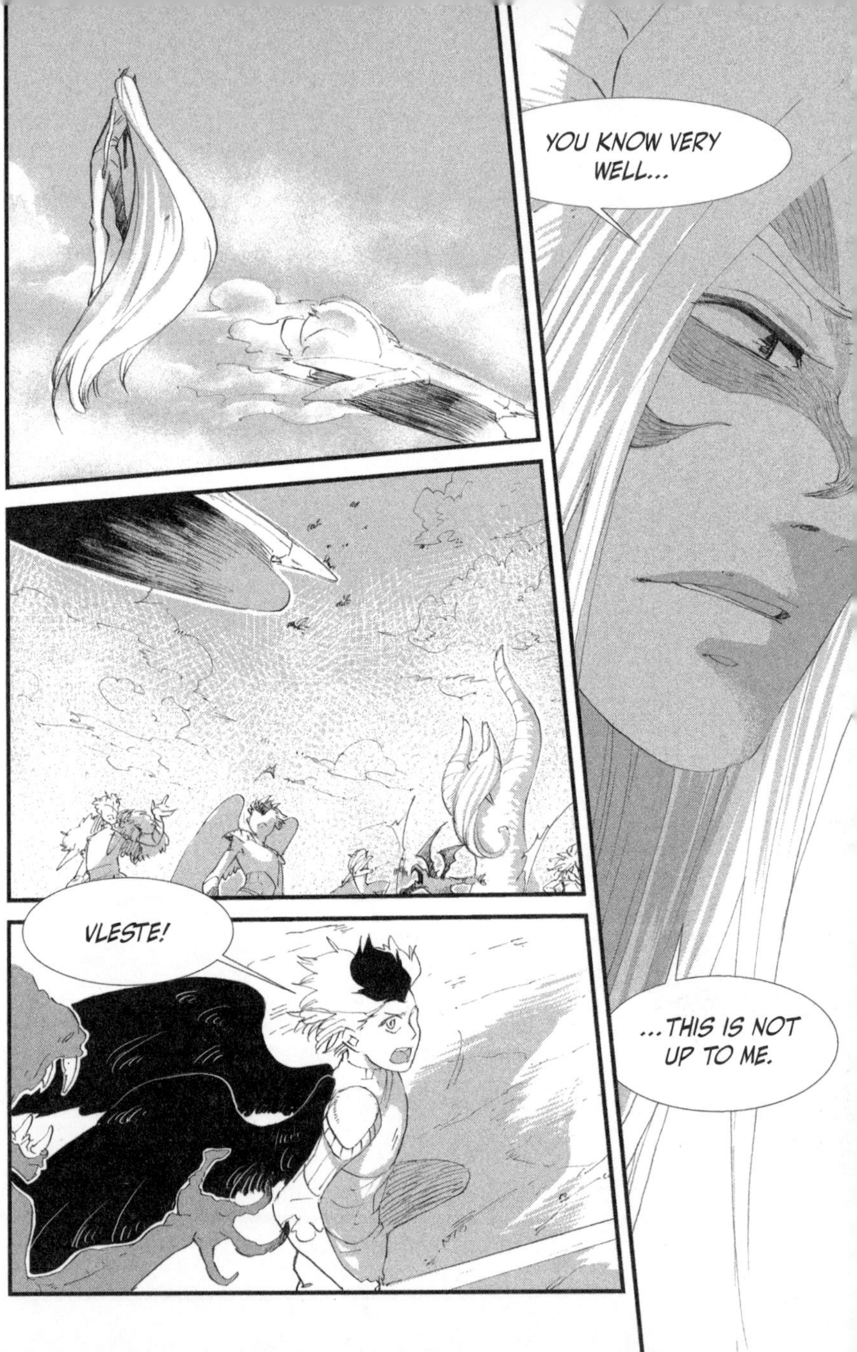
YOU KNOW VERY WELL...
...THIS IS NOT UP TO ME.
VLESTE!

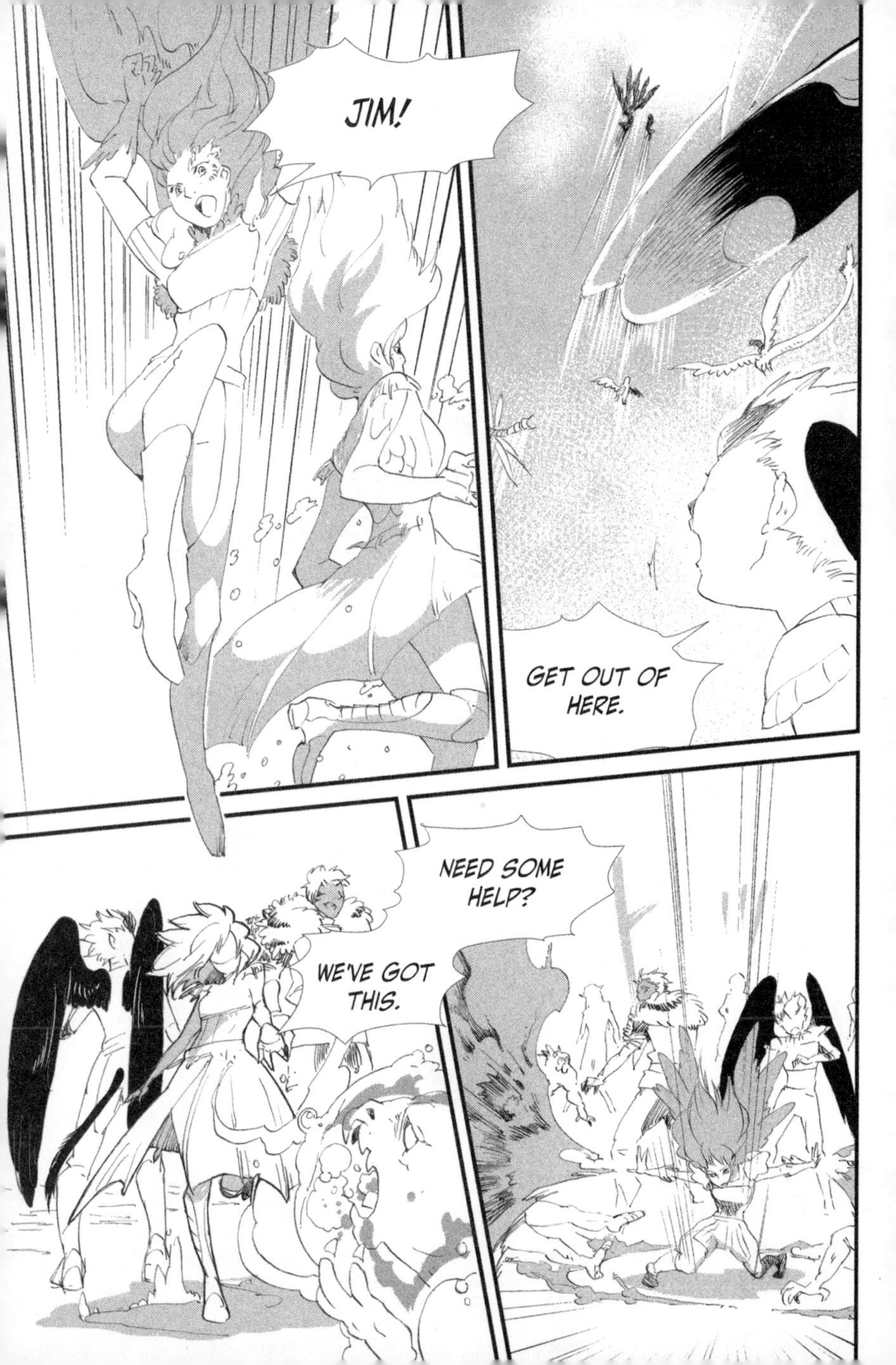
GET OUT OF HERE.
JIM!
NEED SOME HELP?
WE'VE GOT THIS.

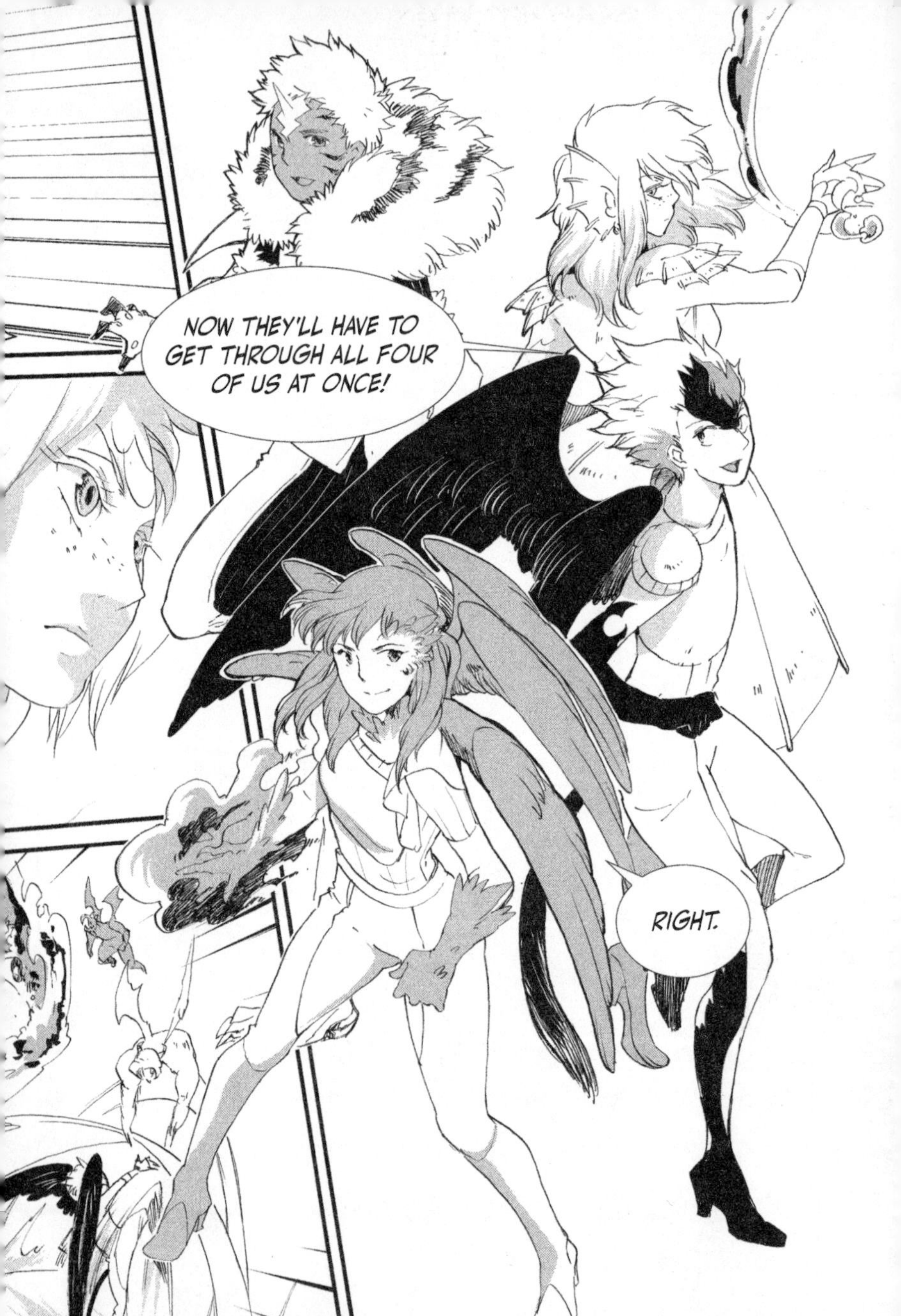
NOW THEY'LL HAVE TO GET THROUGH ALL FOUR OF US AT ONCE!
RIGHT.

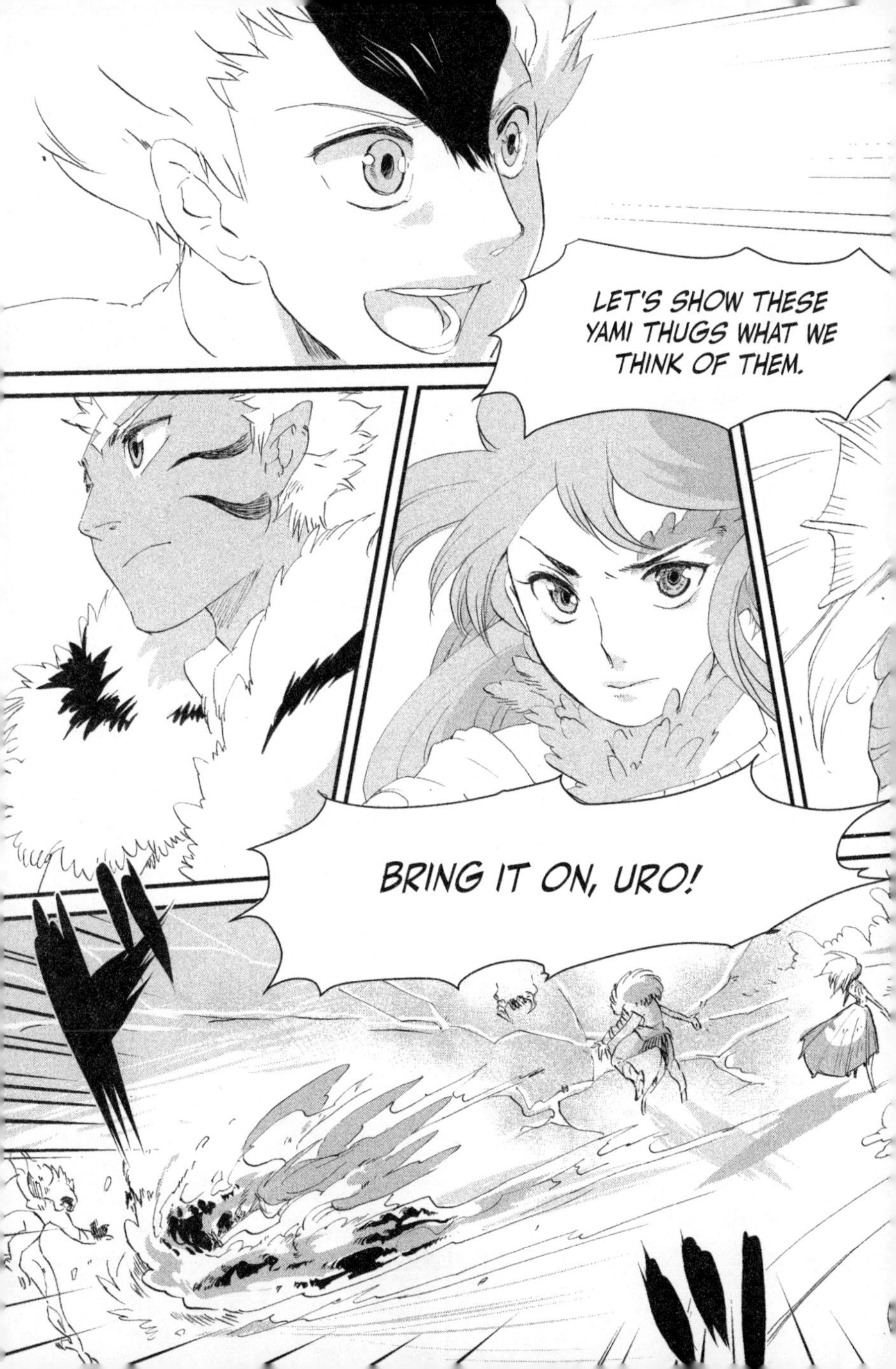
LET'S SHOW THESE YAMI THUGS WHAT WE THINK OF THEM.
BRING IT ON, URO!

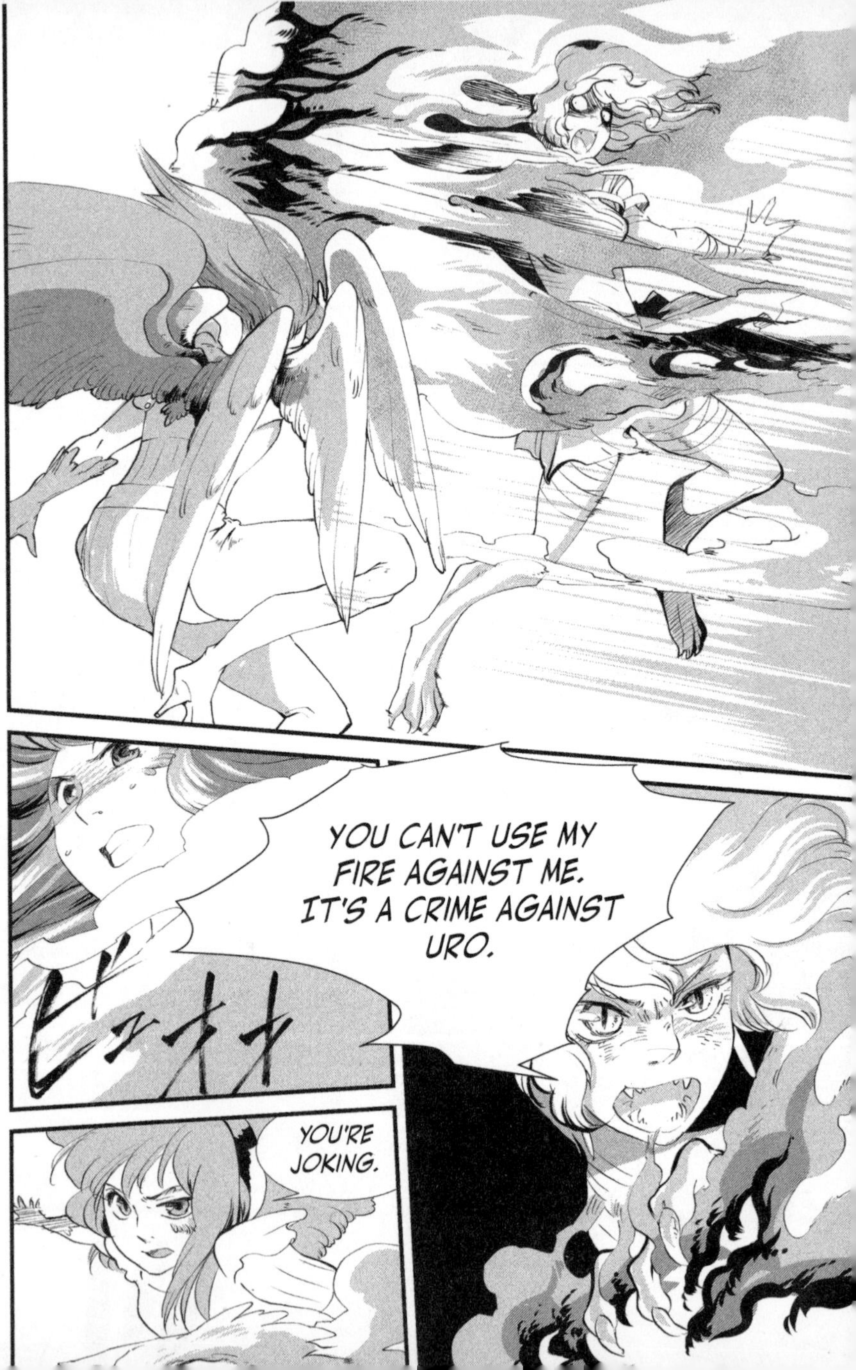
YOU CAN'T USE MY FIRE AGAINST ME. IT'S A CRIME AGAINST URO.
YOU'RE JOKING.

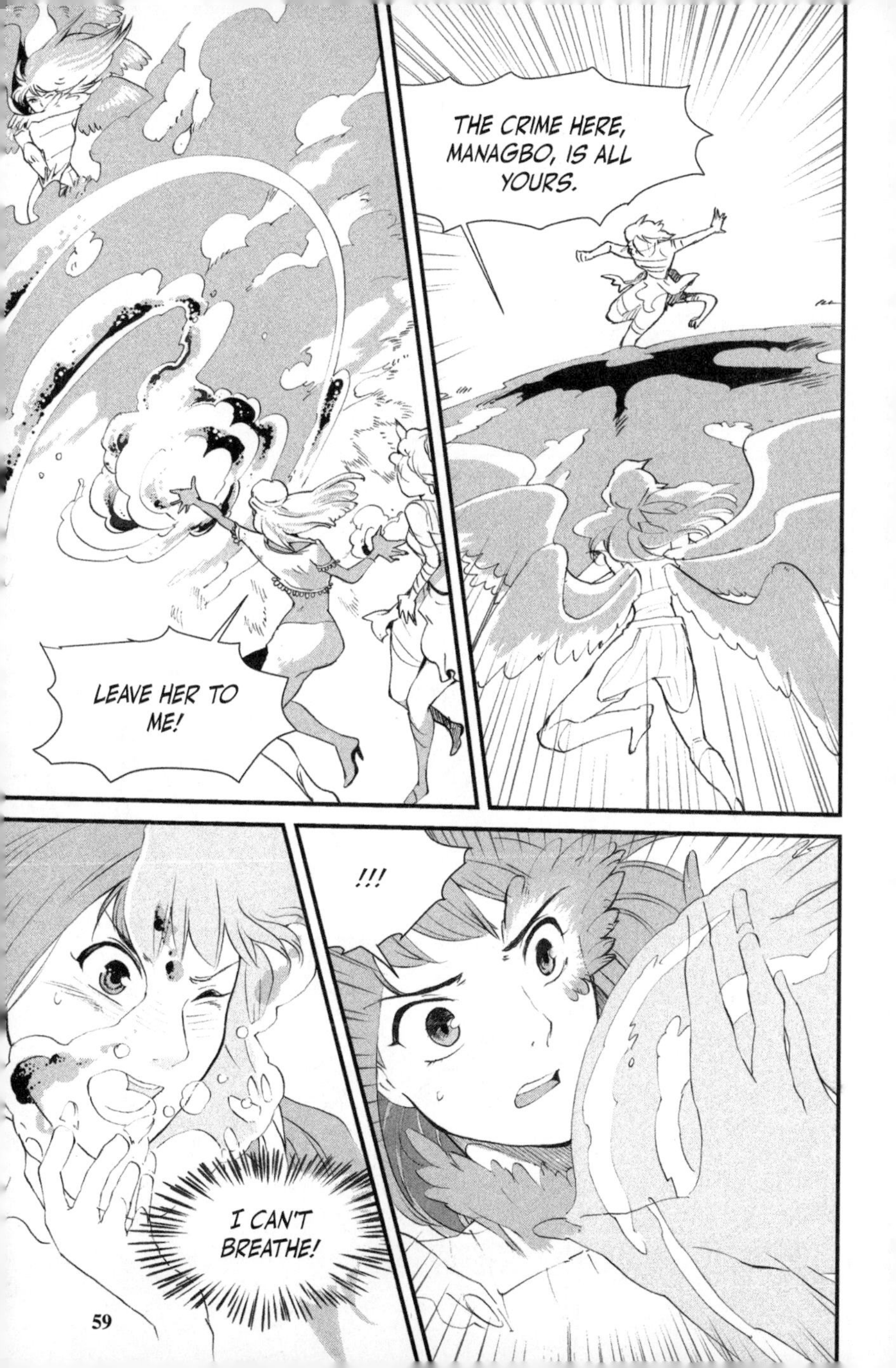
THE CRIME HERE, MANAGBO, IS ALL YOURS.
LEAVE HER TO ME!
!!!
I CAN'T BREATHE!

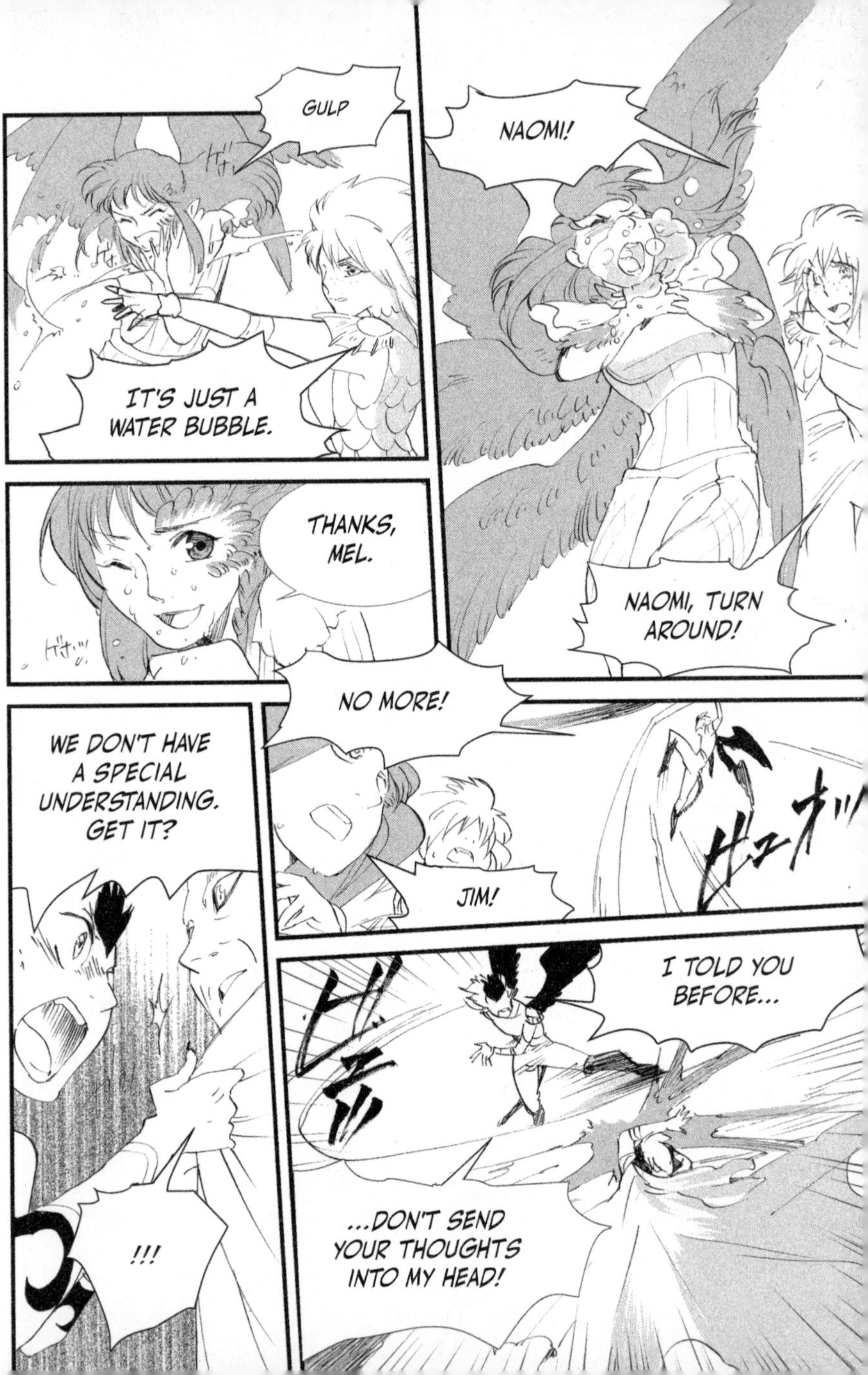
NAOMI!
NAOMI, TURN AROUND!
GULP
IT'S JUST A WATER BUBBLE.
THANKS, MEL.
NO MORE!
JIM!
I TOLD YOU BEFORE...
...DON'T SEND YOUR THOUGHTS INTO MY HEAD!
WE DON'T HAVE A SPECIAL UNDERSTANDING. GET IT?
!!!

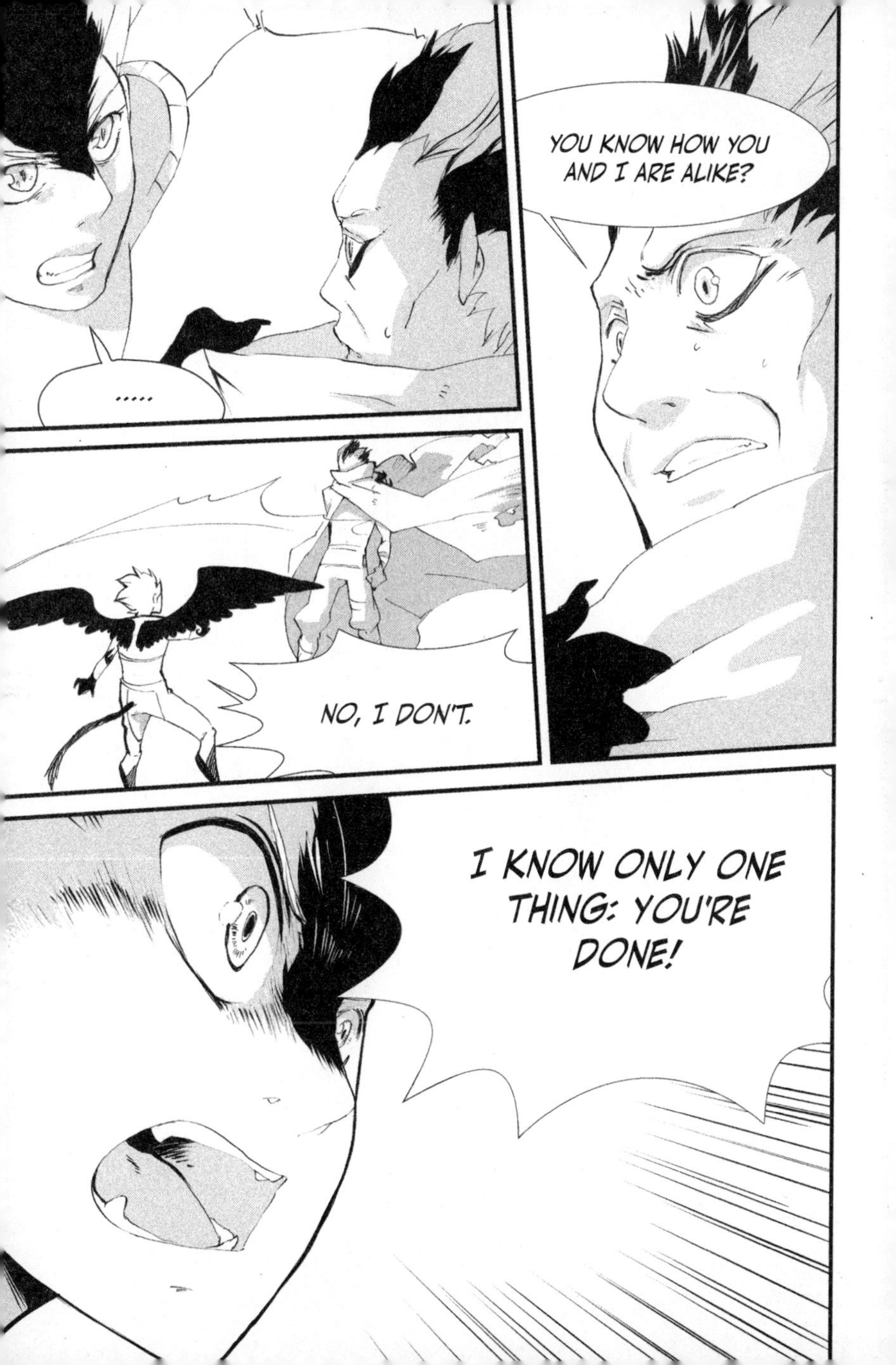
YOU KNOW HOW YOU AND I ARE ALIKE?
......
NO, I DON'T.
I KNOW ONLY ONE THING: YOU'RE DONE!

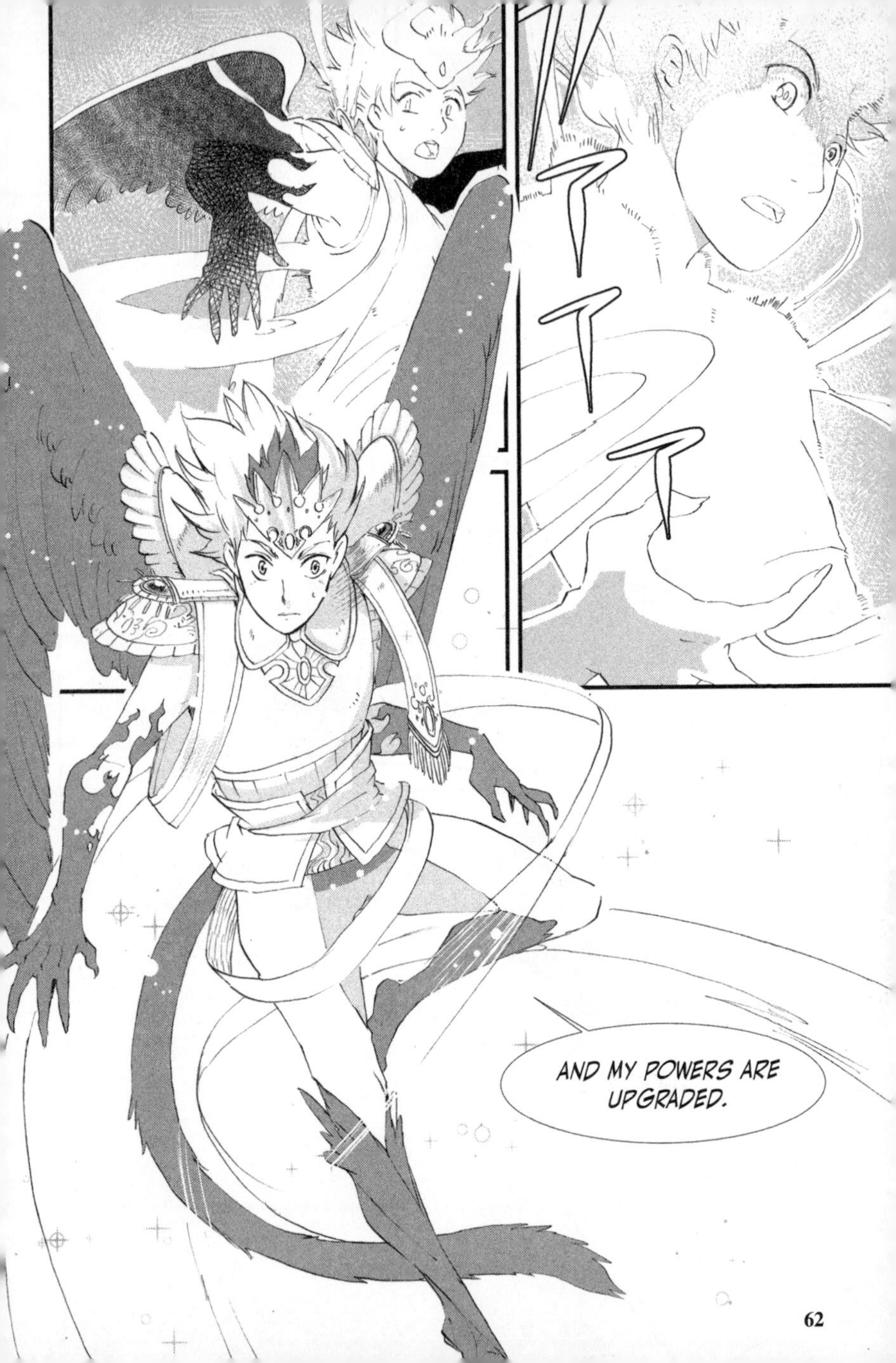
AND MY POWERS ARE UPGRADED.

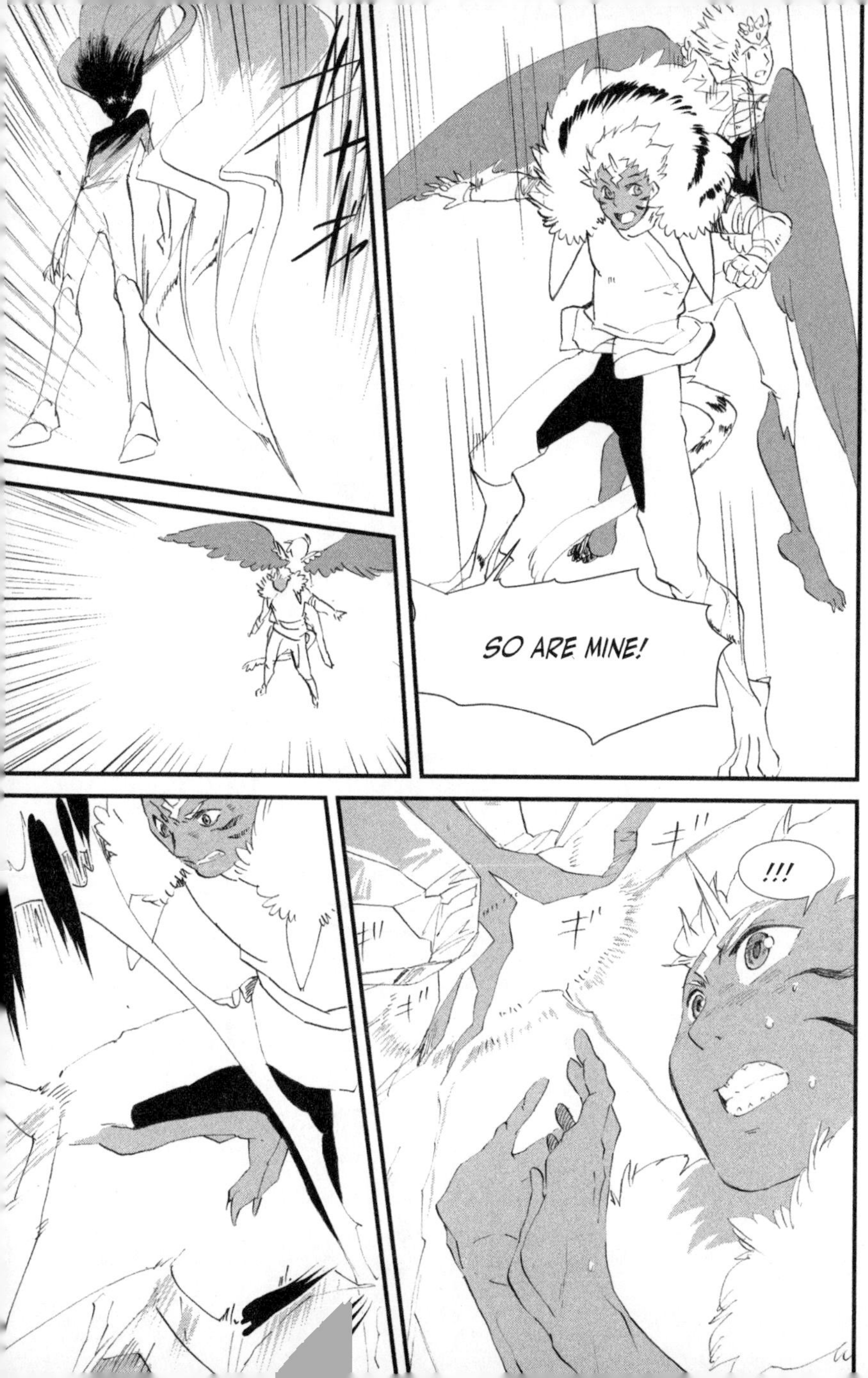
SO ARE MINE!
!!!
ギ
ギ
ギ
ギ

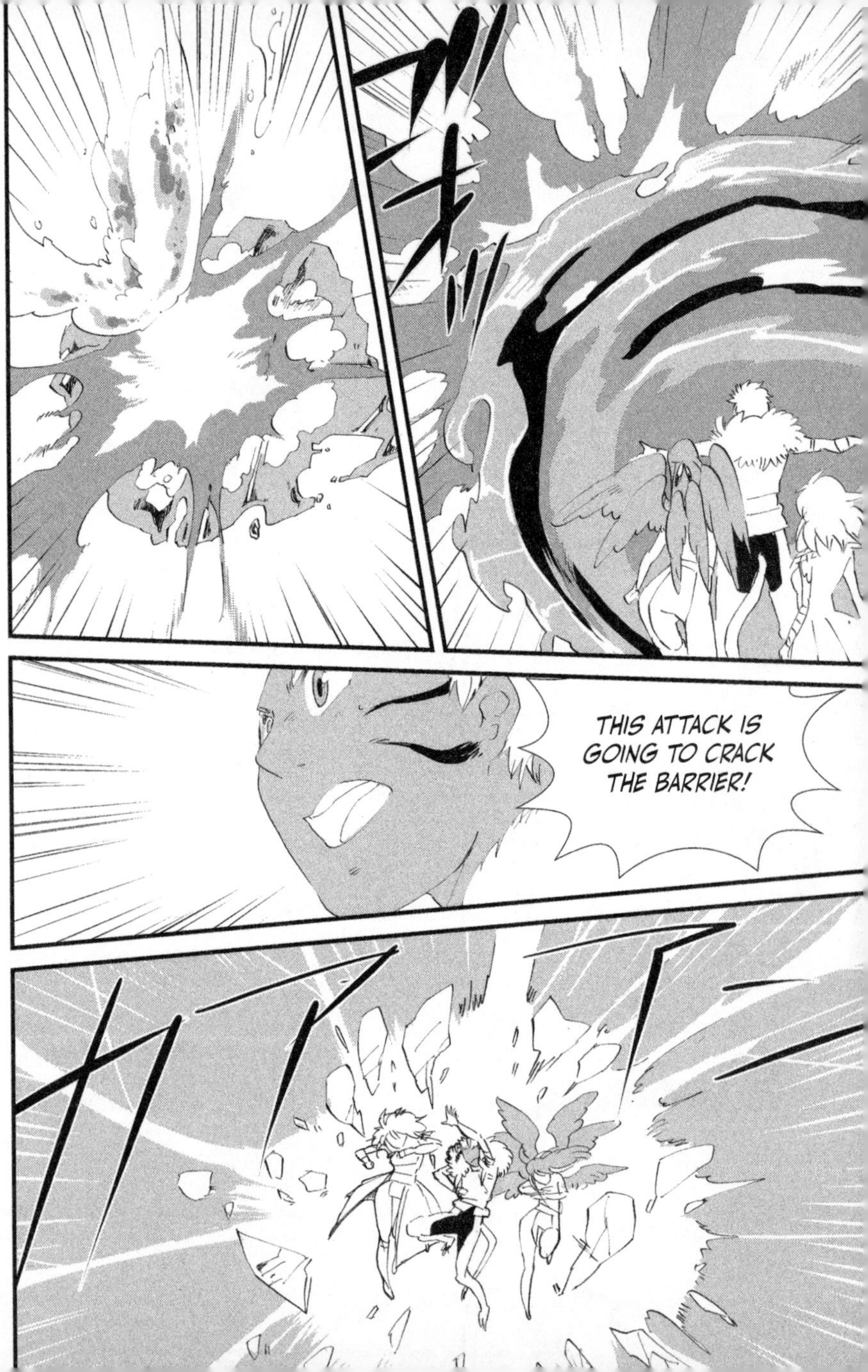
THIS ATTACK IS GOING TO CRACK THE BARRIER!

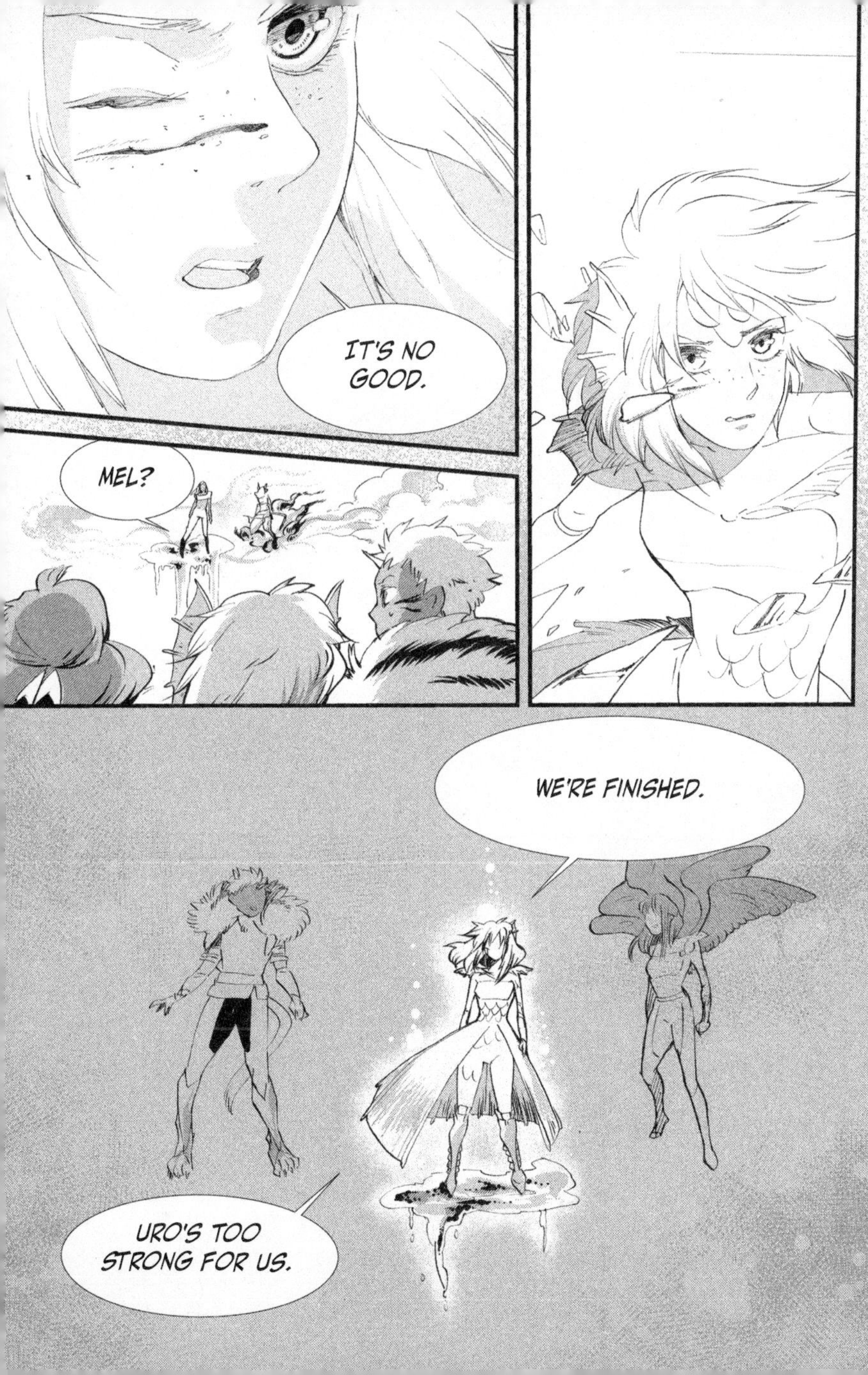
IT'S NO GOOD.
MEL?
WE'RE FINISHED.
URO'S TOO STRONG FOR US.

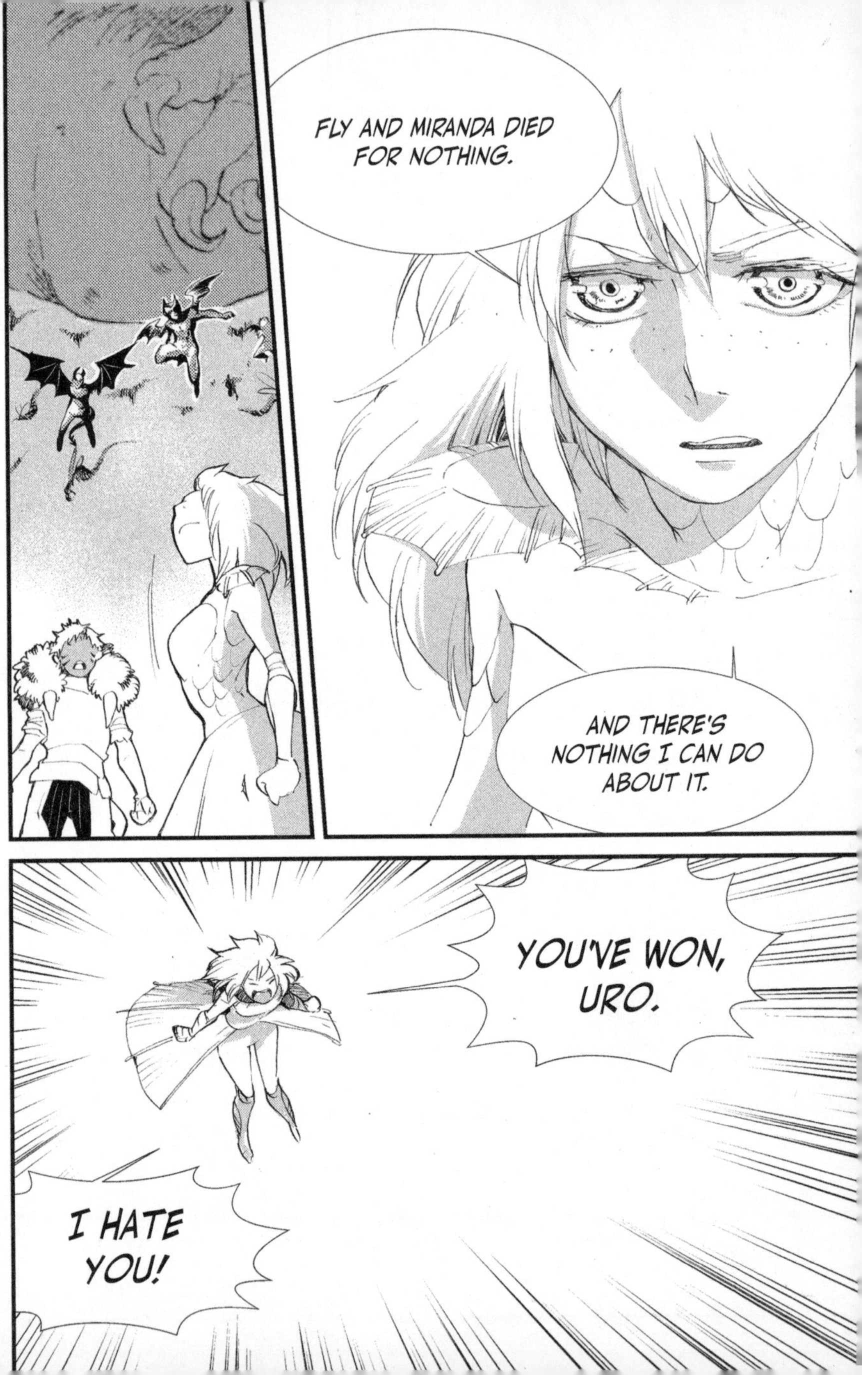
FLY AND MIRANDA DIED FOR NOTHING.
AND THERE'S NOTHING I CAN DO ABOUT IT.
YOU'VE WON, URO.
I HATE YOU!

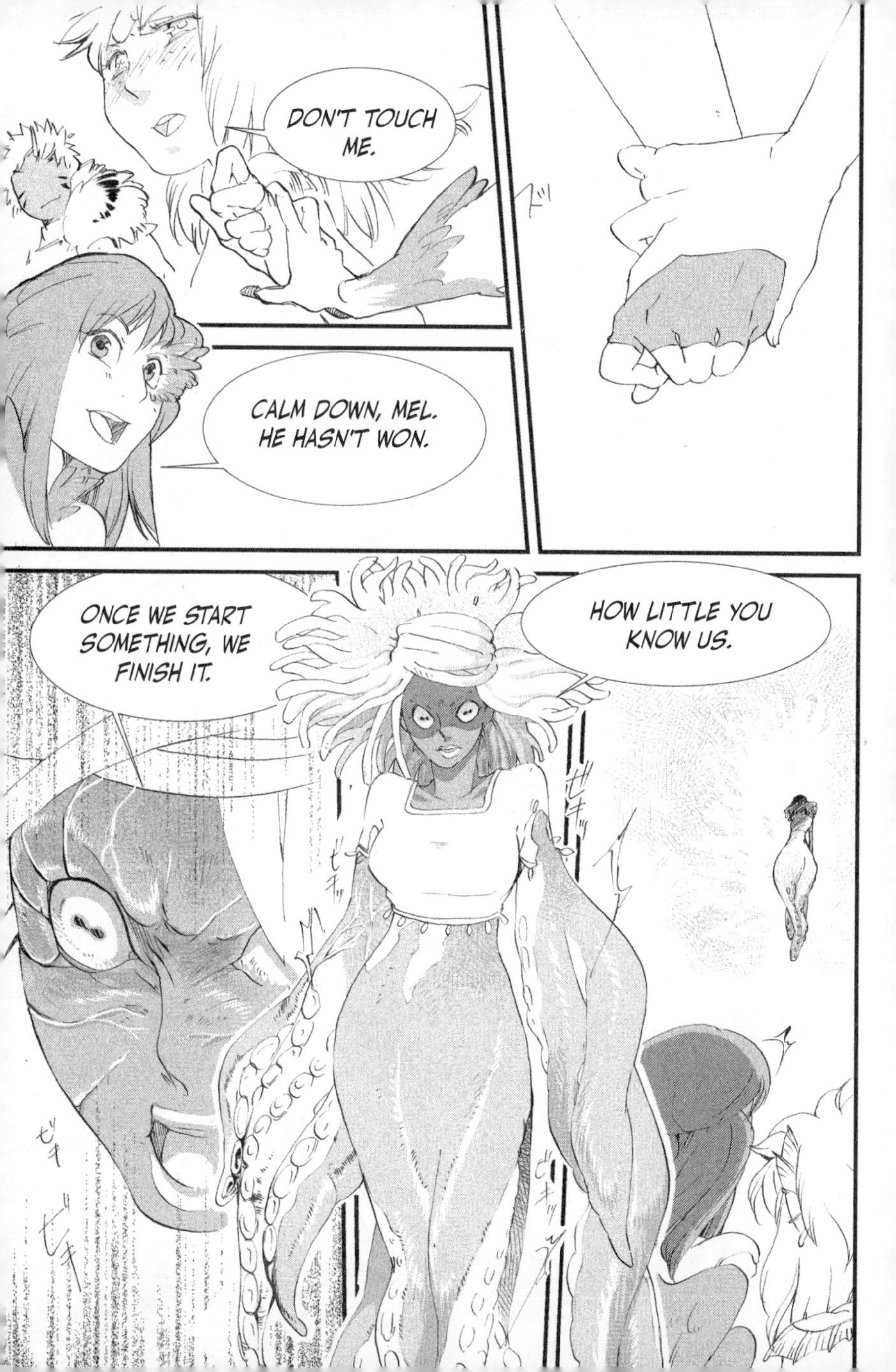
DON'T TOUCH ME.
CALM DOWN, MEL. HE HASN'T WON.
HOW LITTLE YOU KNOW US.
ONCE WE START SOMETHING, WE FINISH IT.

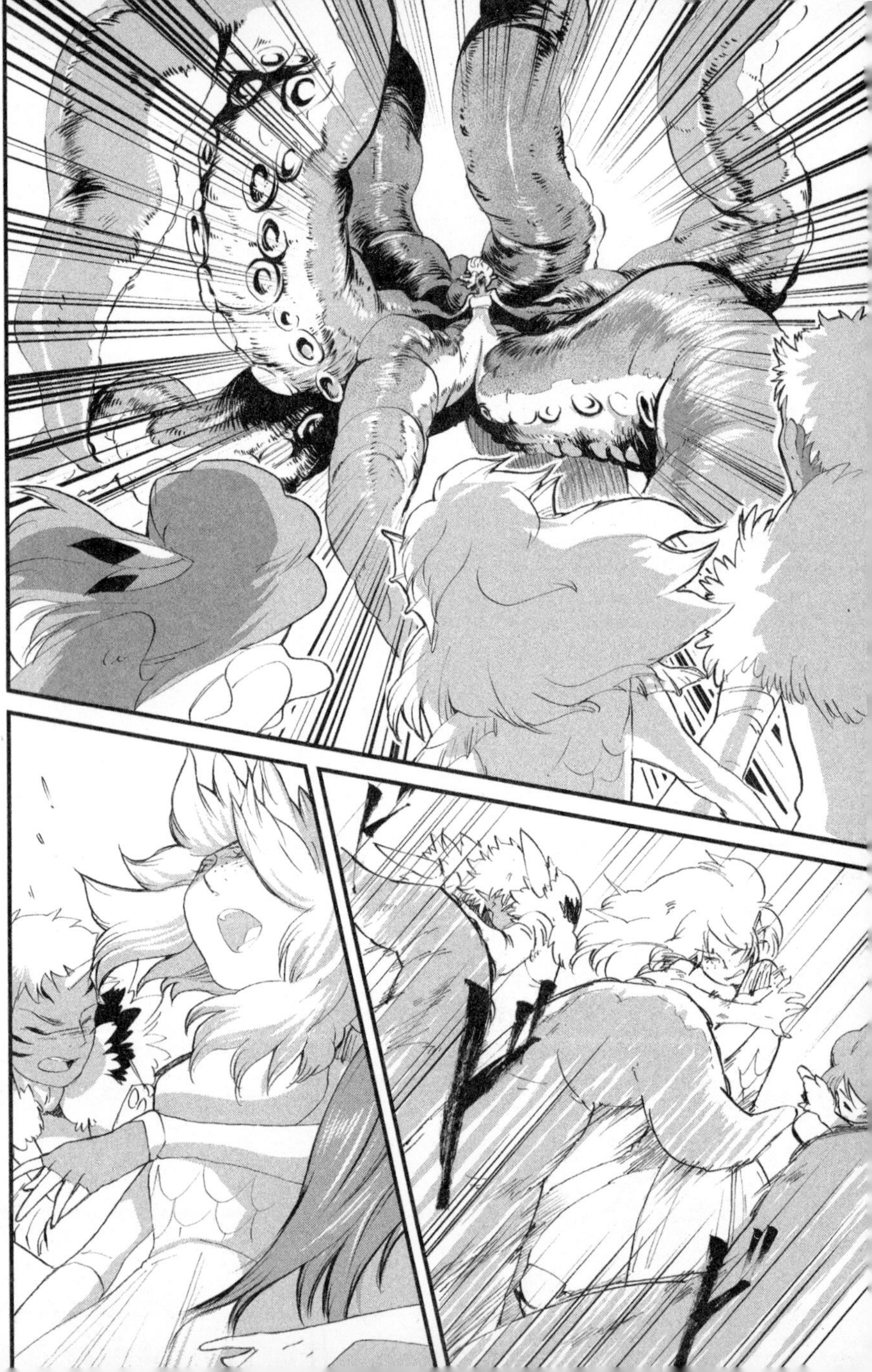

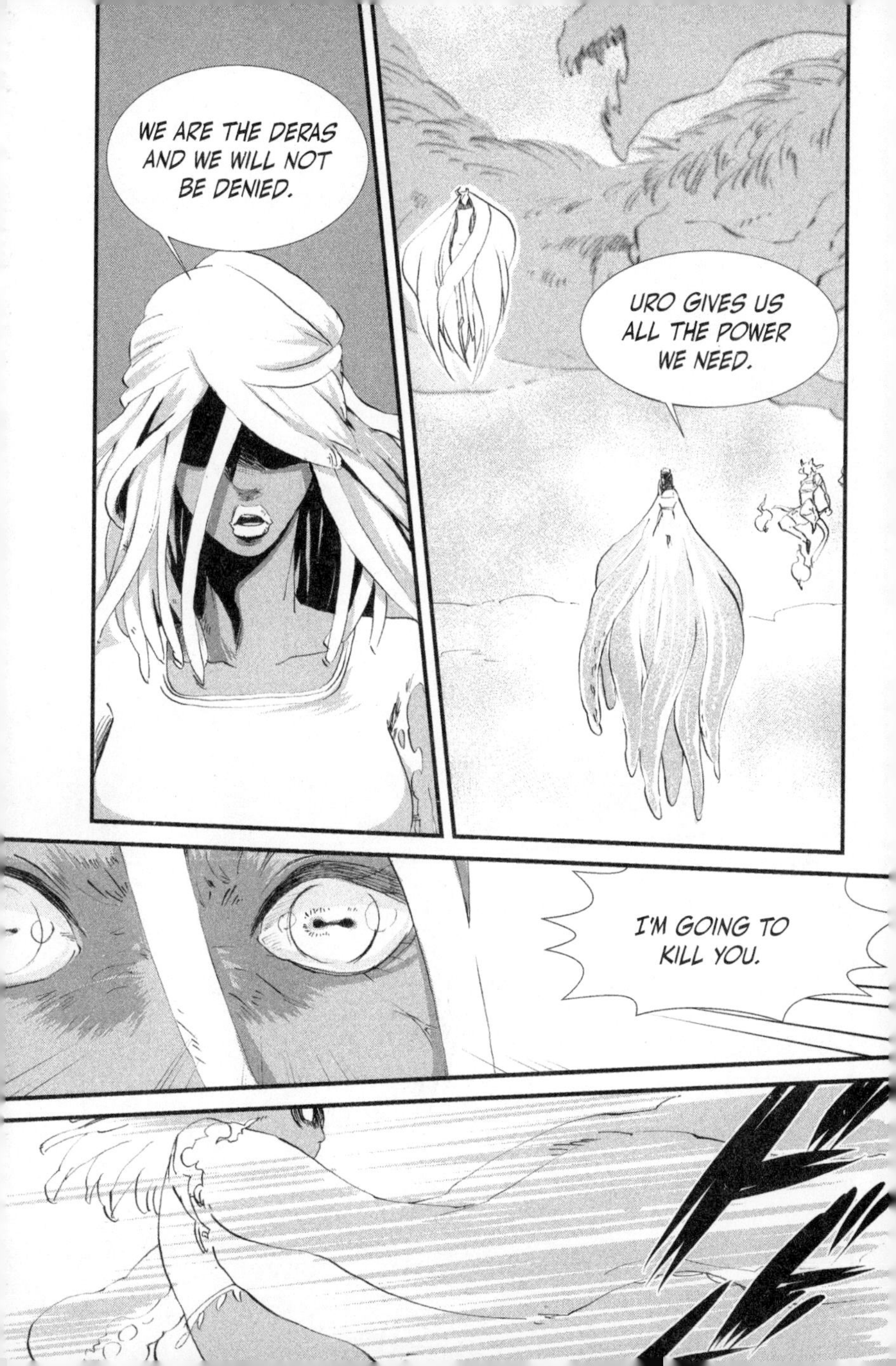
URO GIVES US ALL THE POWER WE NEED.
WE ARE THE DERAS AND WE WILL NOT BE DENIED.
I'M GOING TO KILL YOU.

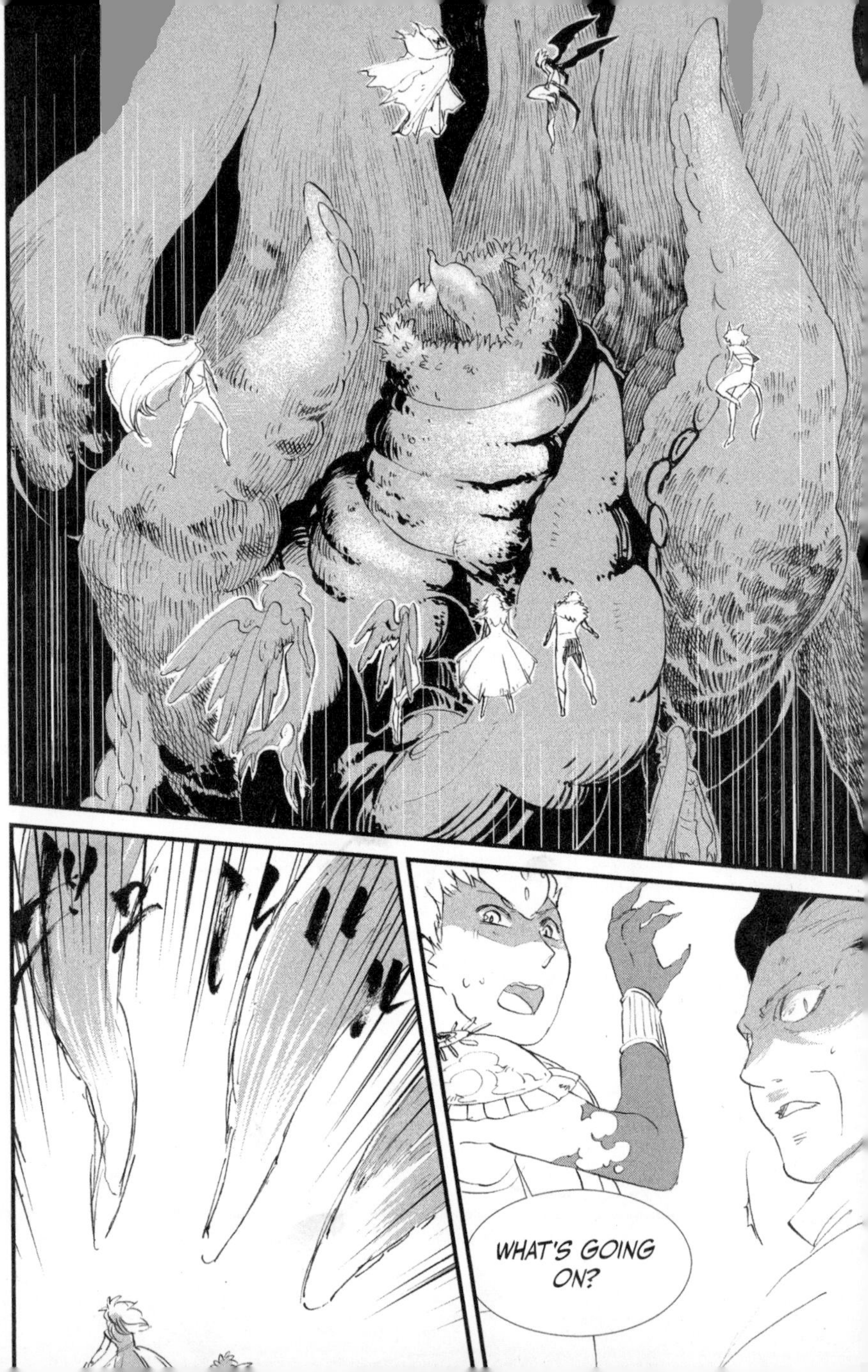
WHAT'S GOING ON?

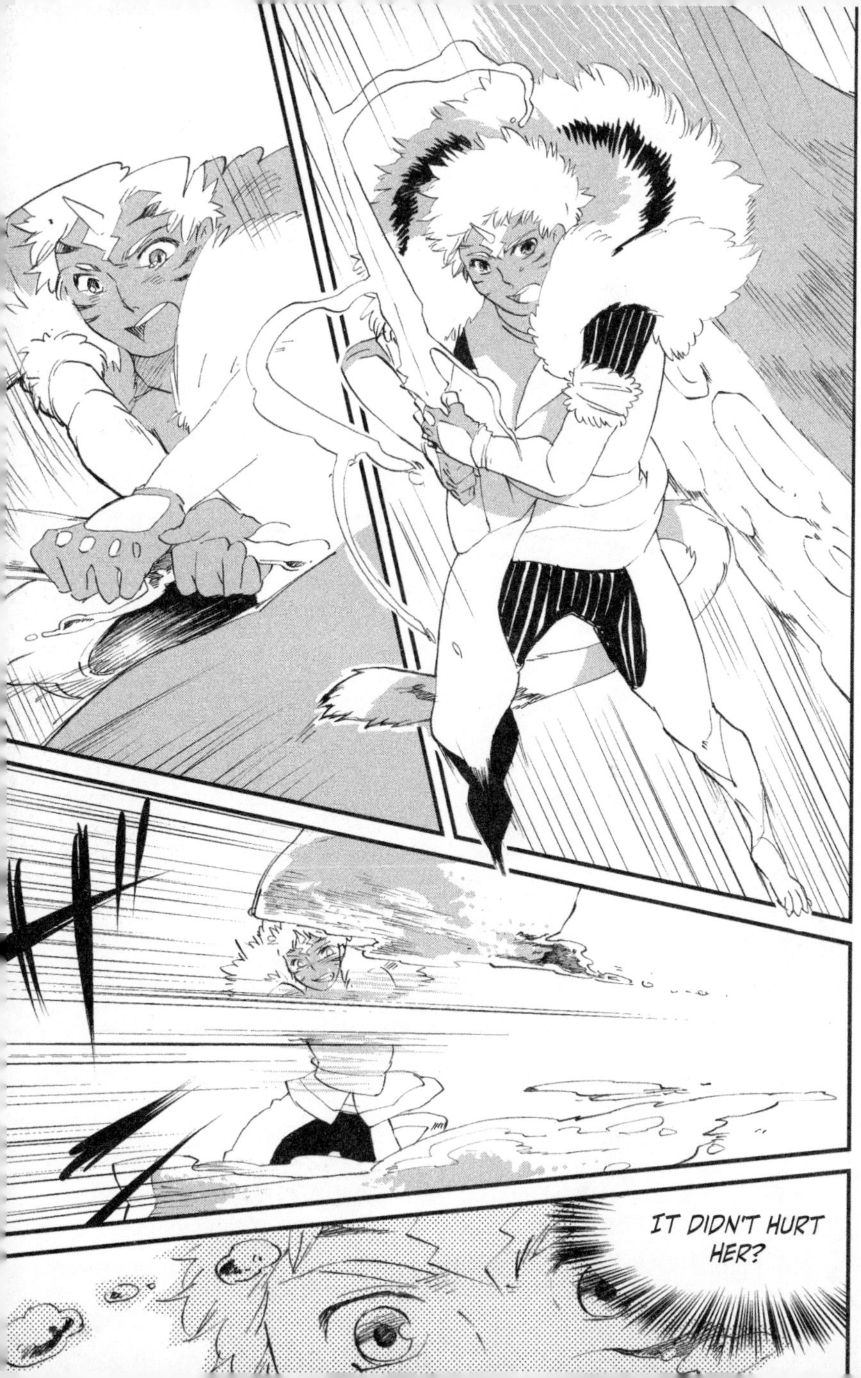
IT DIDN'T HURT HER?

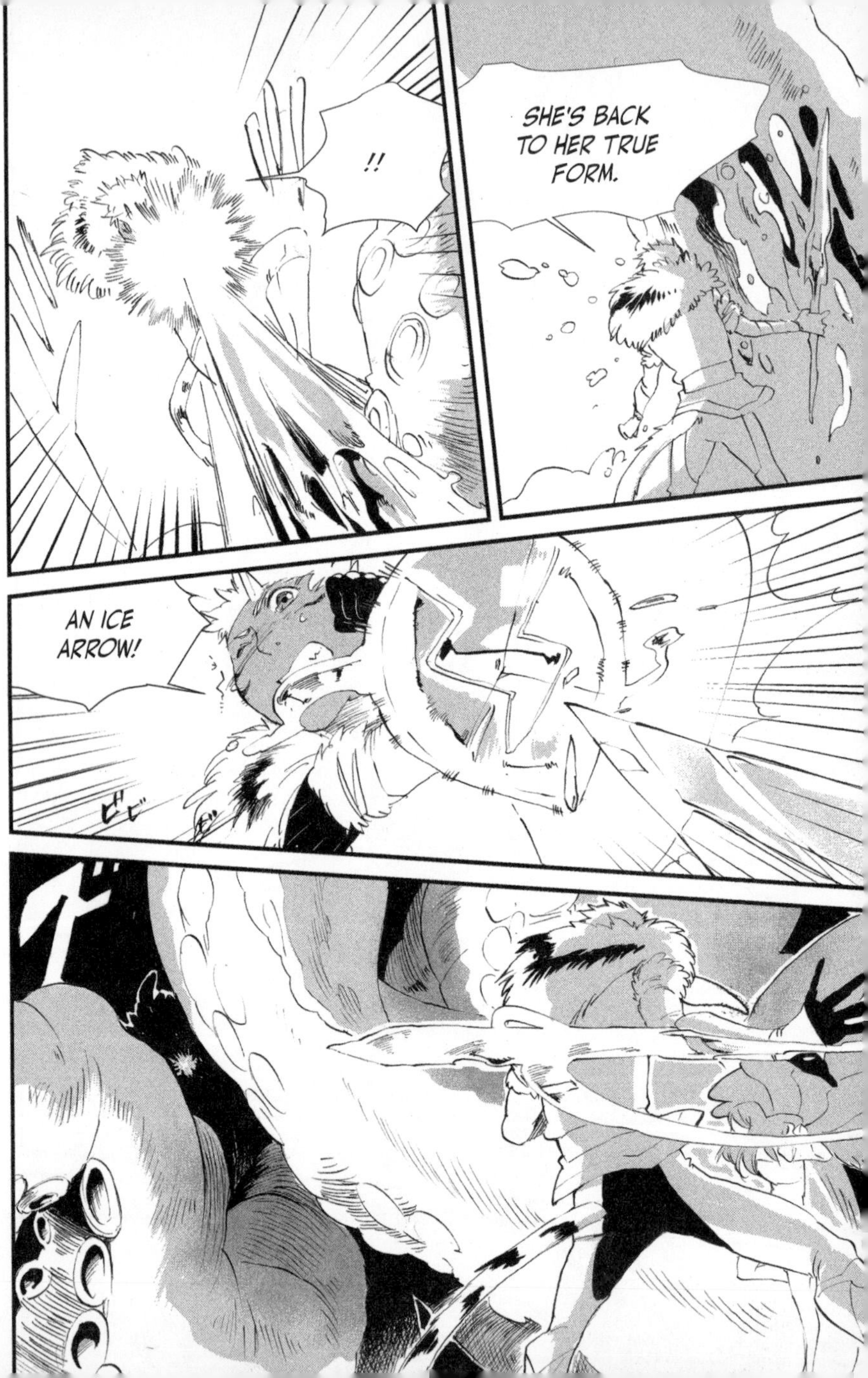
SHE'S BACK TO HER TRUE FORM.
!!
AN ICE ARROW!

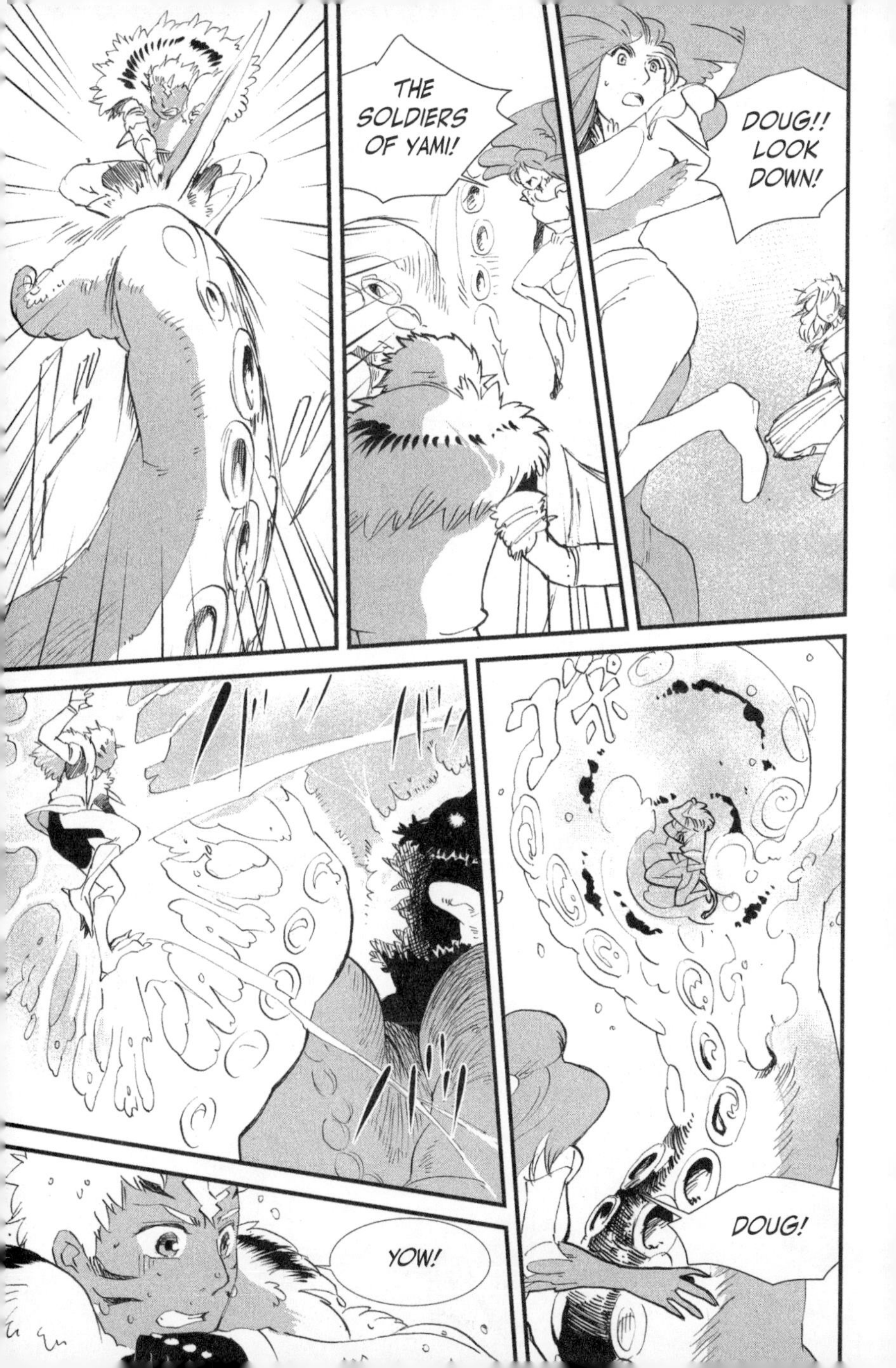
DOUG!! LOOK DOWN!
THE SOLDIERS OF YAMI!
DOUG!
YOW!

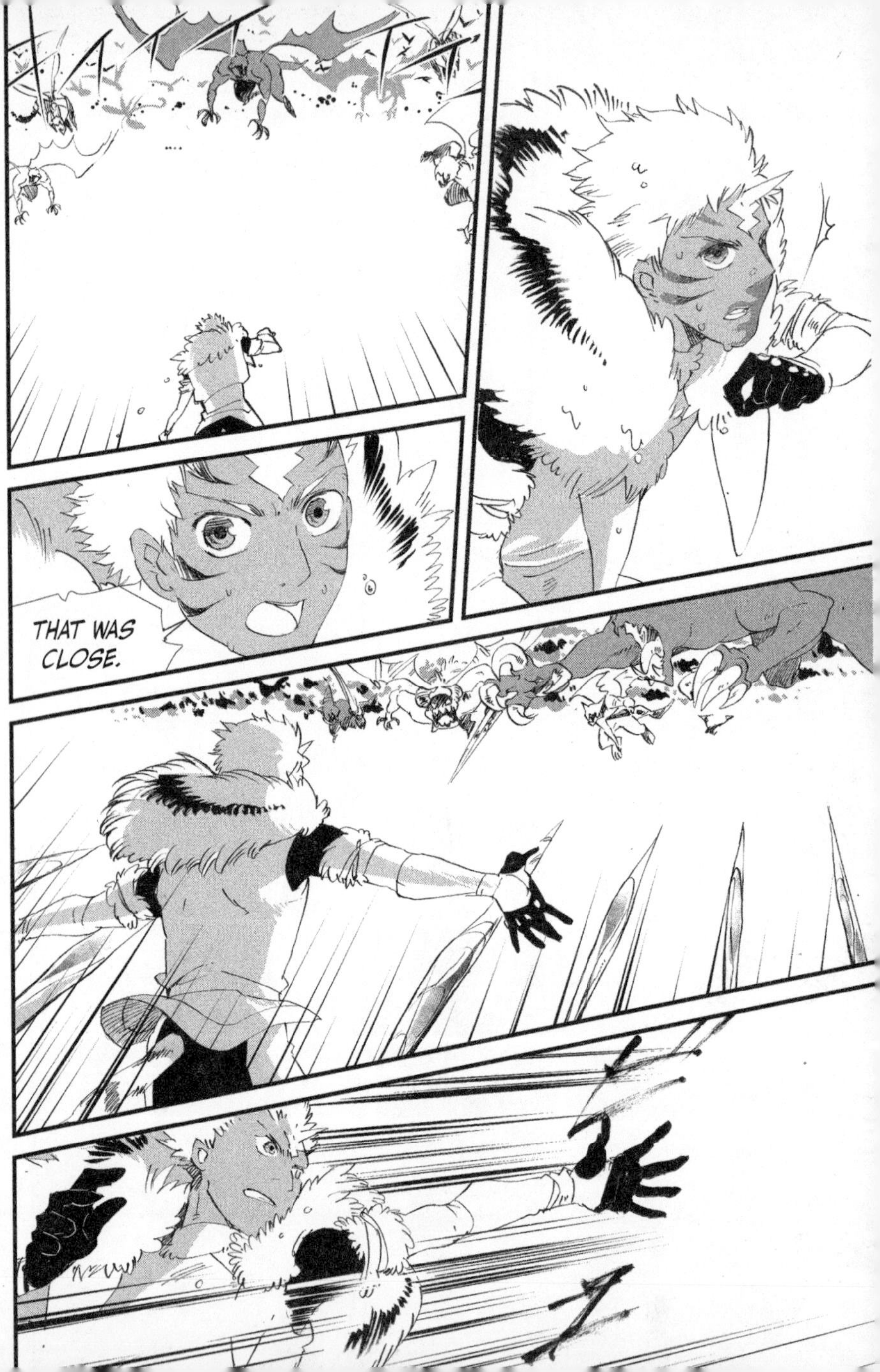
THAT WAS CLOSE.

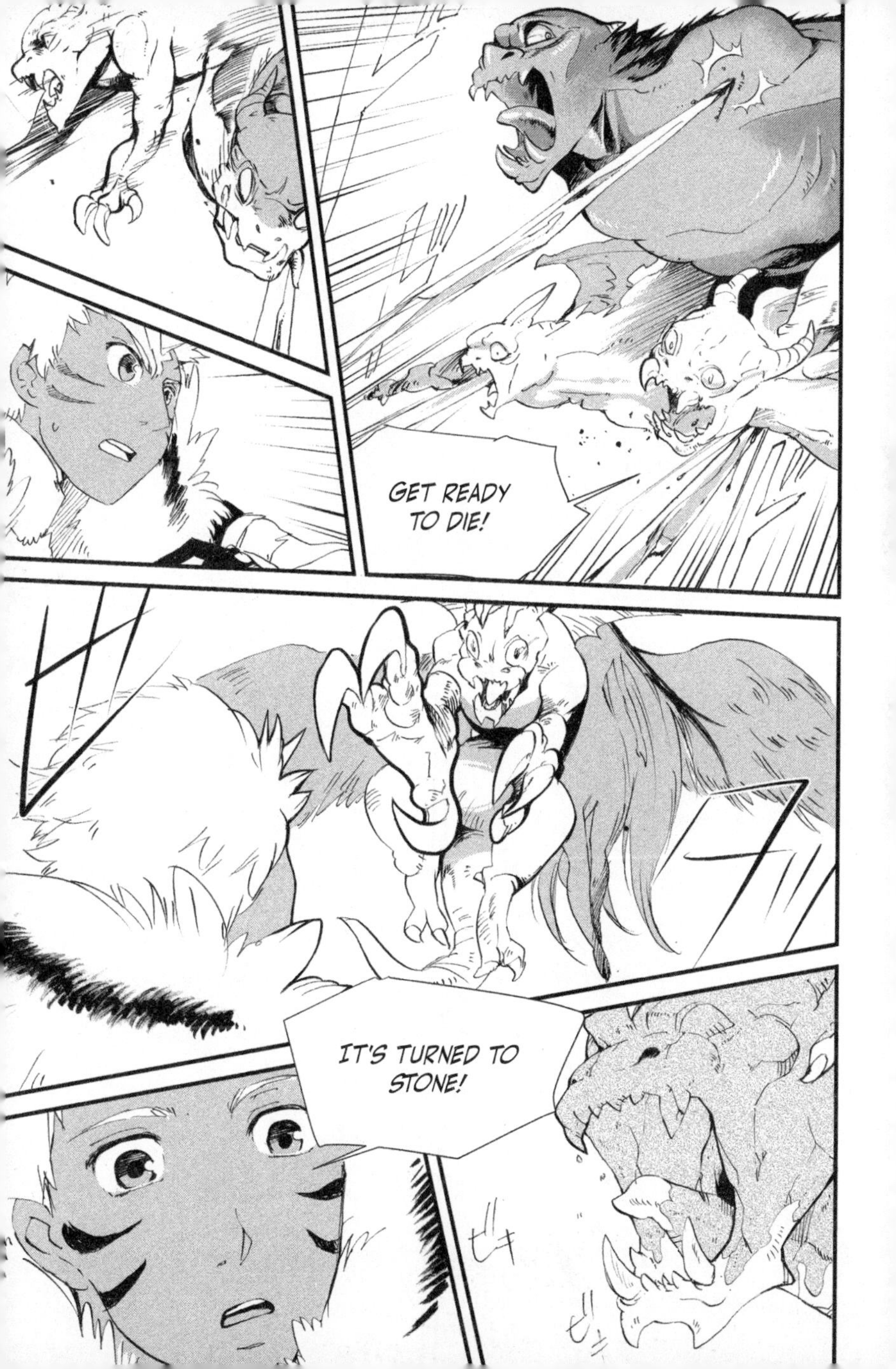
GET READY TO DIE!
IT'S TURNED TO STONE!

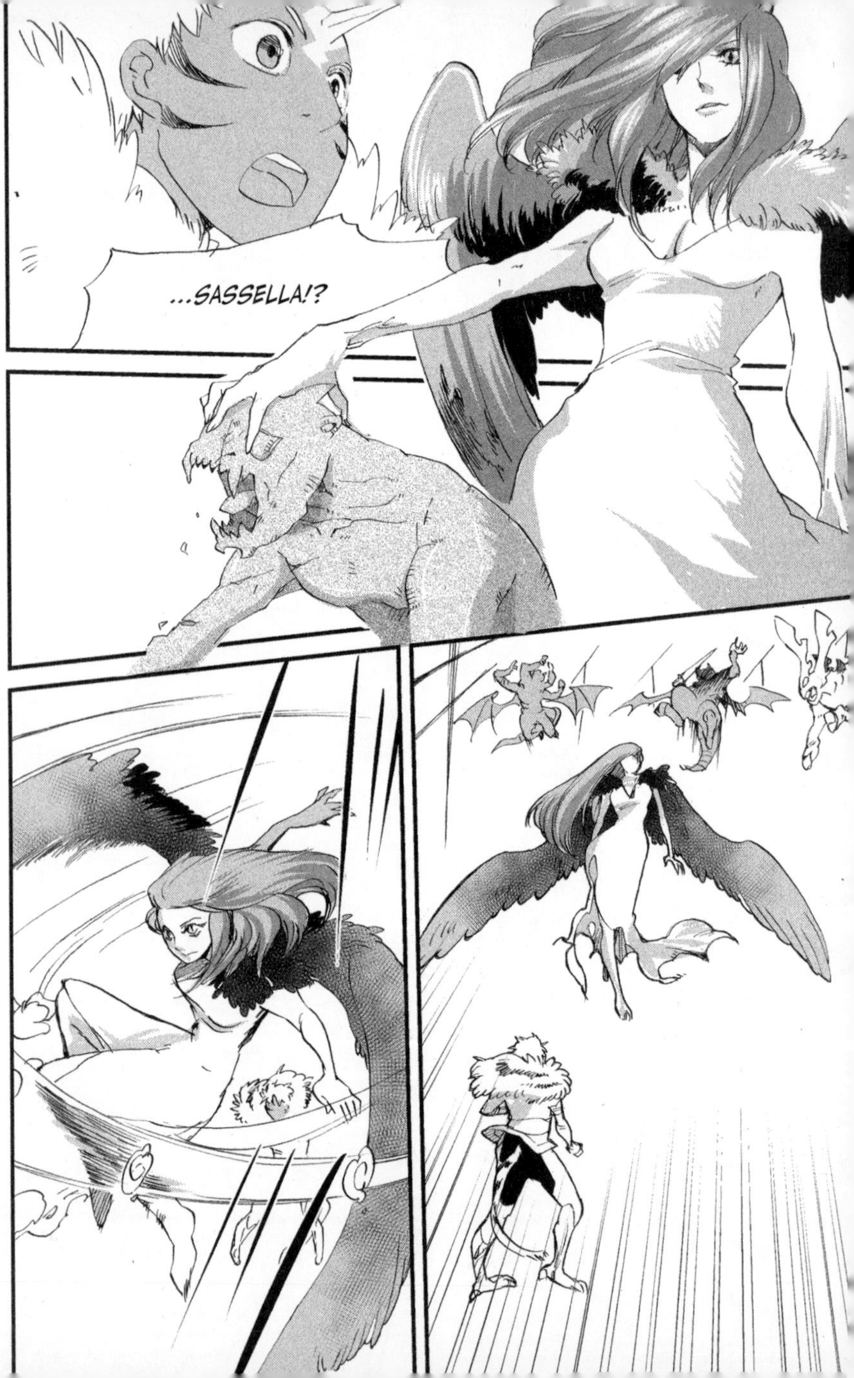
...SASSELLA!?

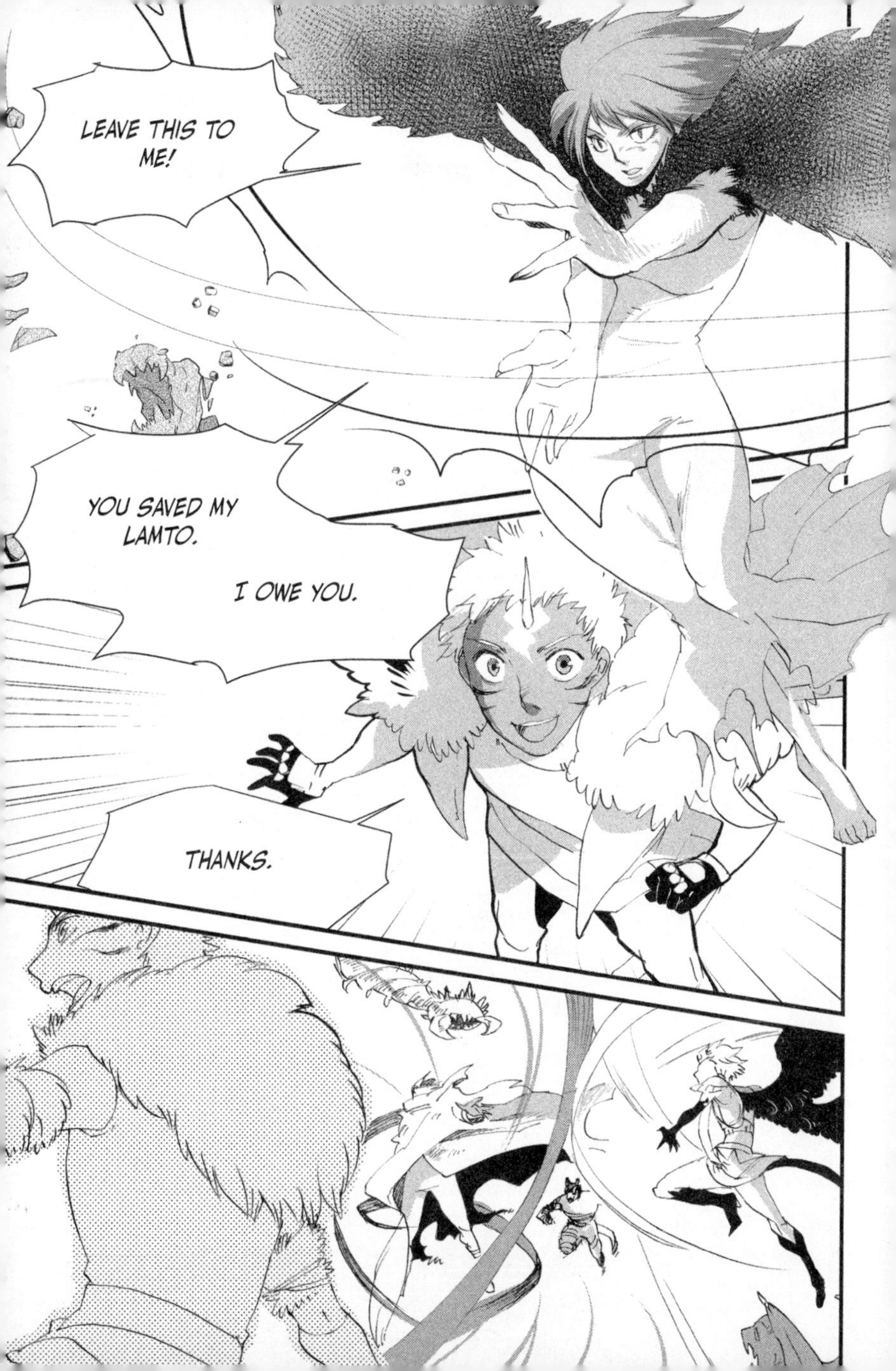
LEAVE THIS TO ME!
YOU SAVED MY LAMTO.
I OWE YOU.
THANKS.

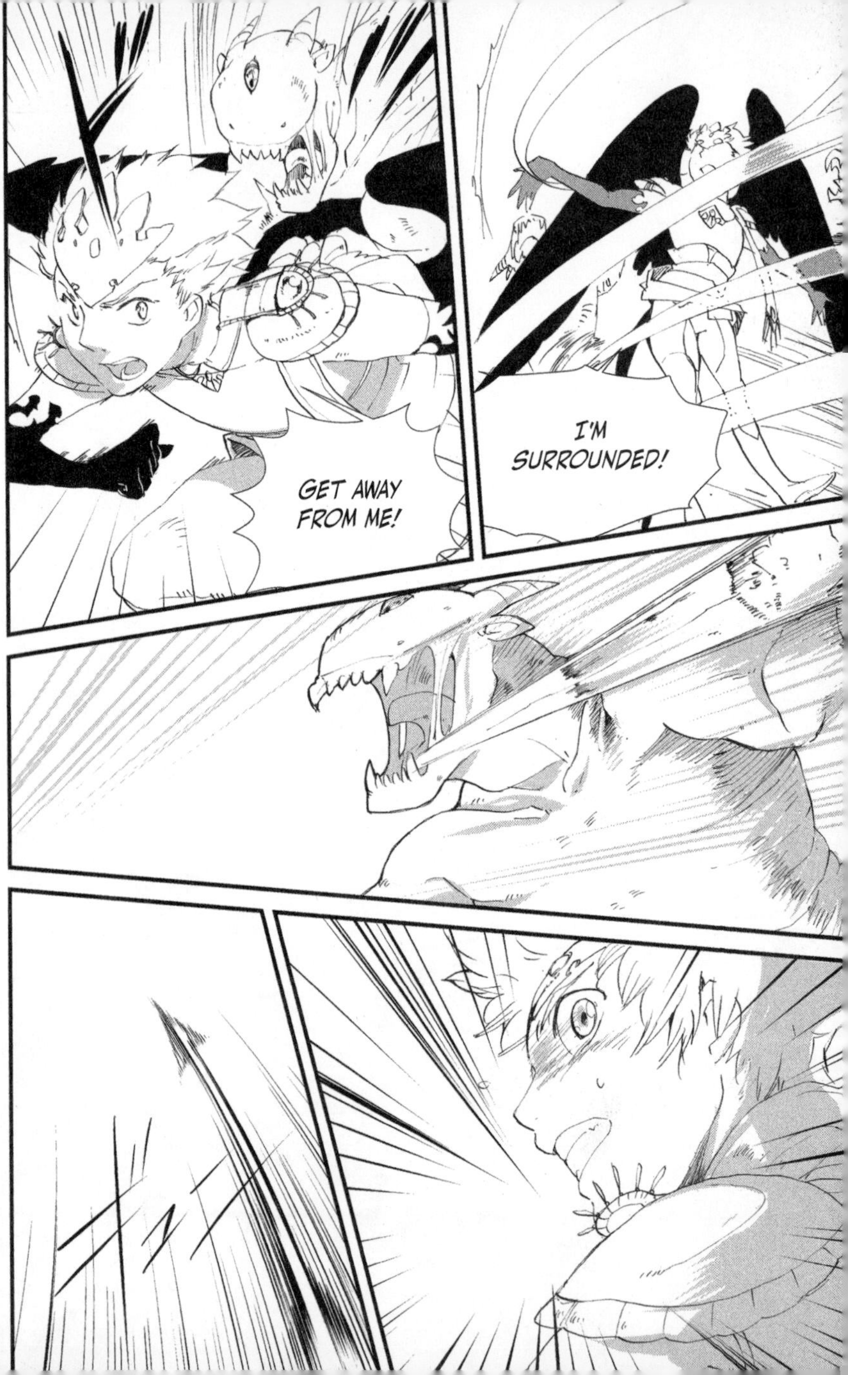
I'M SURROUNDED!
GET AWAY FROM ME!

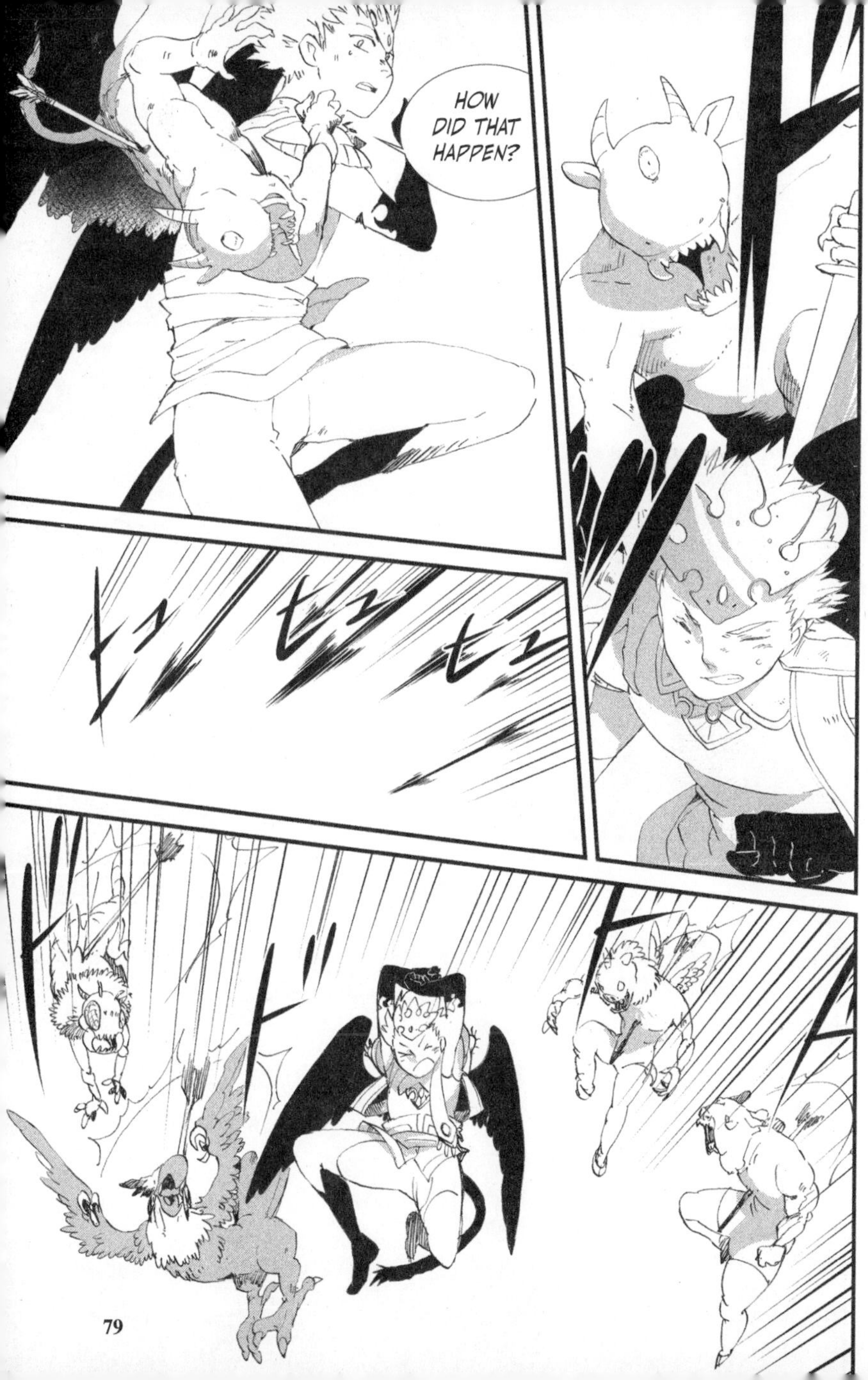
HOW DID THAT HAPPEN?

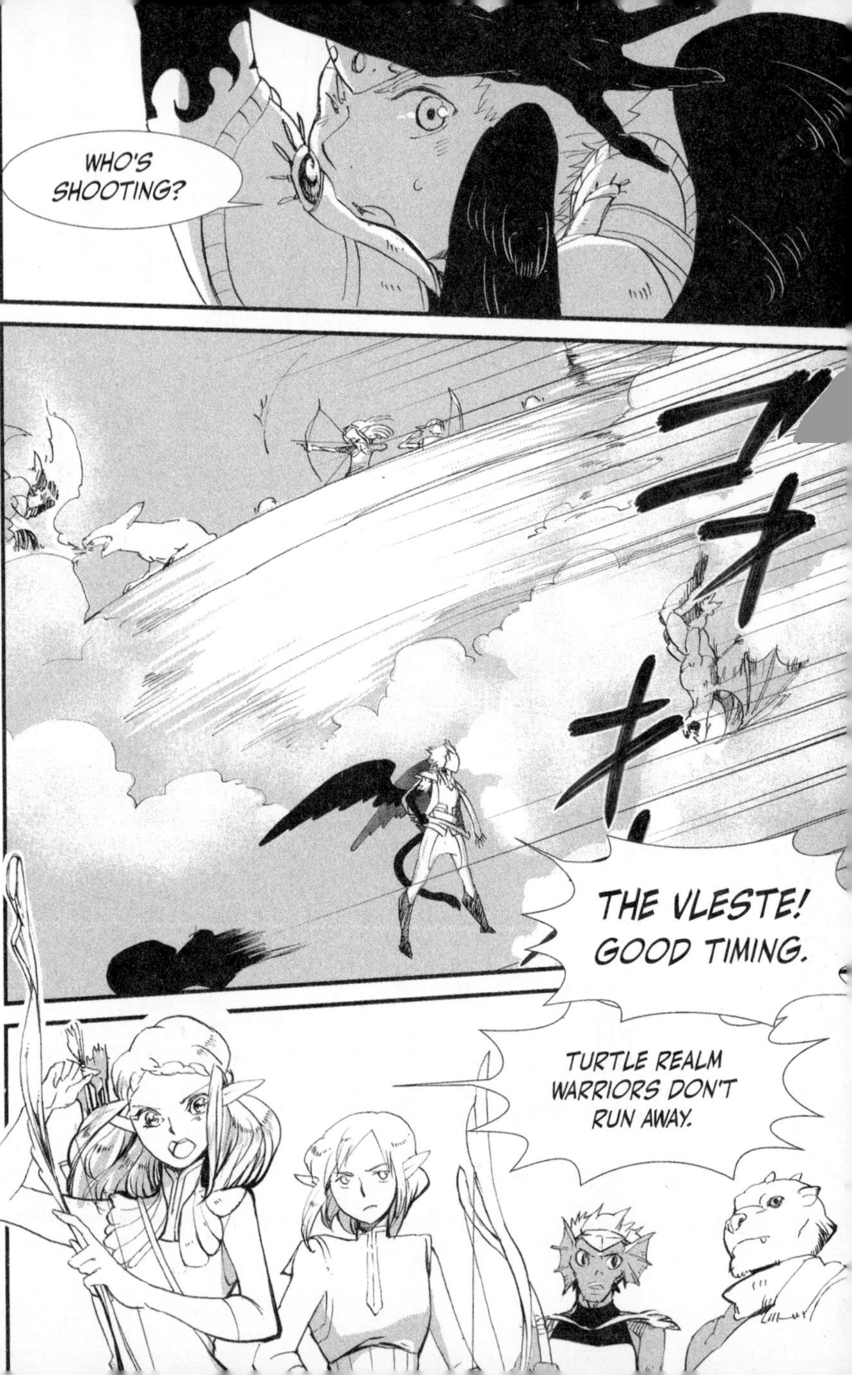
WHO'S SHOOTING?
THE VLESTE! GOOD TIMING.
TURTLE REALM WARRIORS DON'T RUN AWAY.

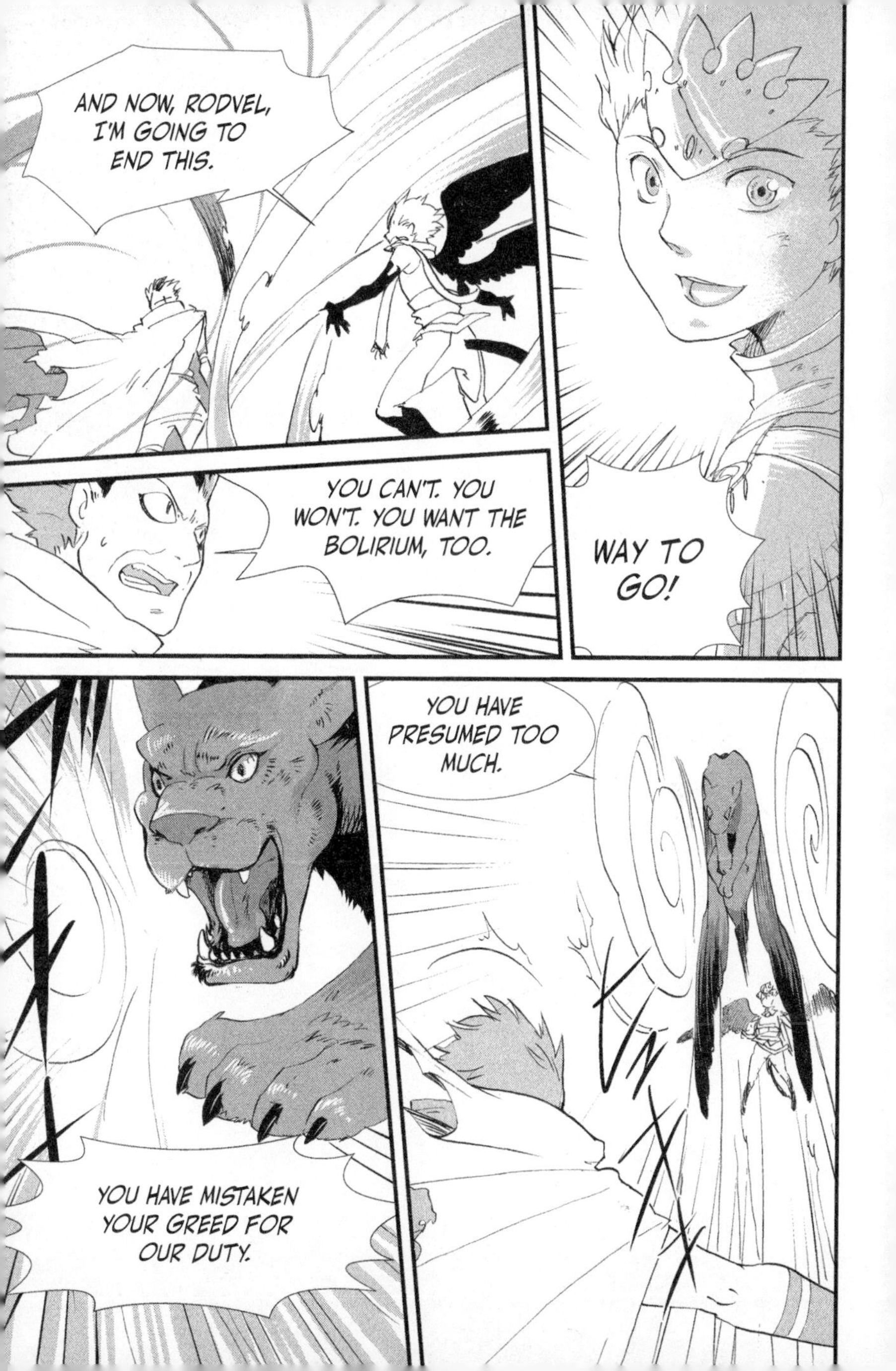
WAY TO GO!
AND NOW, RODVEL, I'M GOING TO END THIS.
YOU CAN'T. YOU WON'T. YOU WANT THE BOLIRIUM, TOO.
YOU HAVE PRESUMED TOO MUCH.
YOU HAVE MISTAKEN YOUR GREED FOR OUR DUTY.

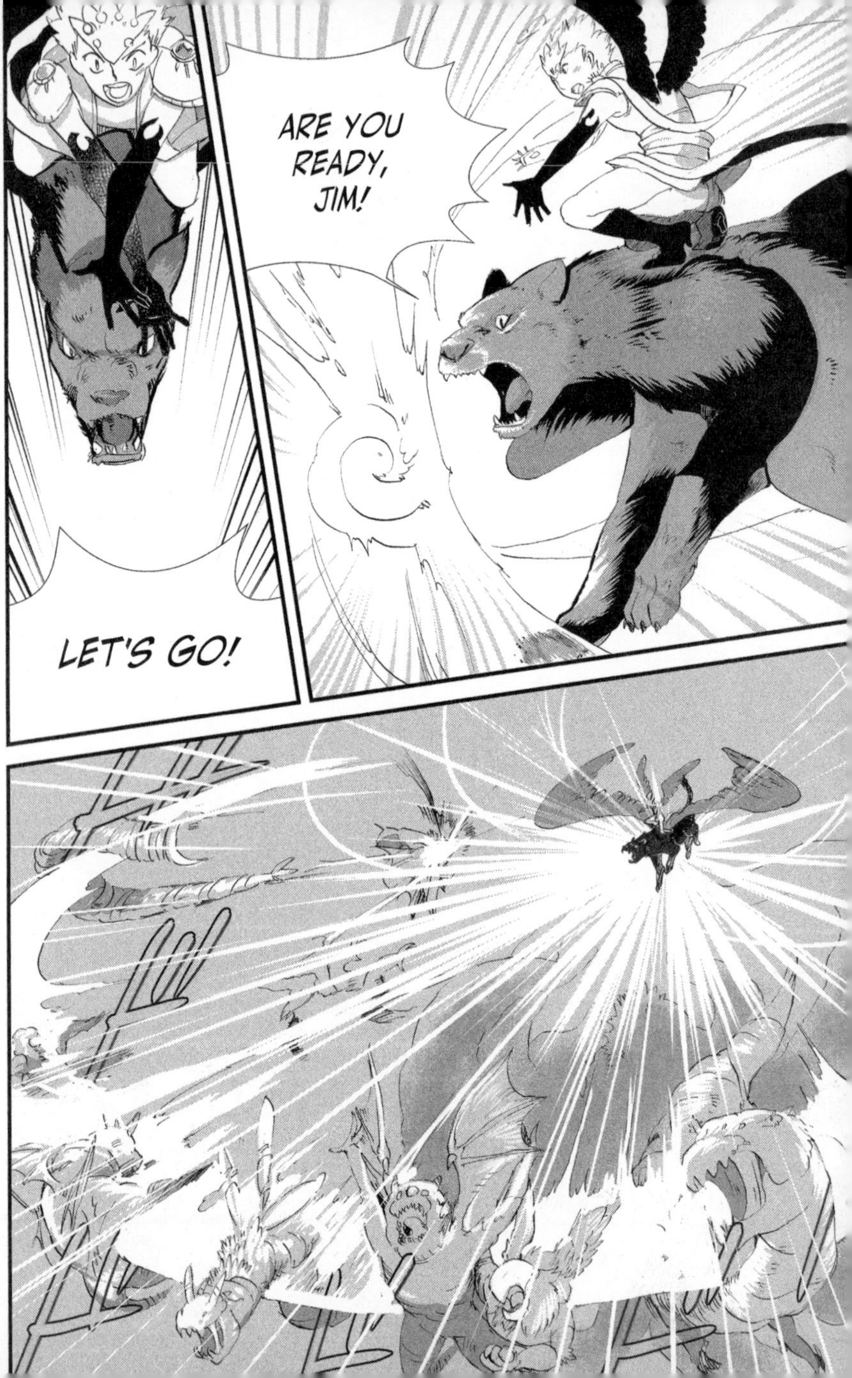
ARE YOU READY, JIM!
LET'S GO!

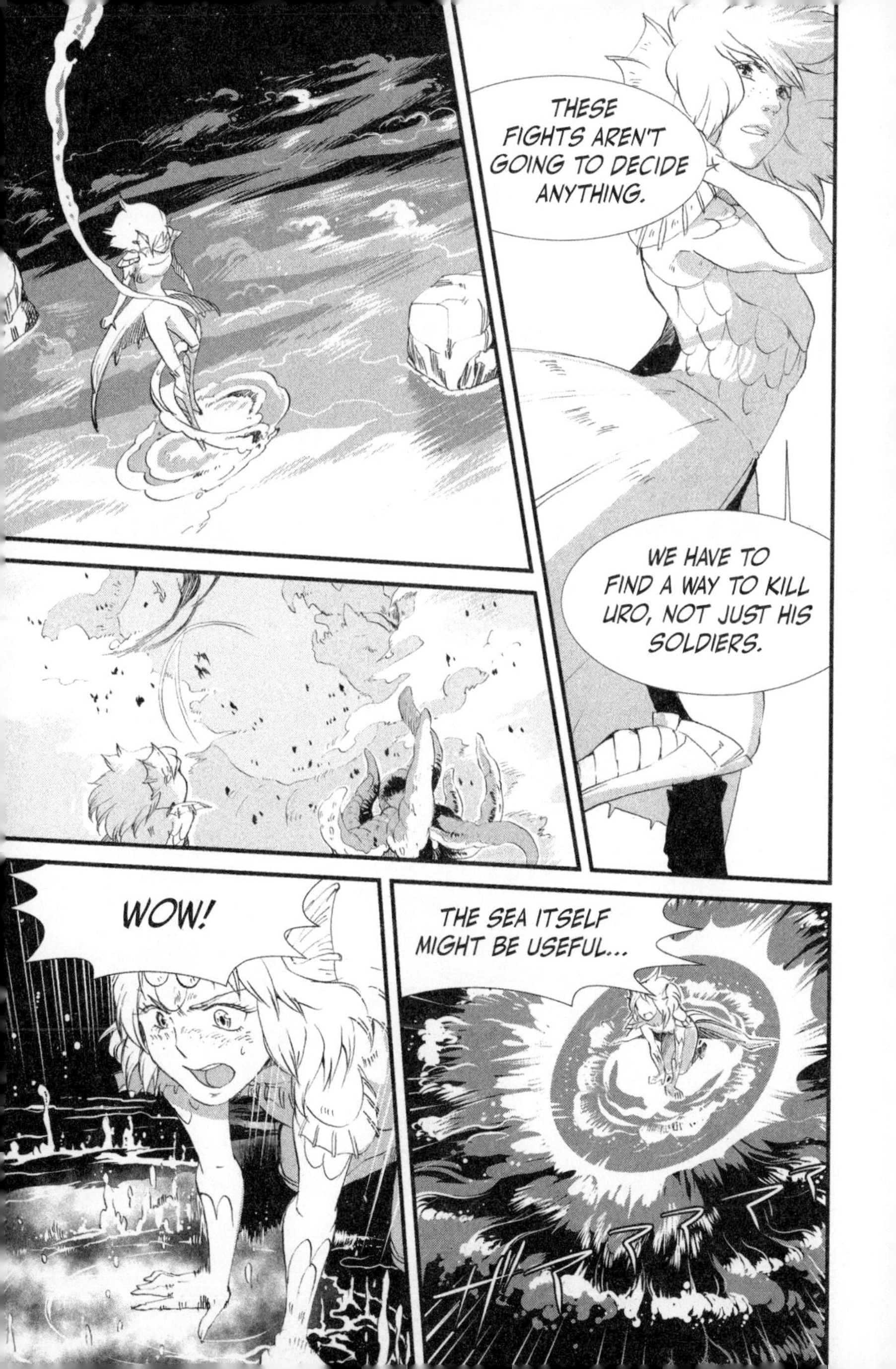
THESE FIGHTS AREN'T GOING TO DECIDE ANYTHING.
WE HAVE TO FIND A WAY TO KILL URO, NOT JUST HIS SOLDIERS.
THE SEA ITSELF MIGHT BE USEFUL...
WOW!

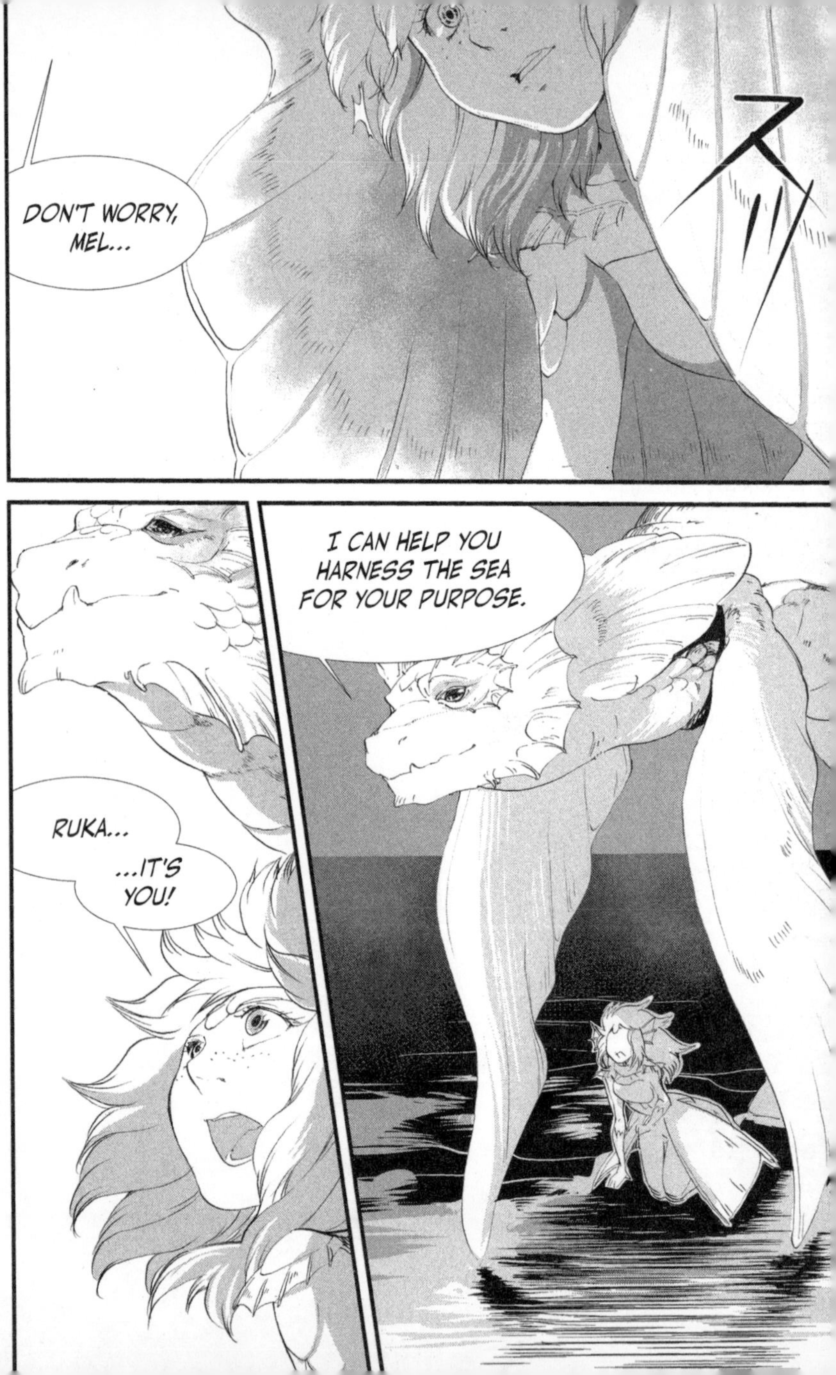
DON'T WORRY, MEL...
I CAN HELP YOU HARNESS THE SEA FOR YOUR PURPOSE.
RUKA...
...IT'S YOU!

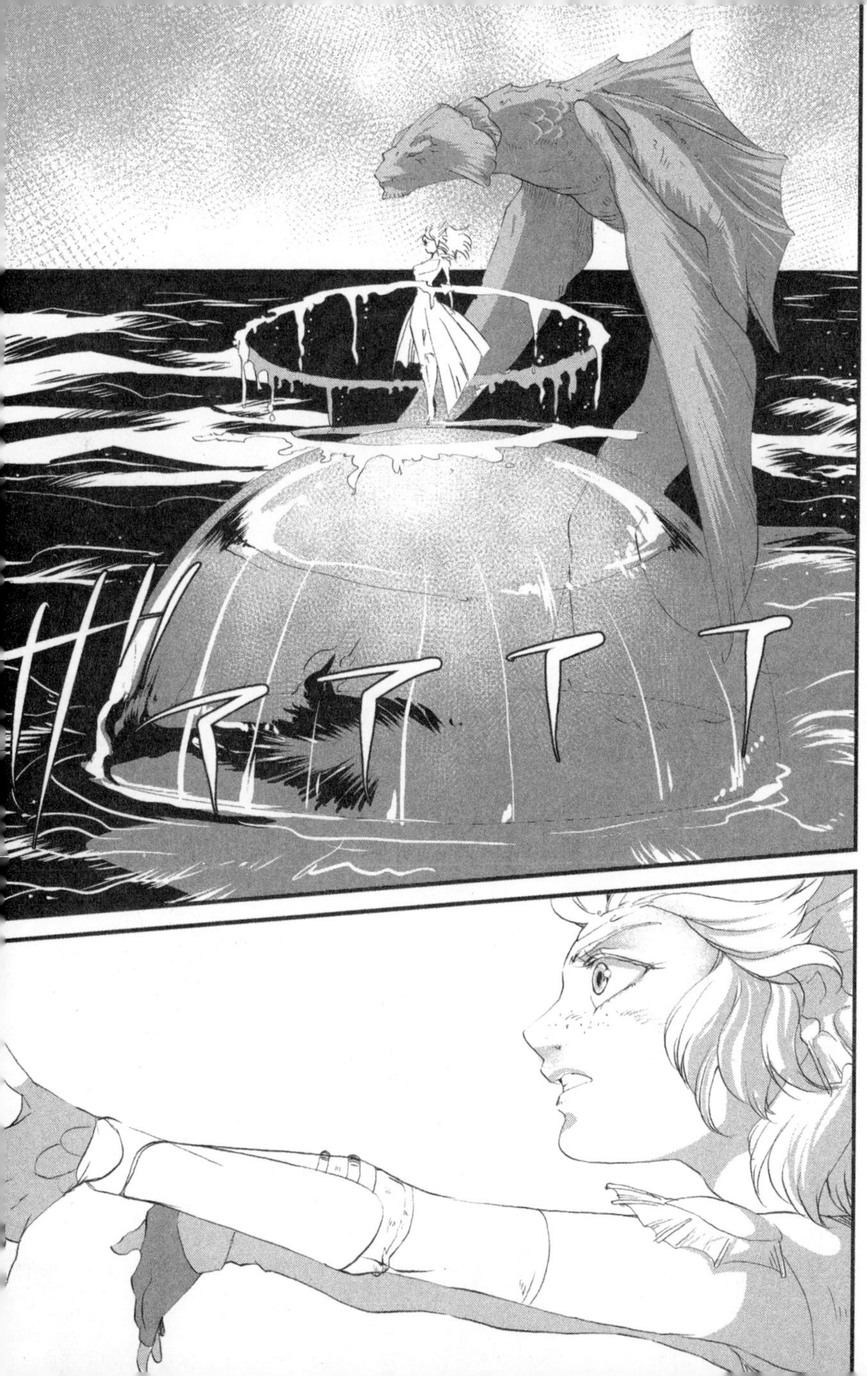

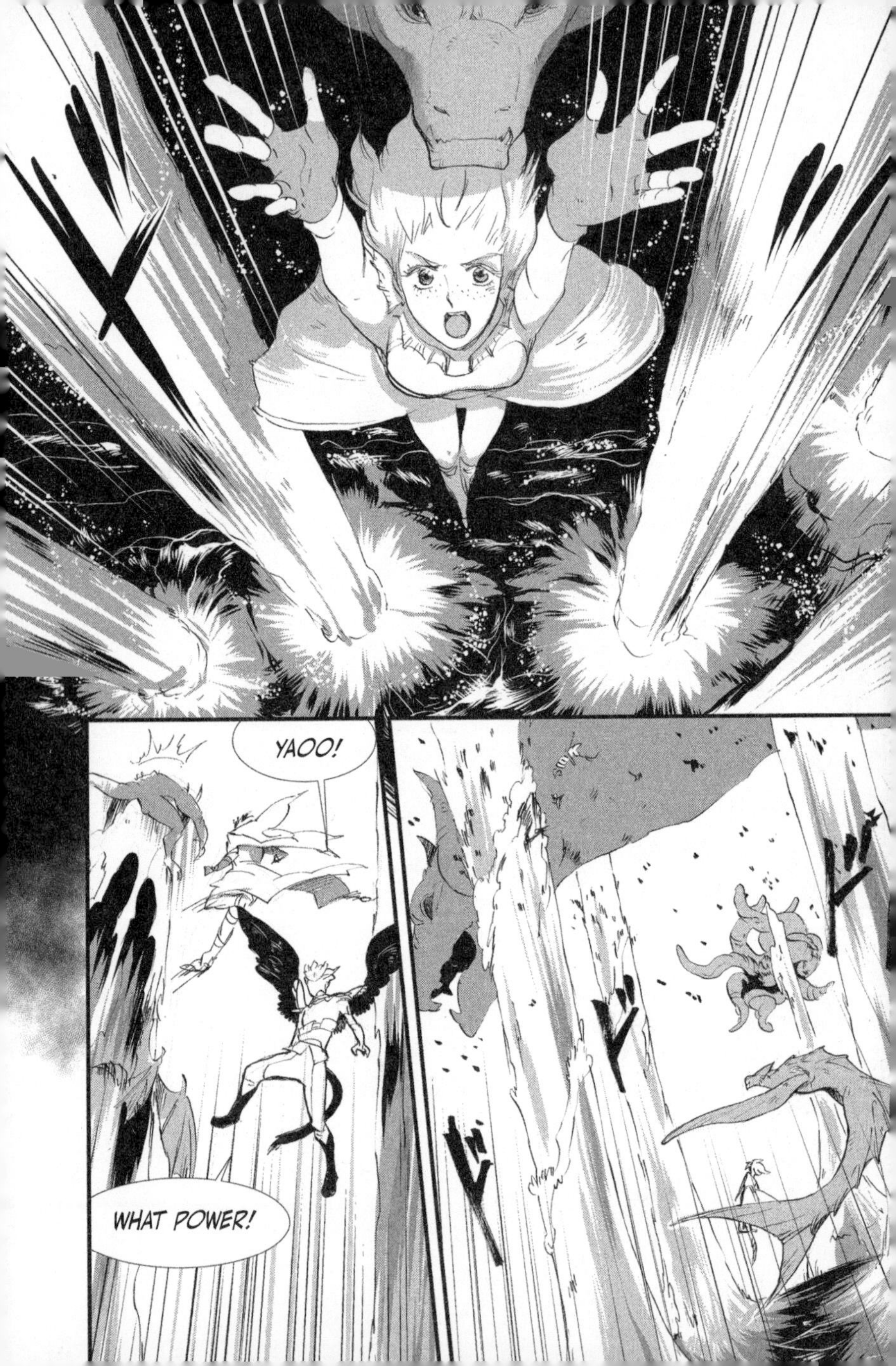
YAOO!
WHAT POWER!

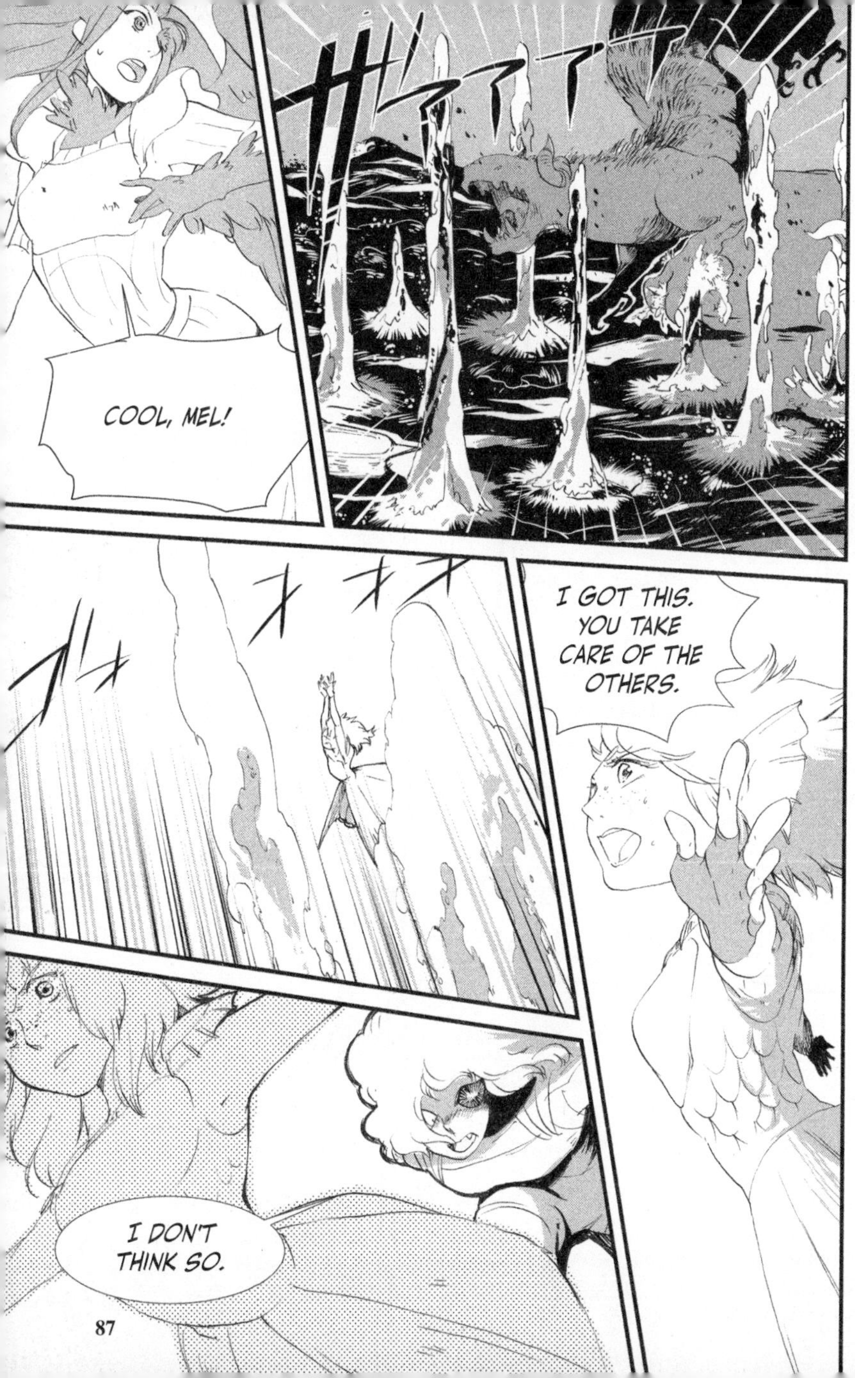
COOL, MEL!
I GOT THIS. YOU TAKE CARE OF THE OTHERS.
I DON'T THINK SO.

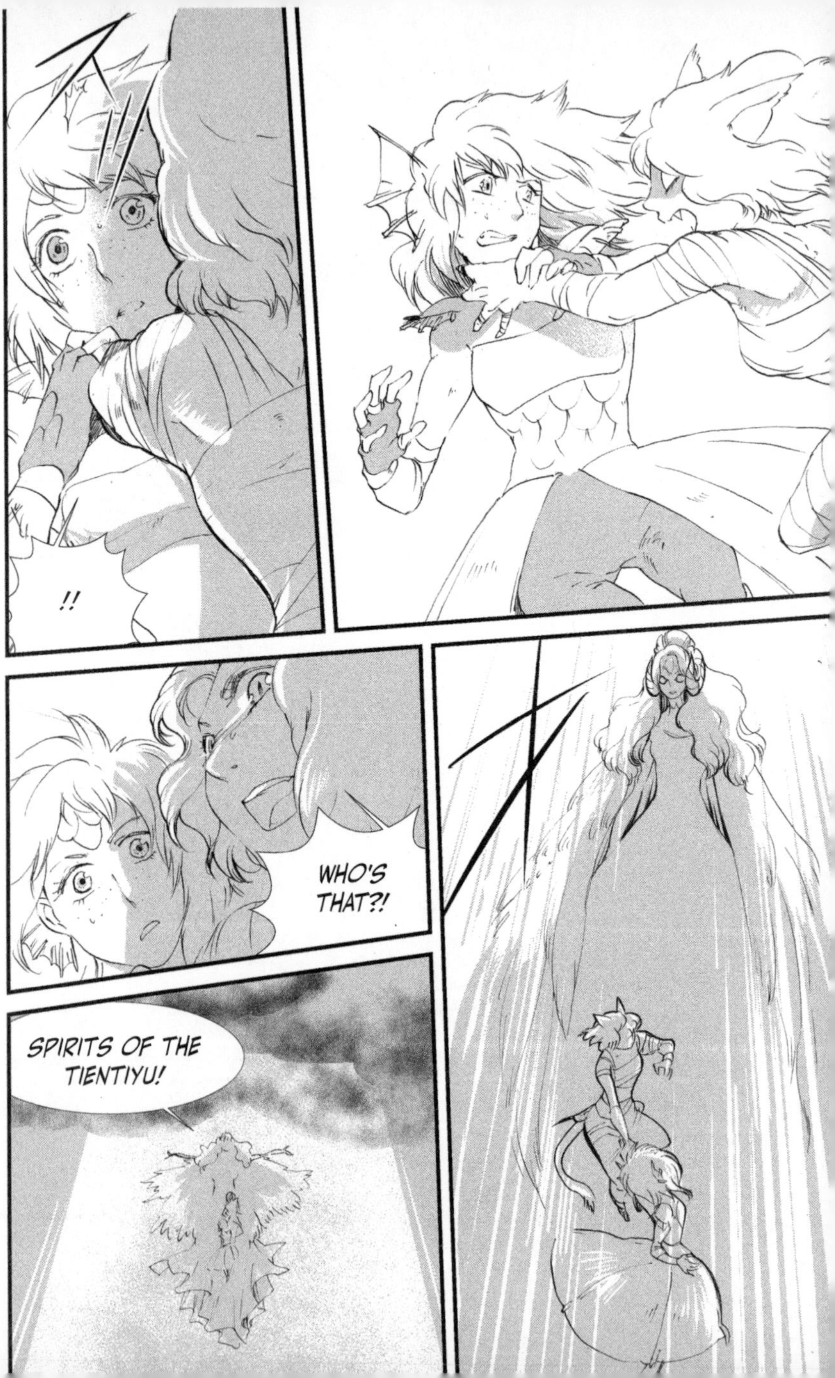
!!
WHO'S THAT?!
SPIRITS OF THE TIENTIYU!

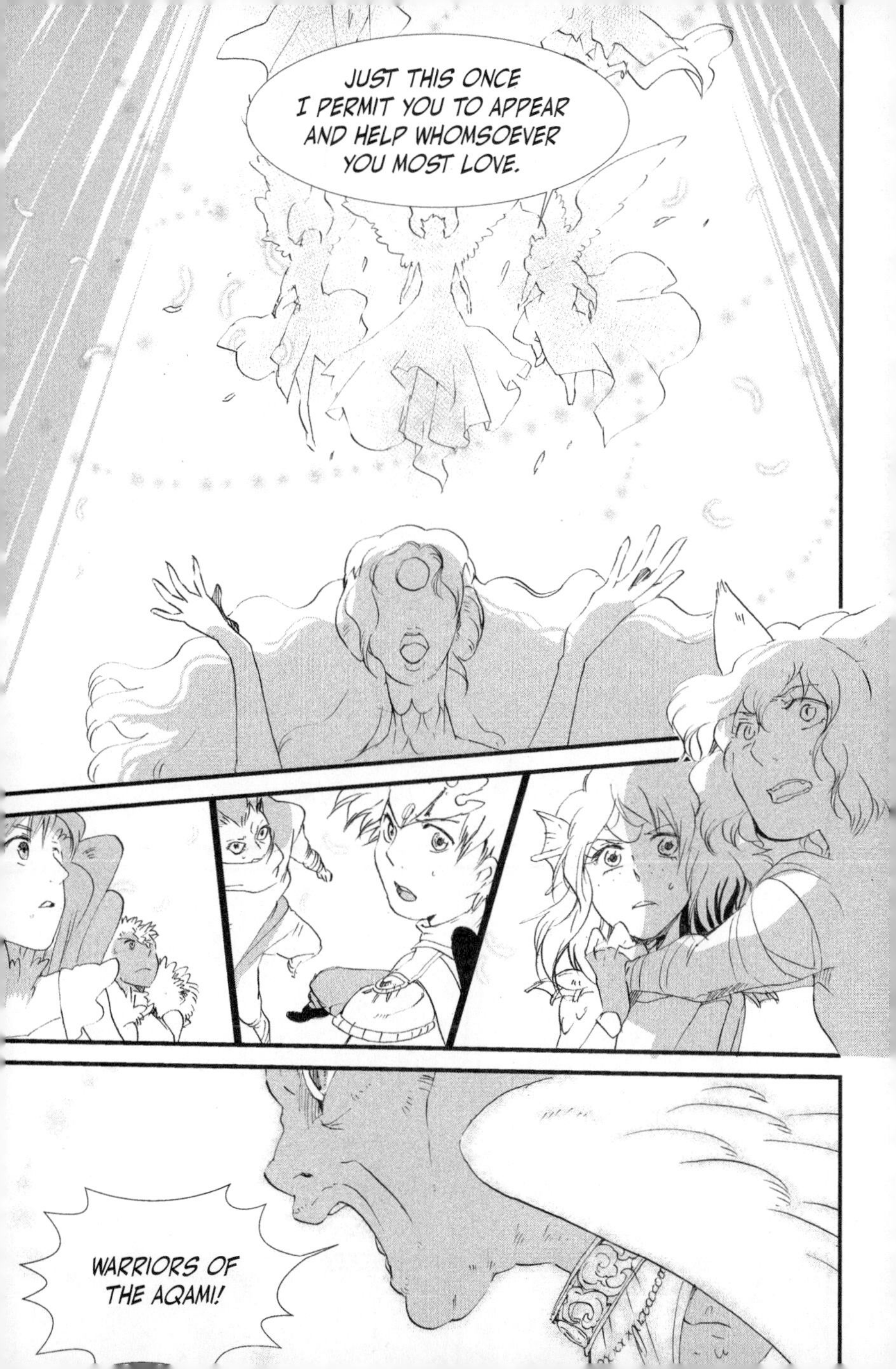
JUST THIS ONCE I PERMIT YOU TO APPEAR AND HELP WHOMSOEVER YOU MOST LOVE.
WARRIORS OF THE AQAMI!

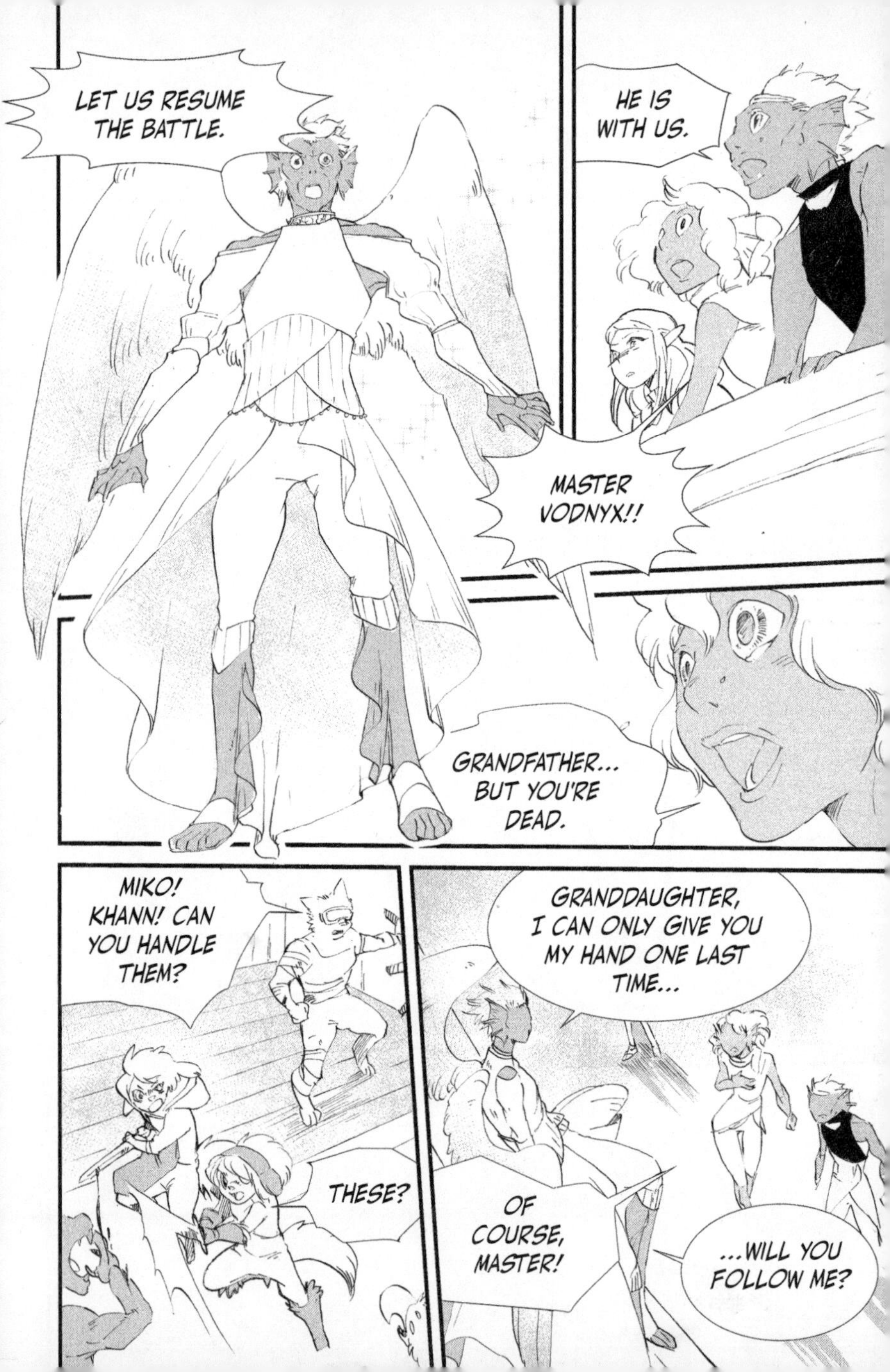
HE IS WITH US.
MASTER VODNYX!!
GRANDFATHER... BUT YOU'RE DEAD.
LET US RESUME THE BATTLE.
GRANDDAUGHTER, I CAN ONLY GIVE YOU MY HAND ONE LAST TIME...
...WILL YOU FOLLOW ME?
OF COURSE, MASTER!
MIKO! KHANN! CAN YOU HANDLE THEM?
THESE?

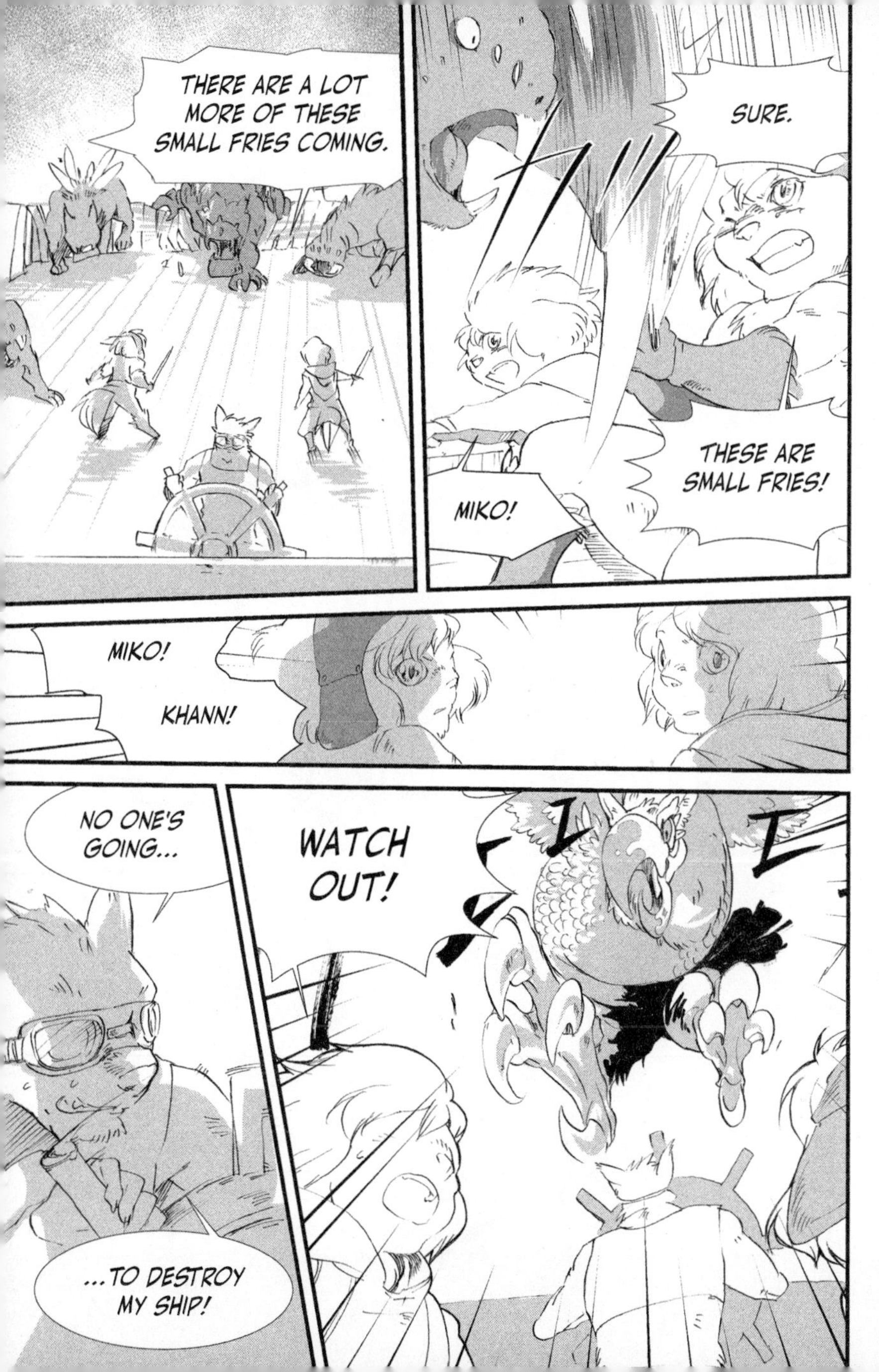
SURE.
THESE ARE SMALL FRIES!
MIKO!
THERE ARE A LOT MORE OF THESE SMALL FRIES COMING.
MIKO!
KHANN!
WATCH OUT!
NO ONE'S GOING...
...TO DESTROY MY SHIP!

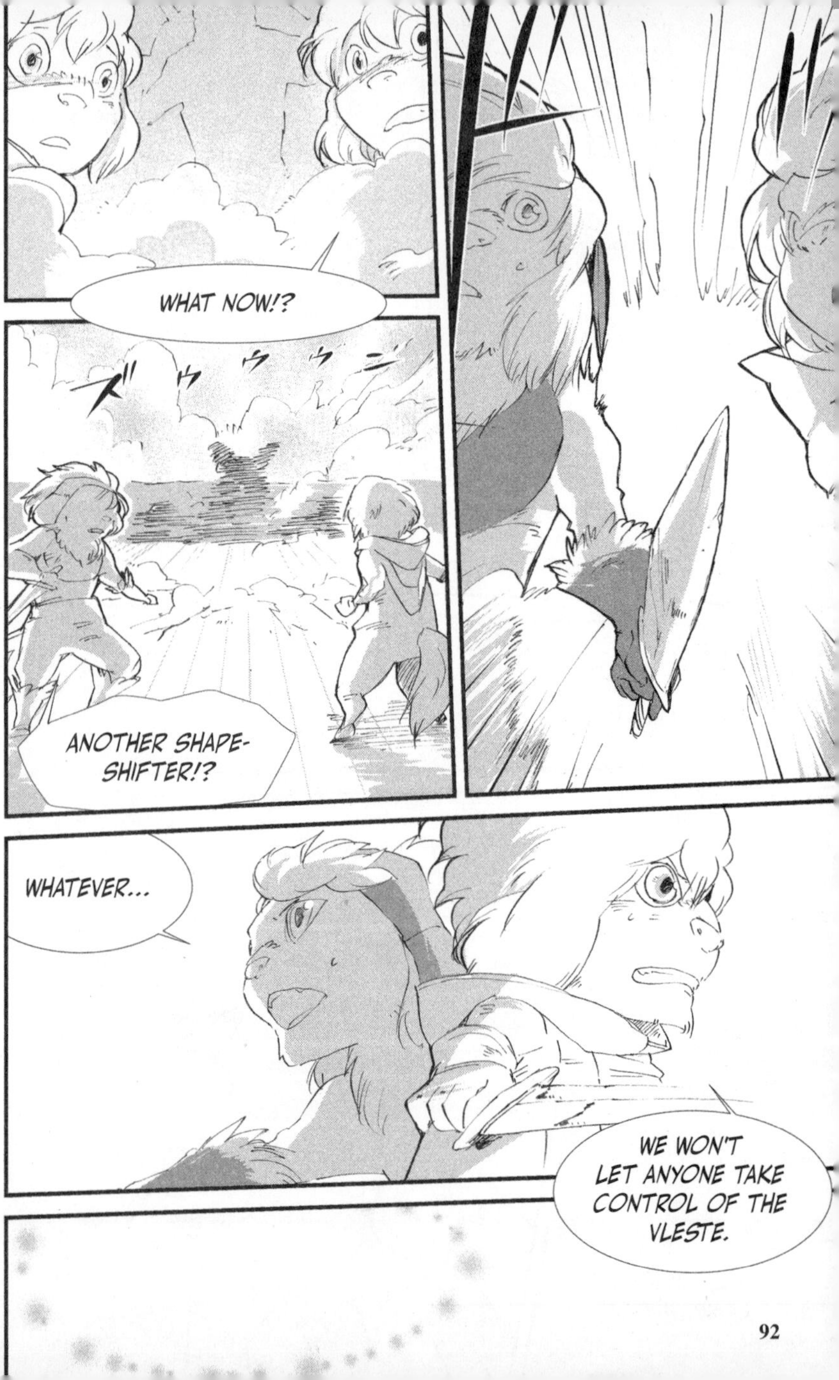
WHAT NOW!?
ズウウウン
ANOTHER SHAPE-SHIFTER!?
WHATEVER...
WE WON'T LET ANYONE TAKE CONTROL OF THE VLESTE.

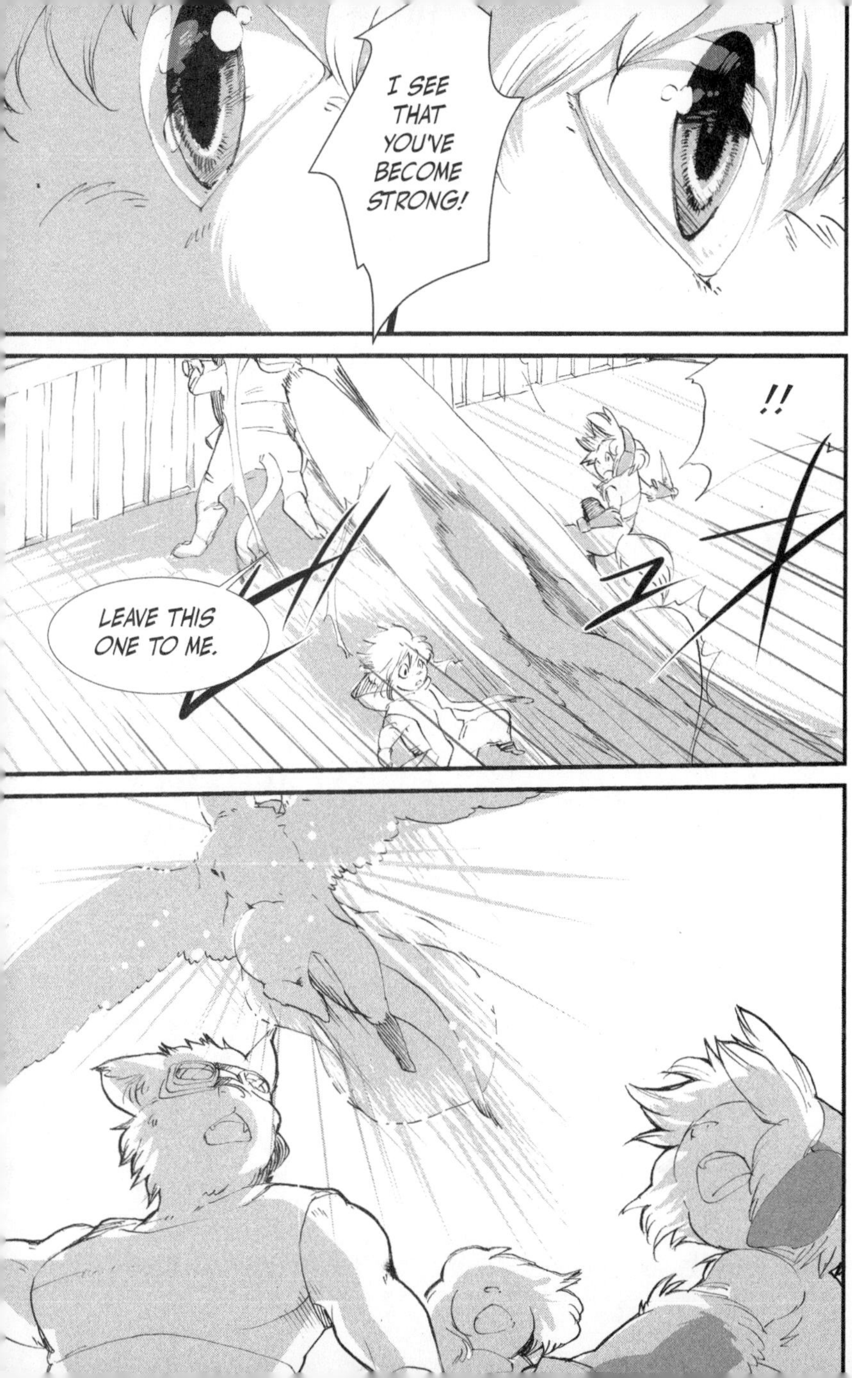
I SEE THAT YOU'VE BECOME STRONG!
!!
LEAVE THIS ONE TO ME.

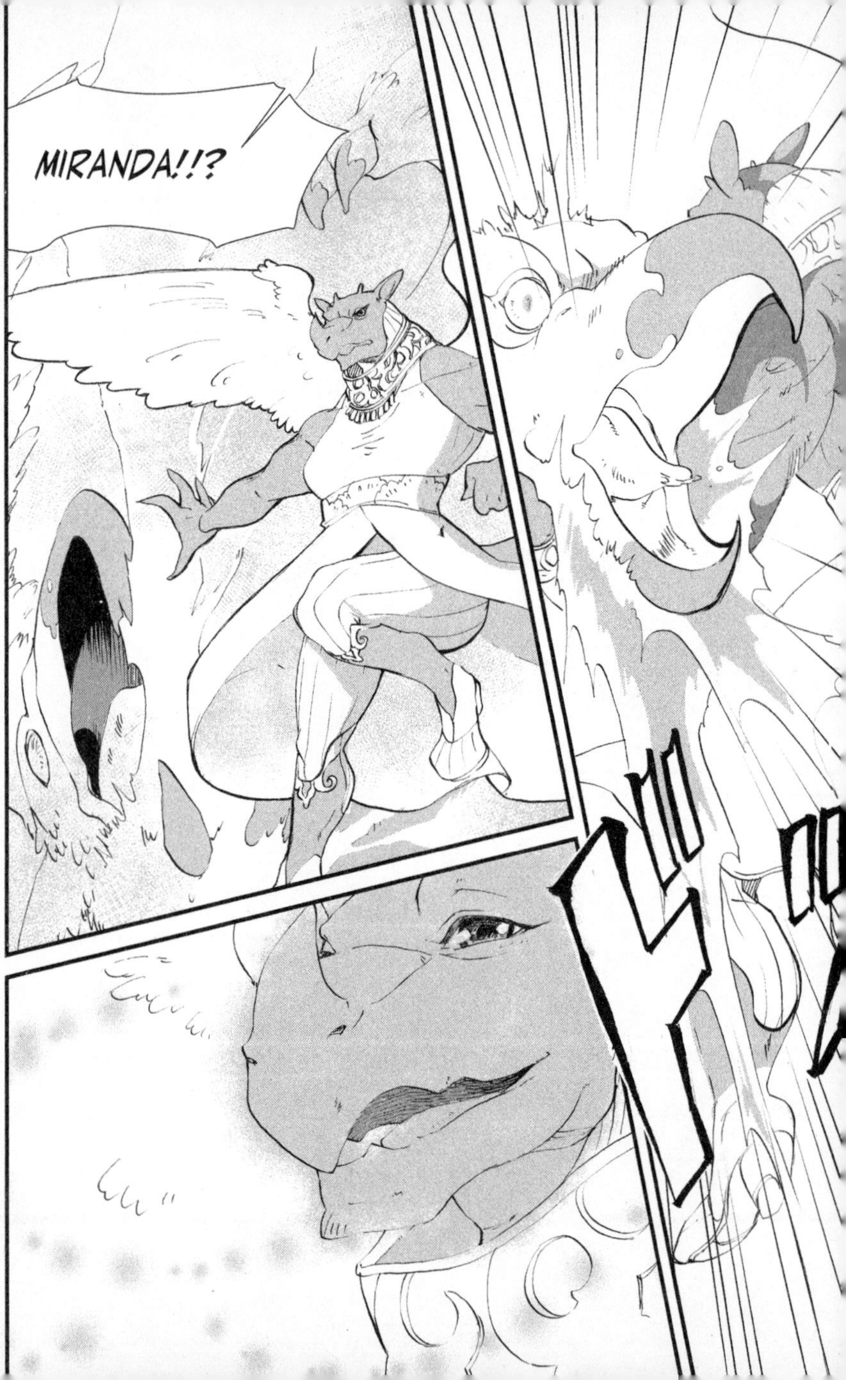
MIRANDA!!?

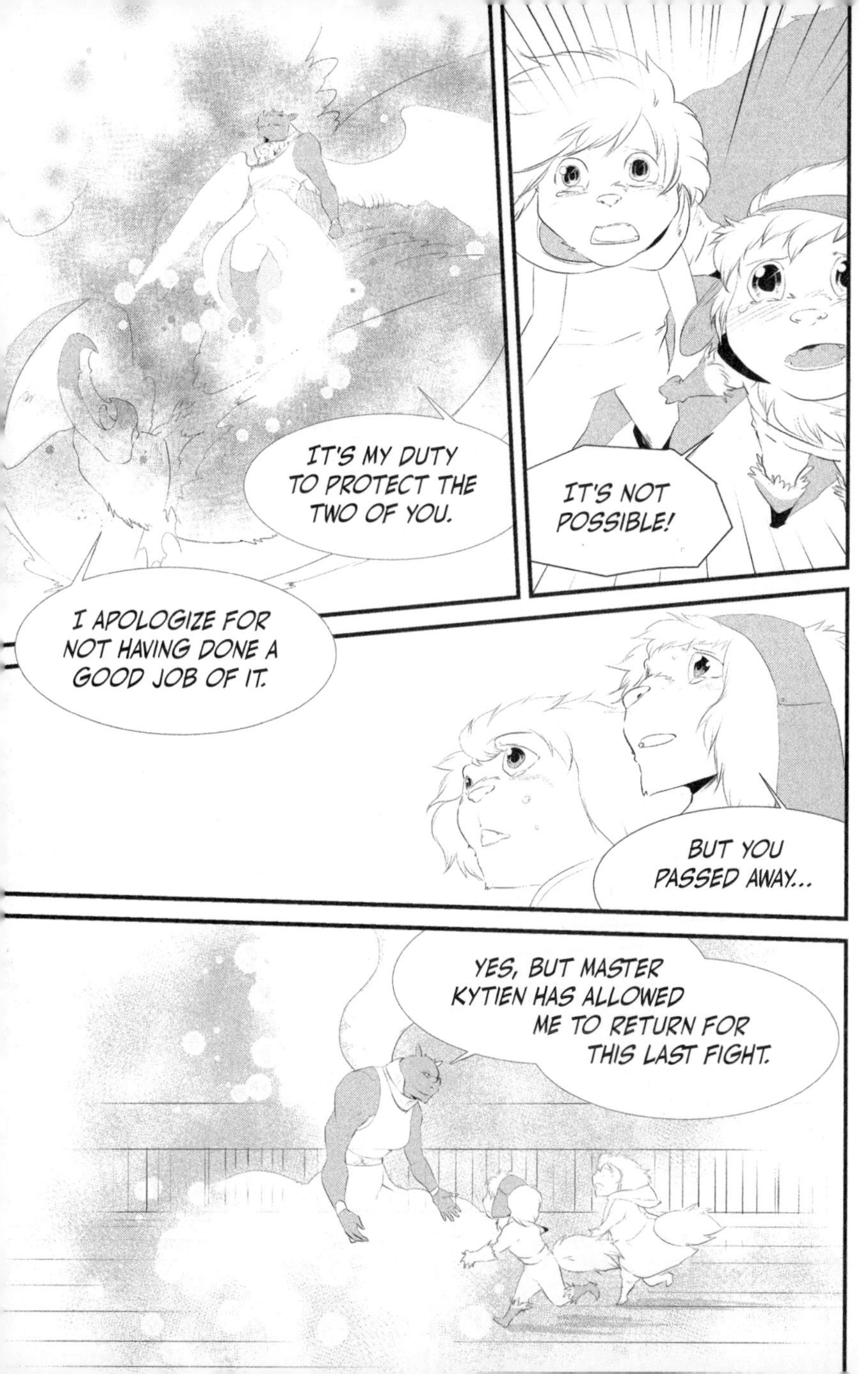
IT'S NOT POSSIBLE!
IT'S MY DUTY TO PROTECT THE TWO OF YOU.
I APOLOGIZE FOR NOT HAVING DONE A GOOD JOB OF IT.
BUT YOU PASSED AWAY...
YES, BUT MASTER KYTIEN HAS ALLOWED ME TO RETURN FOR THIS LAST FIGHT.

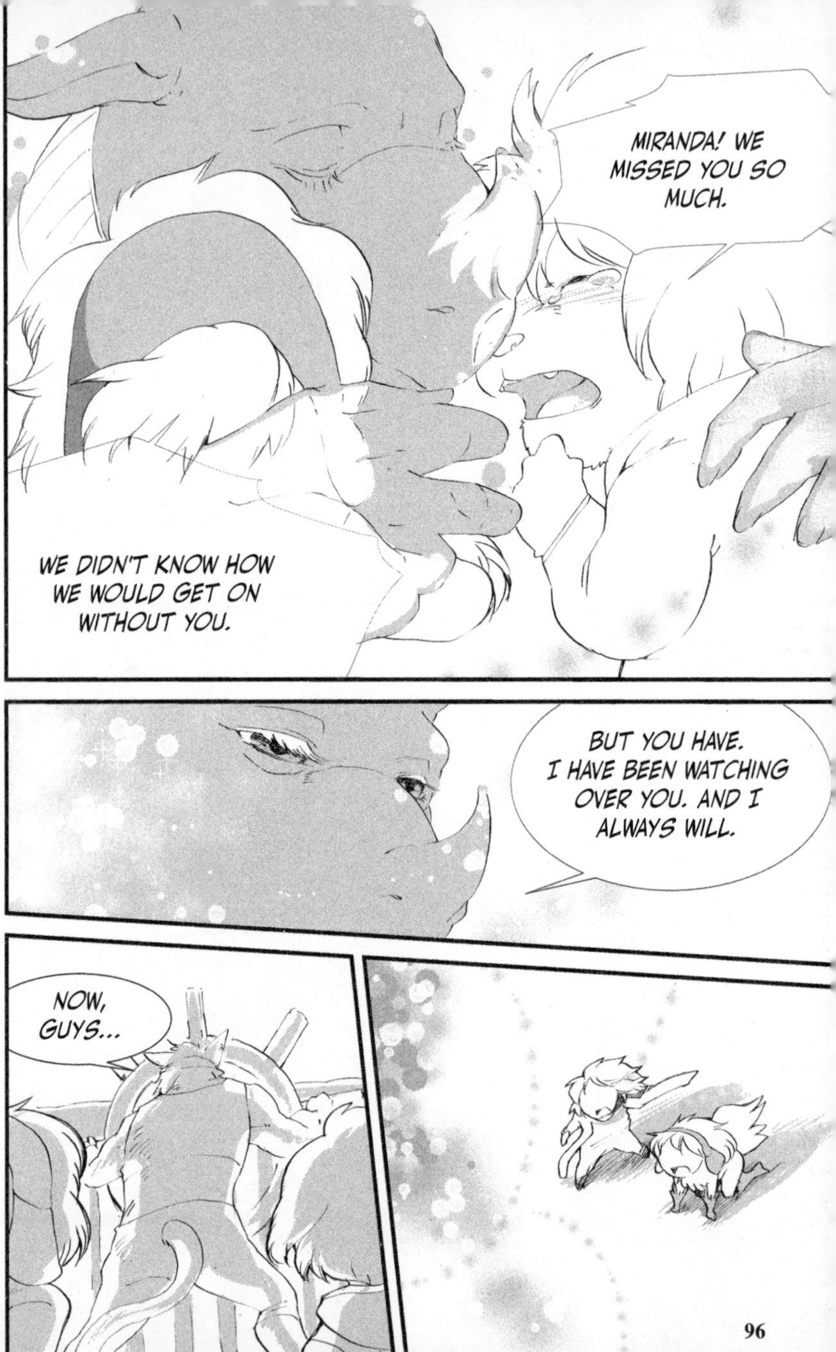
MIRANDA! WE MISSED YOU SO MUCH.
WE DIDN'T KNOW HOW WE WOULD GET ON WITHOUT YOU.
BUT YOU HAVE. I HAVE BEEN WATCHING OVER YOU. AND I ALWAYS WILL.
NOW, GUYS...

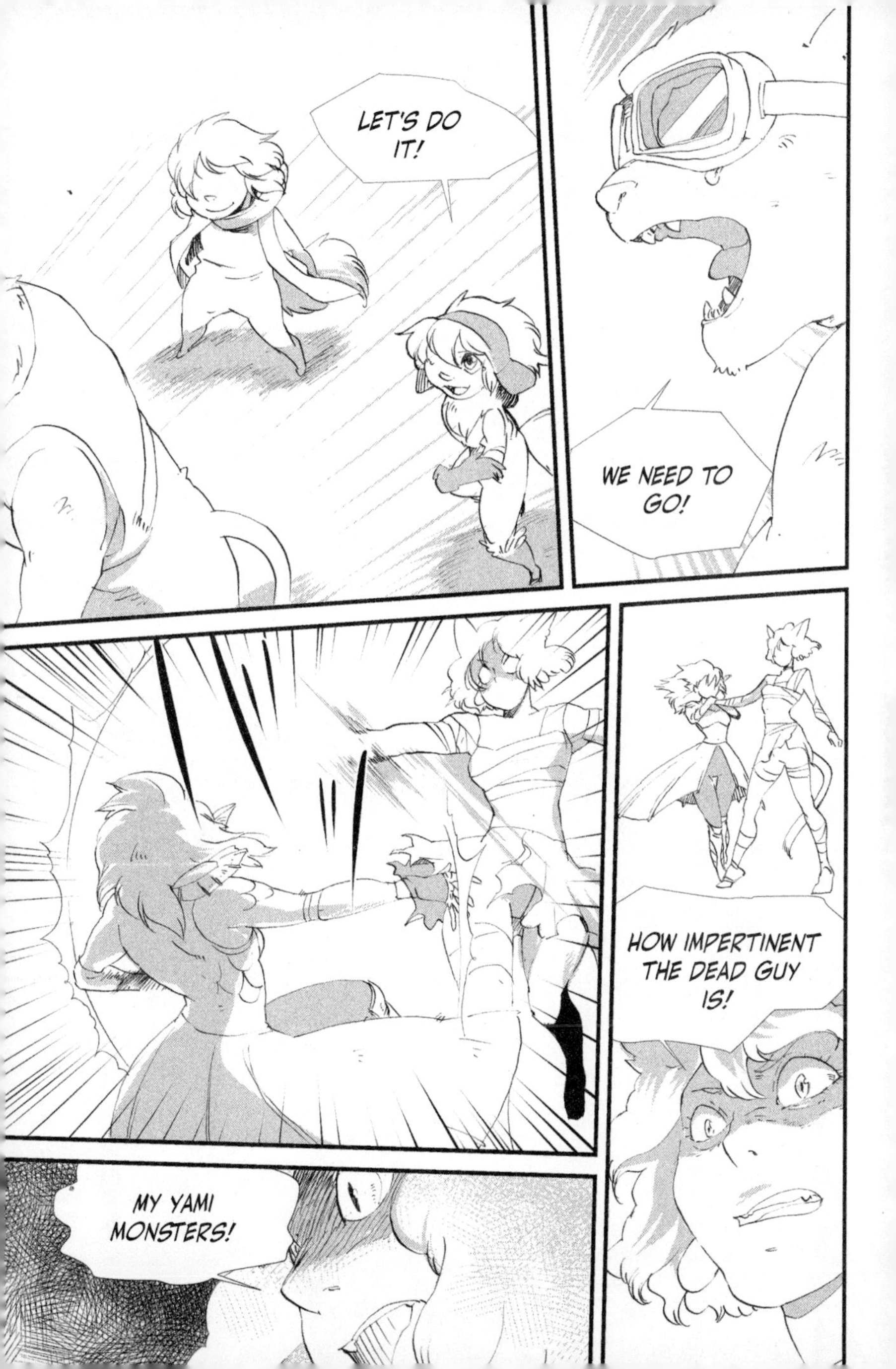
WE NEED TO GO!
LET'S DO IT!
HOW IMPERTINENT THE DEAD GUY IS!
MY YAMI MONSTERS!

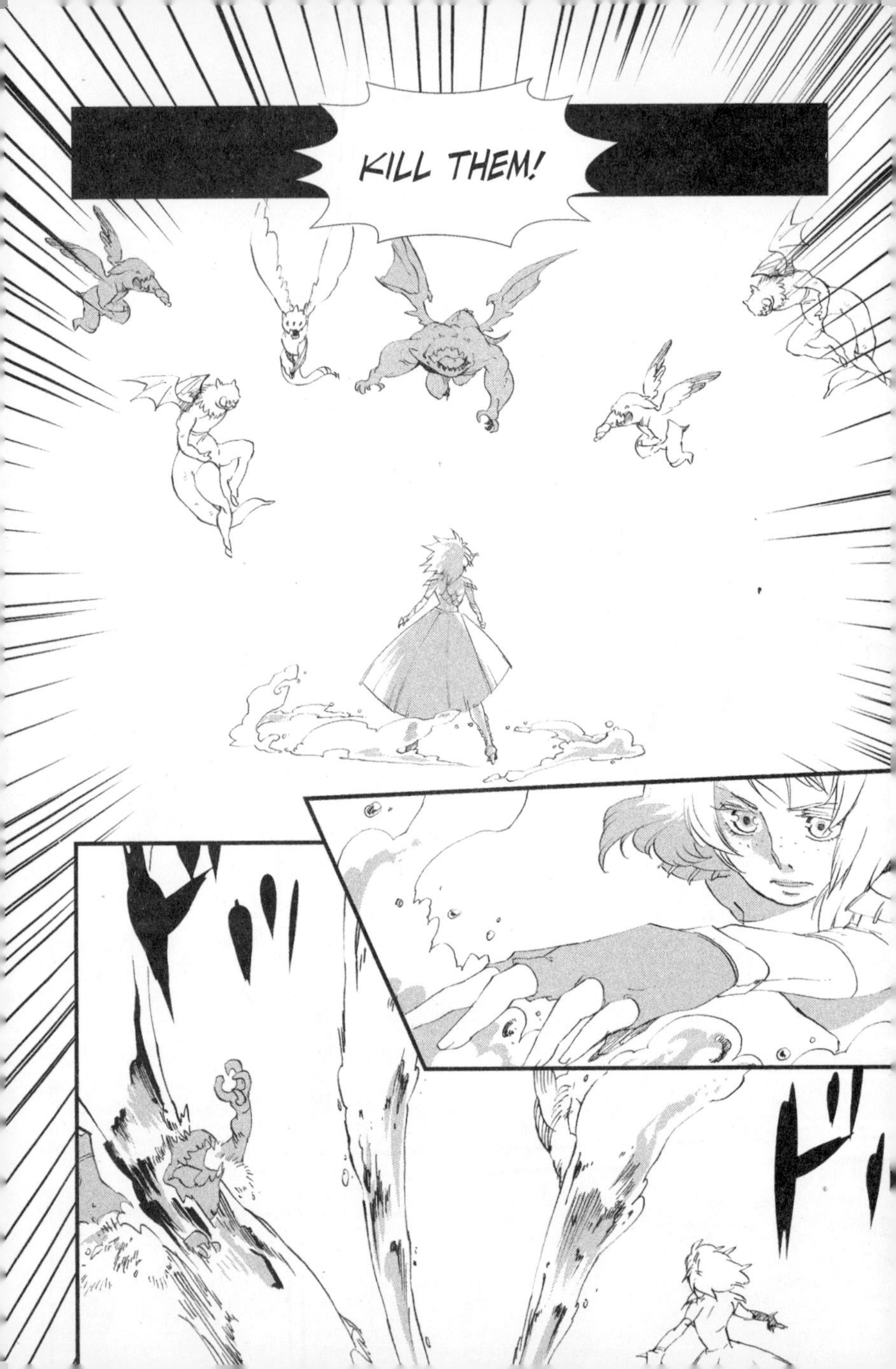
KILL THEM!

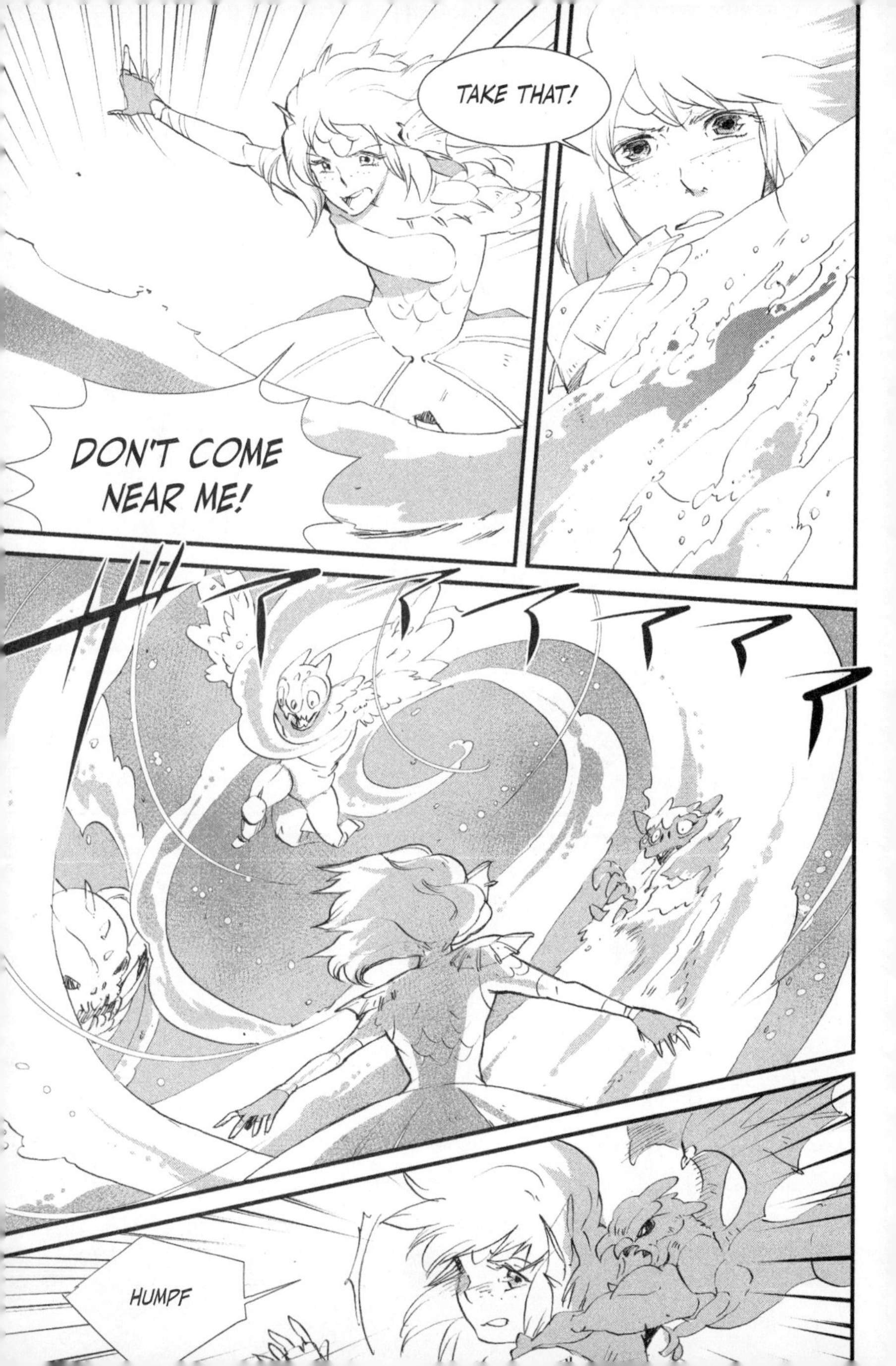
TAKE THAT!
DON'T COME NEAR ME!
HUMPF

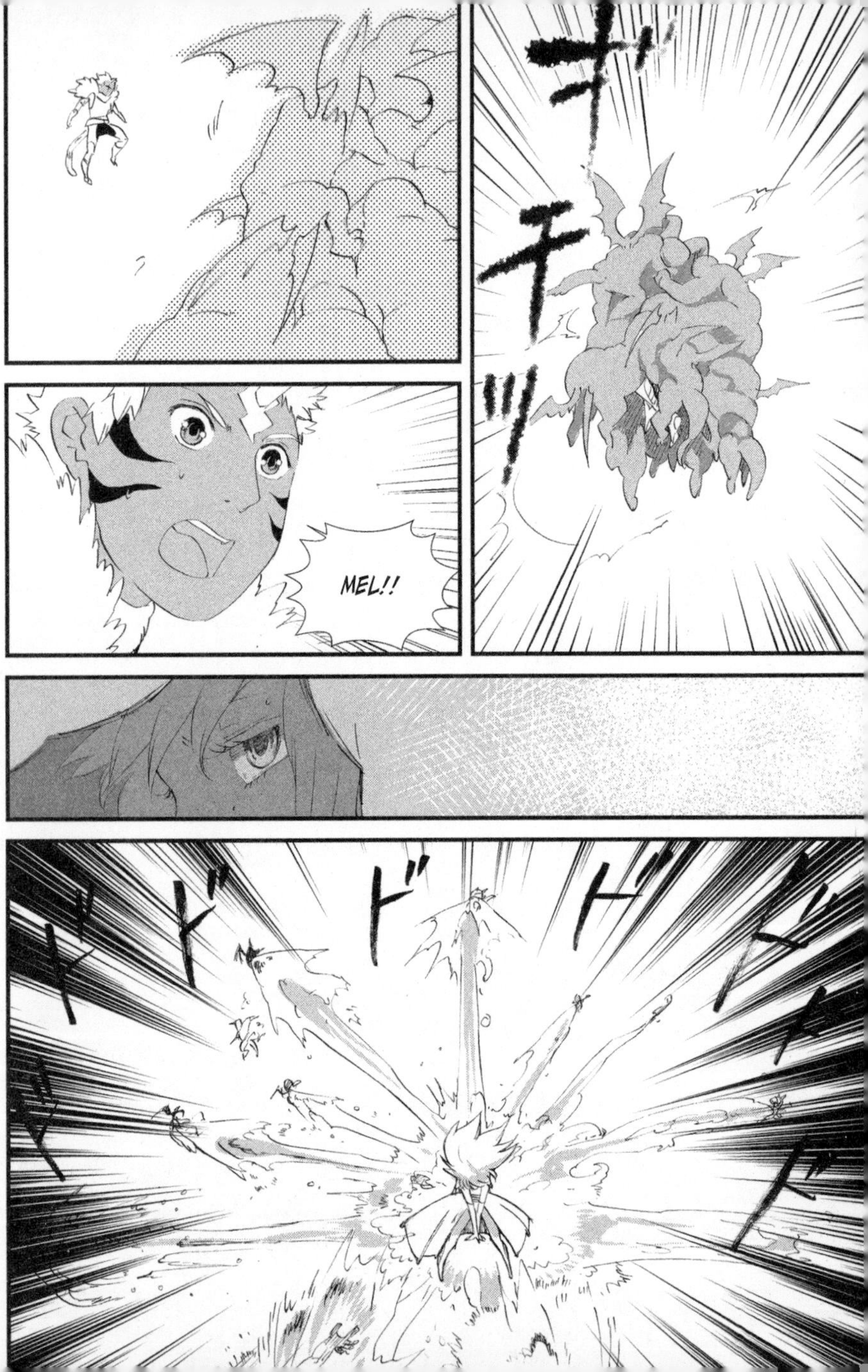
ギチッ!
MEL!!

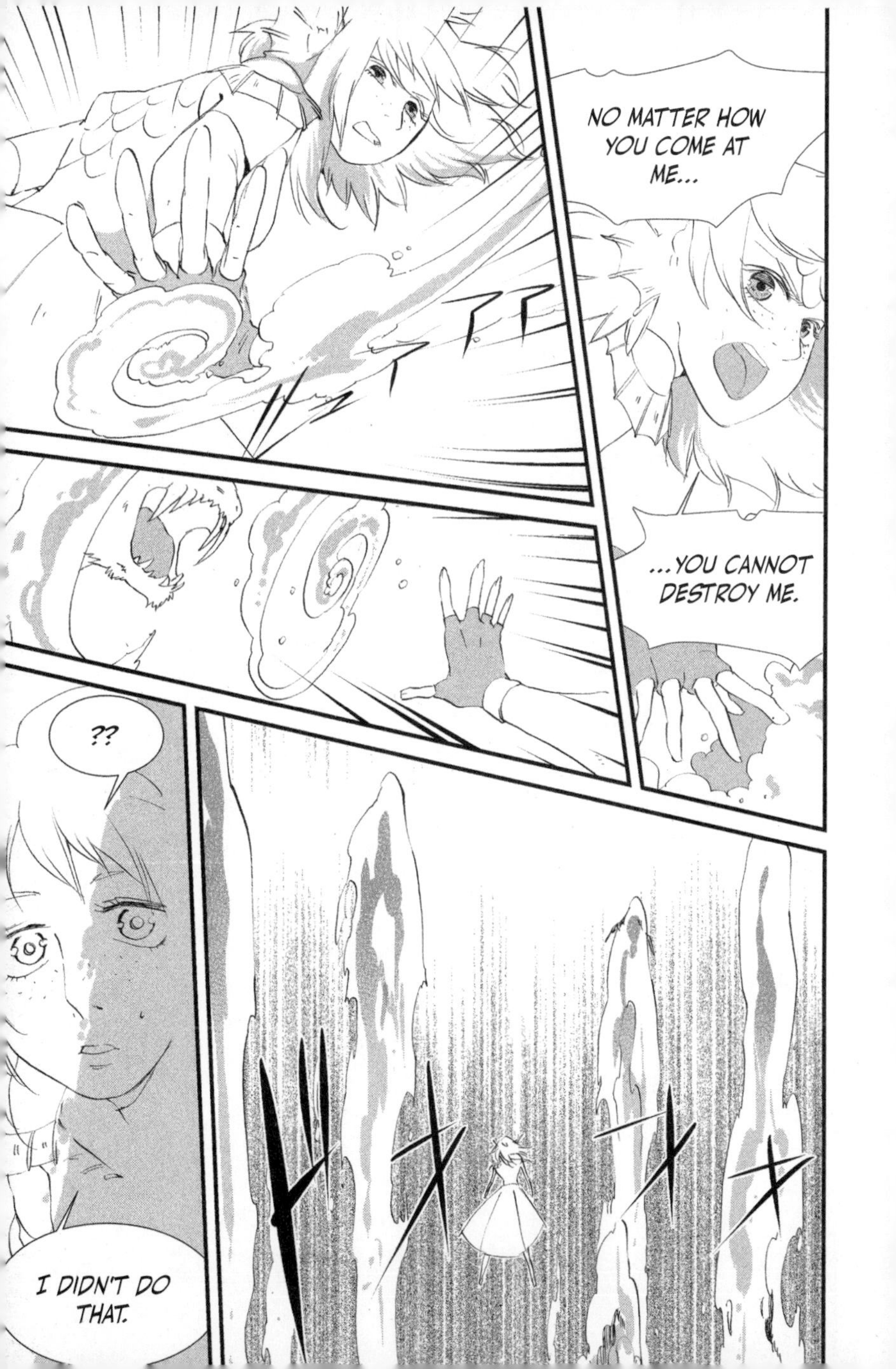
NO MATTER HOW YOU COME AT ME...
...YOU CANNOT DESTROY ME.
??
I DIDN'T DO THAT.

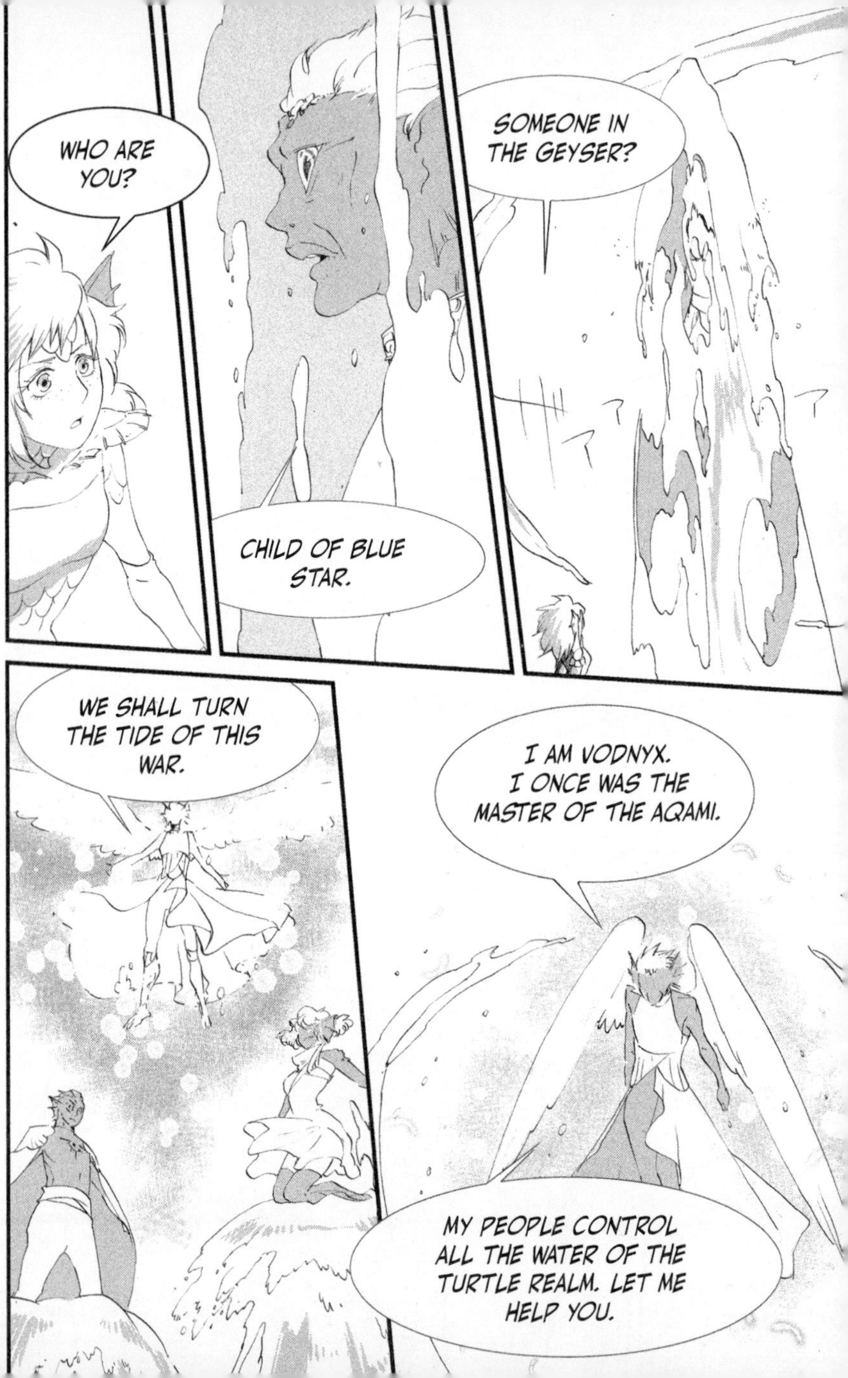
SOMEONE IN THE GEYSER?
CHILD OF BLUE STAR.
WHO ARE YOU?
I AM VODNYX. I ONCE WAS THE MASTER OF THE AQAMI.
MY PEOPLE CONTROL ALL THE WATER OF THE TURTLE REALM. LET ME HELP YOU.
WE SHALL TURN THE TIDE OF THIS WAR.

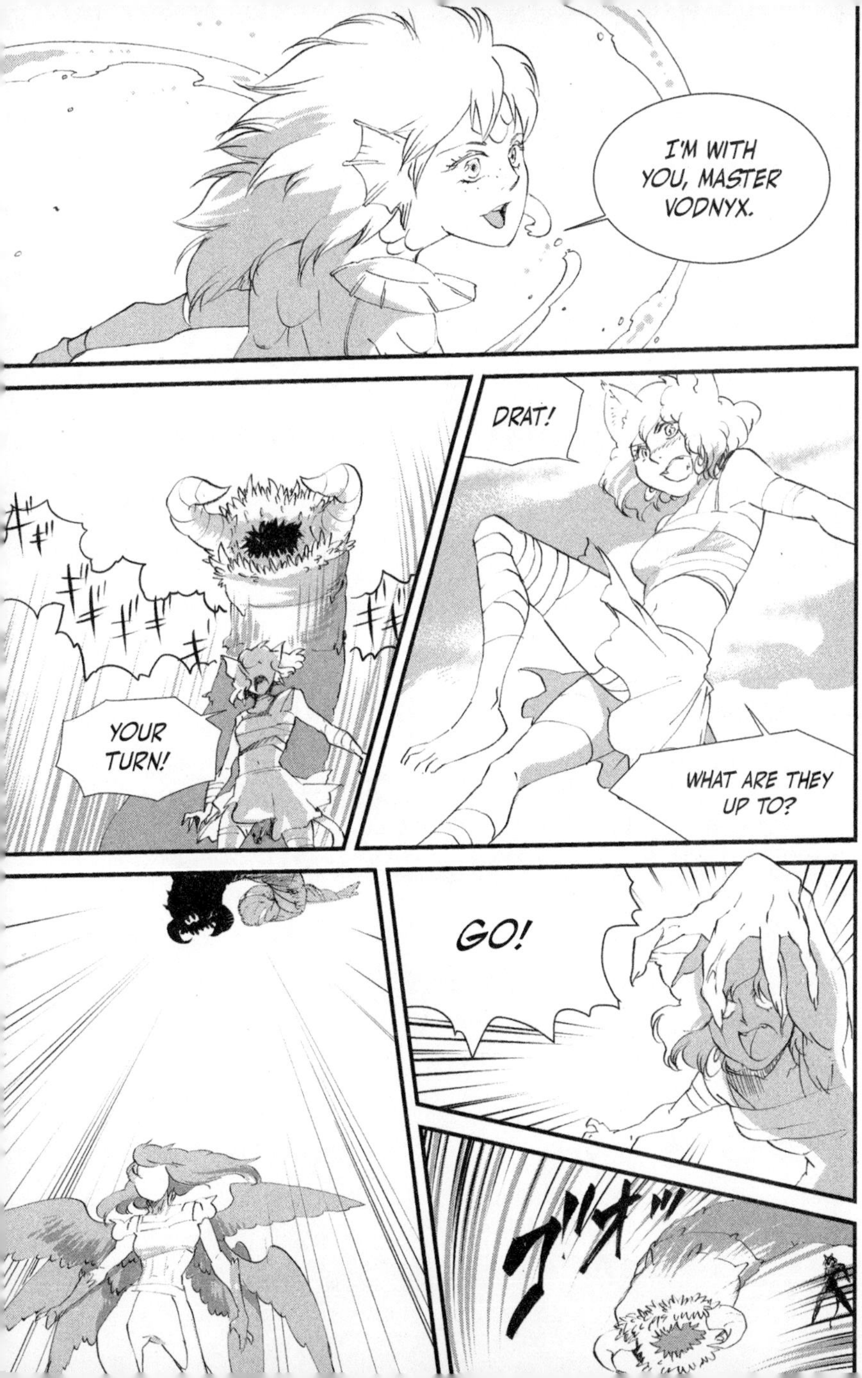
I'M WITH YOU, MASTER VODNYX.
DRAT!
WHAT ARE THEY UP TO?
YOUR TURN!
GO!

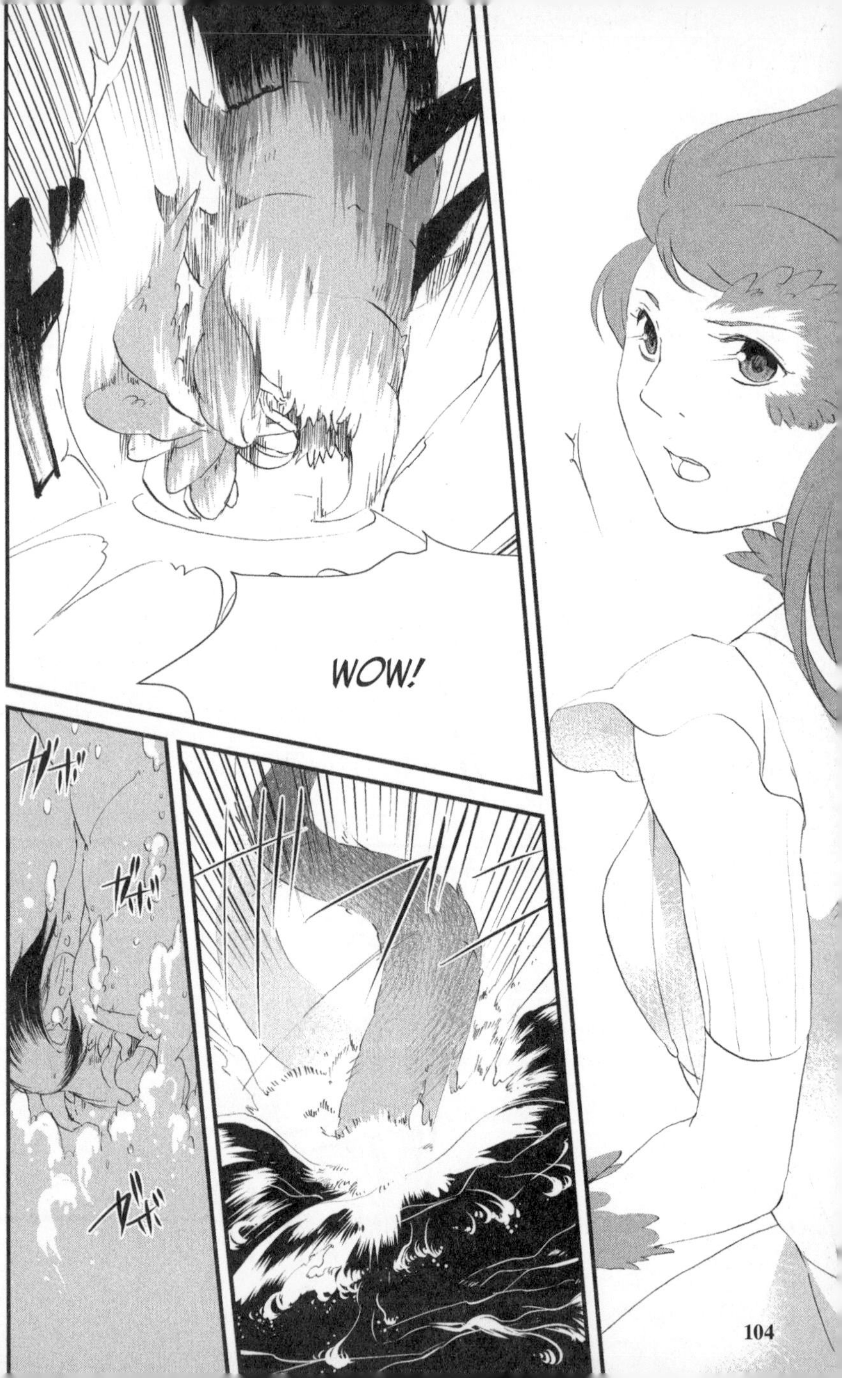
WOW!

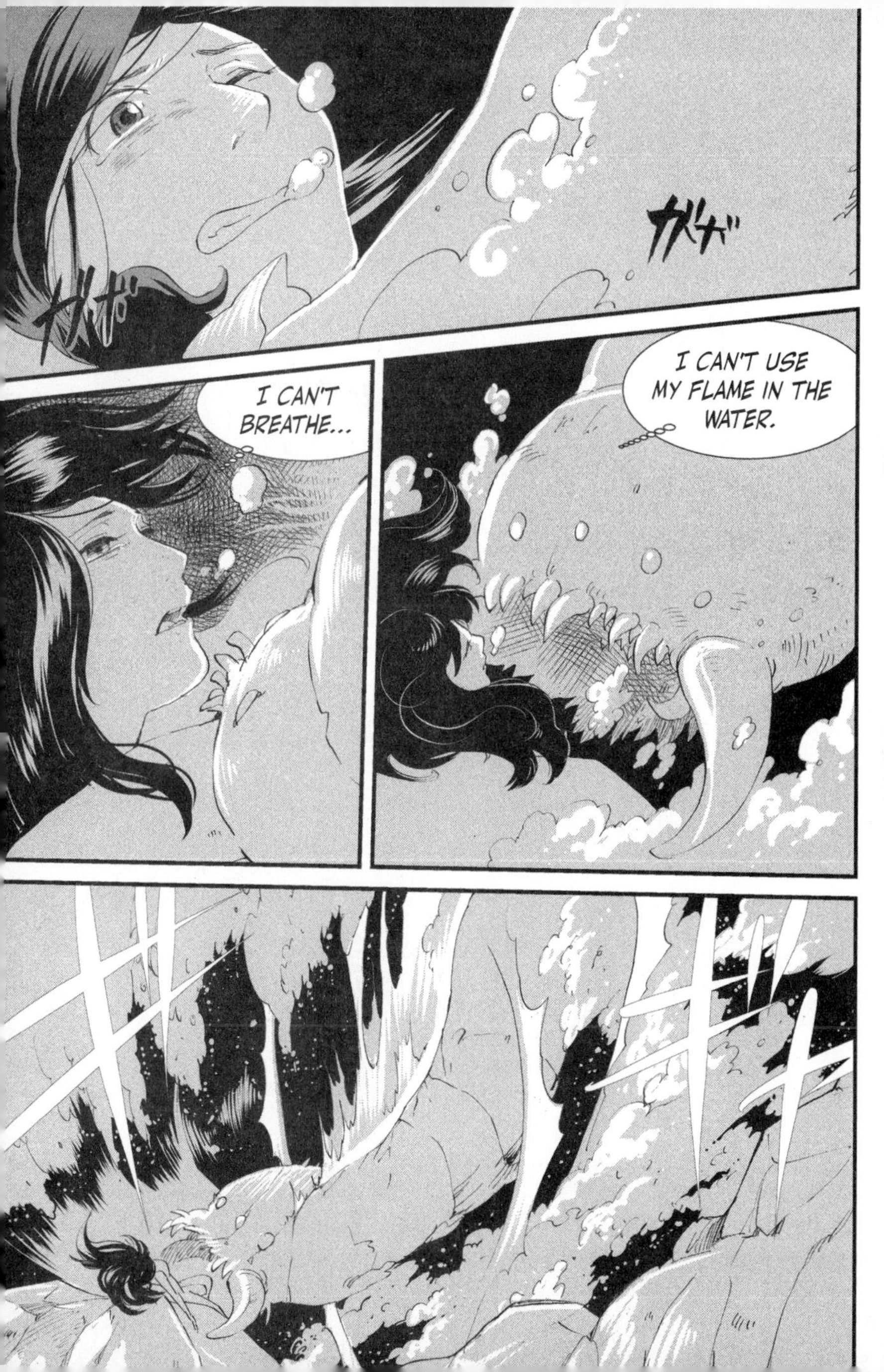
I CAN'T USE MY FLAME IN THE WATER.
I CAN'T BREATHE...

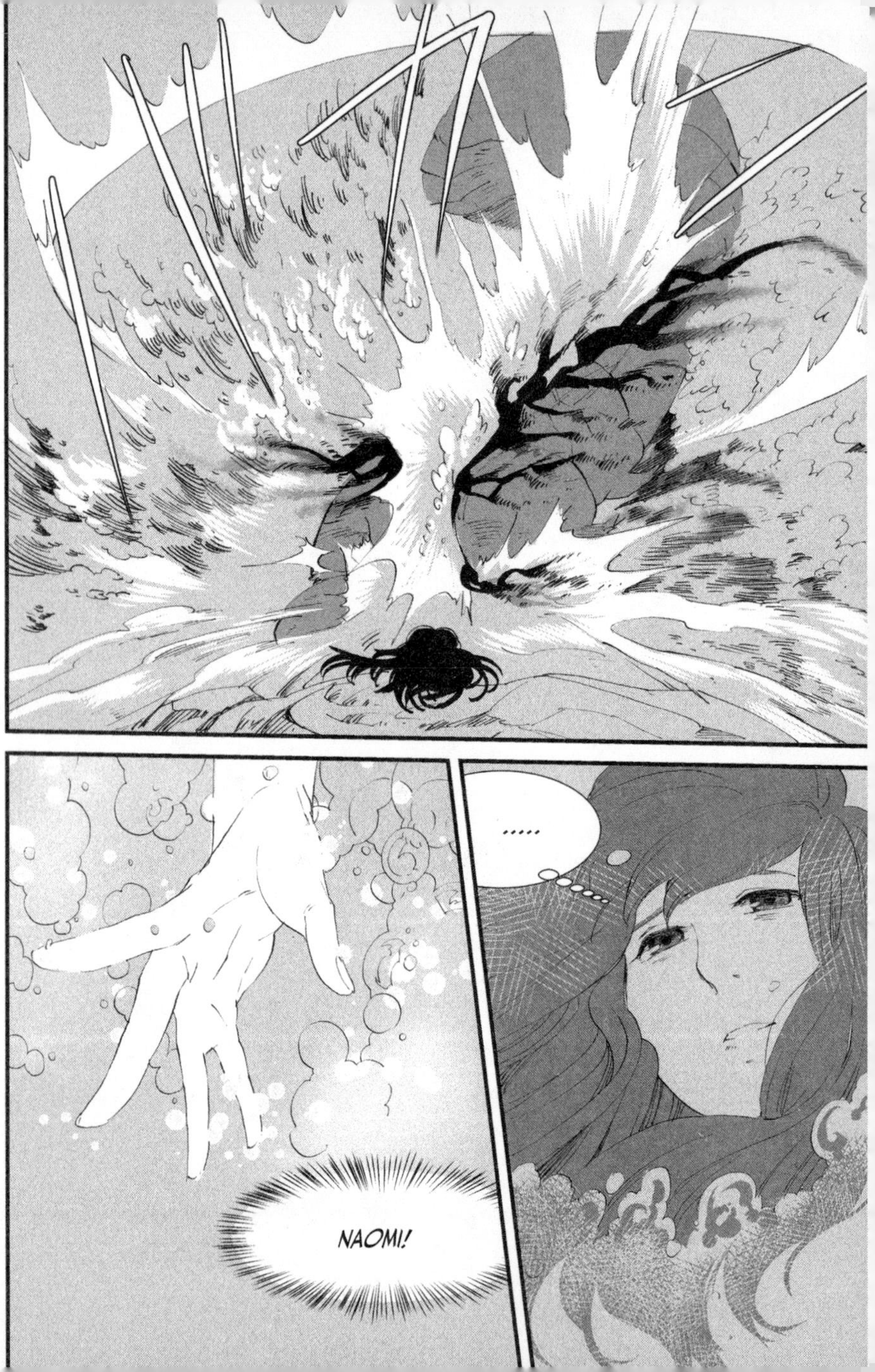
......
NAOMI!

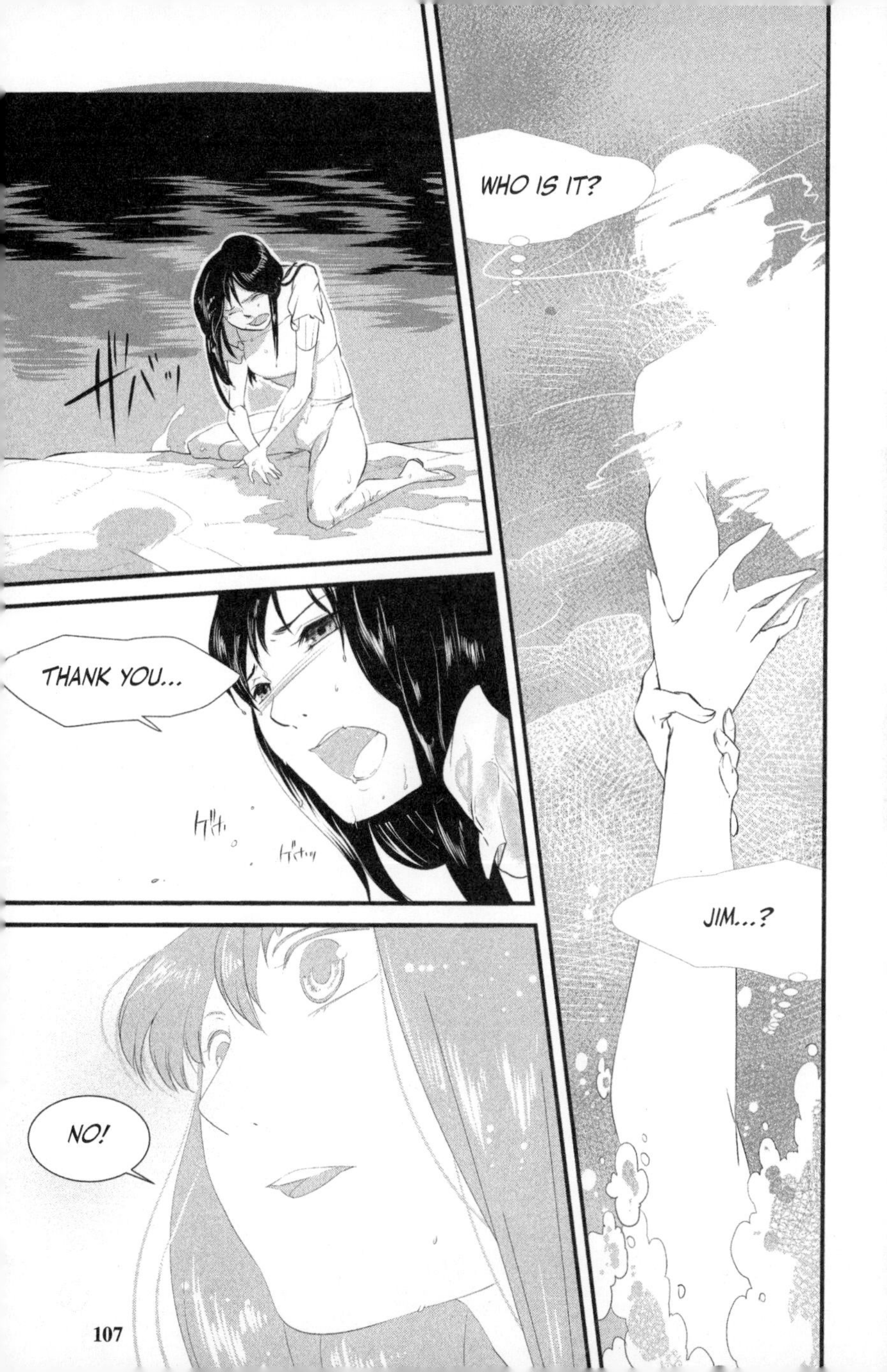
WHO IS IT?
JIM...?
ザバッ
THANK YOU...
ゲホ
ゲホッ
NO!

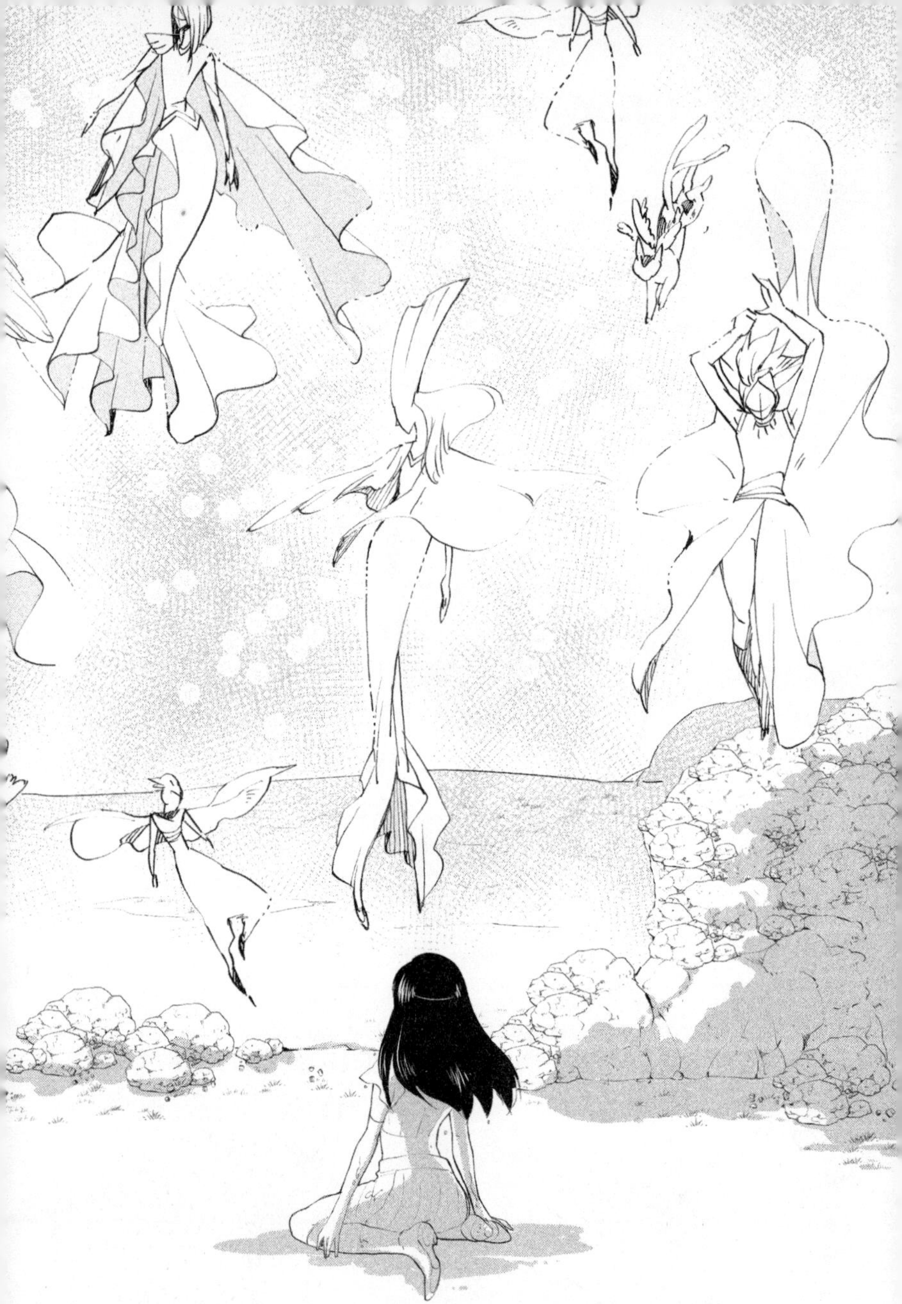

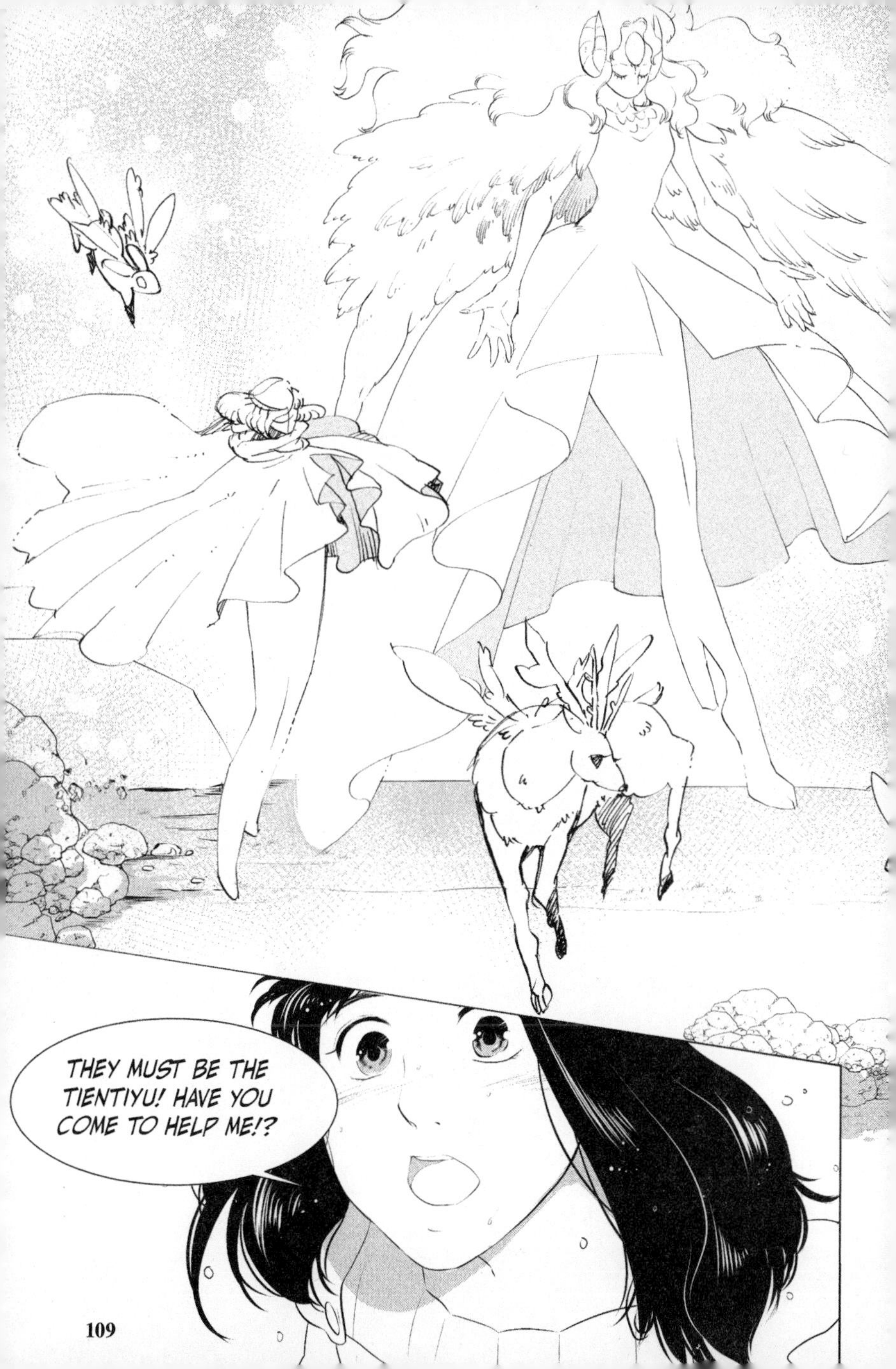
THEY MUST BE THE TIENTIYU! HAVE YOU COME TO HELP ME!?

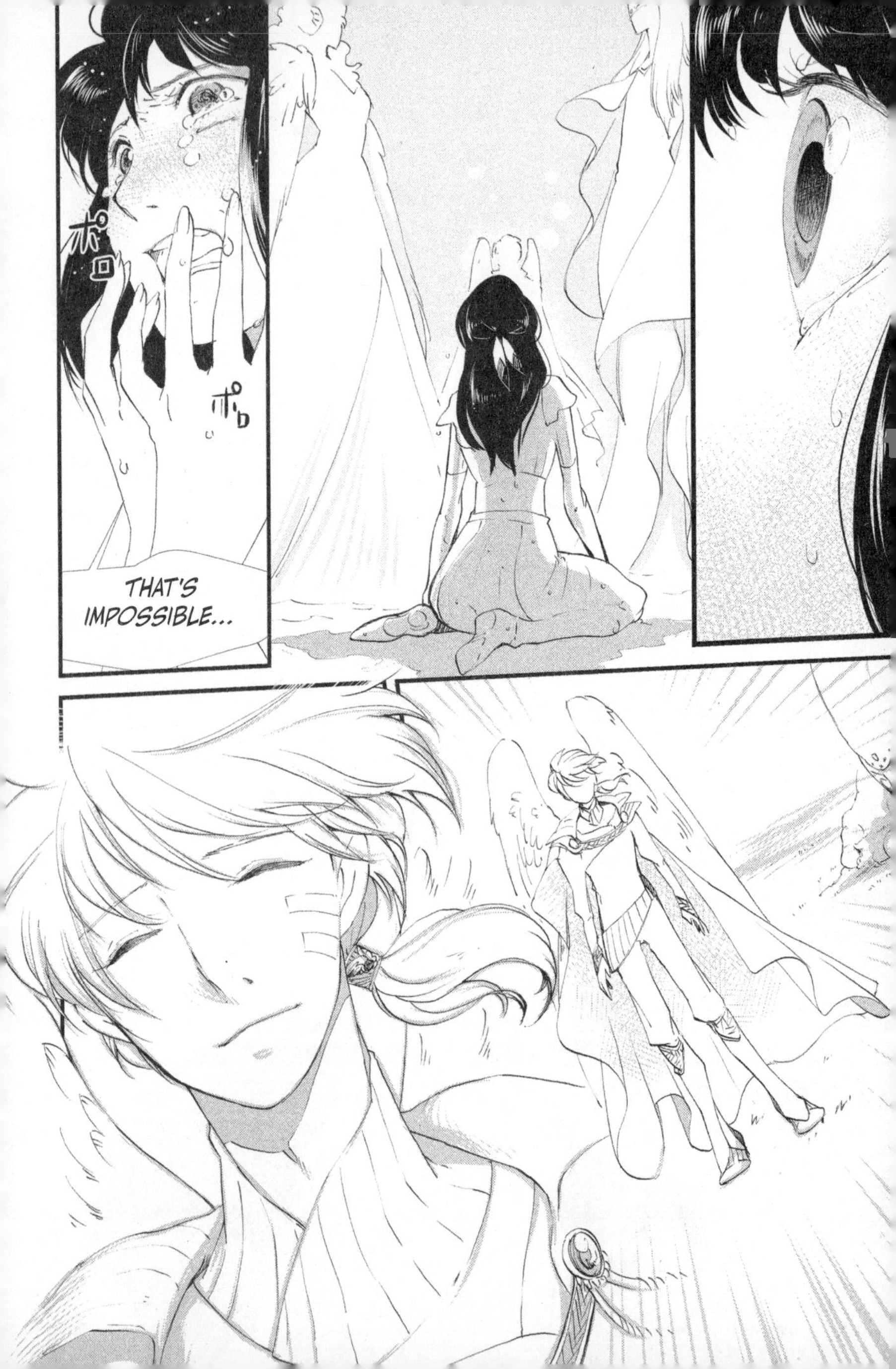
ポロ
ぽろ
THAT'S IMPOSSIBLE...

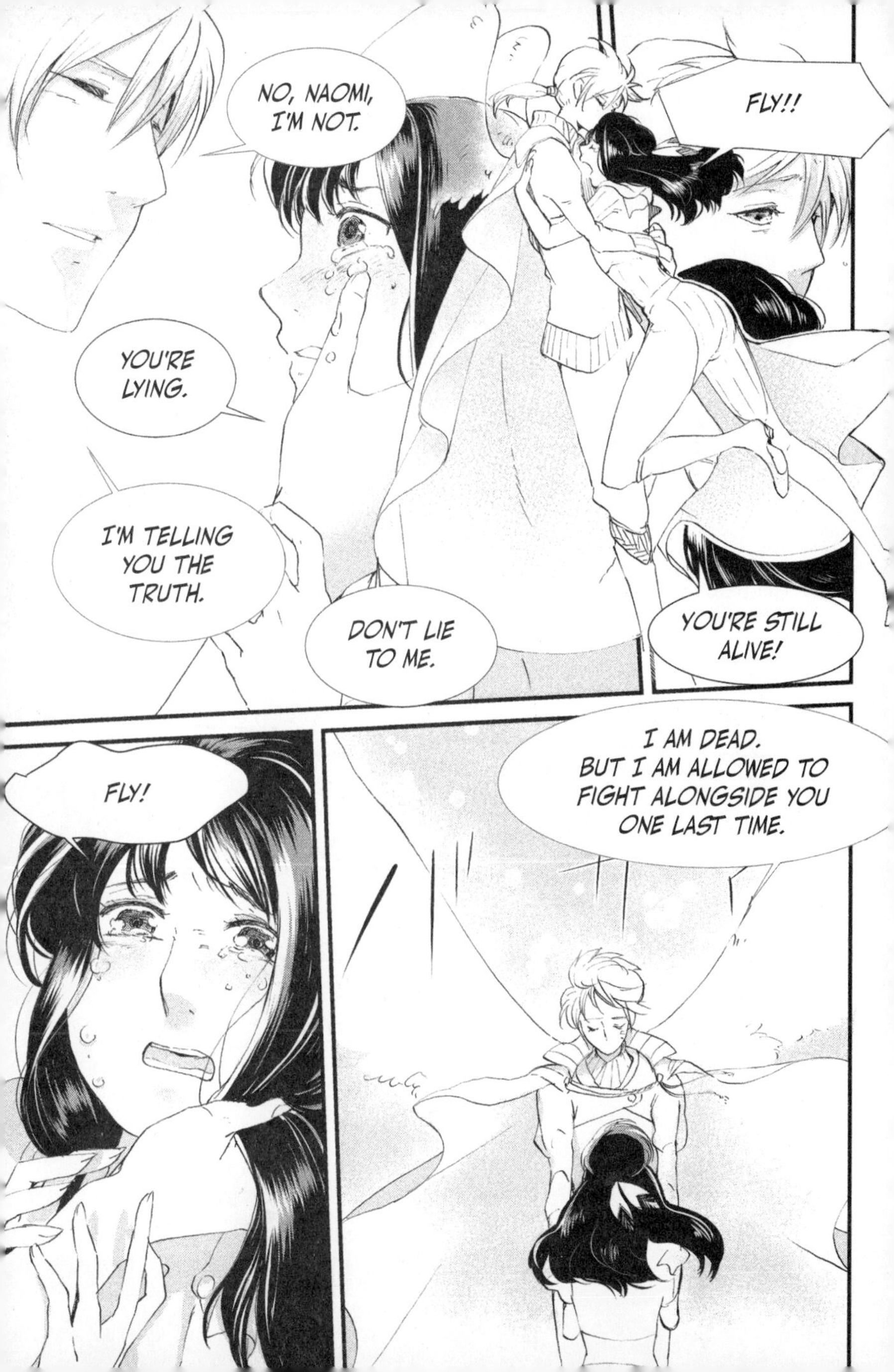
FLY!!
YOU'RE STILL ALIVE!
NO, NAOMI, I'M NOT.
YOU'RE LYING.
I'M TELLING YOU THE TRUTH.
DON'T LIE TO ME.
I AM DEAD. BUT I AM ALLOWED TO FIGHT ALONGSIDE YOU ONE LAST TIME.
FLY!

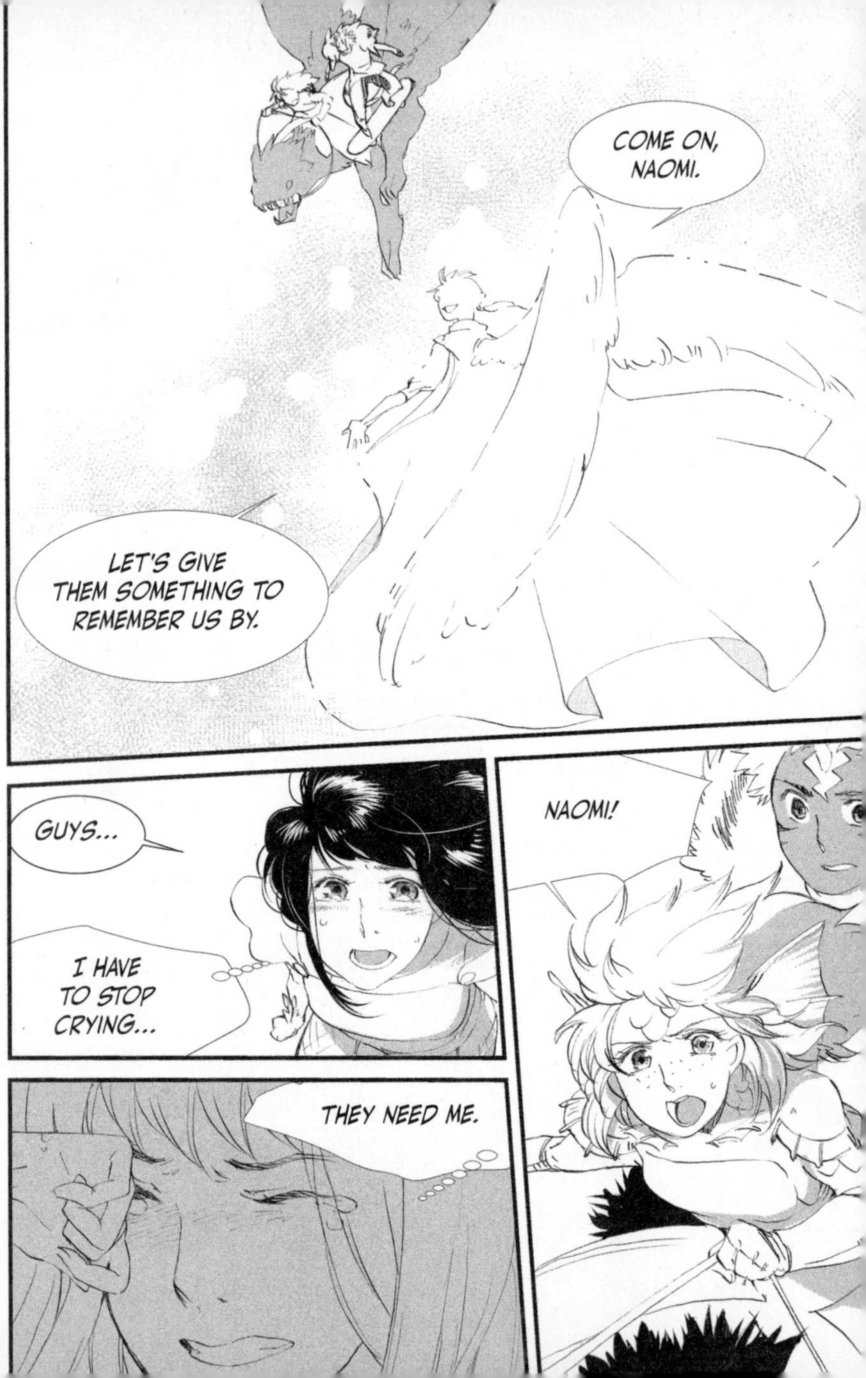
COME ON, NAOMI.
LET'S GIVE THEM SOMETHING TO REMEMBER US BY.
NAOMI!
GUYS...
I HAVE TO STOP CRYING...
THEY NEED ME.

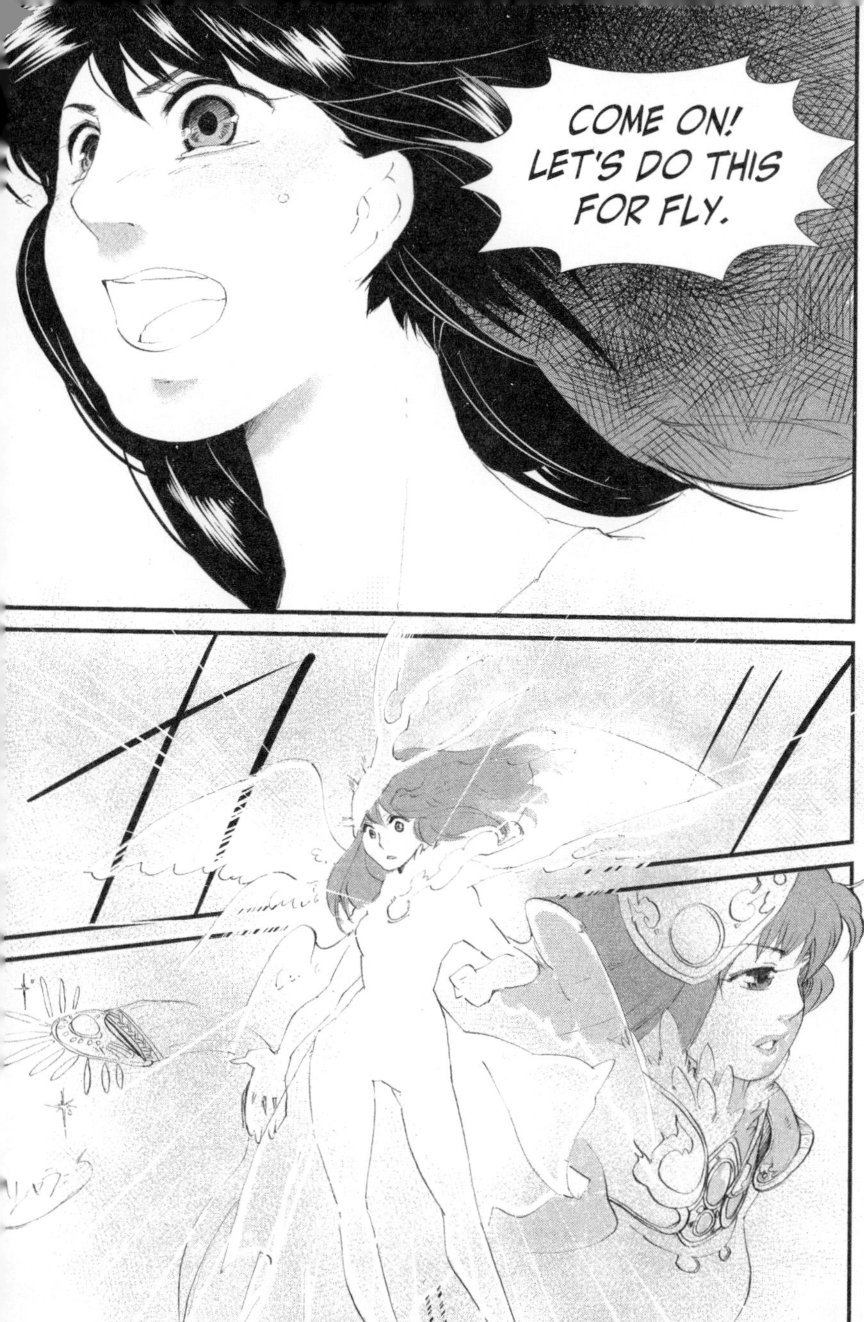
COME ON! LET'S DO THIS FOR FLY.

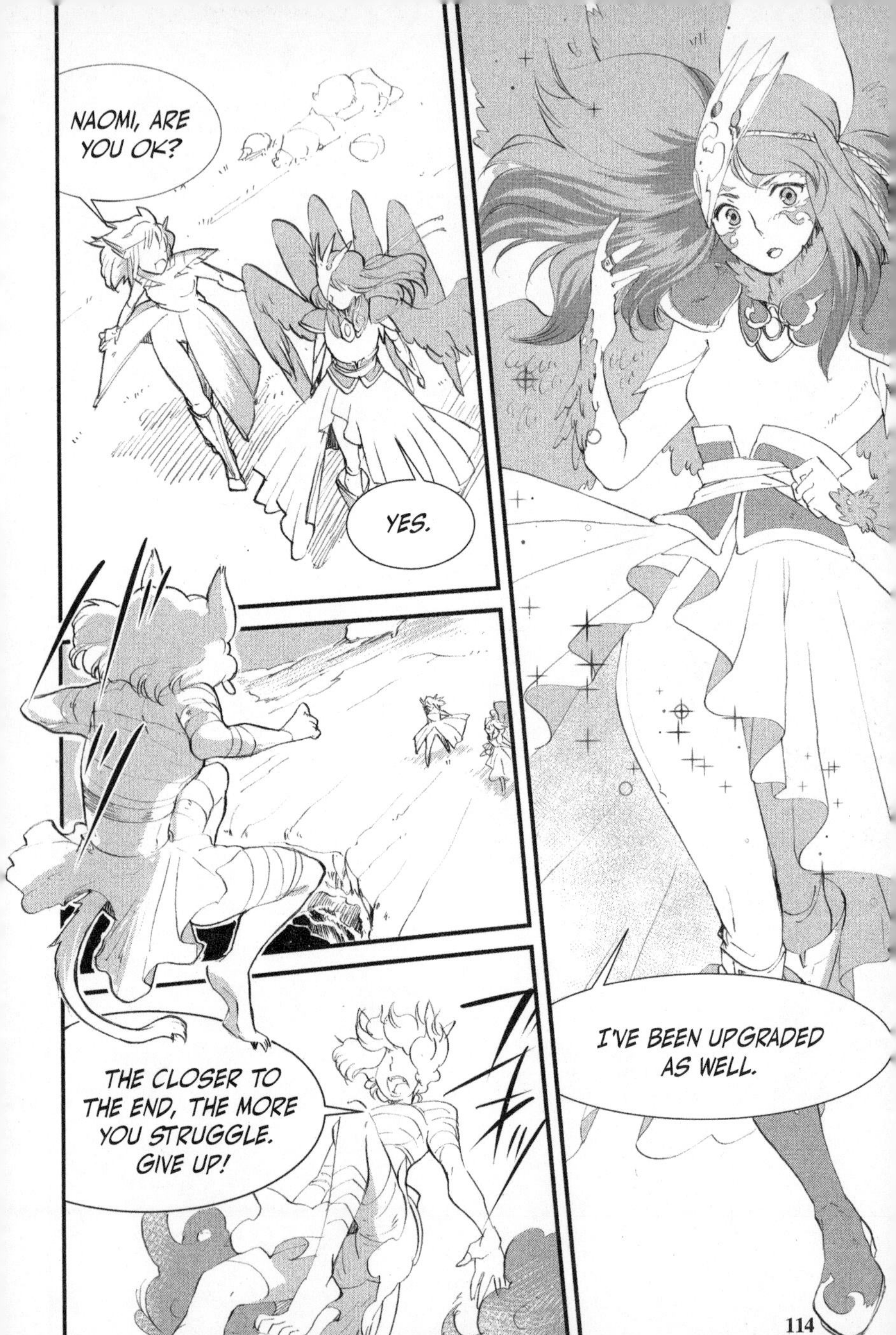
I'VE BEEN UPGRADED AS WELL.
NAOMI, ARE YOU OK?
YES.
THE CLOSER TO THE END, THE MORE YOU STRUGGLE. GIVE UP!

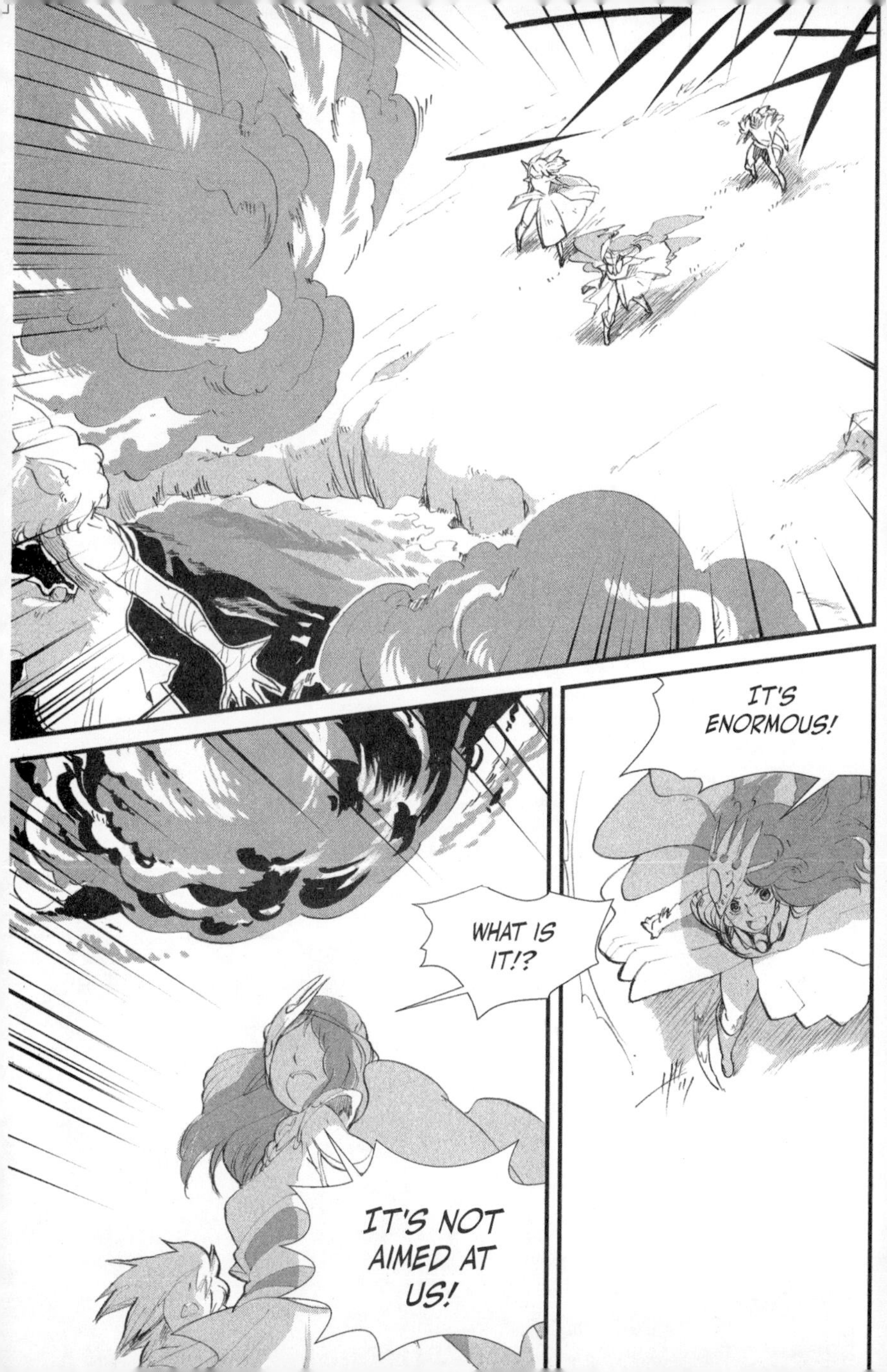
IT'S ENORMOUS!
WHAT IS IT!?
IT'S NOT AIMED AT US!

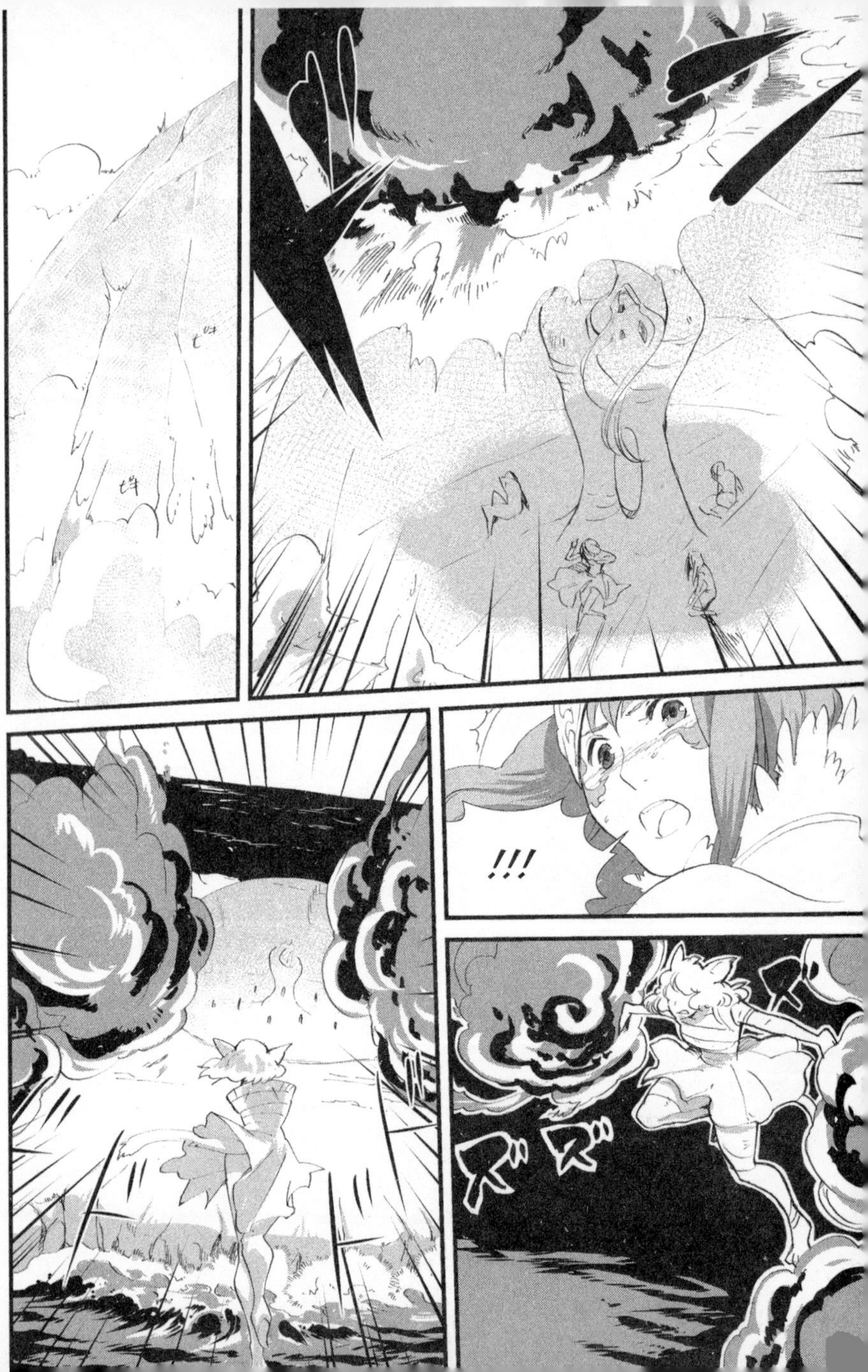
ピキ
ピキ
!!!

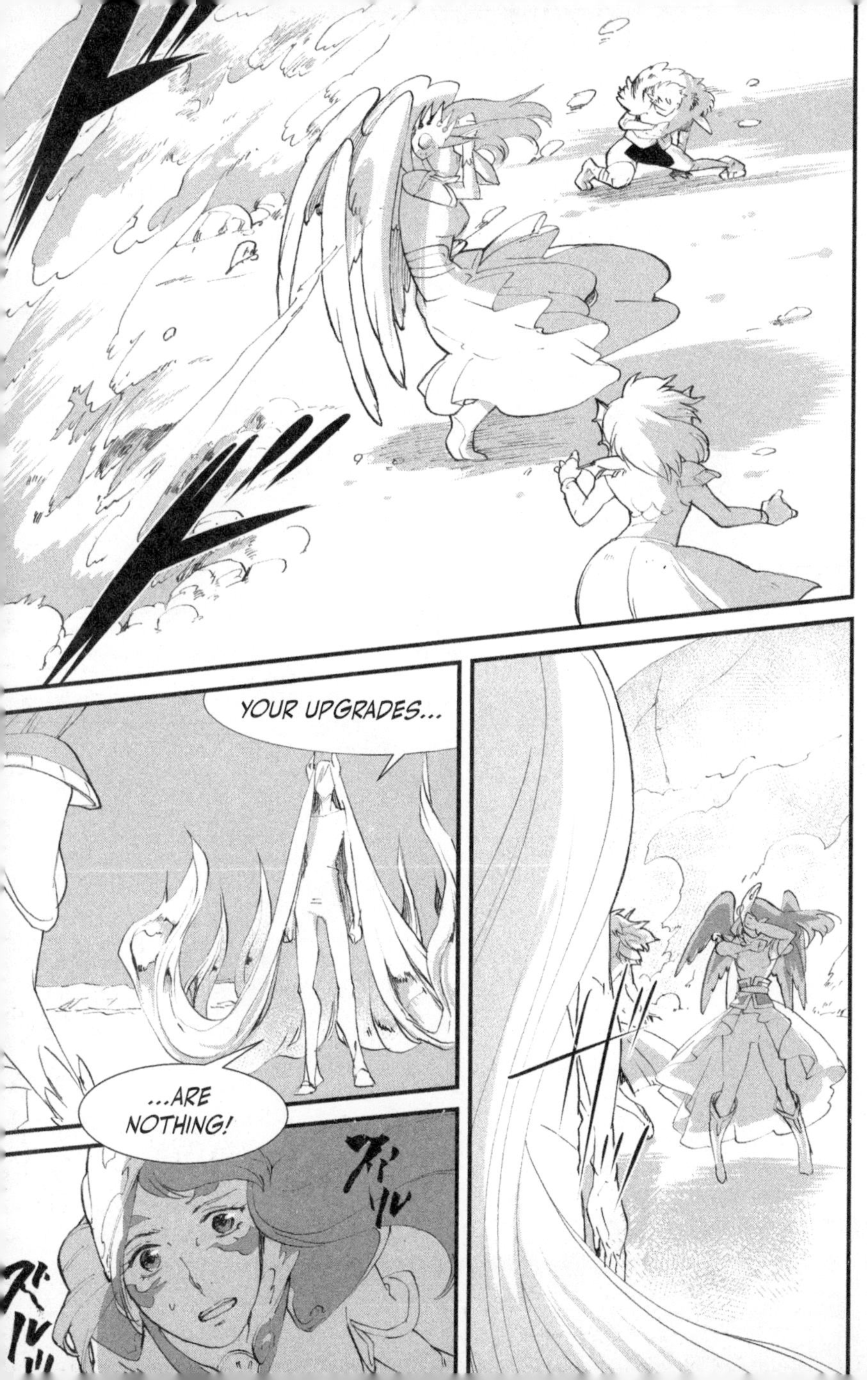
YOUR UPGRADES...
...ARE NOTHING!

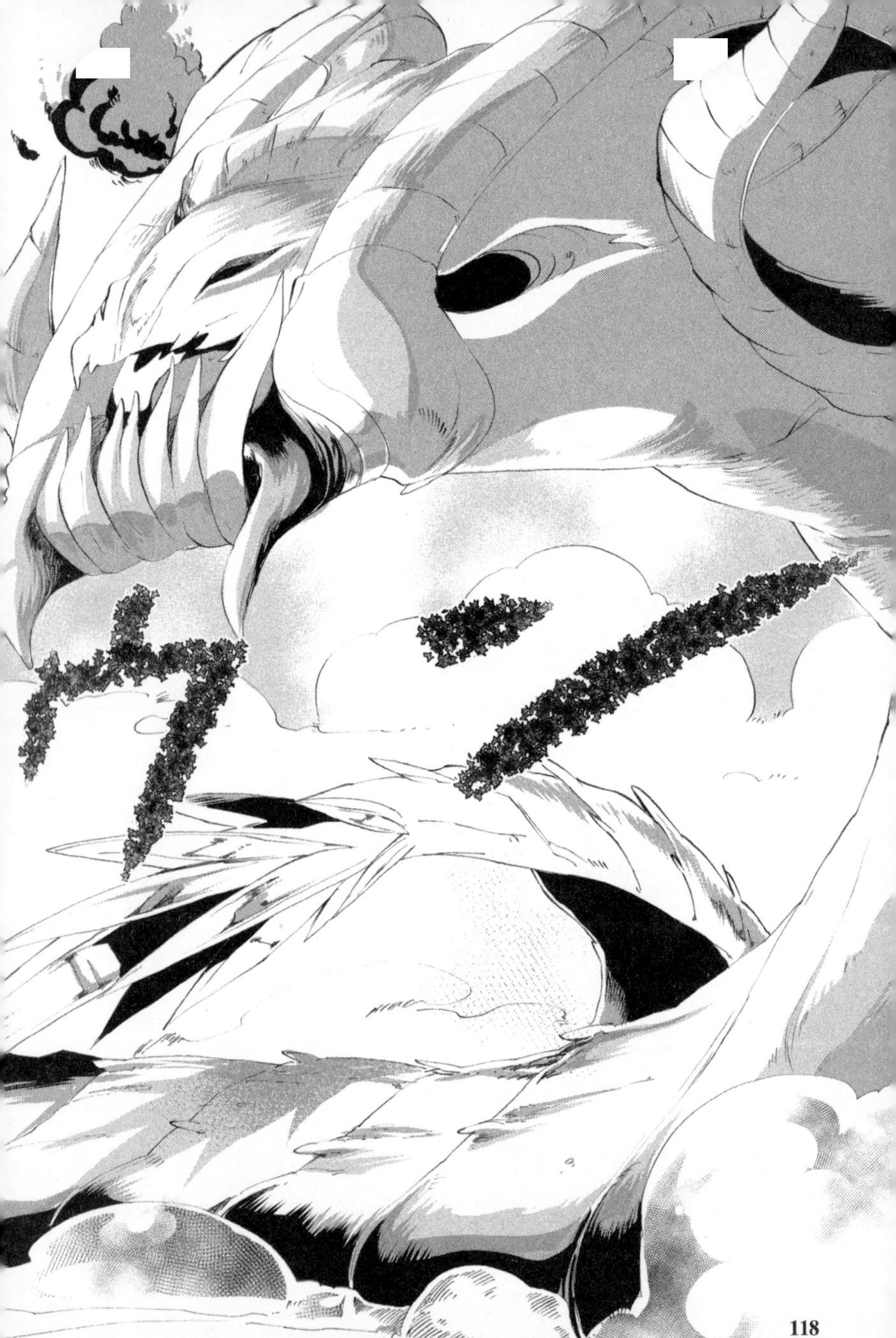
サン

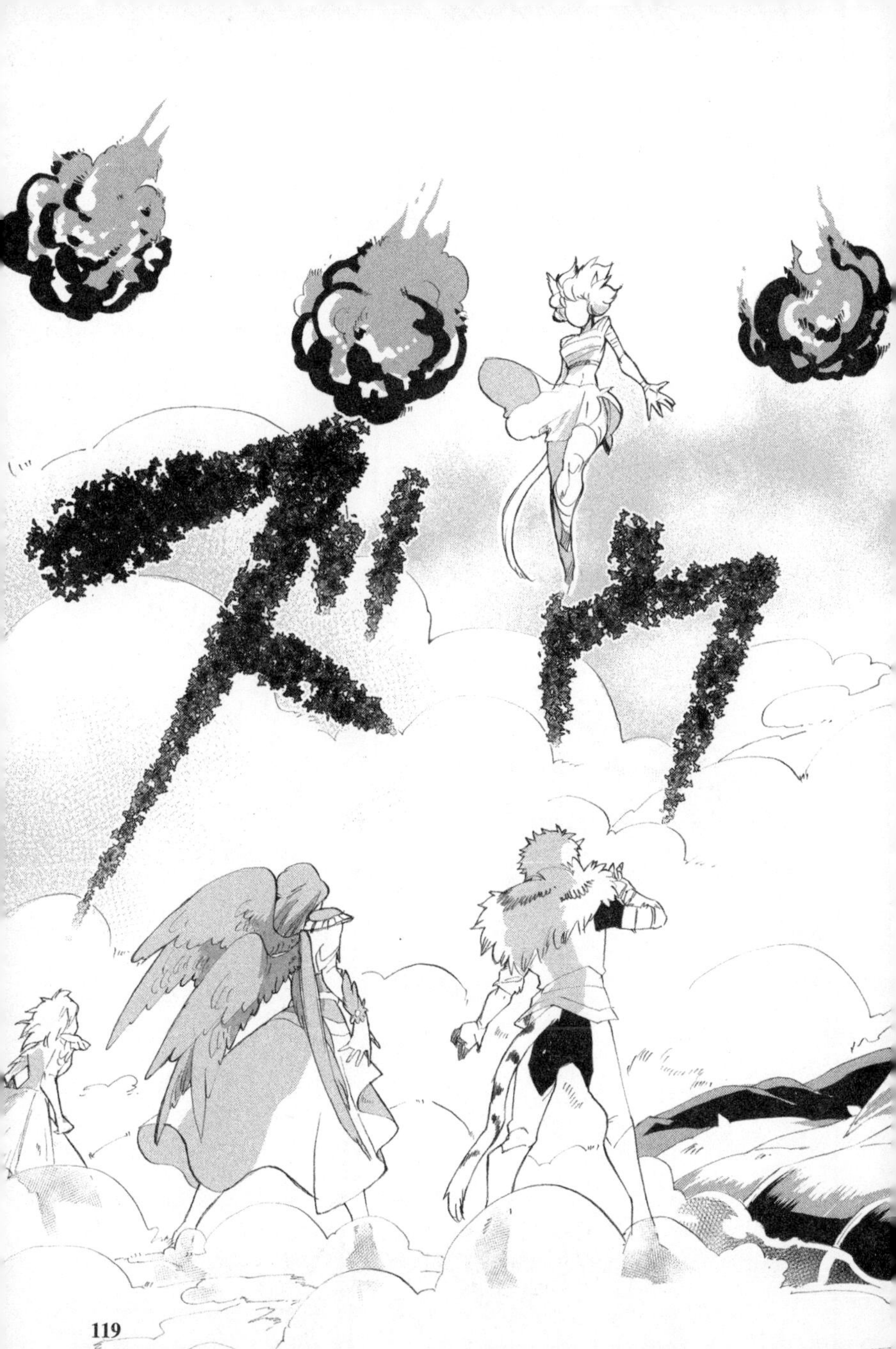

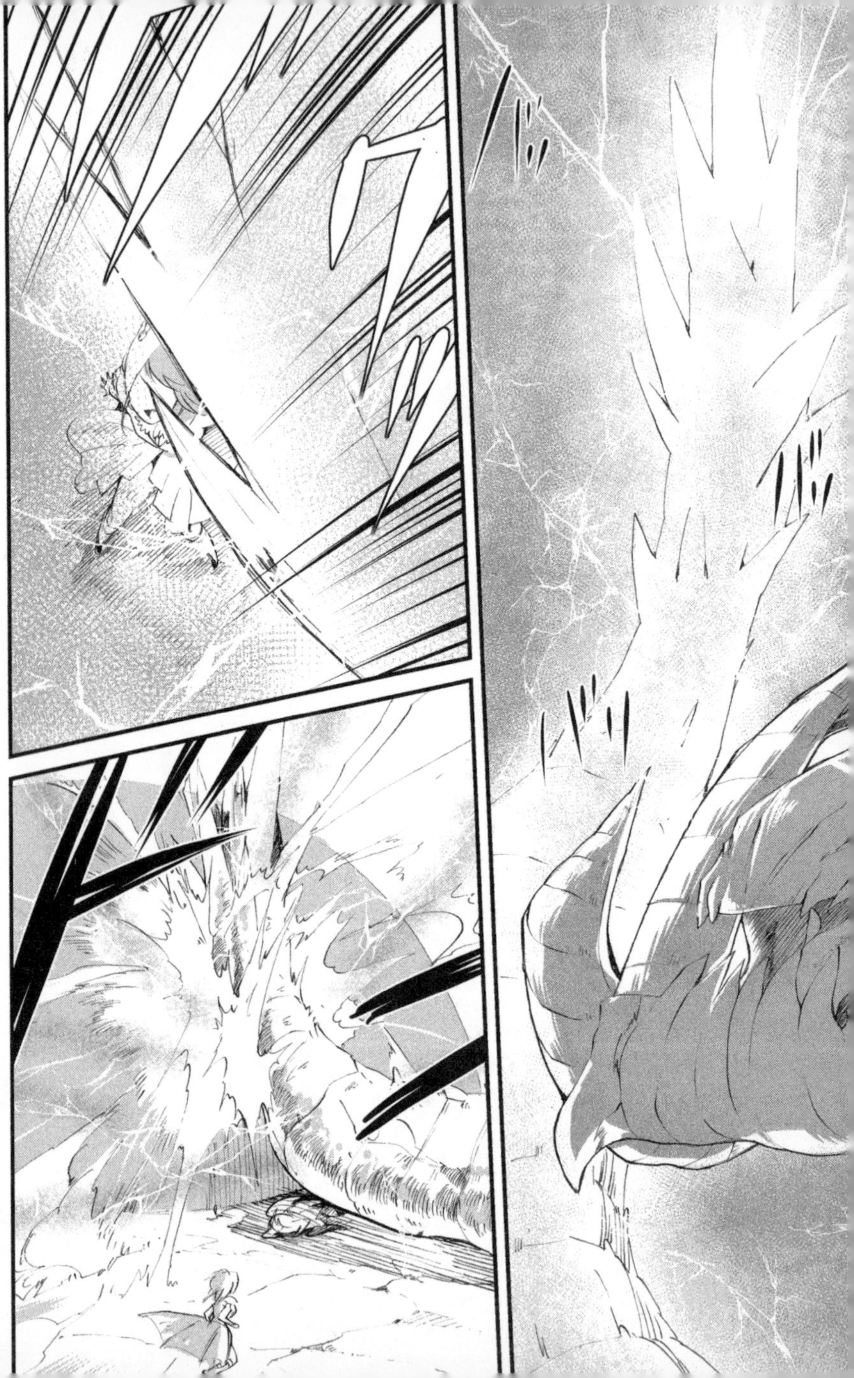

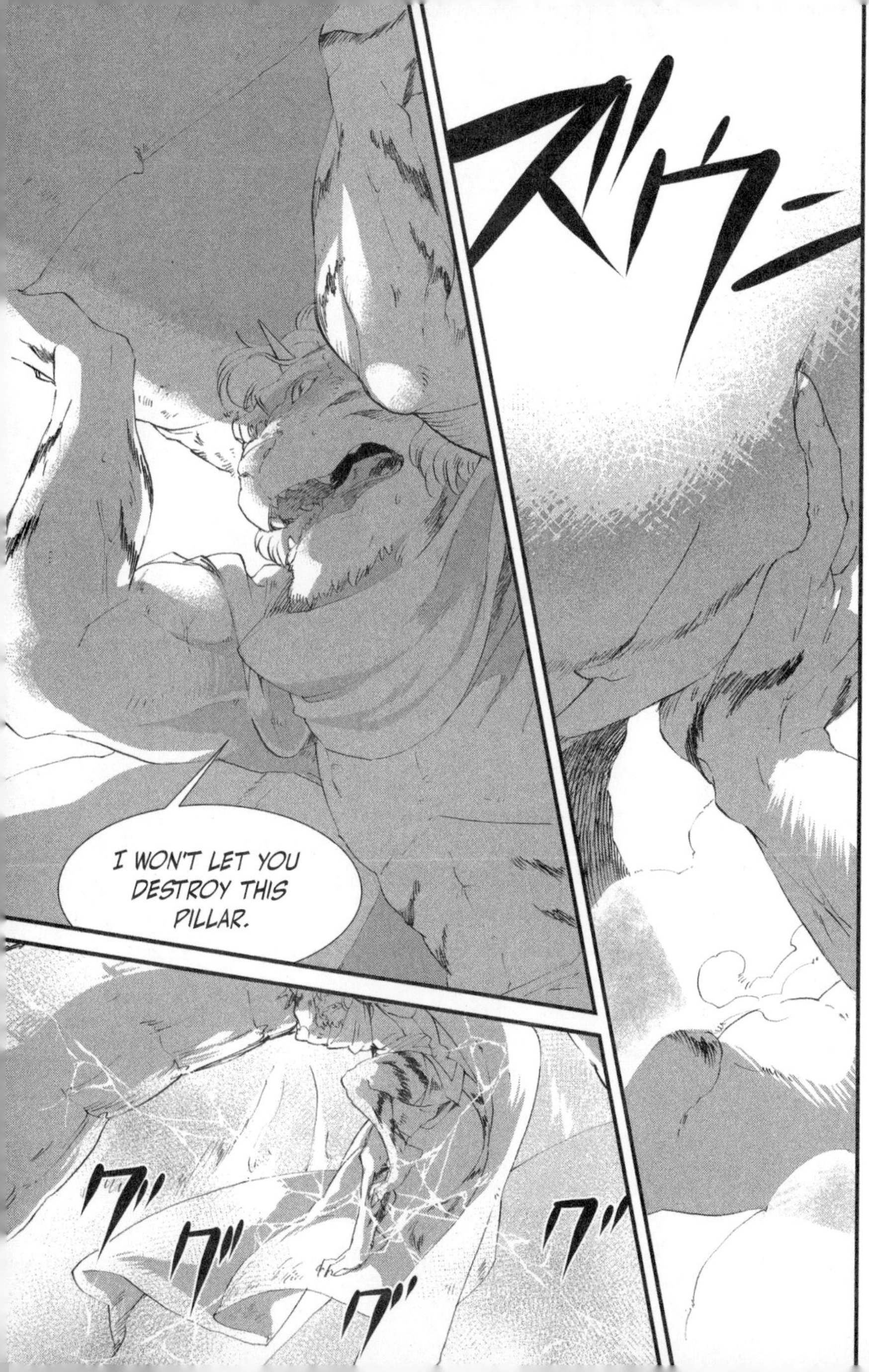
I WON'T LET YOU DESTROY THIS PILLAR.

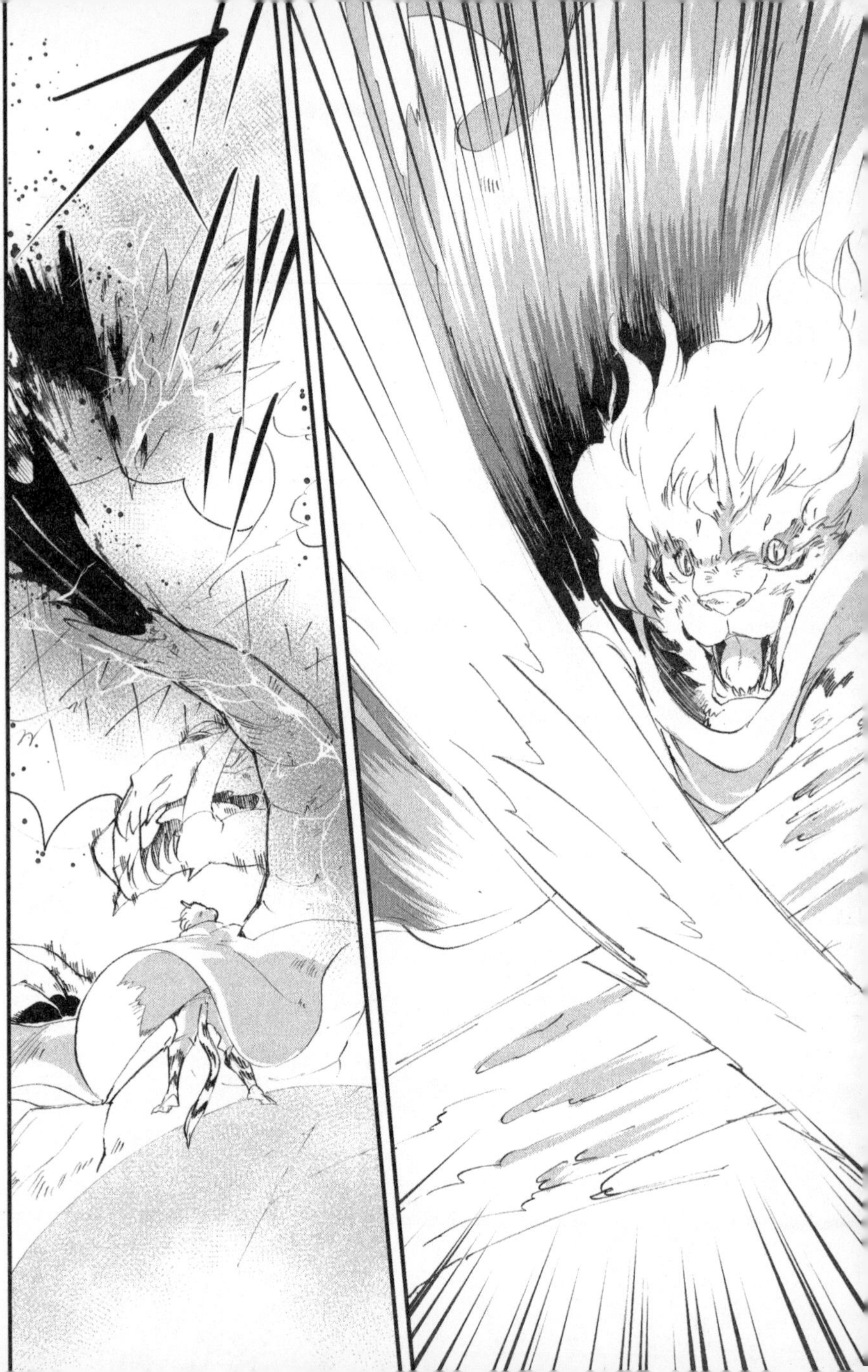

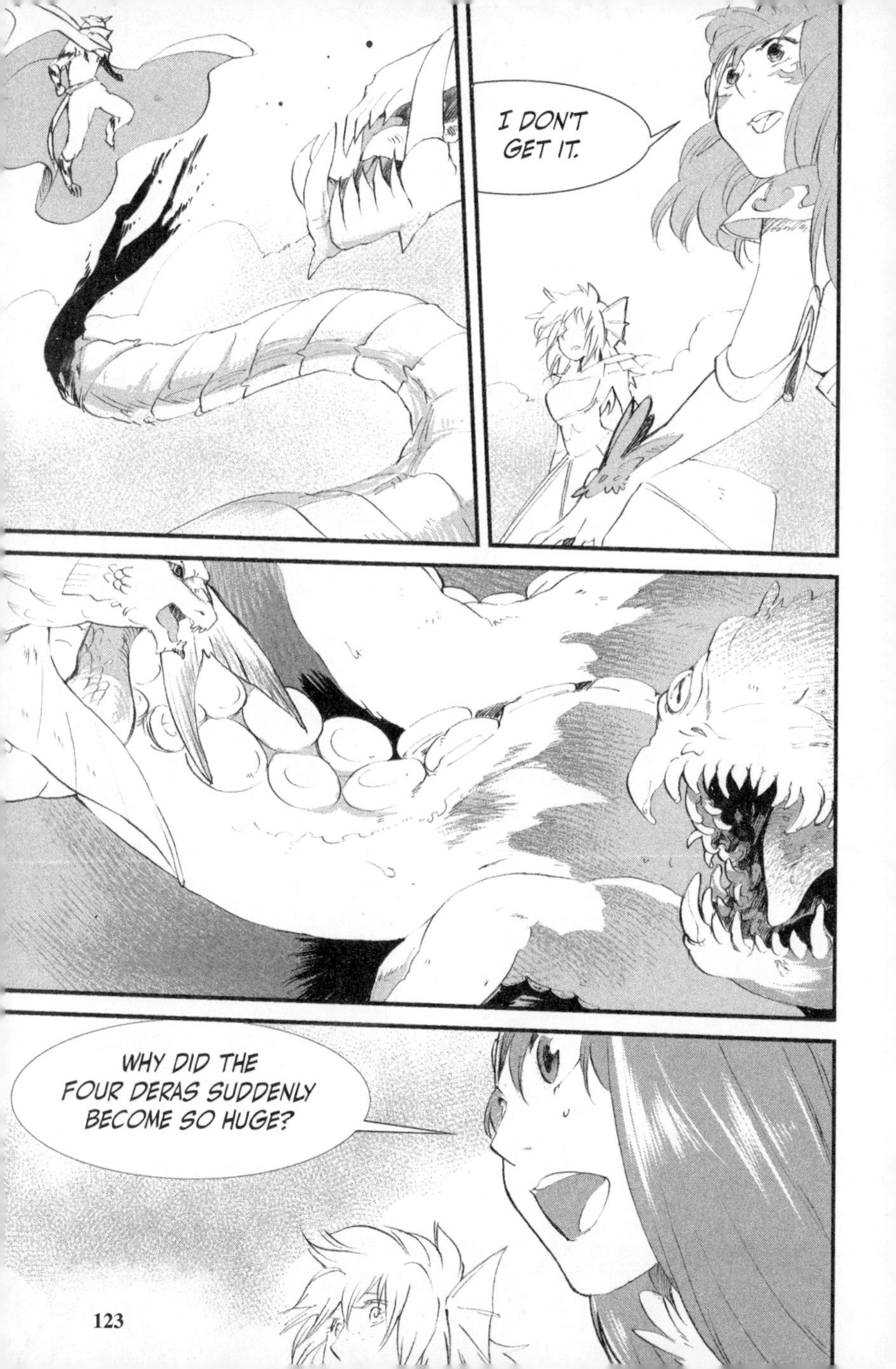
I DON'T GET IT.
WHY DID THE FOUR DERAS SUDDENLY BECOME SO HUGE?

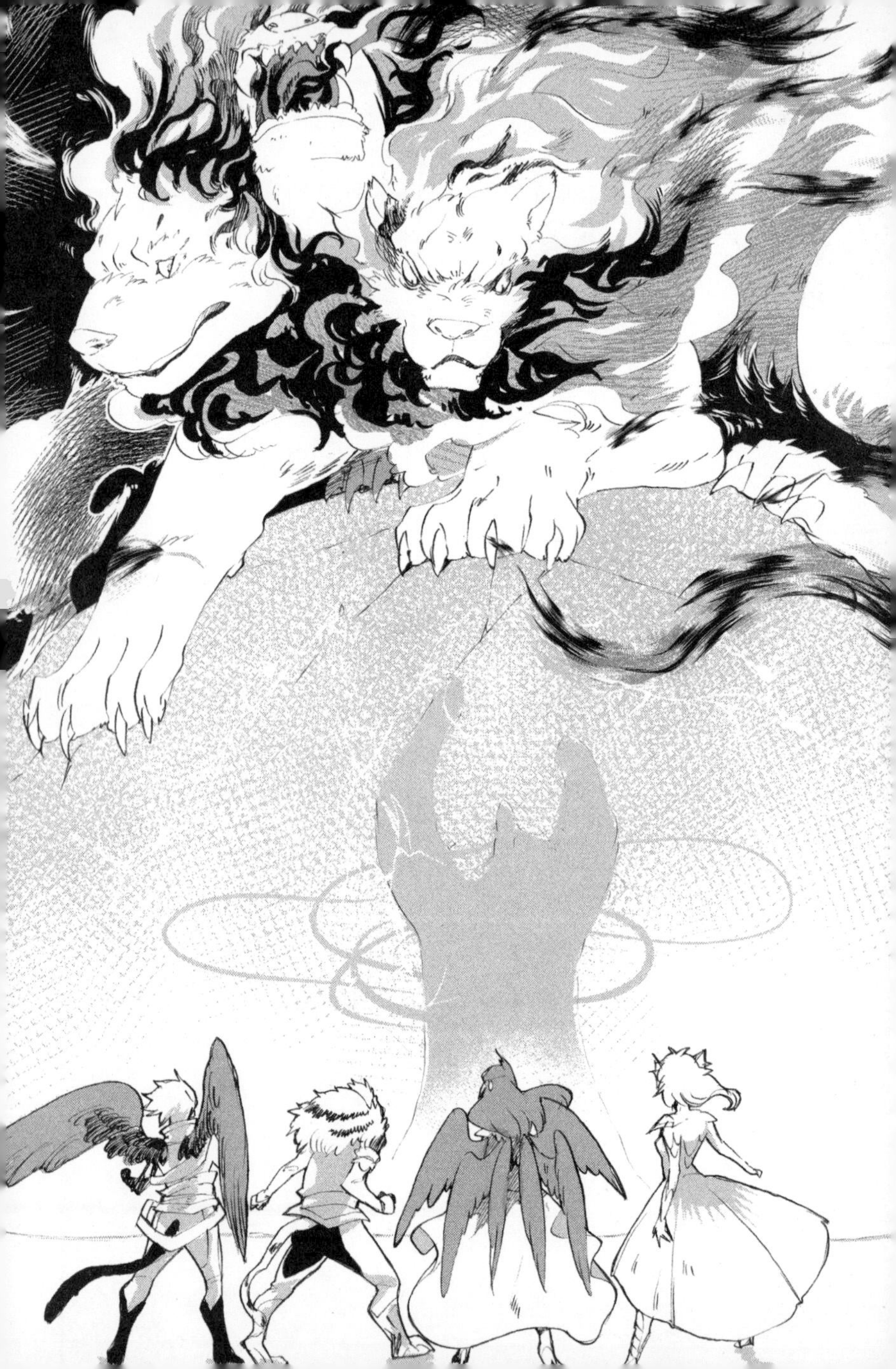

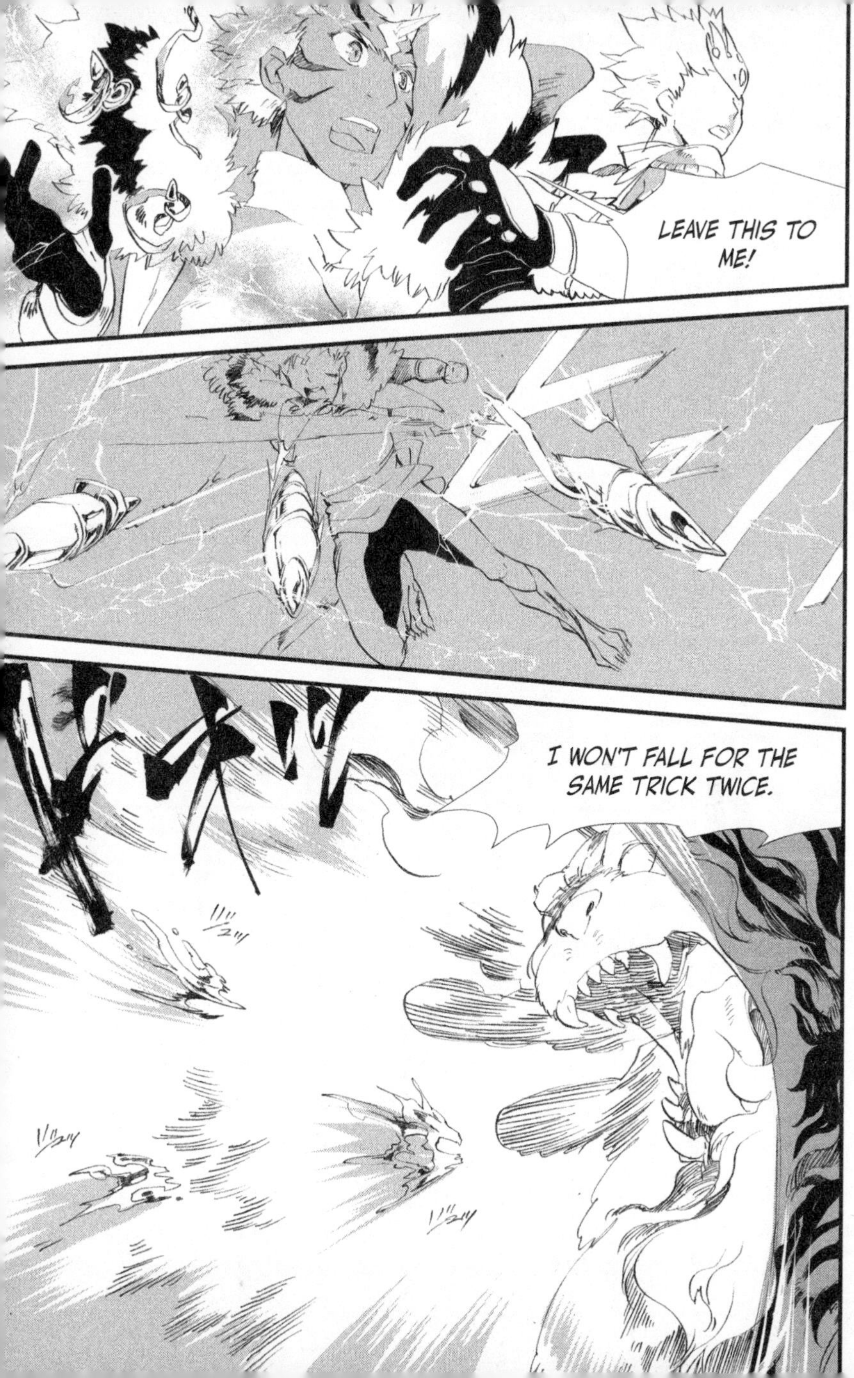
LEAVE THIS TO ME!
I WON'T FALL FOR THE SAME TRICK TWICE.

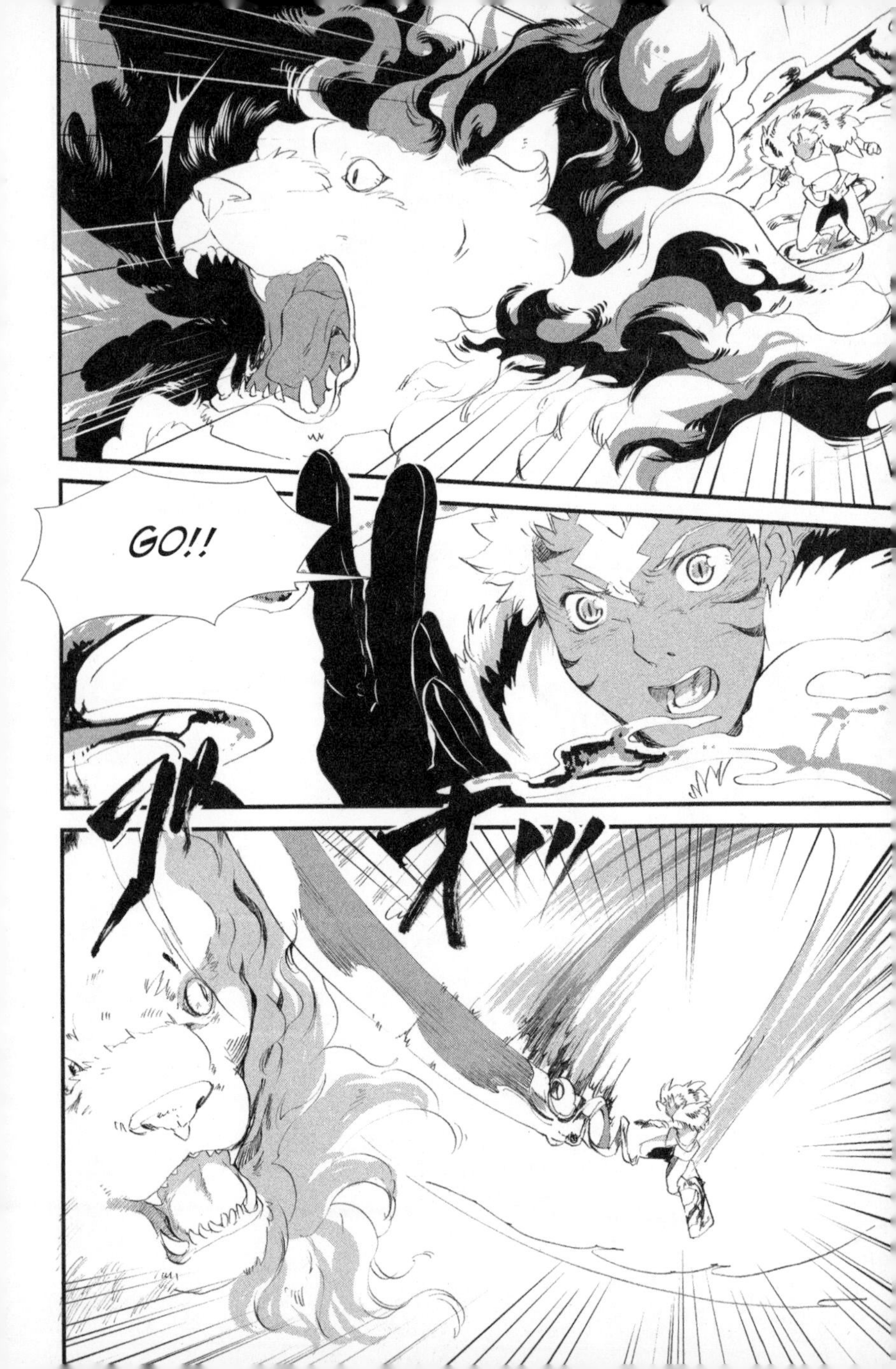
GO!!

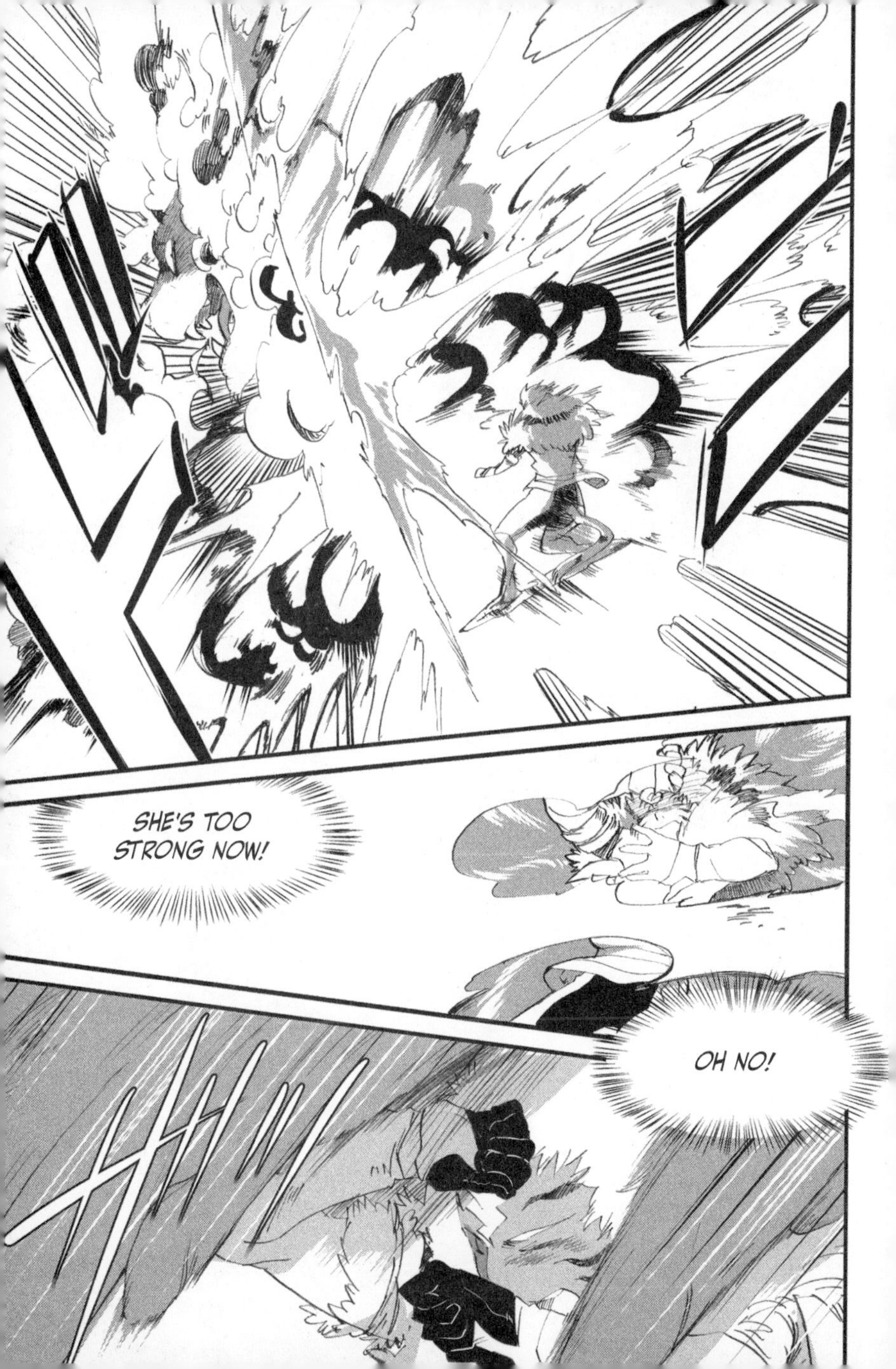
SHE'S TOO
STRONG NOW!
OH NO!

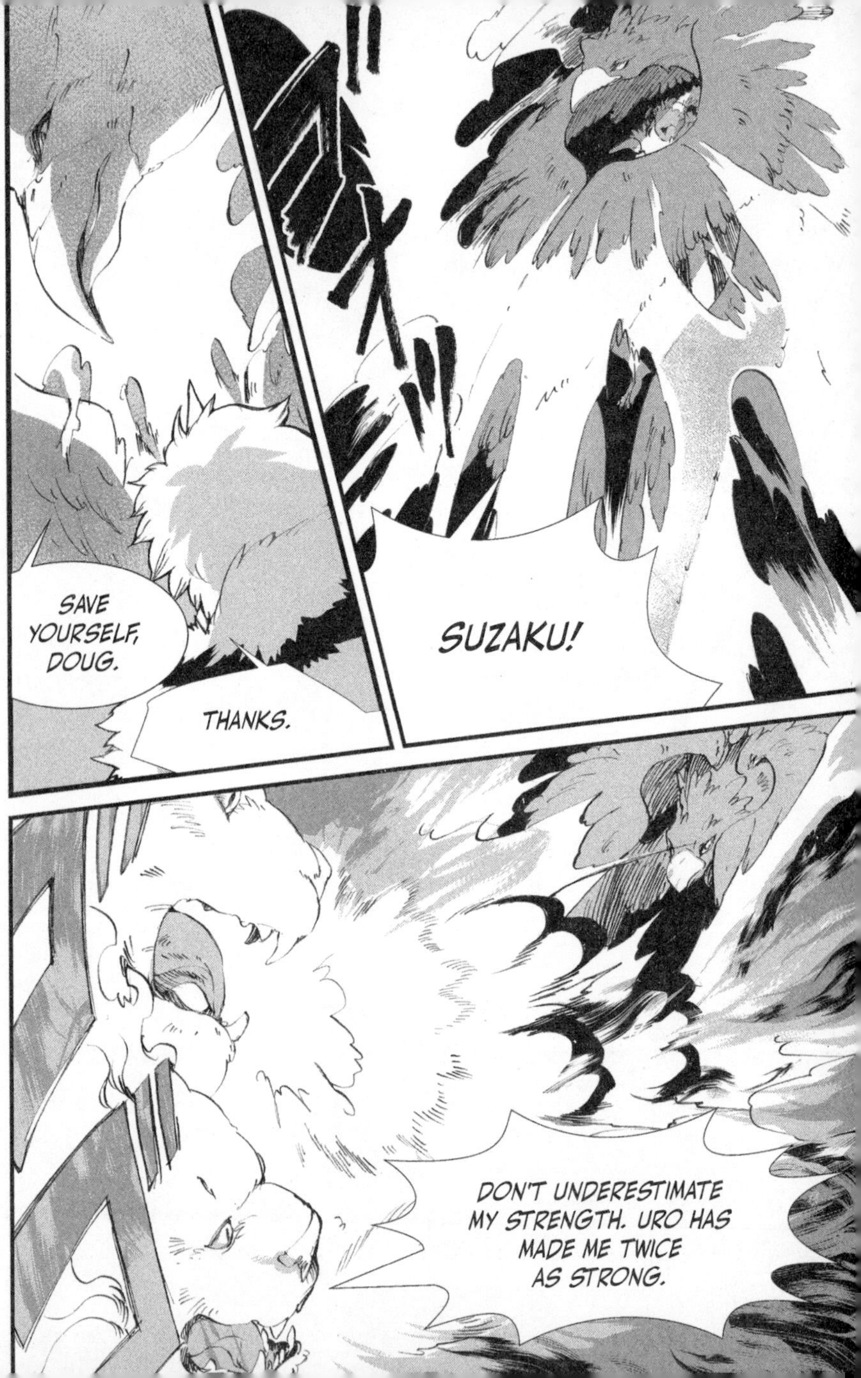
SUZAKU!
SAVE YOURSELF, DOUG.
THANKS.
DON'T UNDERESTIMATE MY STRENGTH. URO HAS MADE ME TWICE AS STRONG.

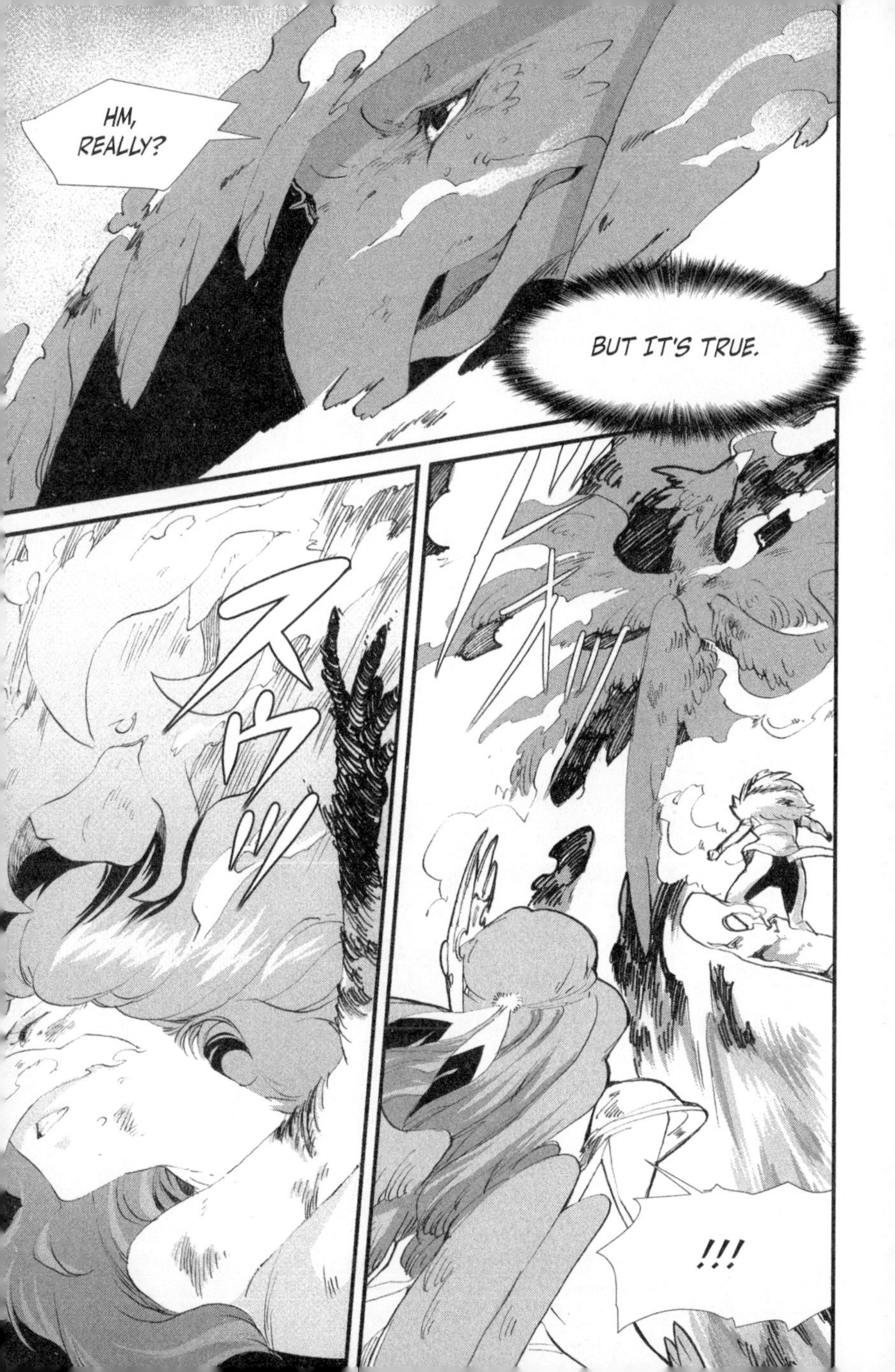
HM, REALLY?
BUT IT'S TRUE.
ドォッ
!!!
スゥッ

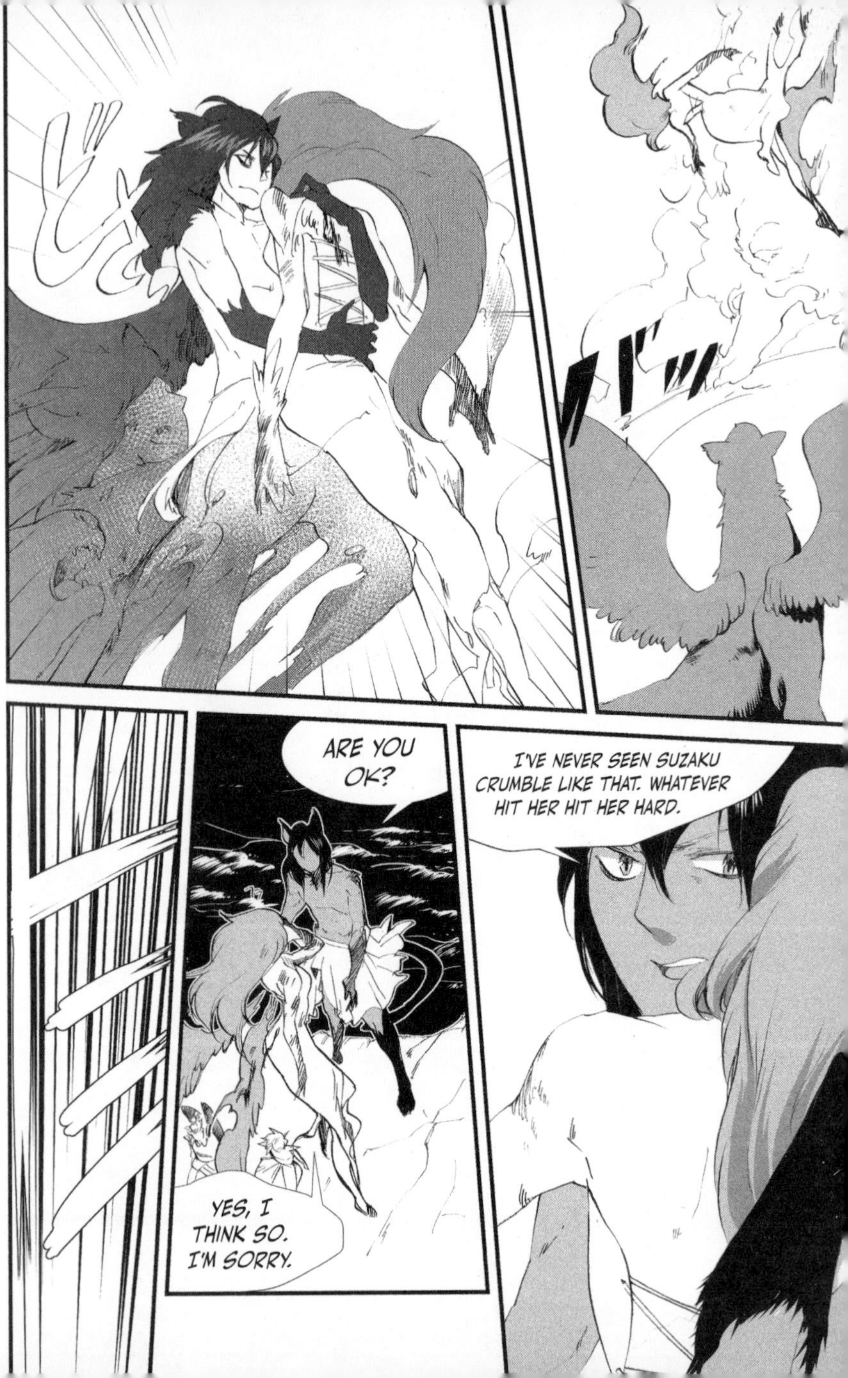

I'VE NEVER SEEN SUZAKU CRUMBLE LIKE THAT. WHATEVER HIT HER HIT HER HARD.
ARE YOU OK?
YES, I THINK SO. I'M SORRY.

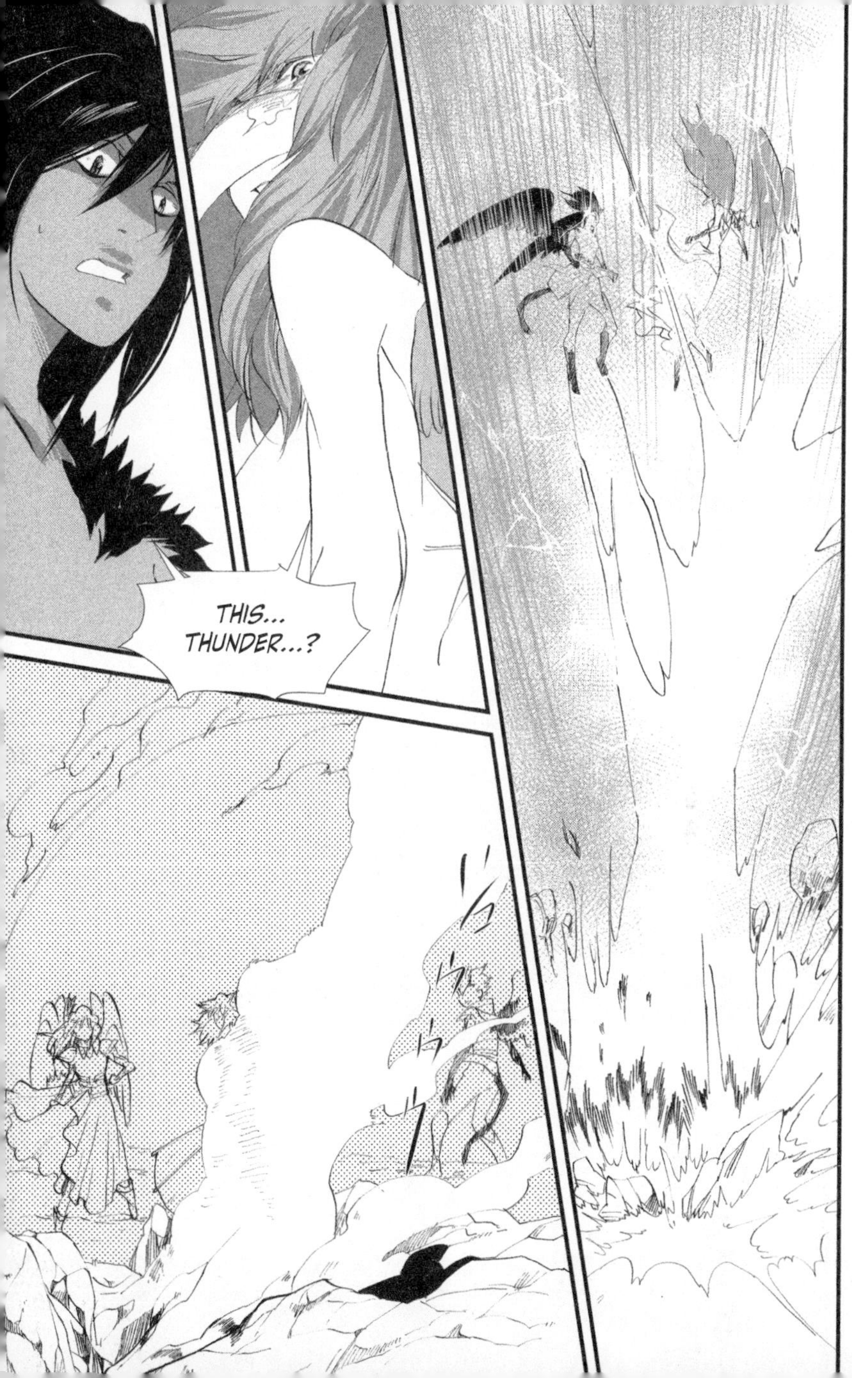
THIS...
THUNDER...?

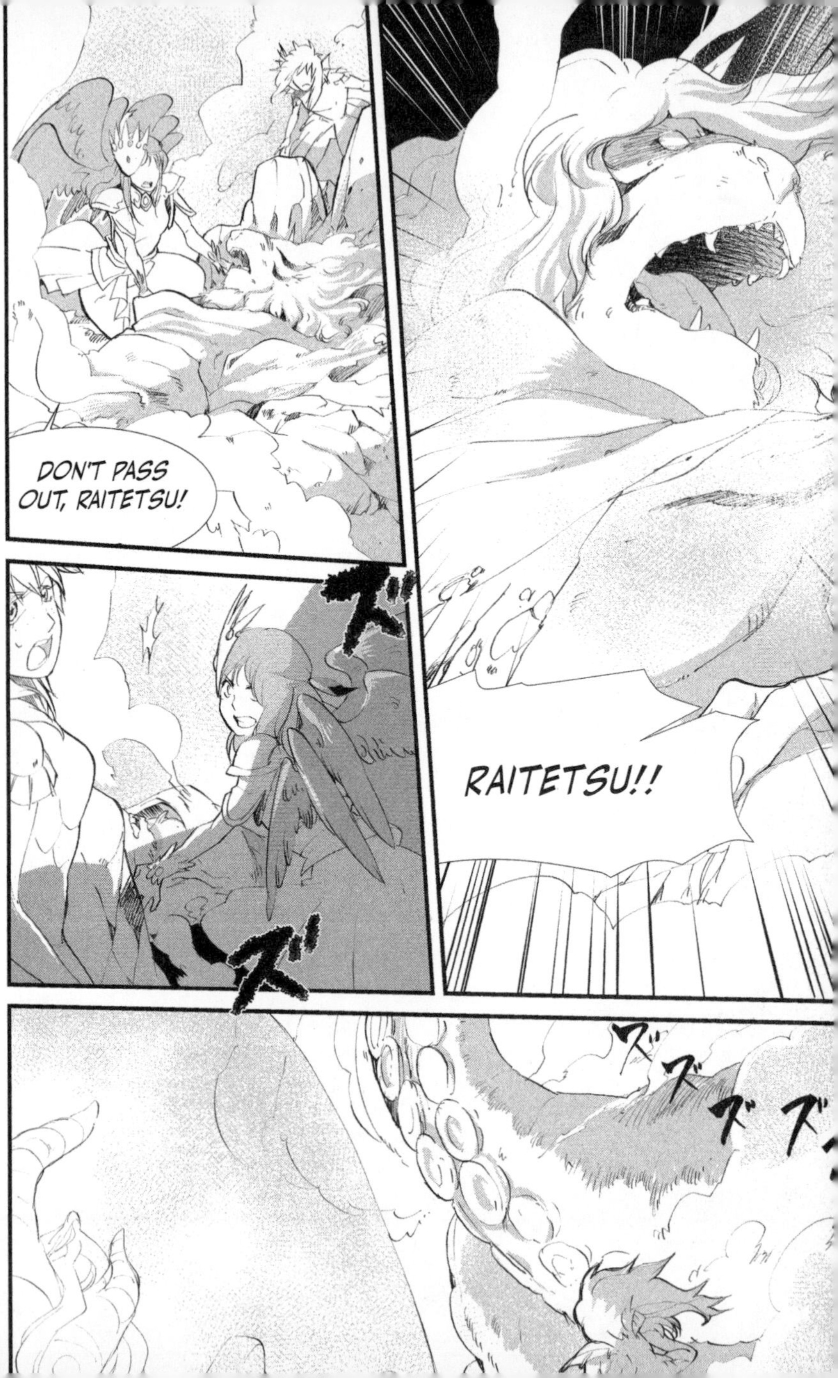
RAITETSU!!
DON'T PASS OUT, RAITETSU!
ズ
ズ
ズ
ズ
ズ
ズ

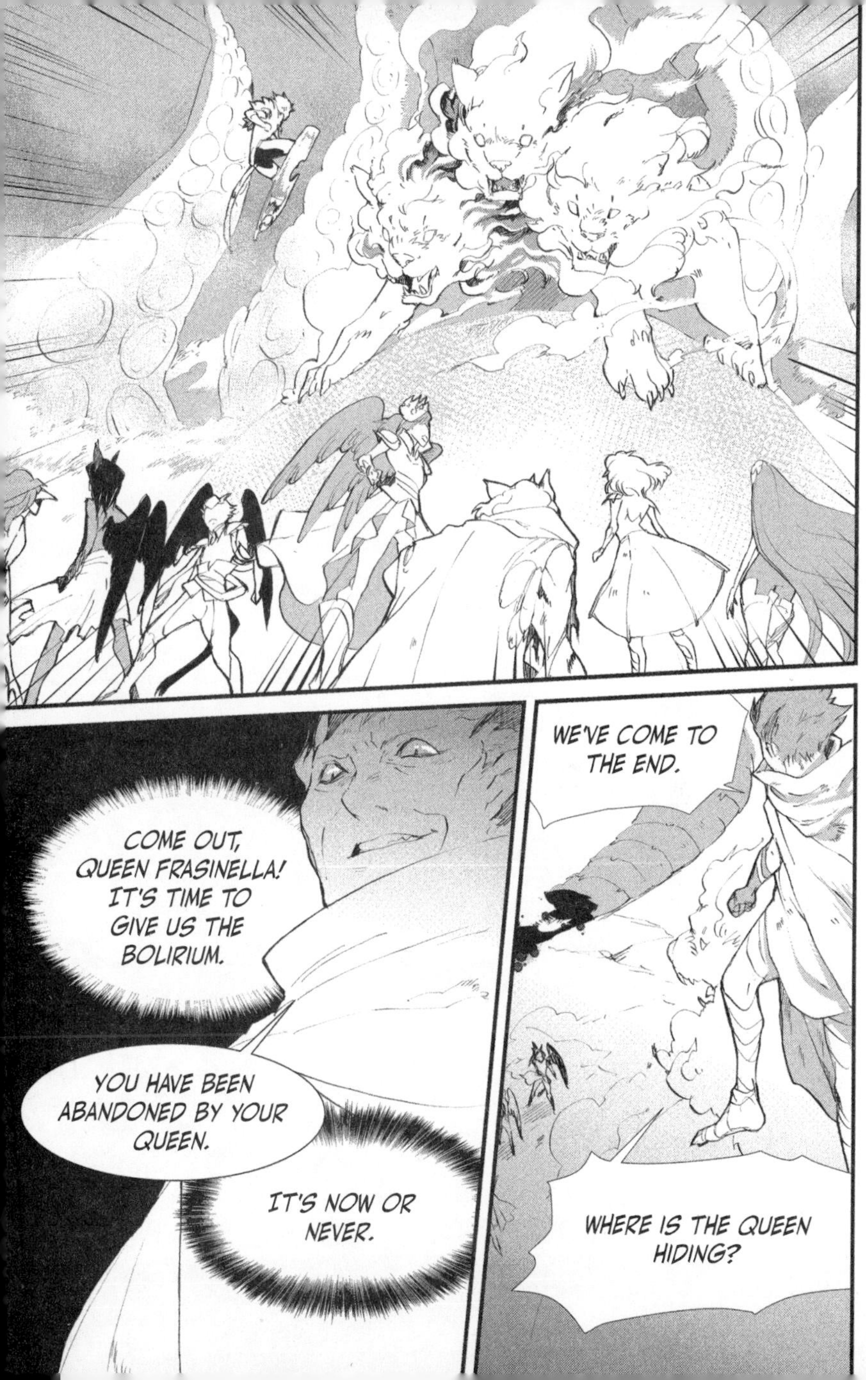
WE'VE COME TO THE END.
WHERE IS THE QUEEN HIDING?
COME OUT, QUEEN FRASINELLA! IT'S TIME TO GIVE US THE BOLIRIUM.
YOU HAVE BEEN ABANDONED BY YOUR QUEEN.
IT'S NOW OR NEVER.

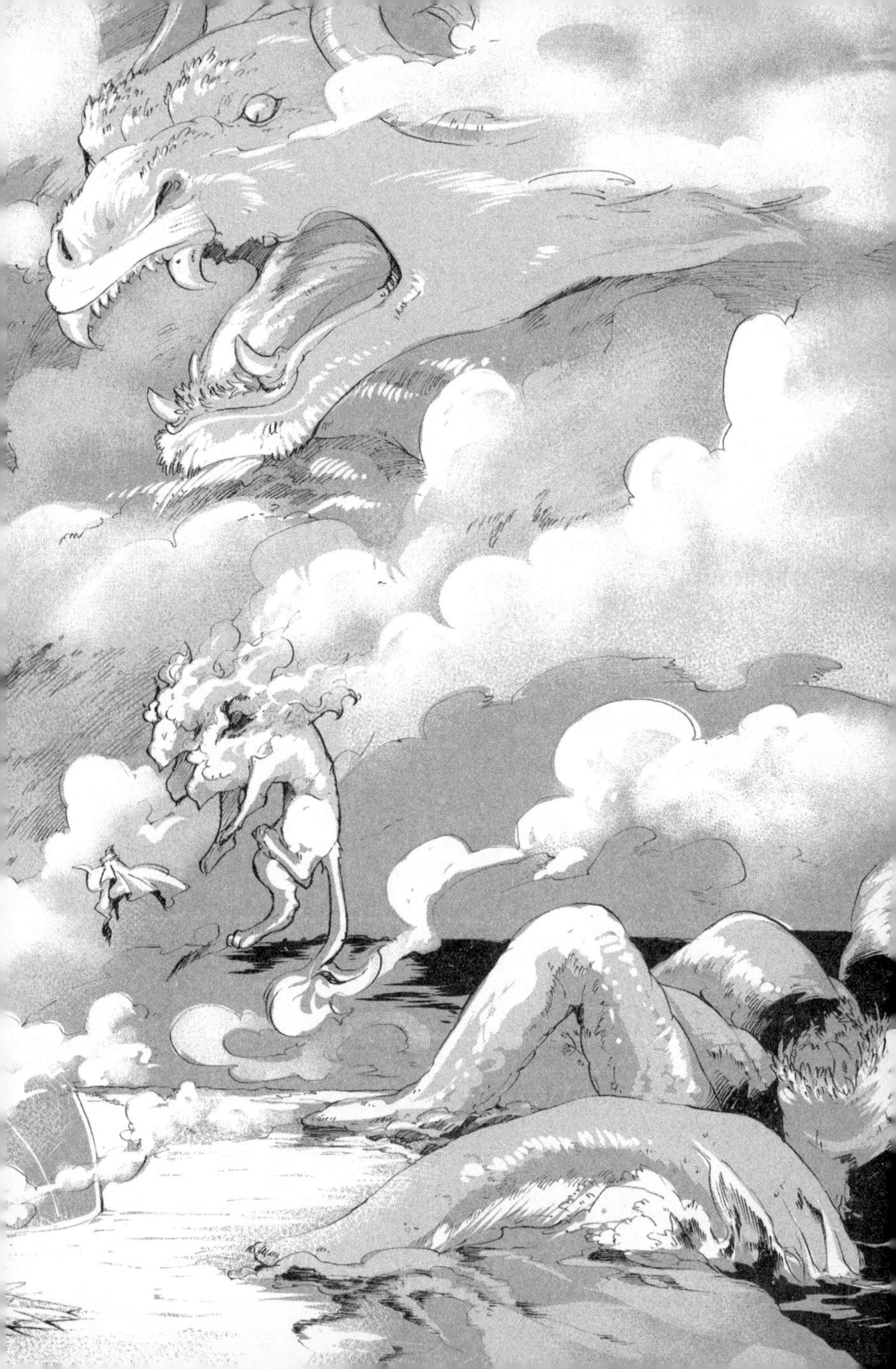

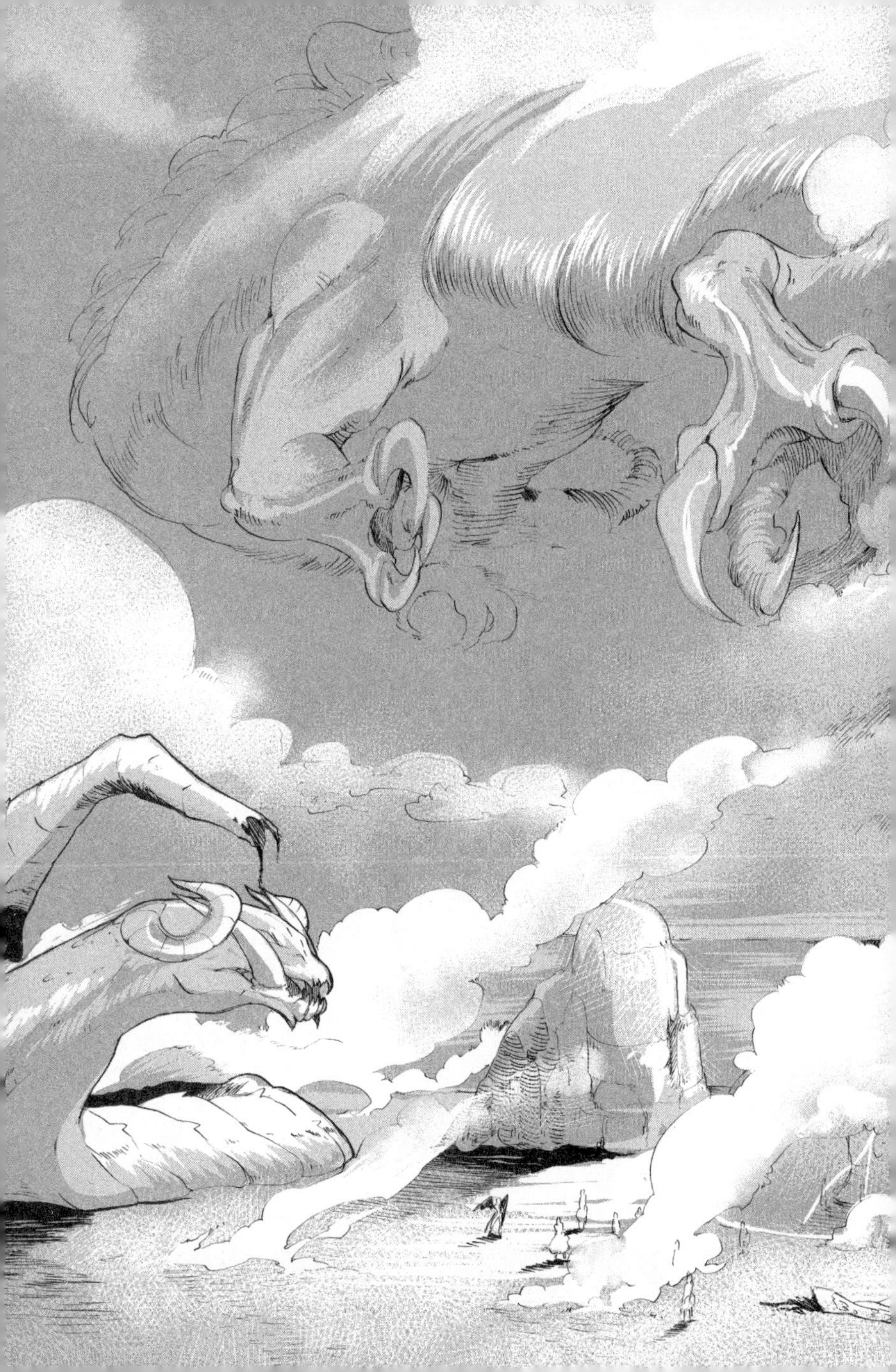

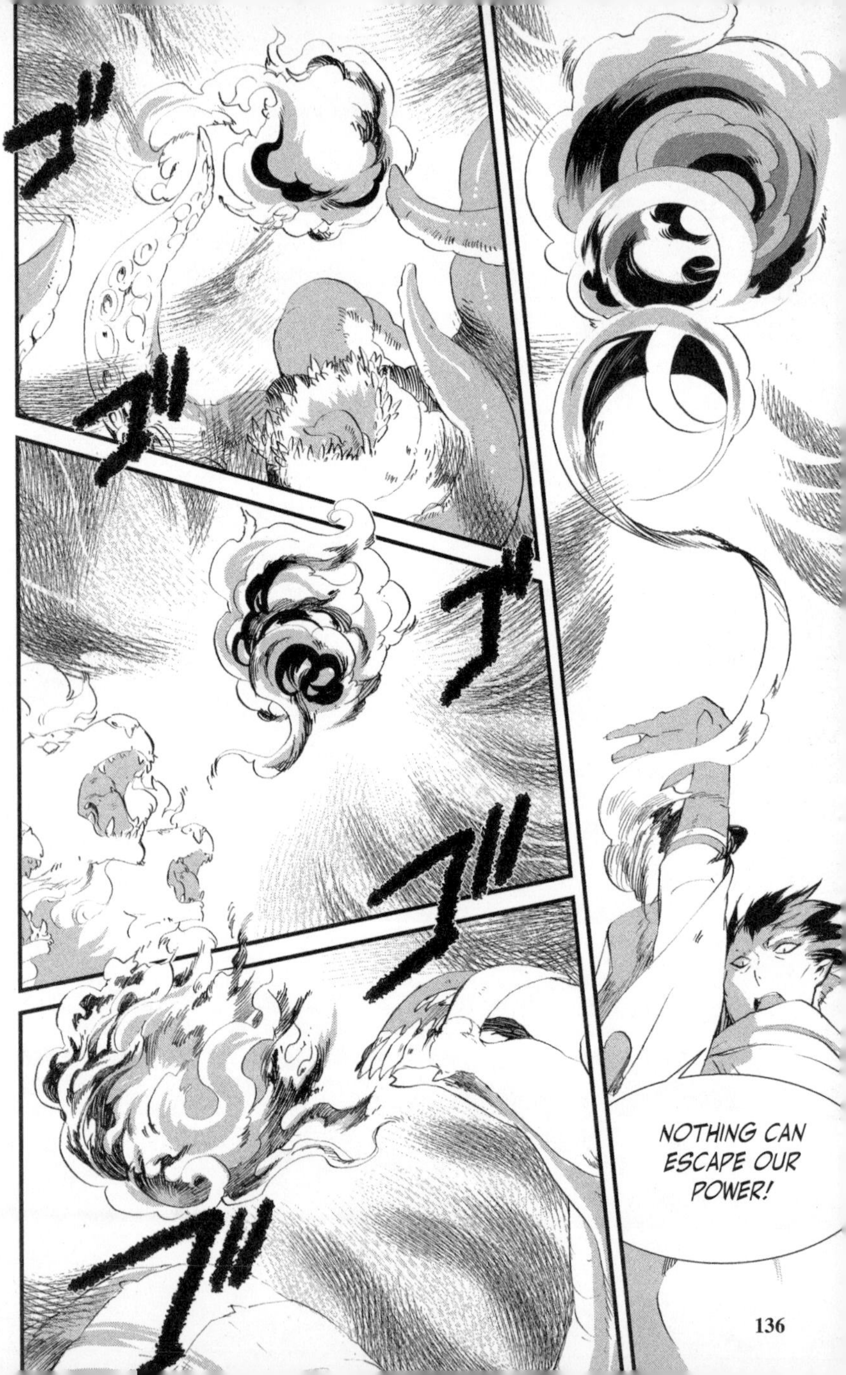
NOTHING CAN ESCAPE OUR POWER!

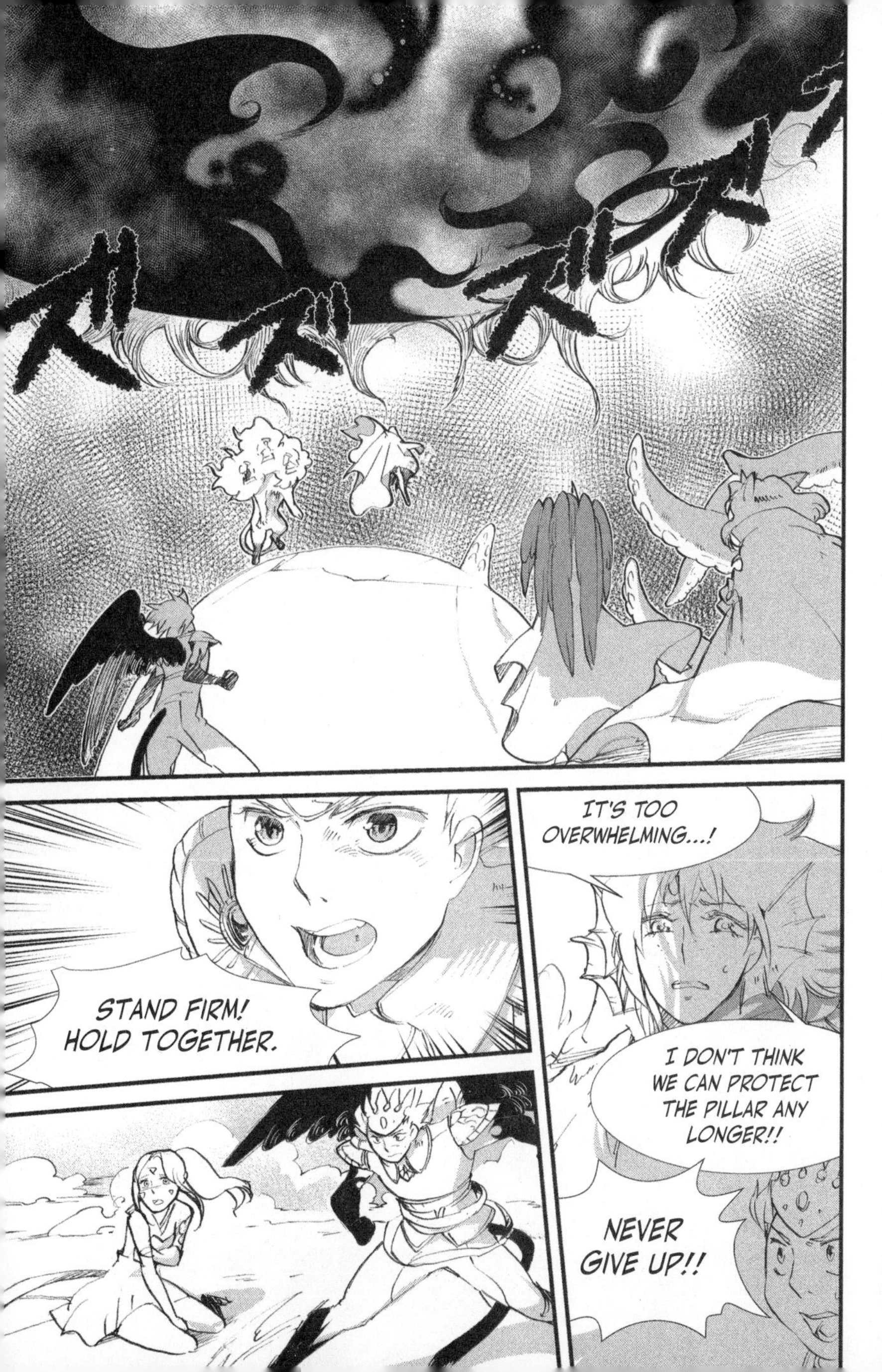
IT'S TOO OVERWHELMING...!
I DON'T THINK WE CAN PROTECT THE PILLAR ANY LONGER!!
NEVER GIVE UP!!
STAND FIRM! HOLD TOGETHER.

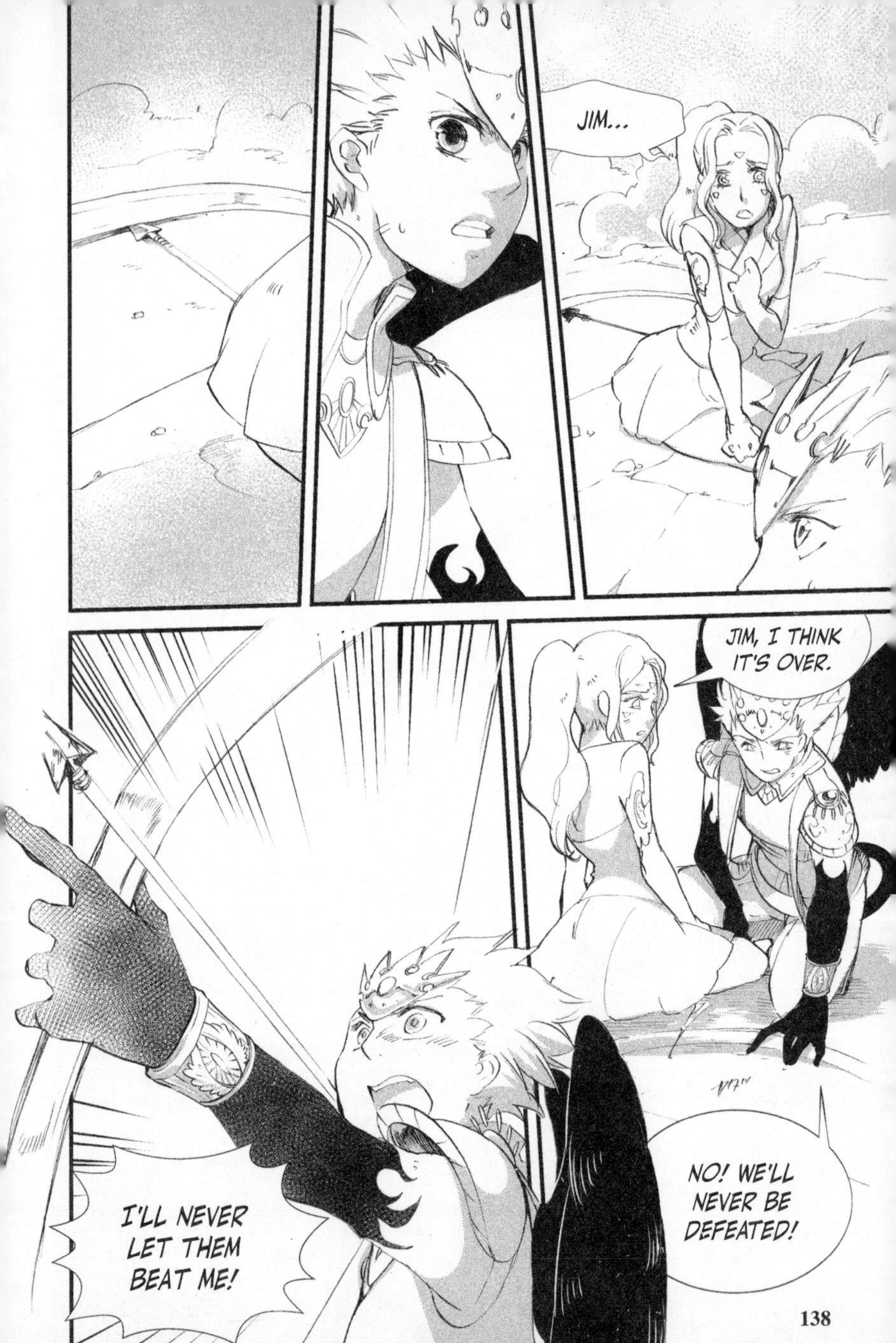
JIM...
JIM, I THINK IT'S OVER.
NO! WE'LL NEVER BE DEFEATED!
I'LL NEVER LET THEM BEAT ME!

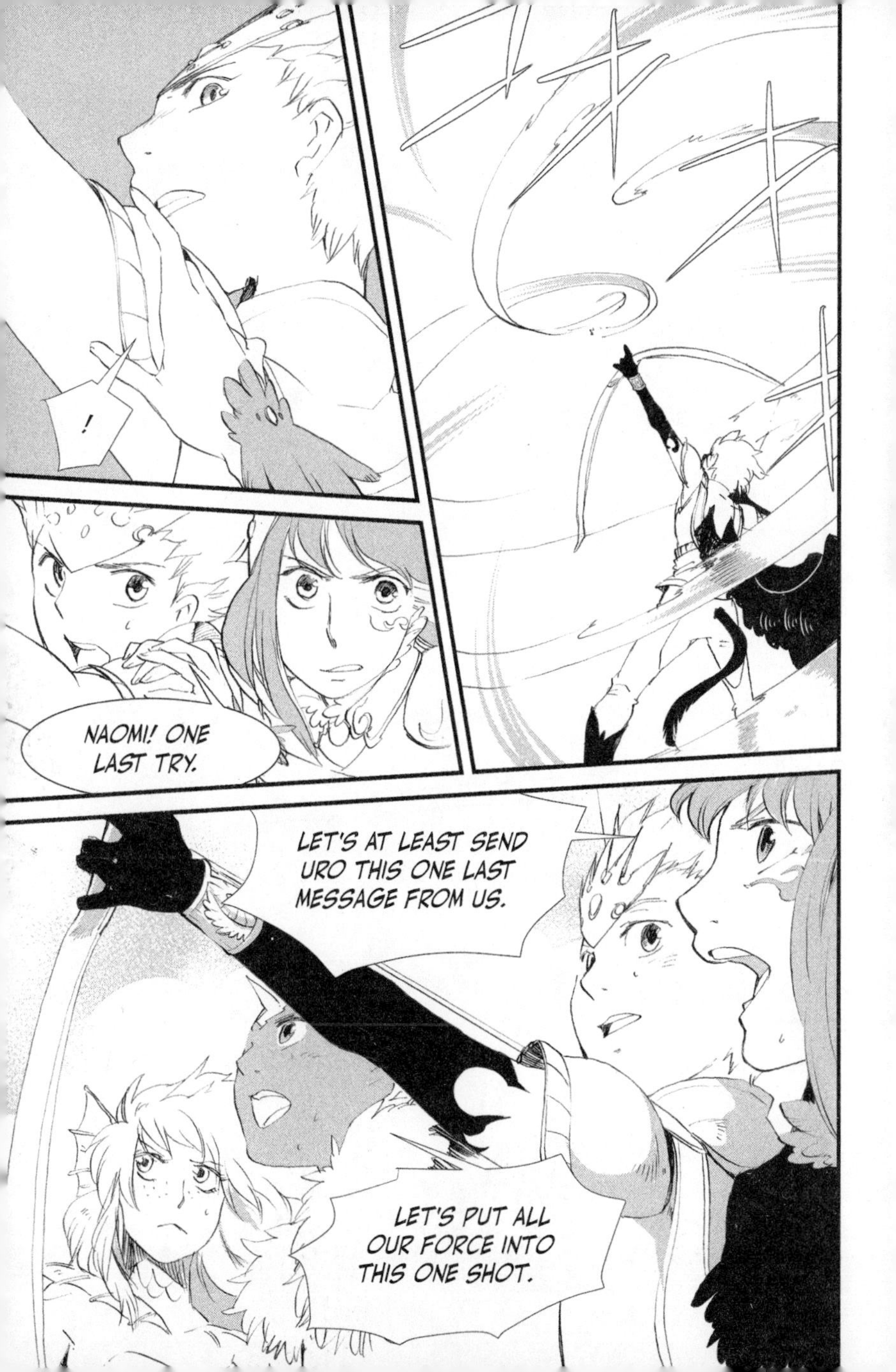
!
NAOMI! ONE LAST TRY.
LET'S AT LEAST SEND URO THIS ONE LAST MESSAGE FROM US.
LET'S PUT ALL OUR FORCE INTO THIS ONE SHOT.

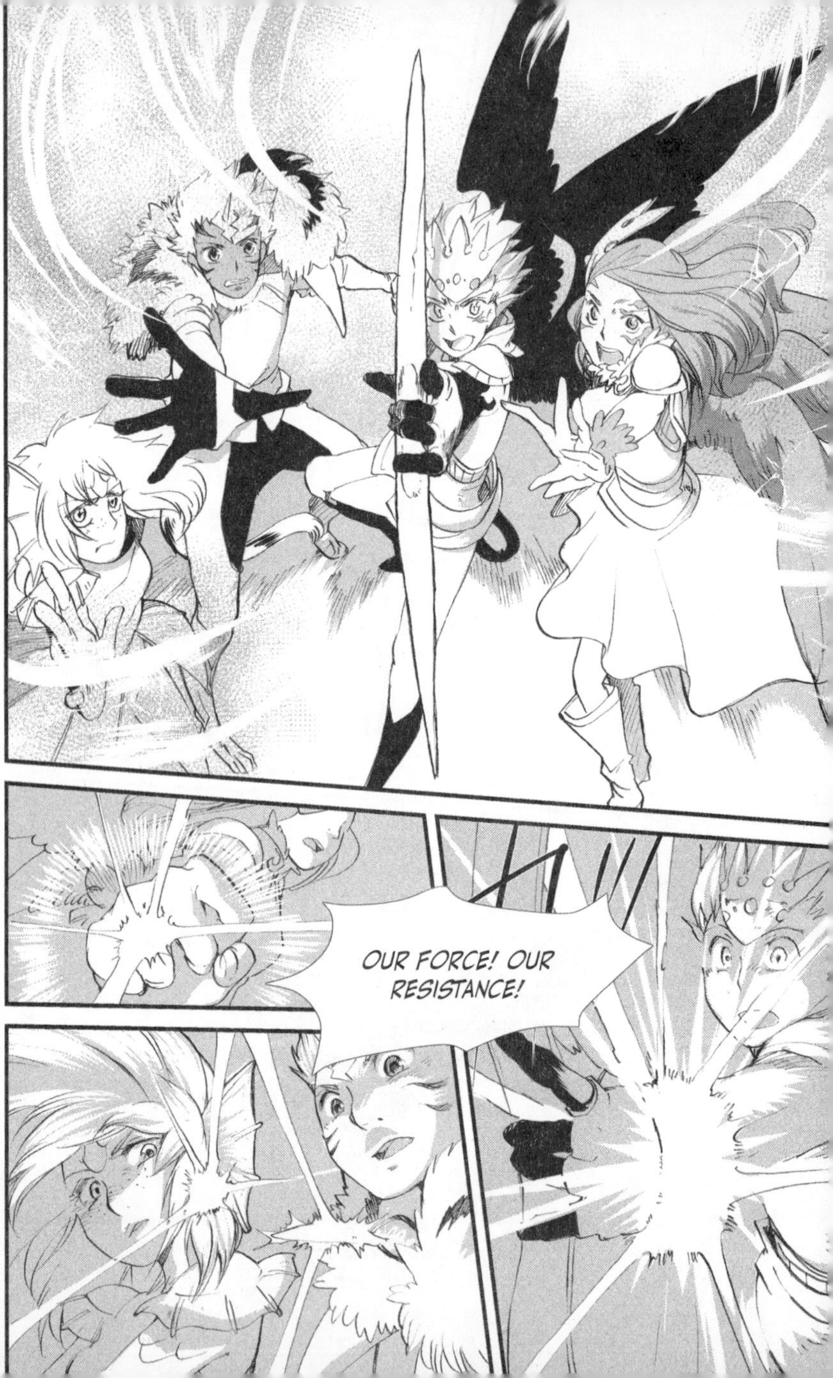
OUR FORCE! OUR RESISTANCE!

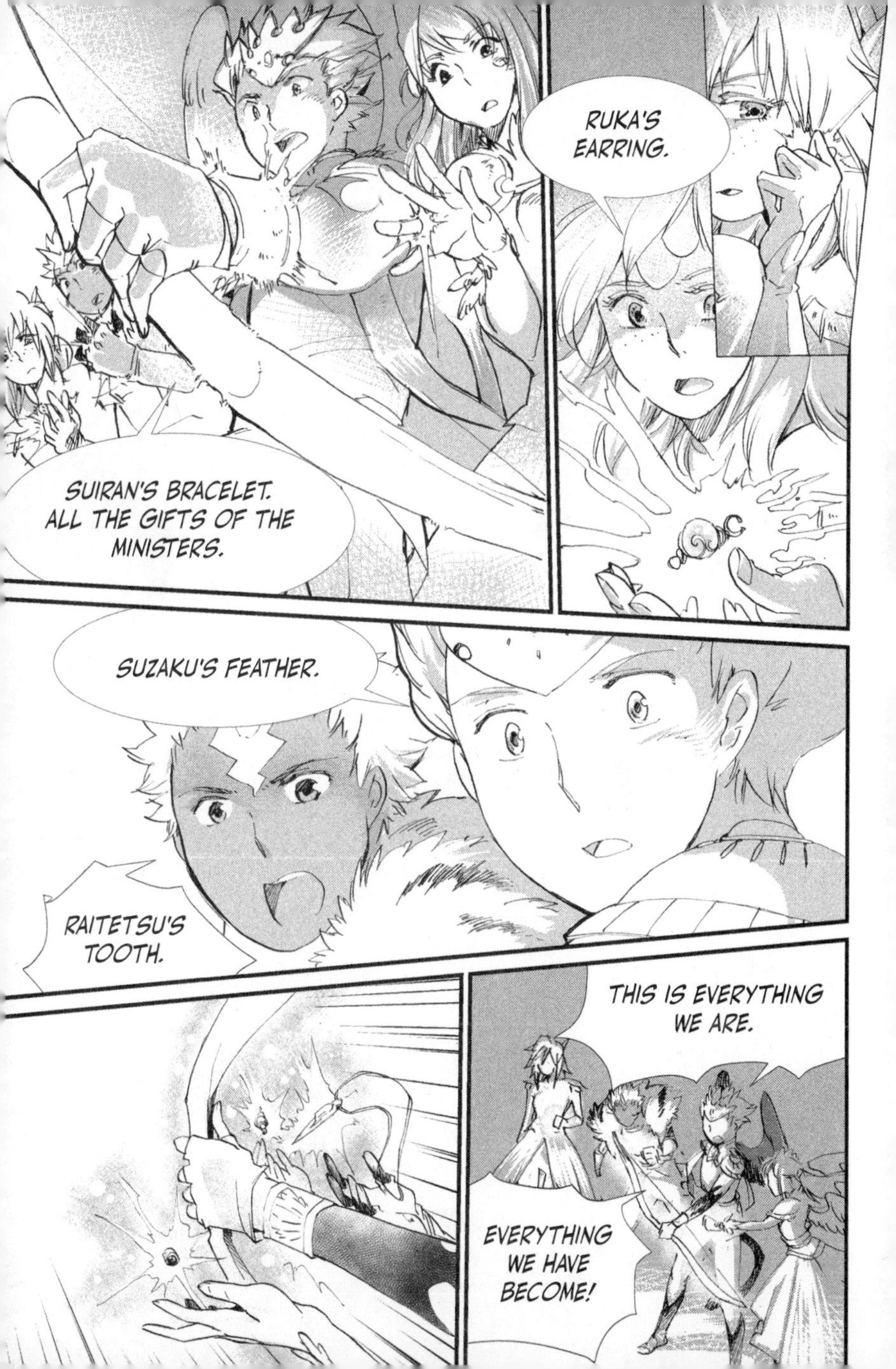
RUKA'S EARRING.
SUIRAN'S BRACELET. ALL THE GIFTS OF THE MINISTERS.
SUZAKU'S FEATHER.
RAITETSU'S TOOTH.
THIS IS EVERYTHING WE ARE.
EVERYTHING WE HAVE BECOME!

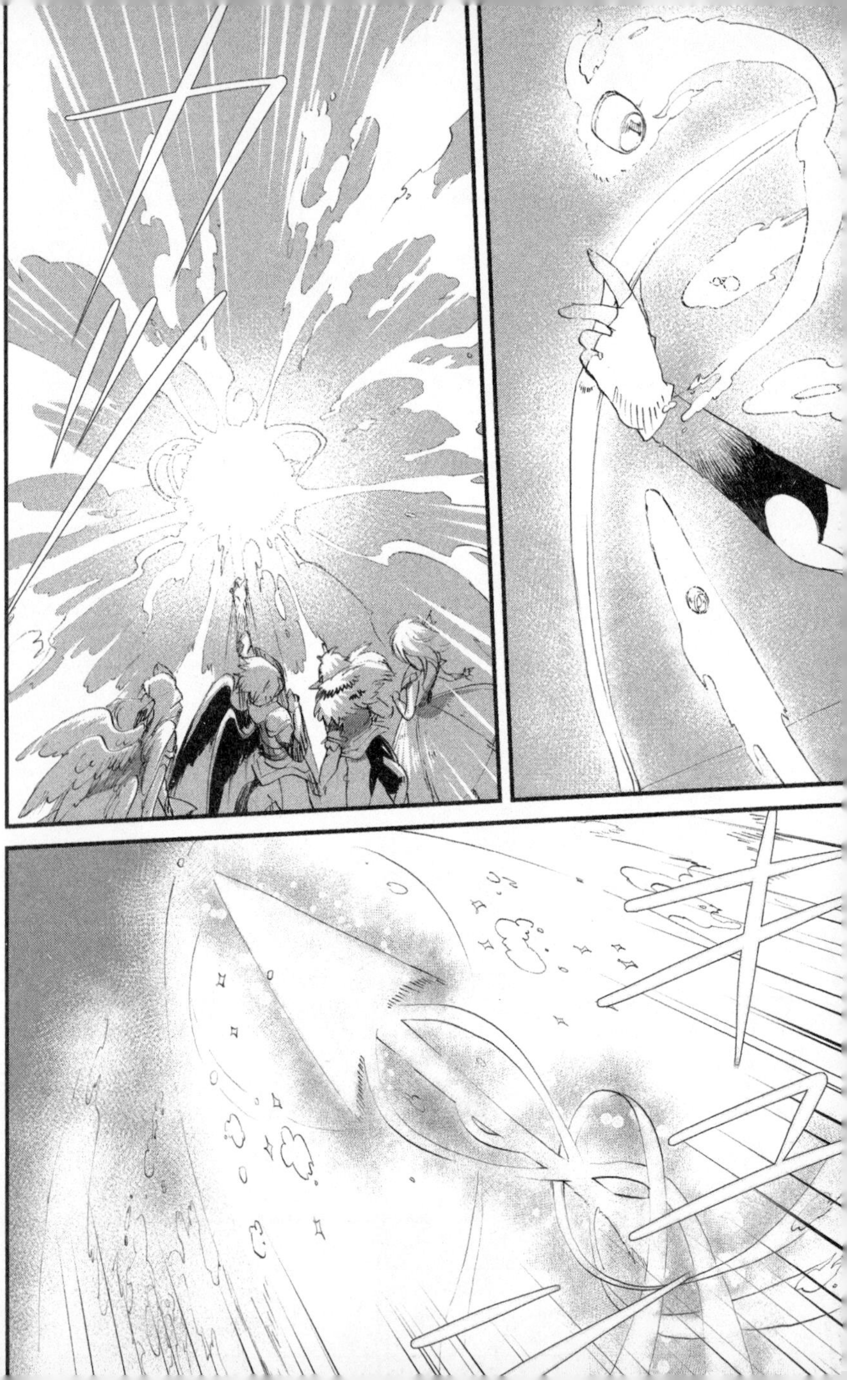

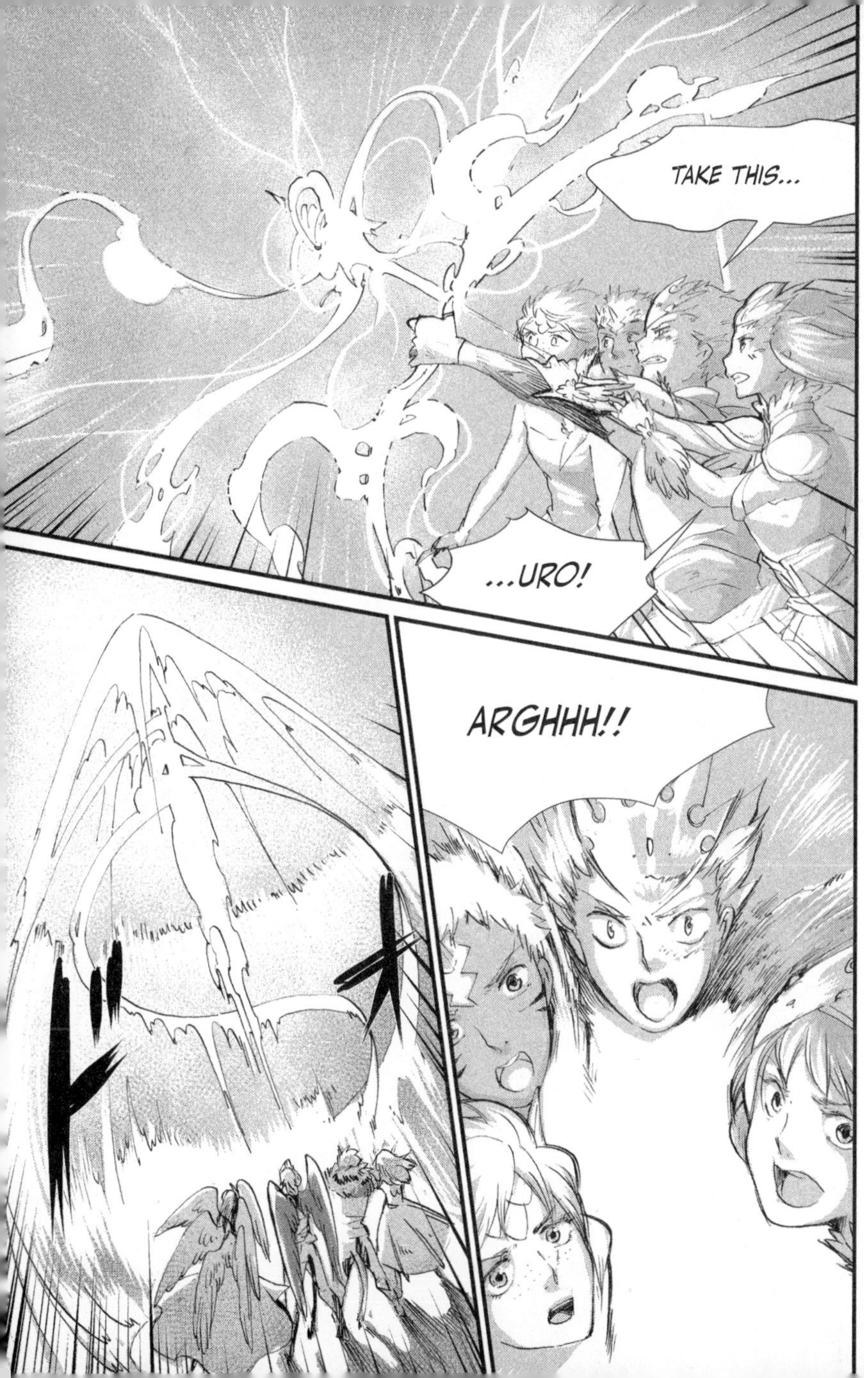
TAKE THIS...
...URO!
ARGHHH!!
ド

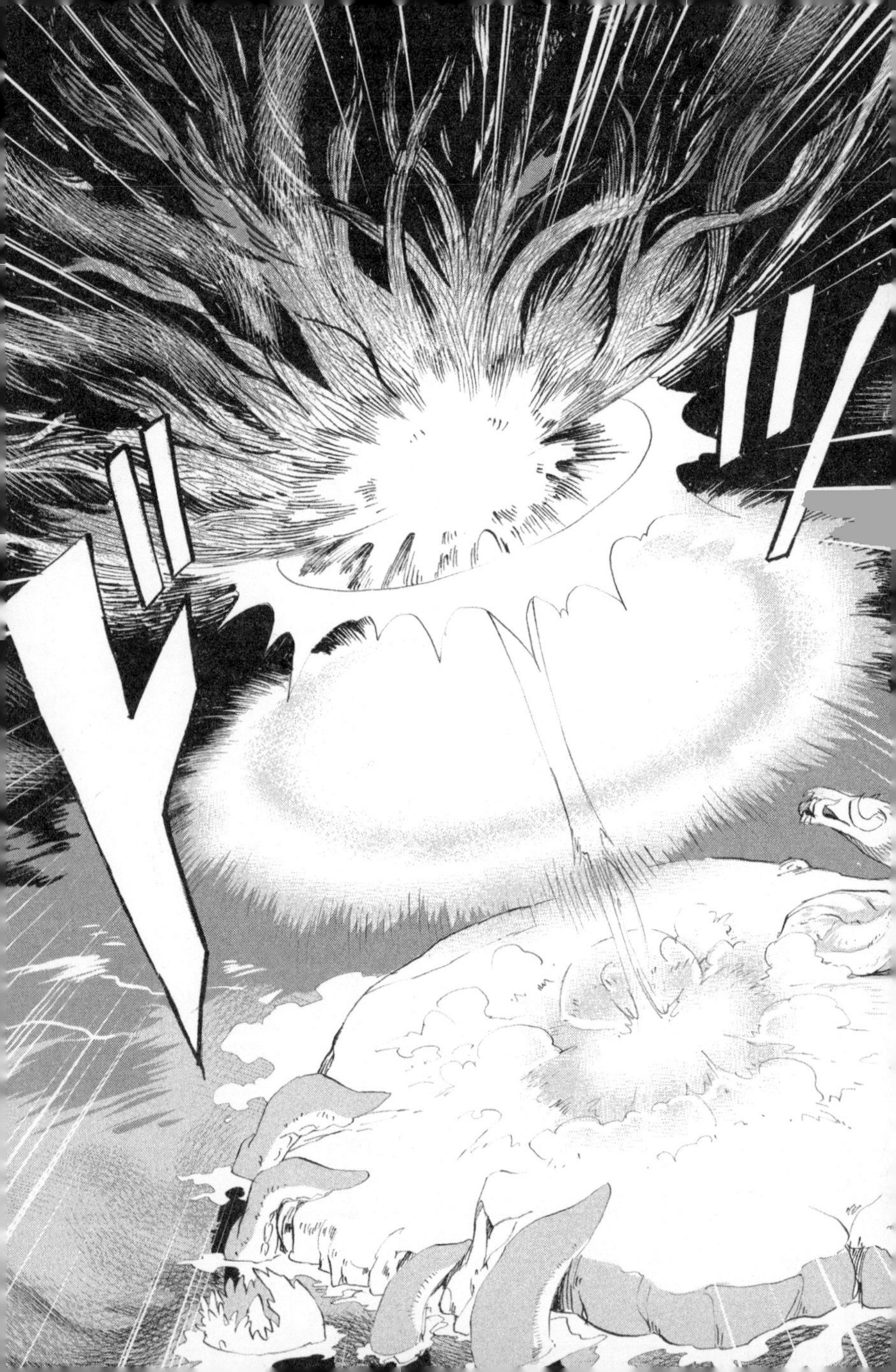

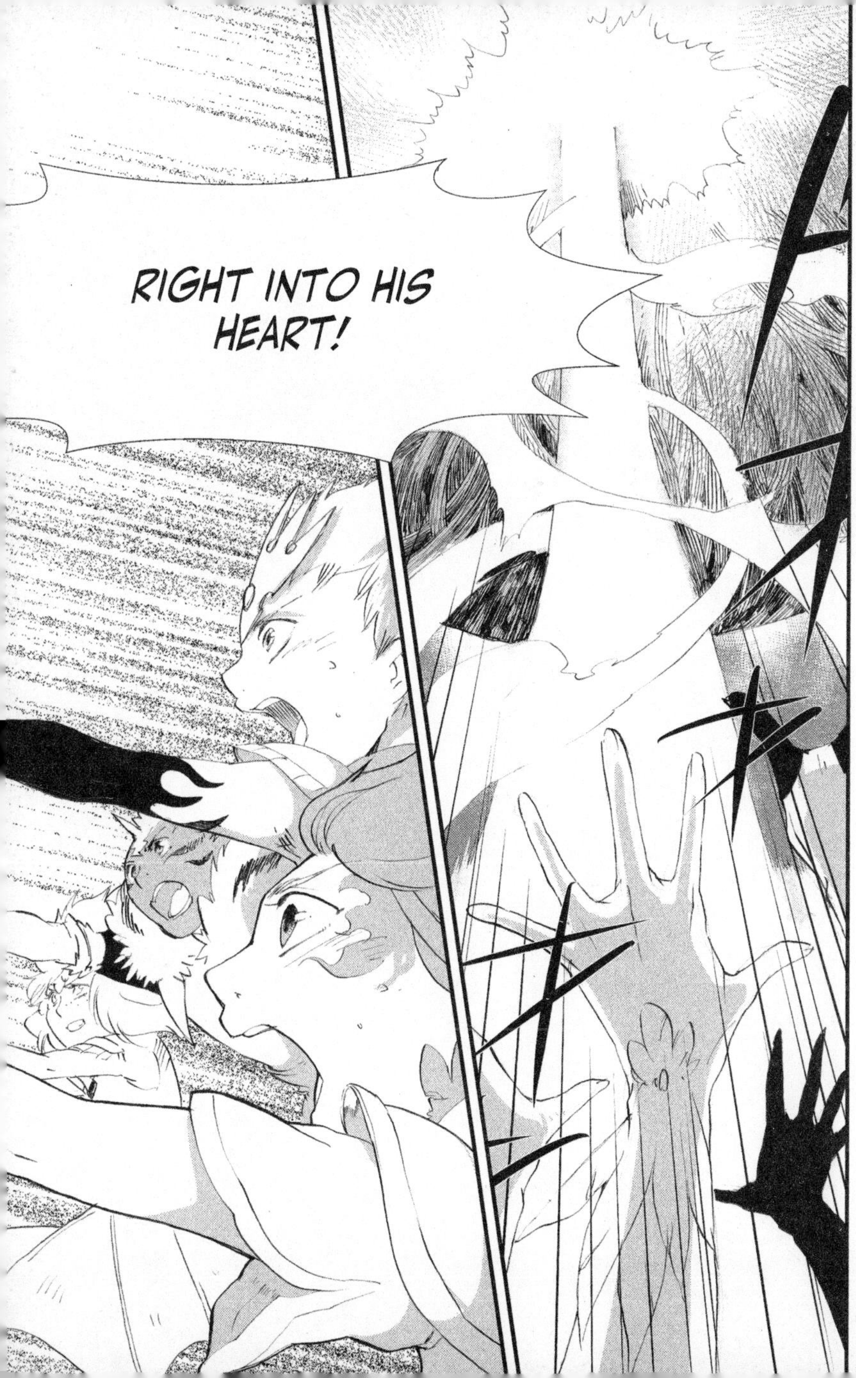
RIGHT INTO HIS HEART!

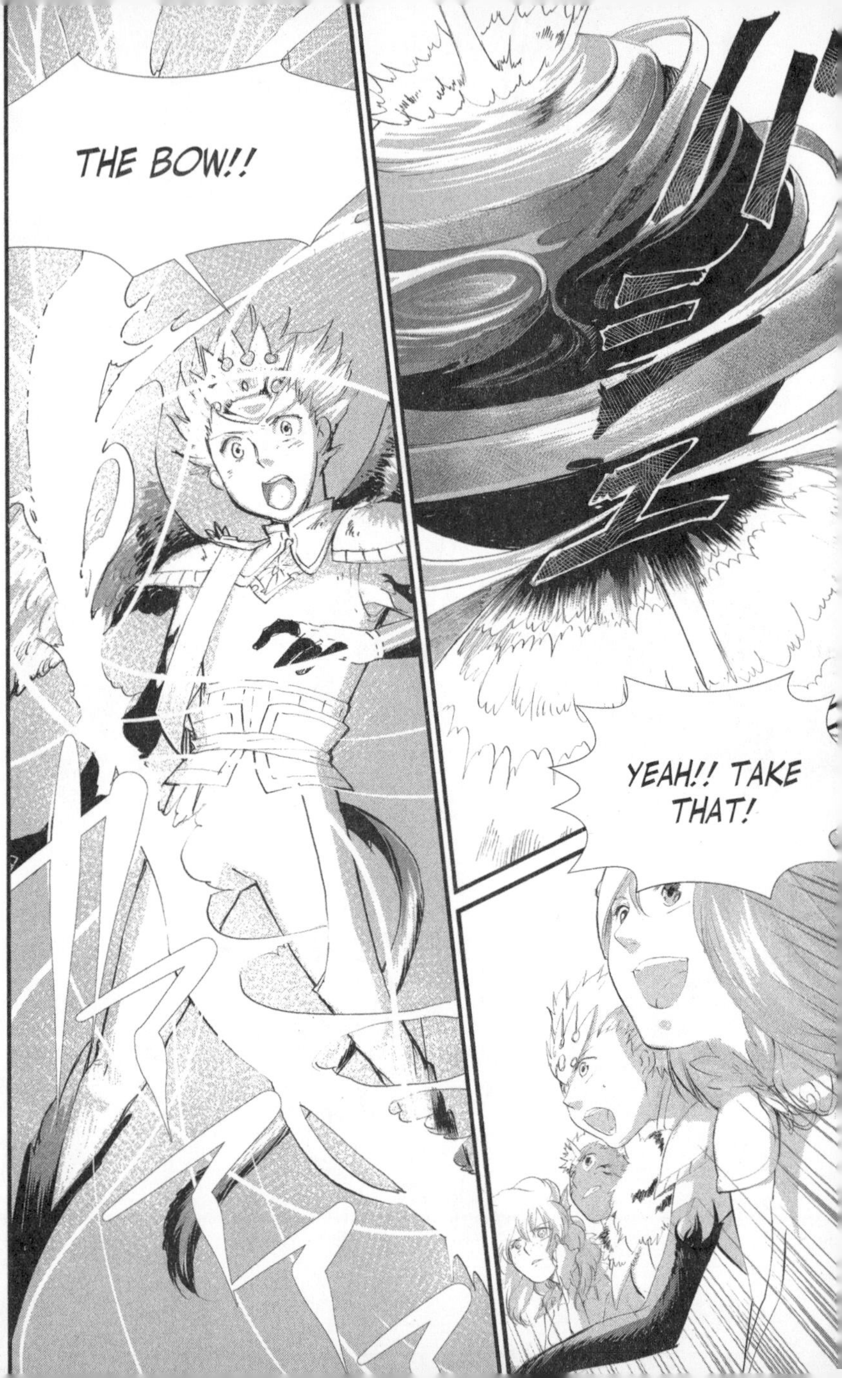
YEAH!! TAKE THAT!
THE BOW!!

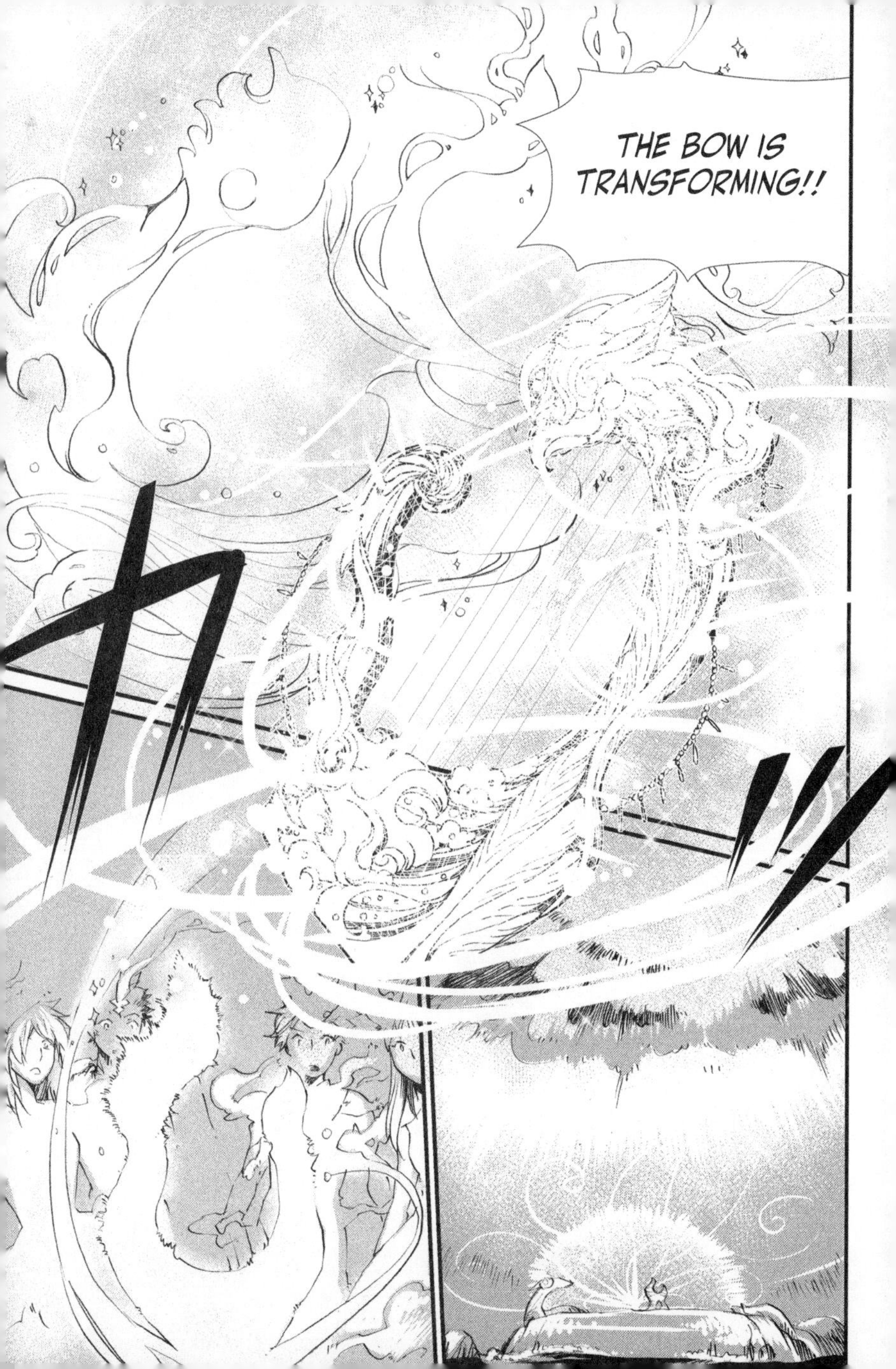
THE BOW IS TRANSFORMING!!

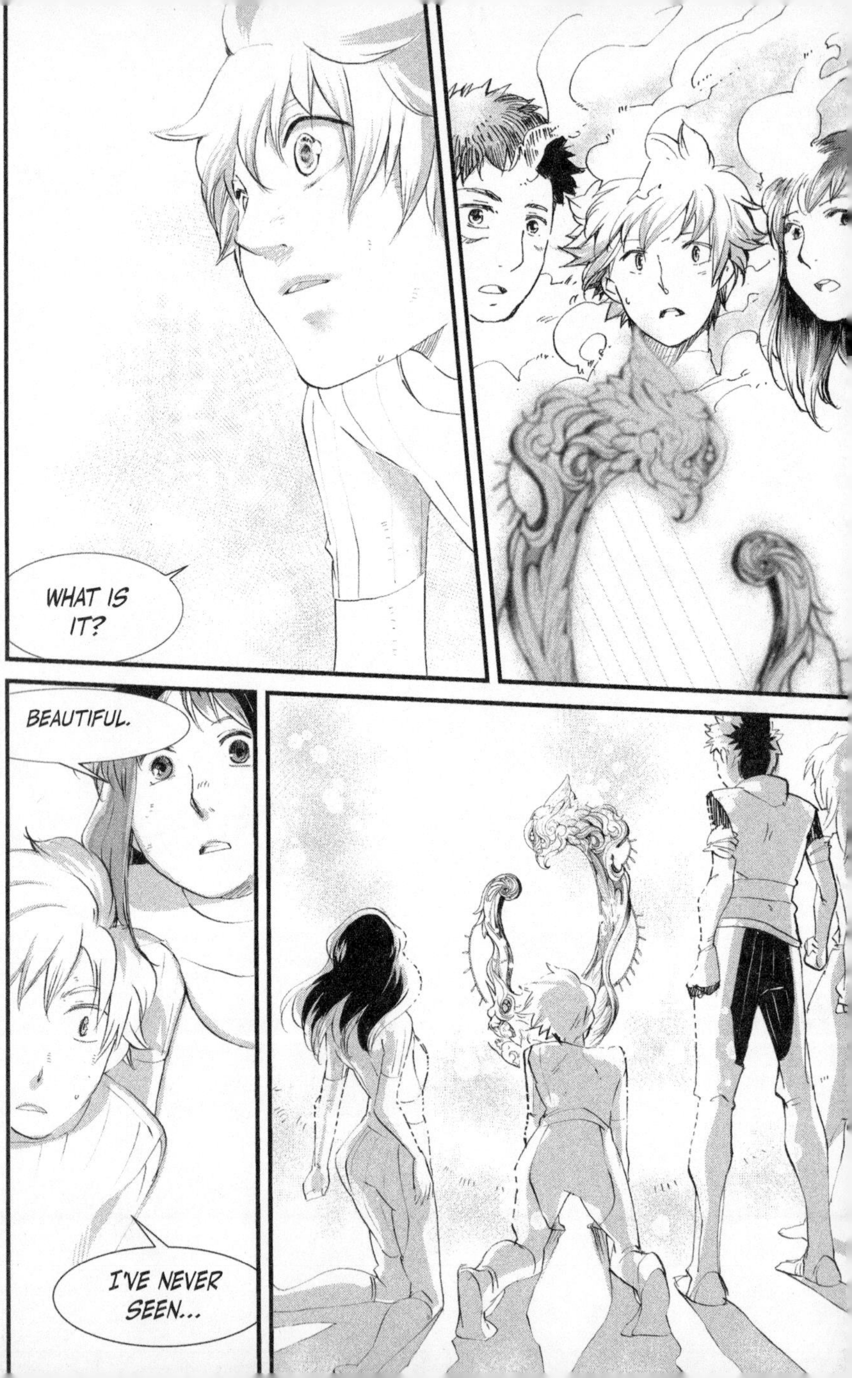
WHAT IS IT?
BEAUTIFUL.
I'VE NEVER SEEN...

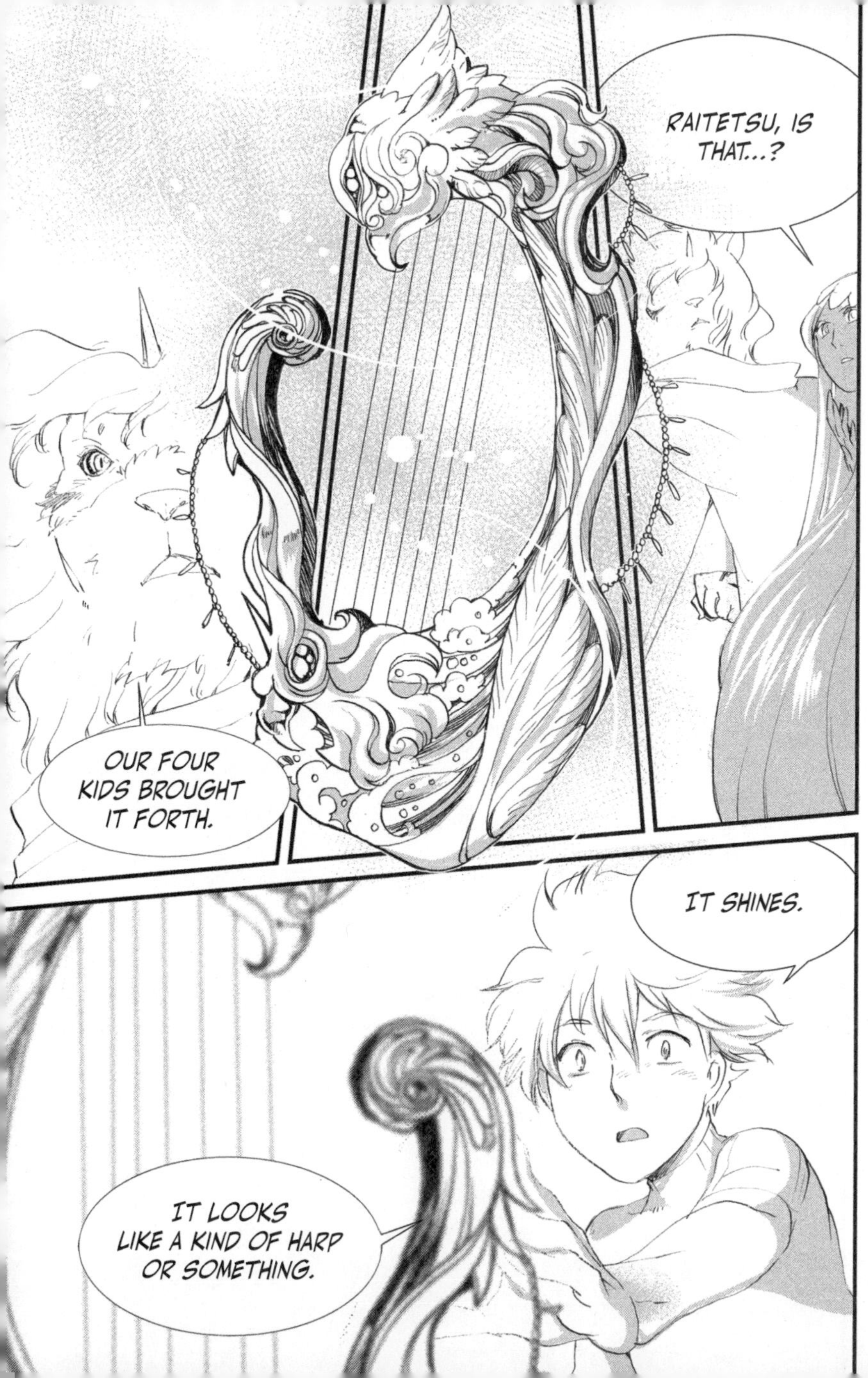
RAITETSU, IS THAT...?
OUR FOUR KIDS BROUGHT IT FORTH.
IT SHINES.
IT LOOKS LIKE A KIND OF HARP OR SOMETHING.

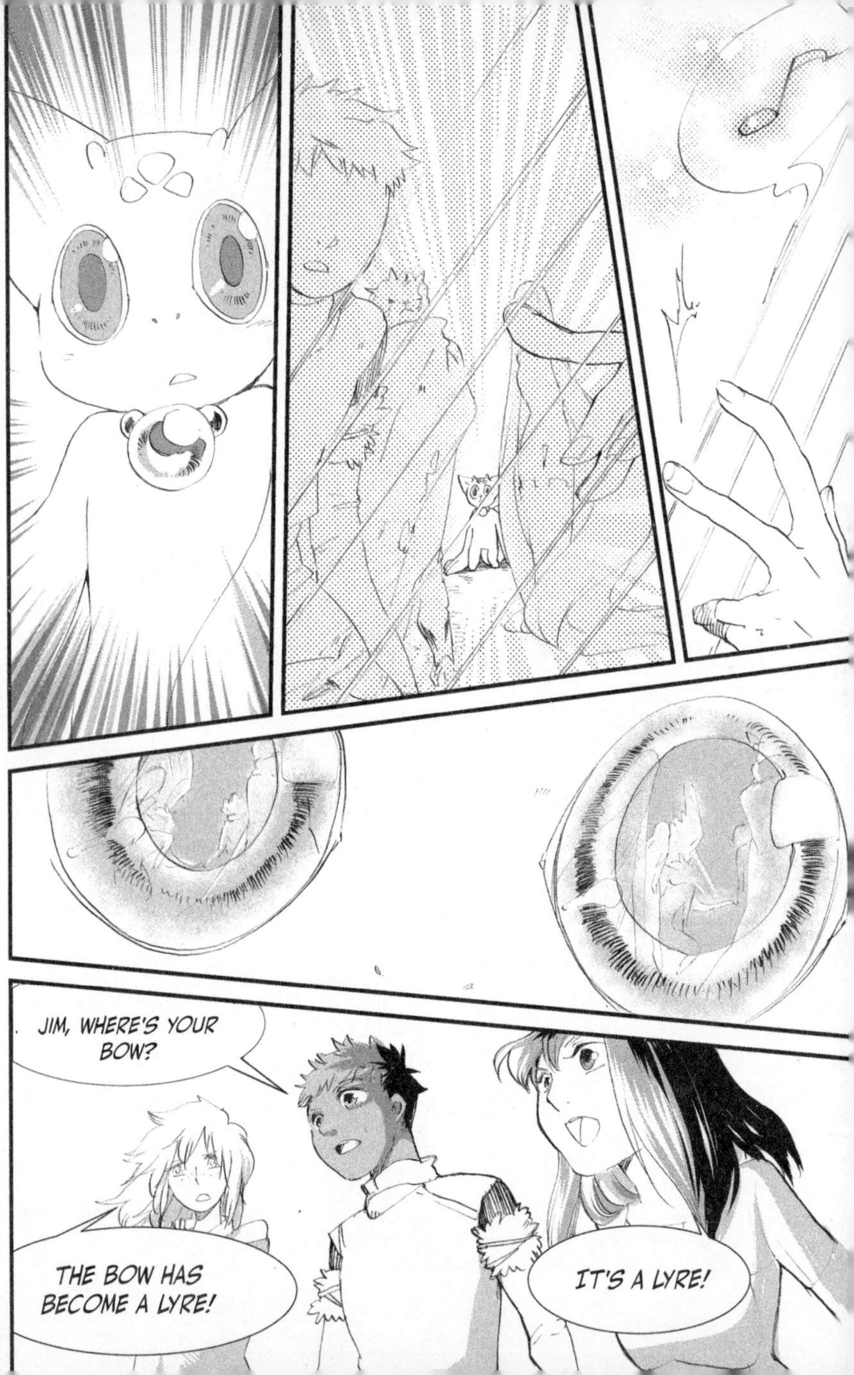
JIM, WHERE'S YOUR BOW?
IT'S A LYRE!
THE BOW HAS BECOME A LYRE!

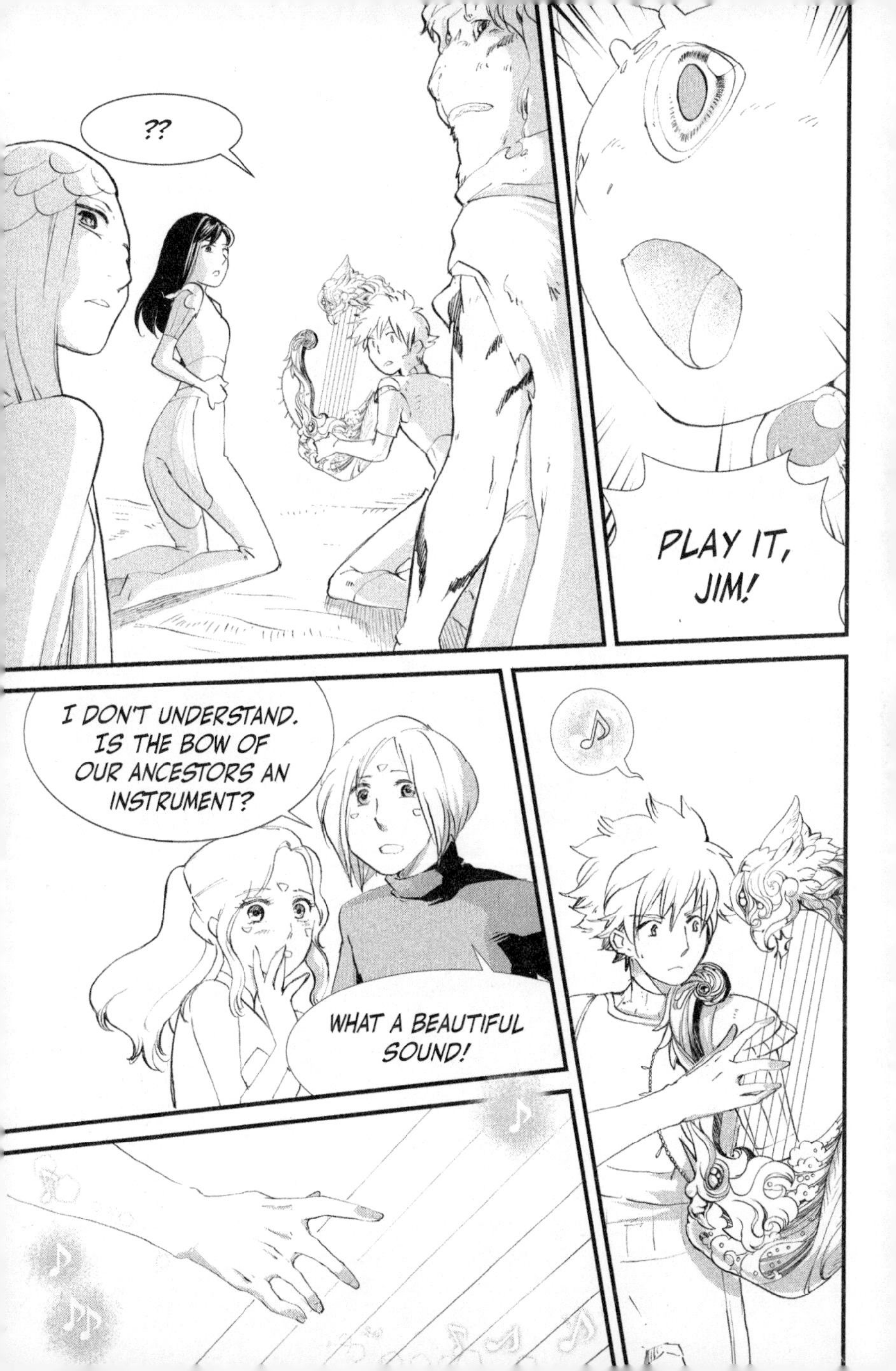
PLAY IT, JIM!
??
♪
I DON'T UNDERSTAND. IS THE BOW OF OUR ANCESTORS AN INSTRUMENT?
WHAT A BEAUTIFUL SOUND!

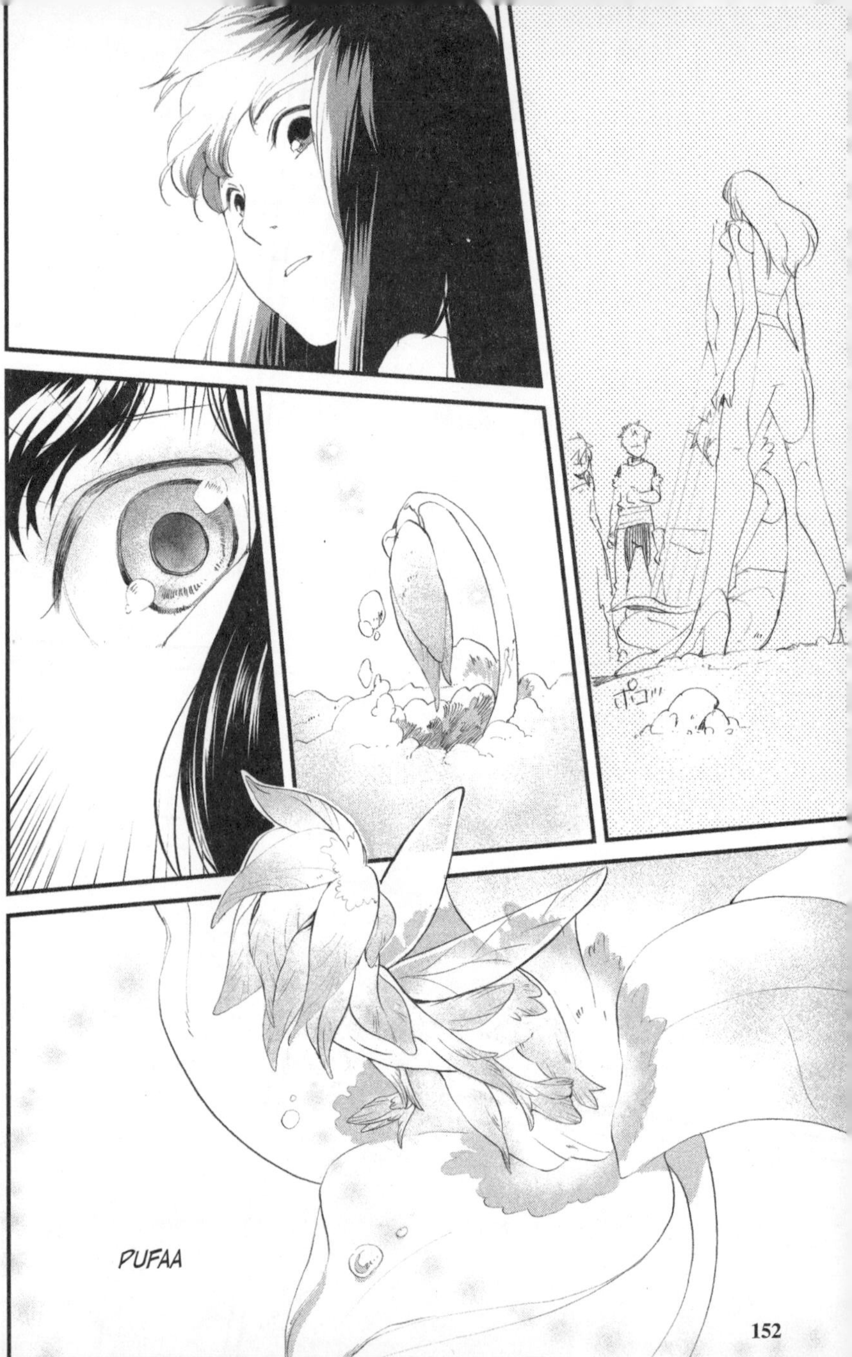
ポコ゛
PUFAA

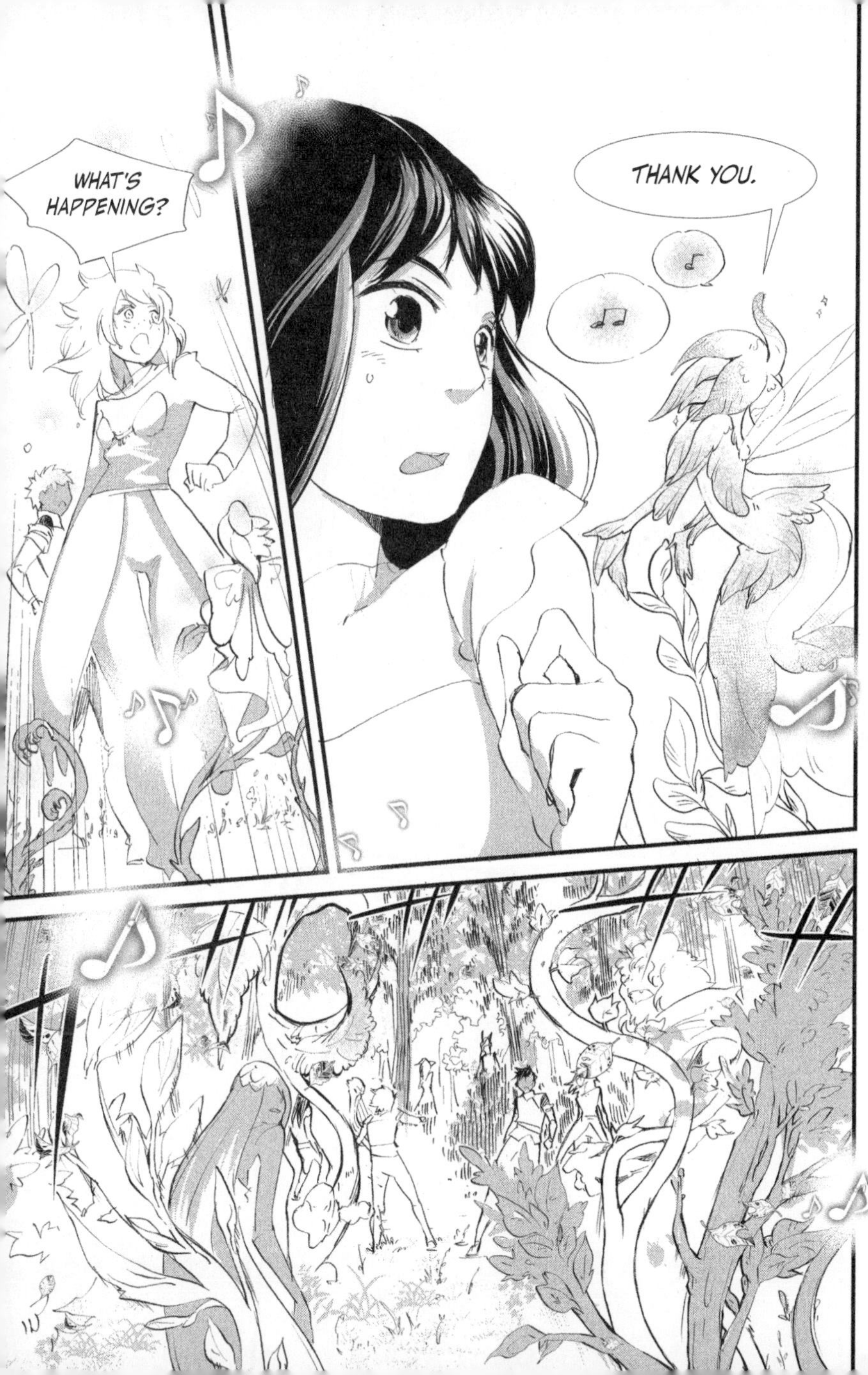
THANK YOU.
WHAT'S HAPPENING?

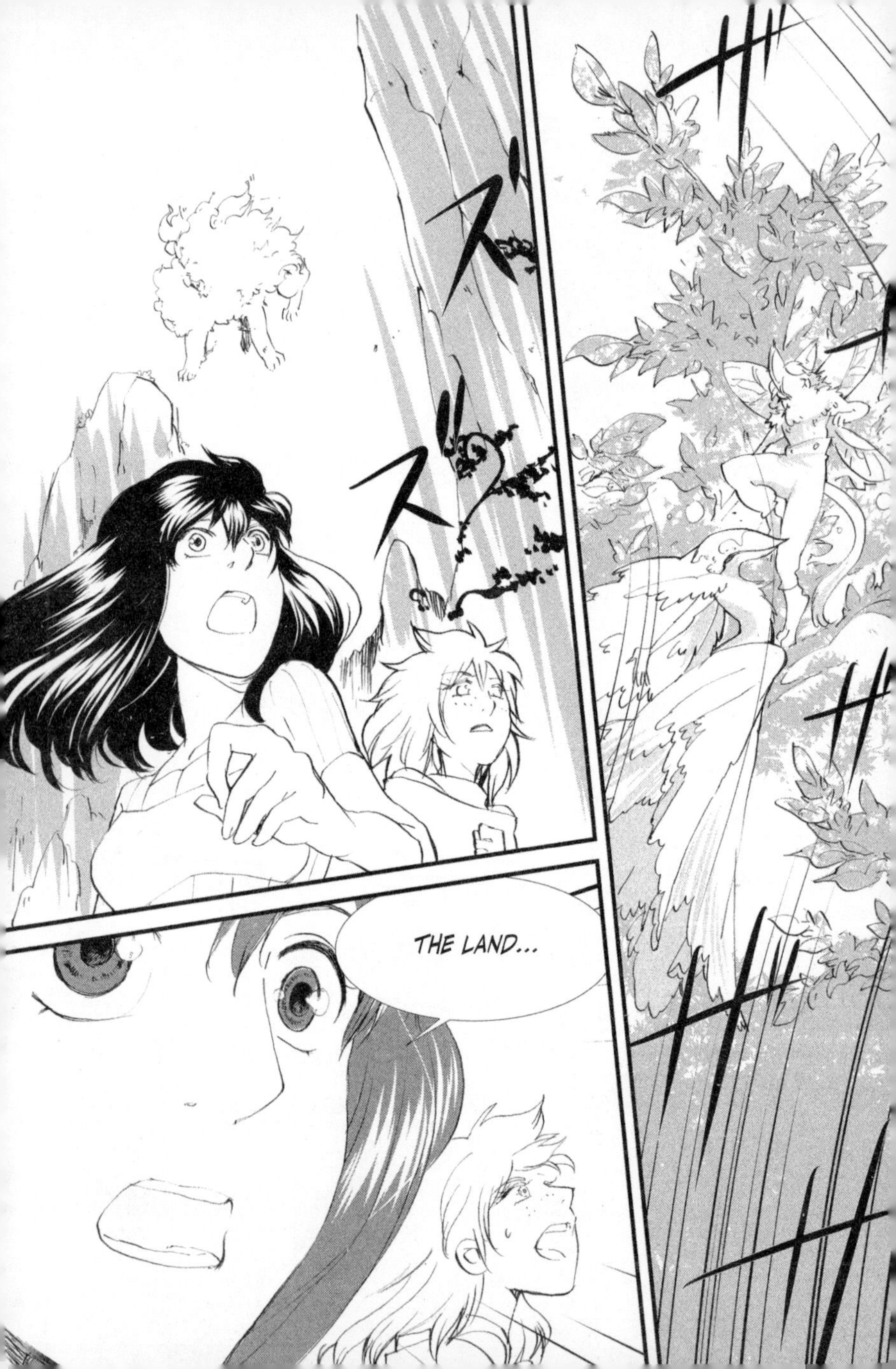
THE LAND...

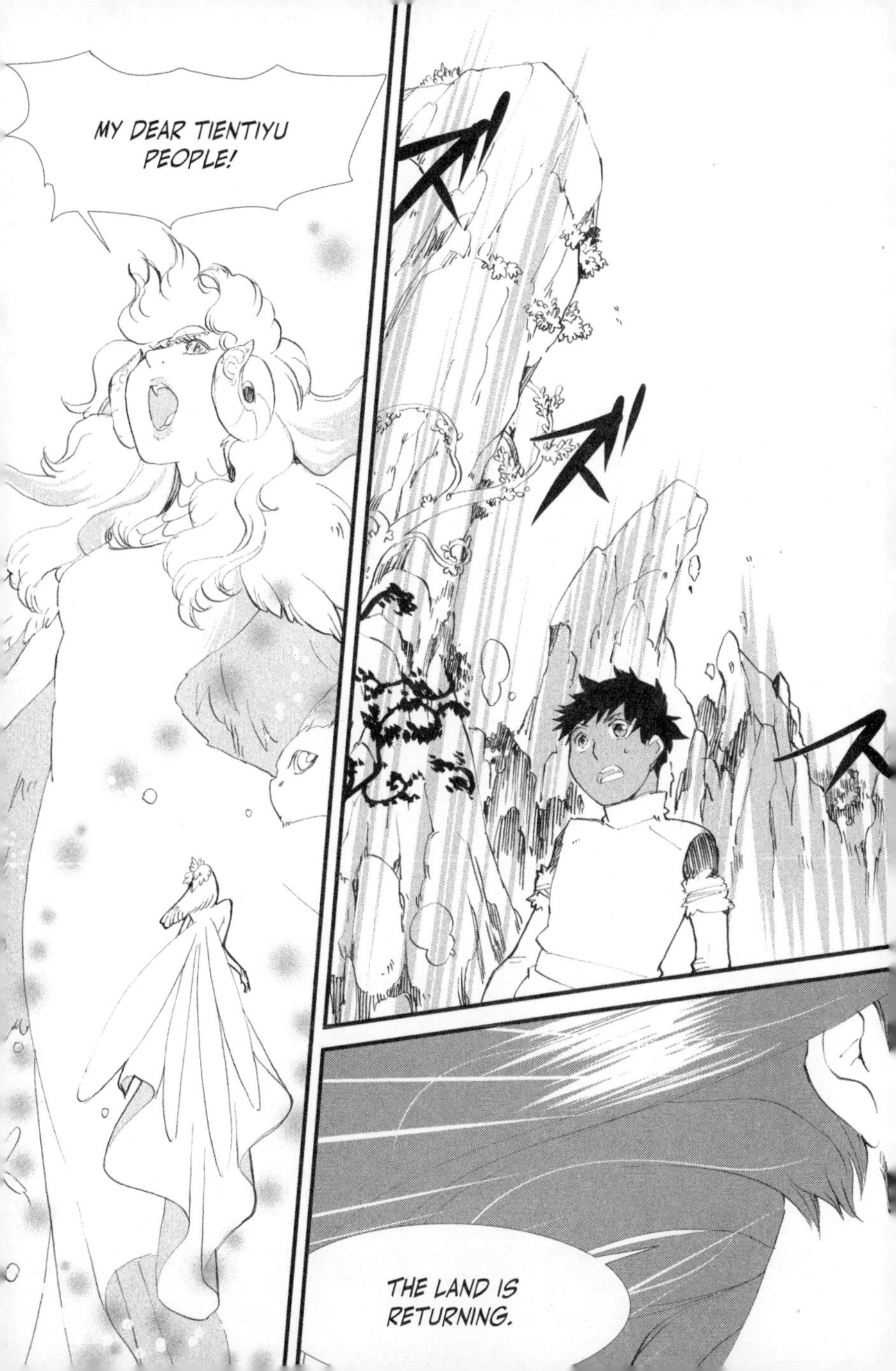
THE LAND IS RETURNING.
MY DEAR TIENTIYU PEOPLE!

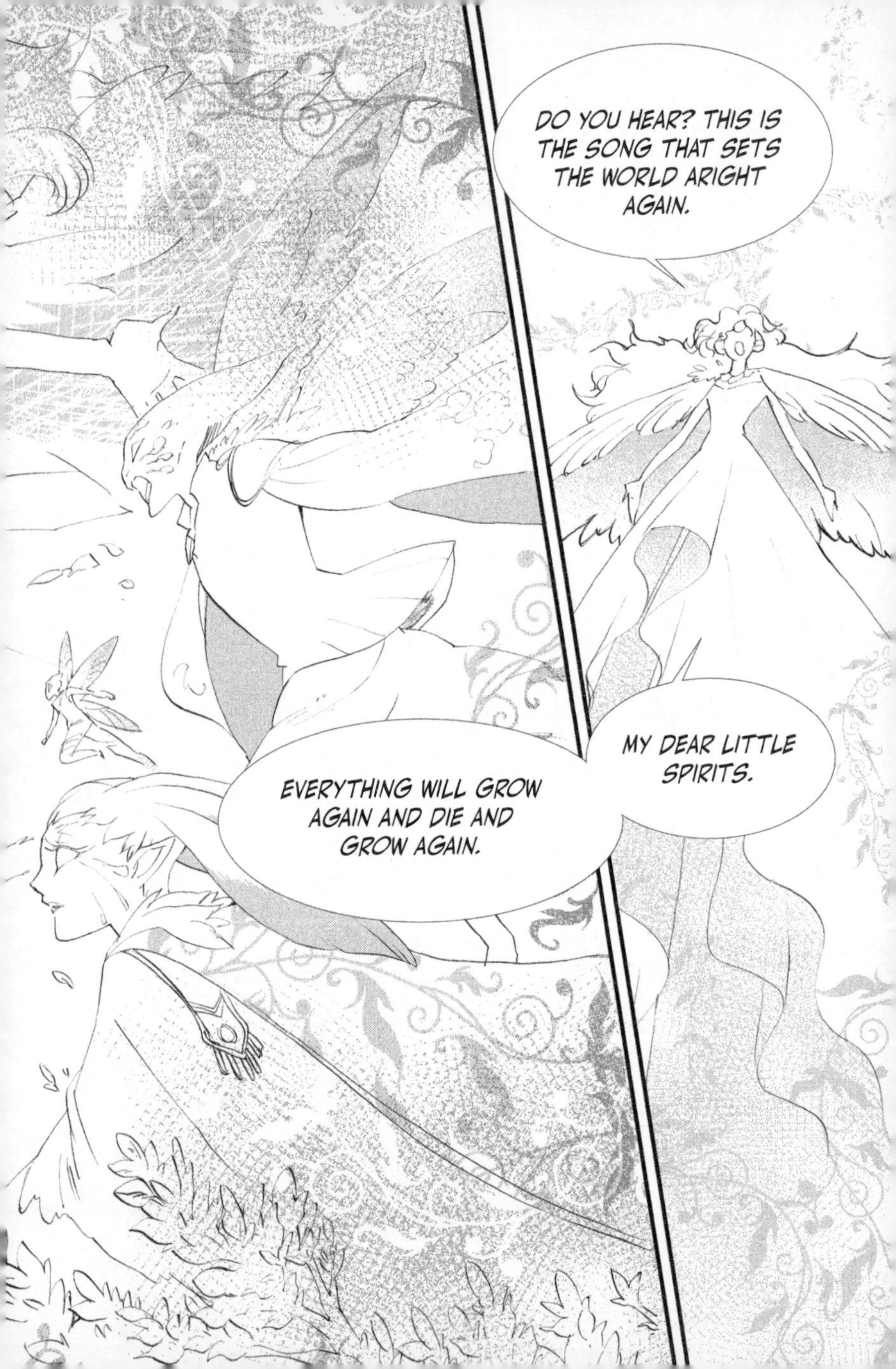
DO YOU HEAR? THIS IS THE SONG THAT SETS THE WORLD ARIGHT AGAIN.
MY DEAR LITTLE SPIRITS.
EVERYTHING WILL GROW AGAIN AND DIE AND GROW AGAIN.

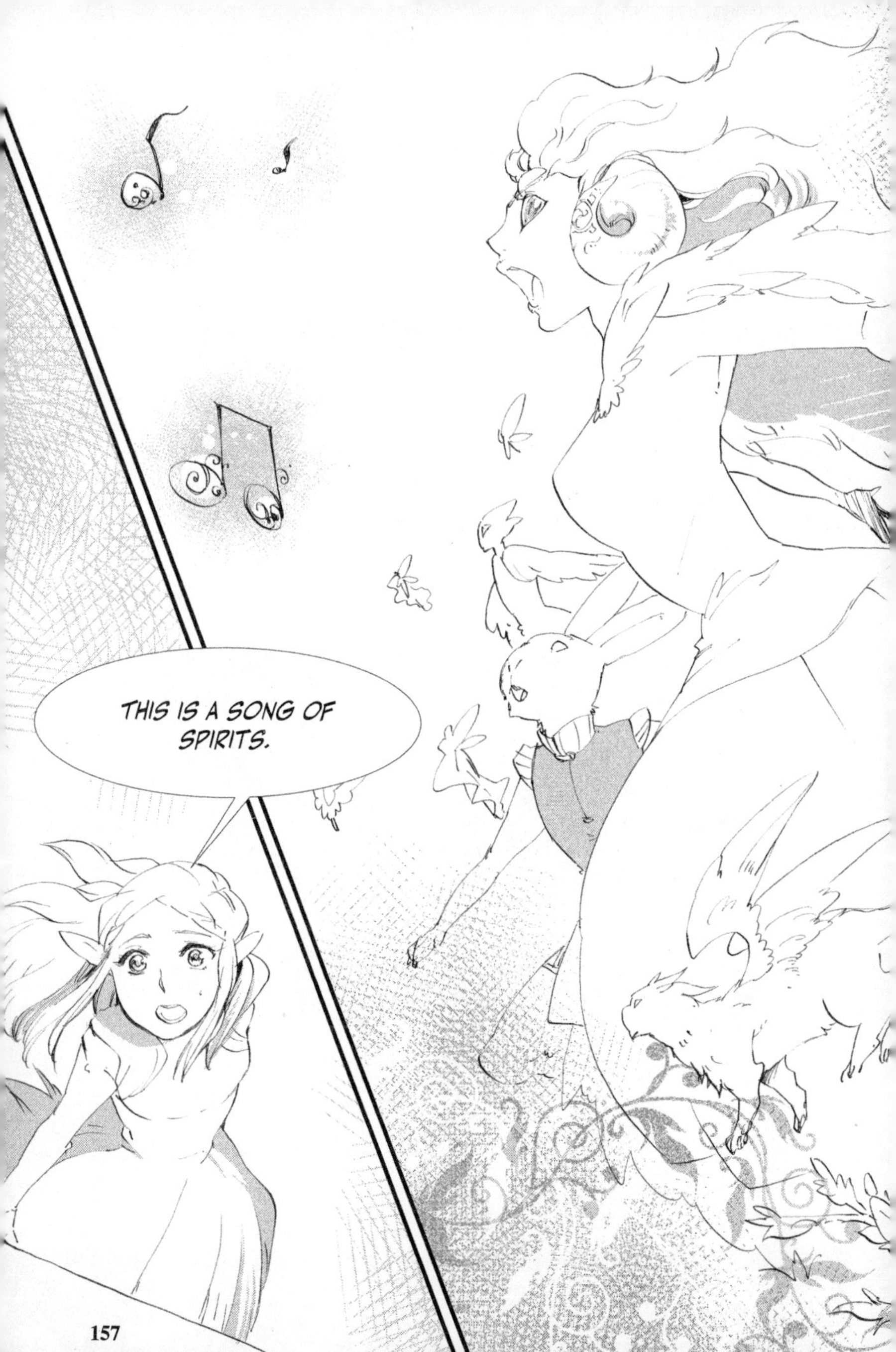
THIS IS A SONG OF SPIRITS.

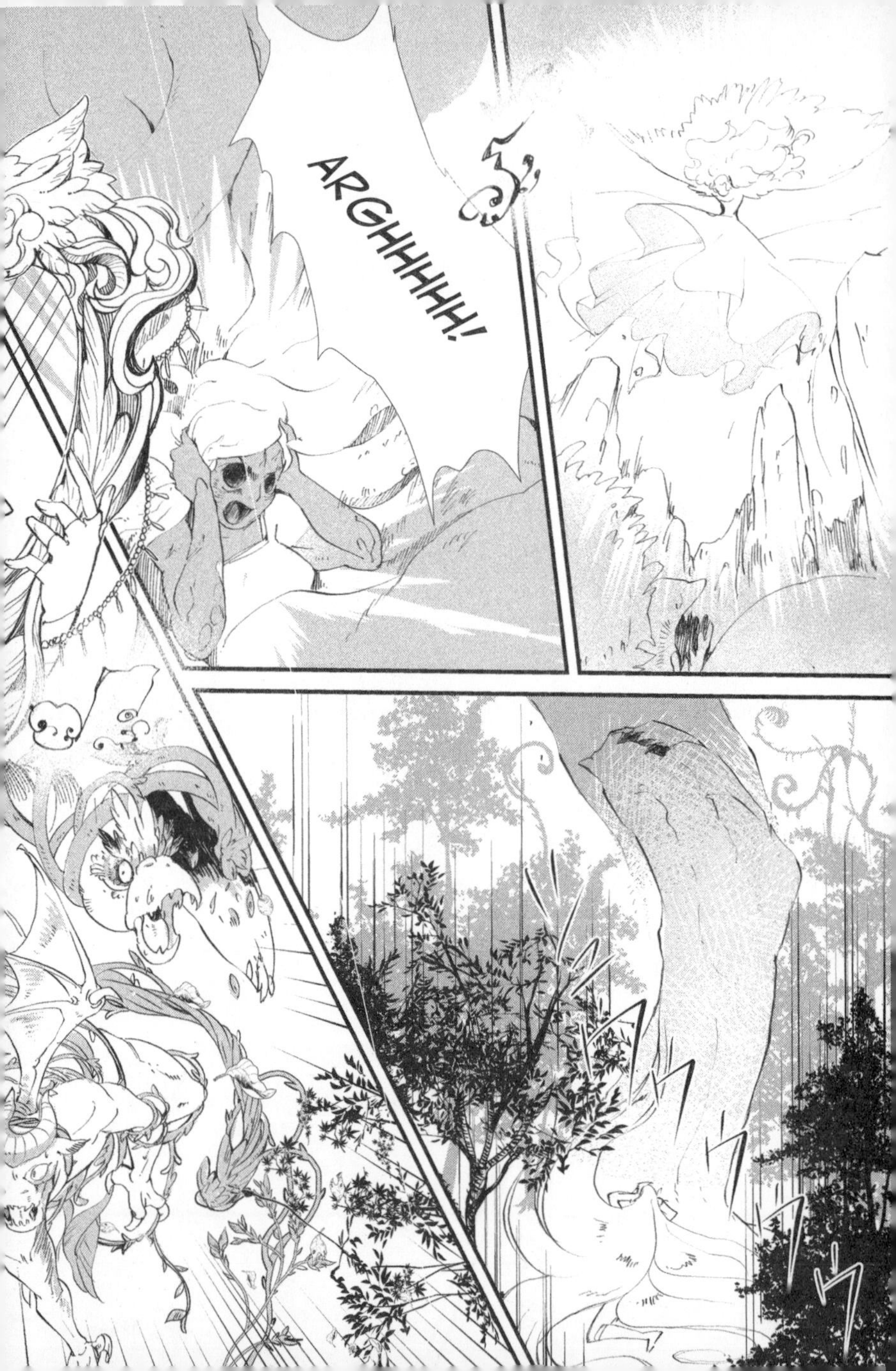
ARGHHHHH!

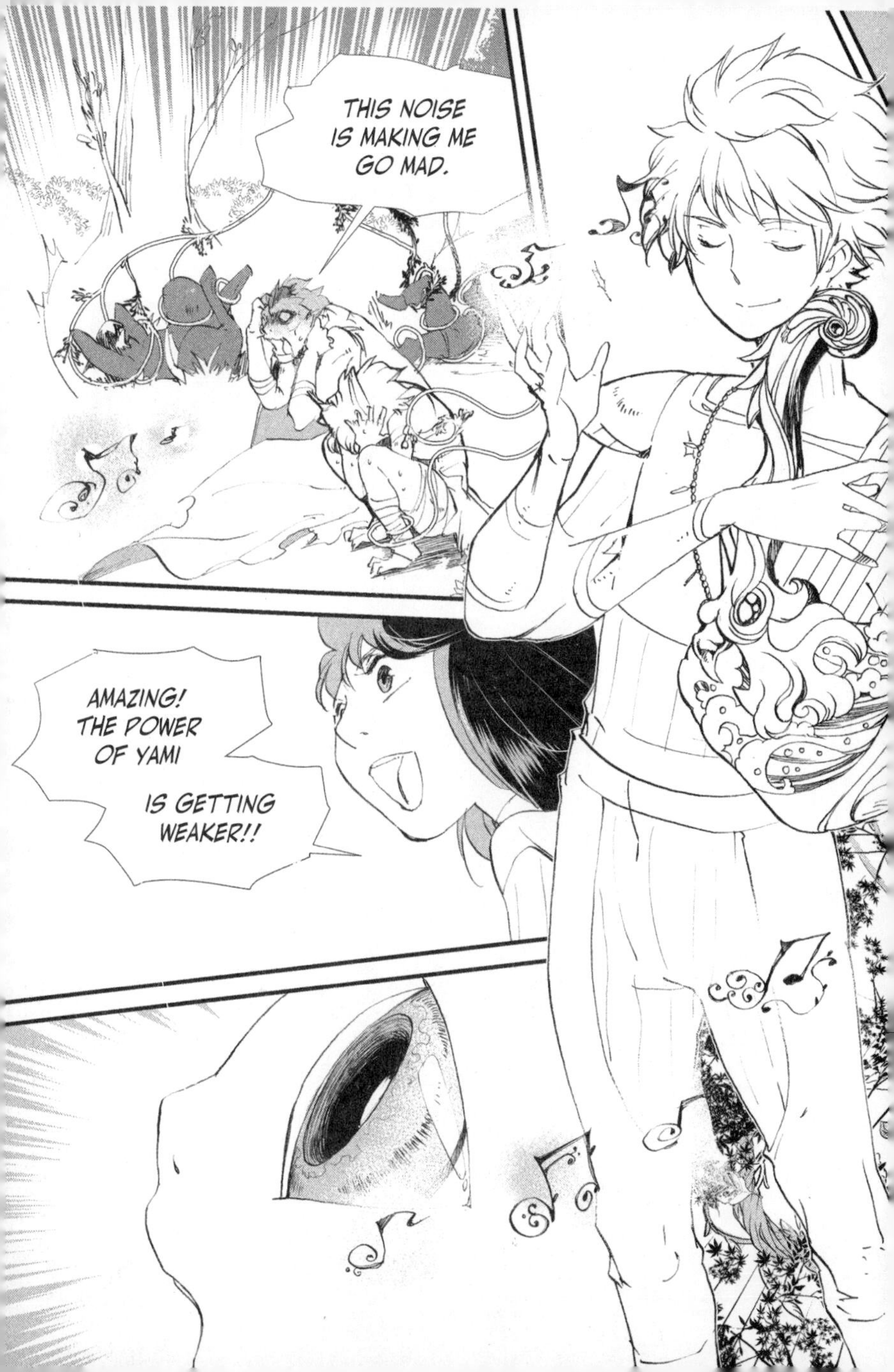
THIS NOISE IS MAKING ME GO MAD.
AMAZING! THE POWER OF YAMI
IS GETTING WEAKER!!

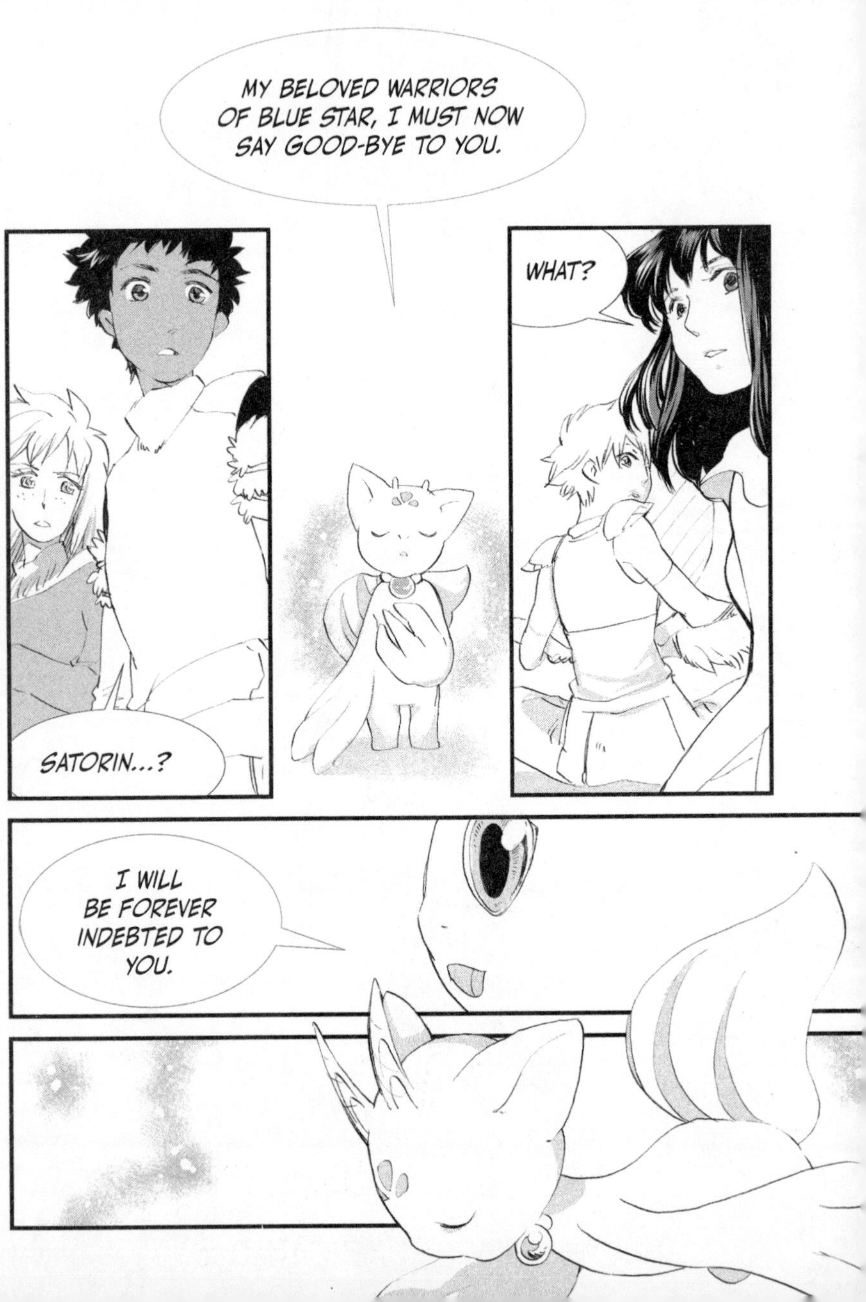
MY BELOVED WARRIORS OF BLUE STAR, I MUST NOW SAY GOOD-BYE TO YOU.
WHAT?
SATORIN...?
I WILL BE FOREVER INDEBTED TO YOU.

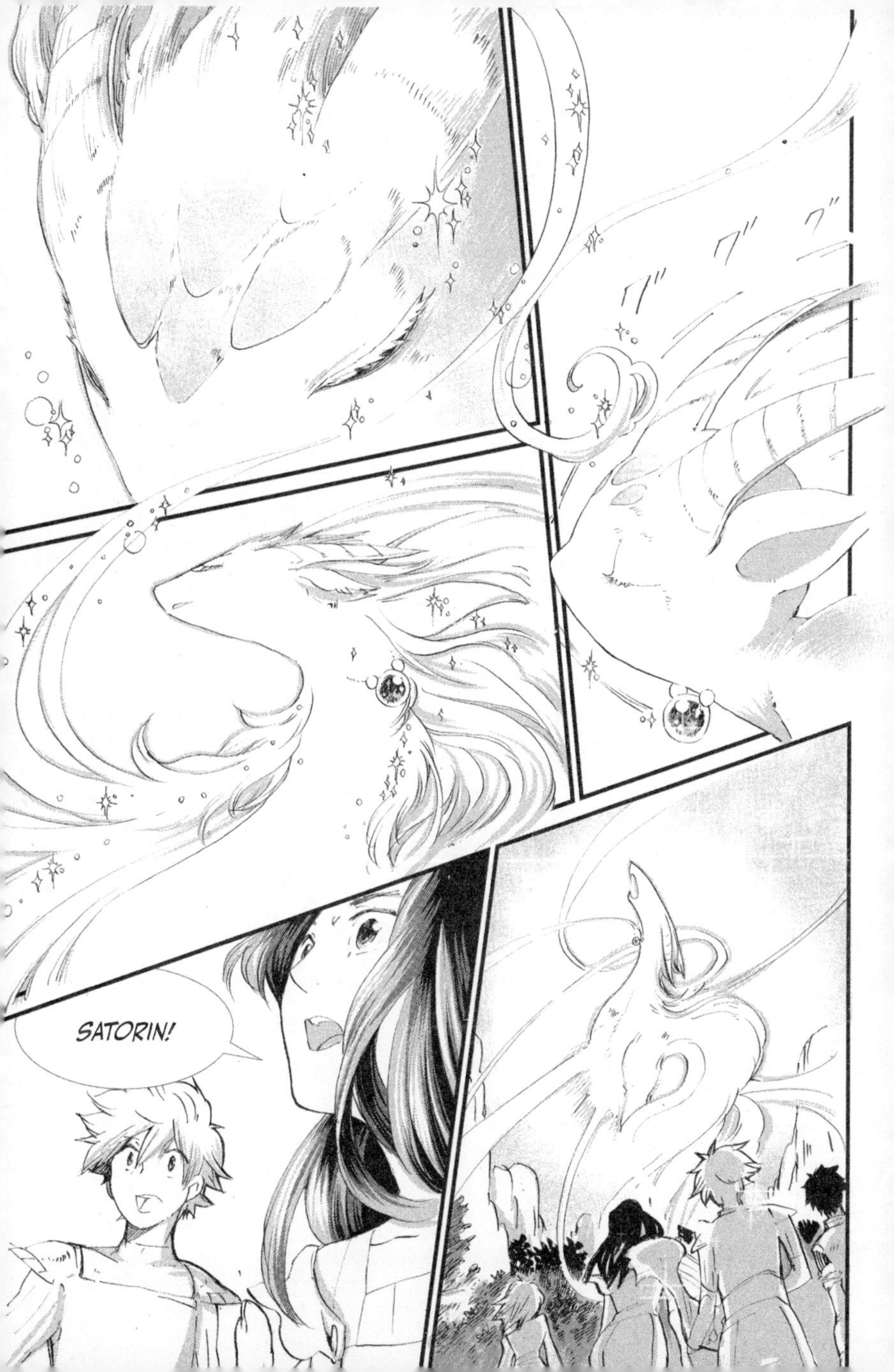
SATORIN!

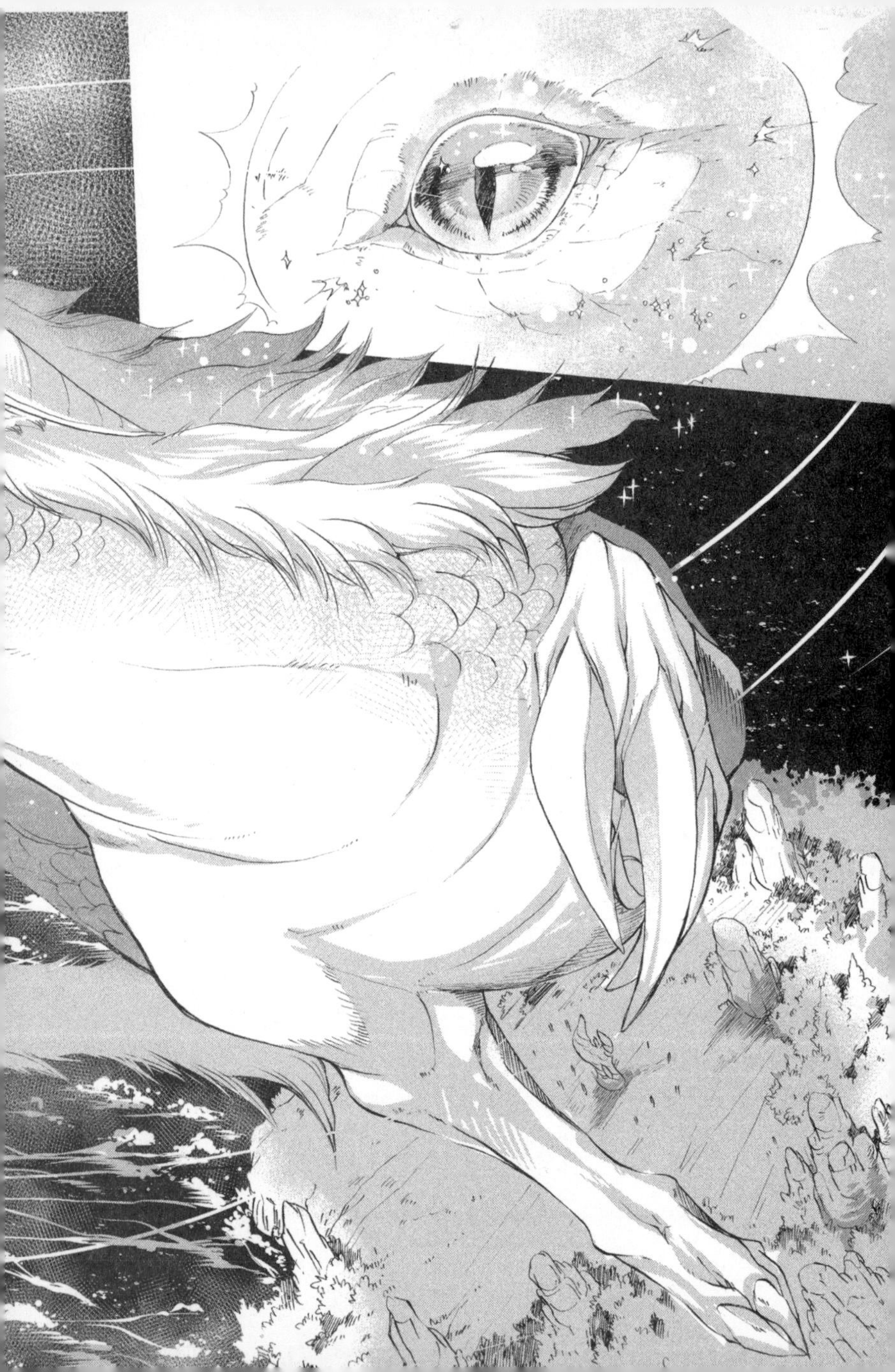

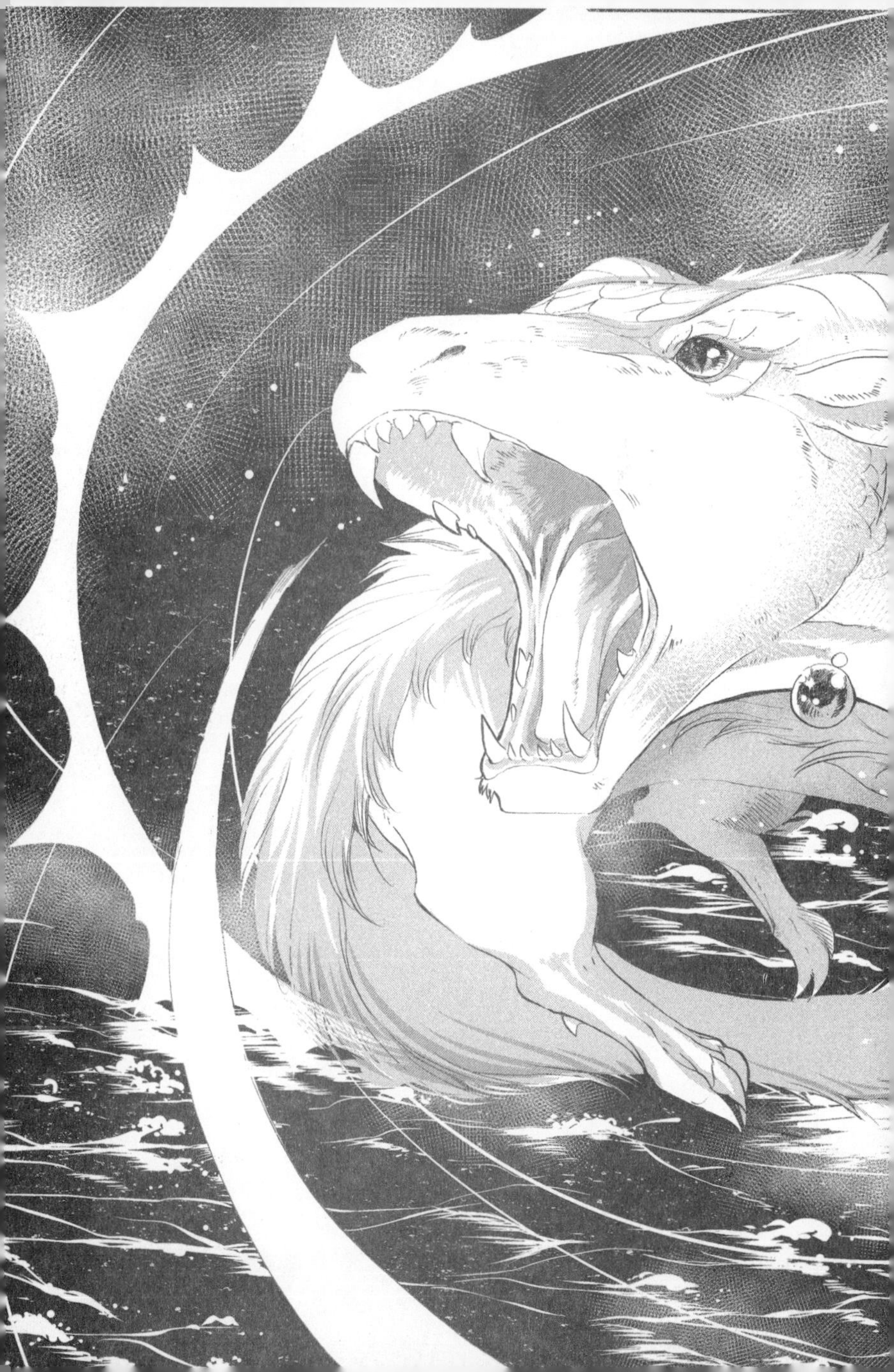

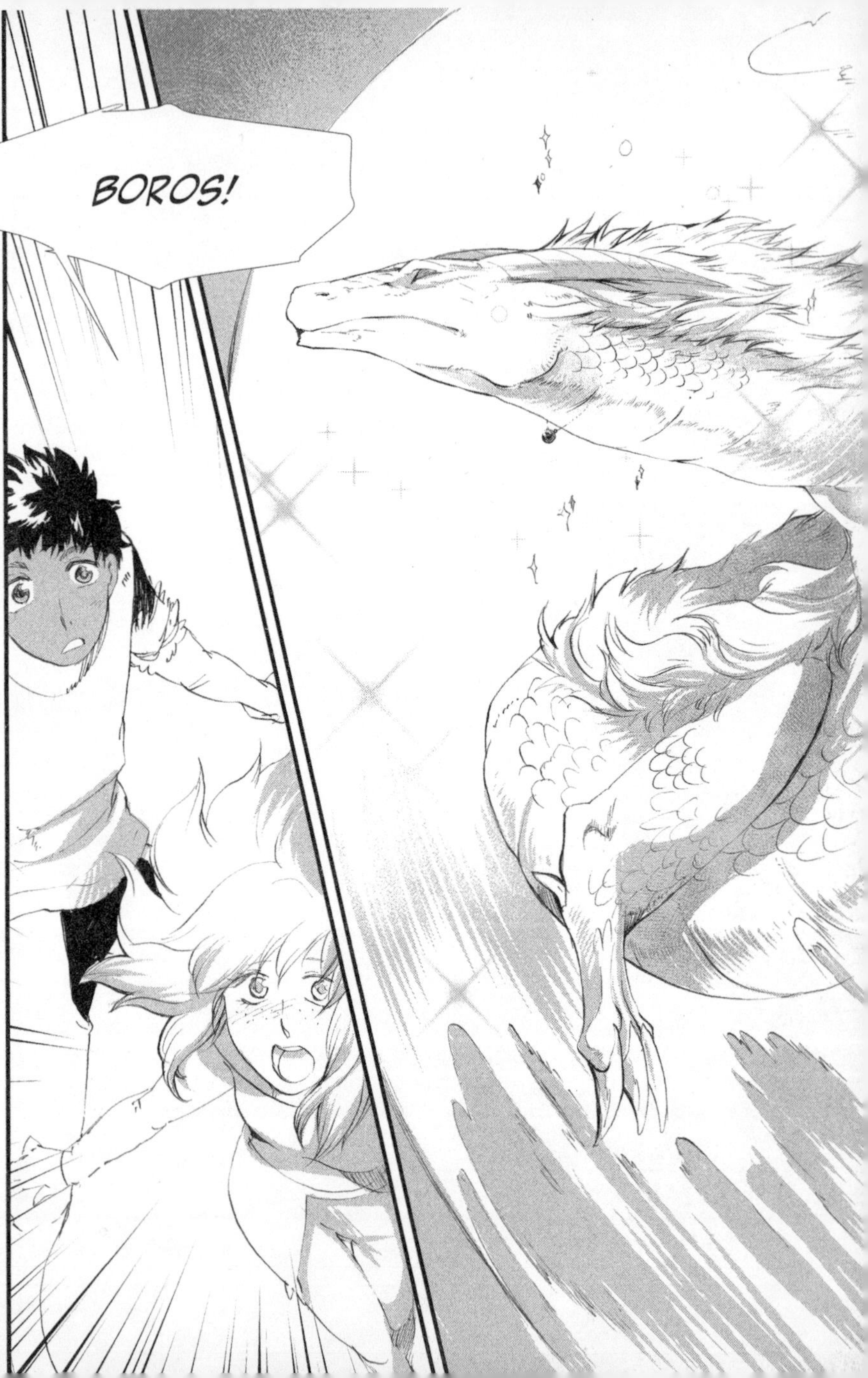
BOROS!

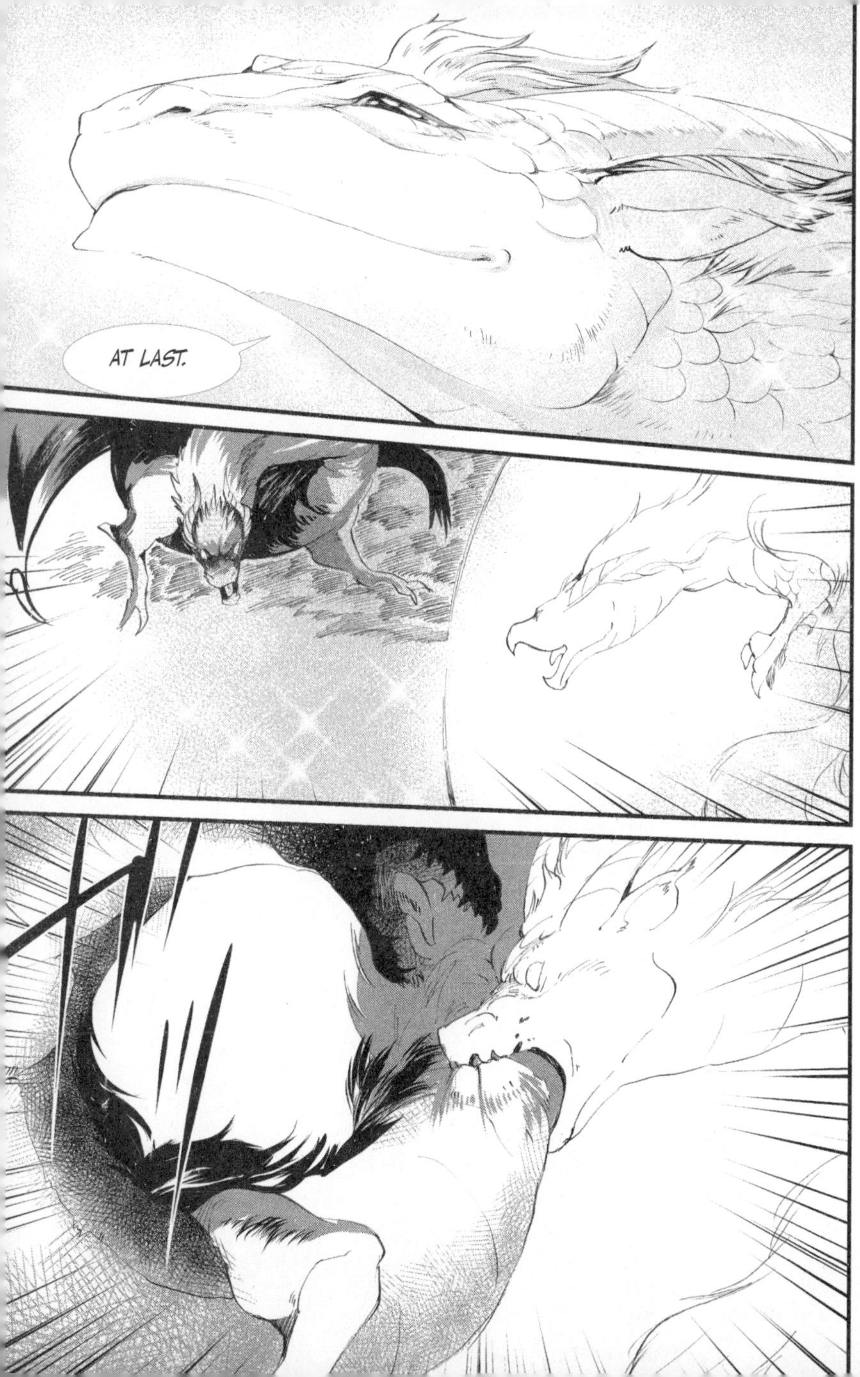
AT LAST.

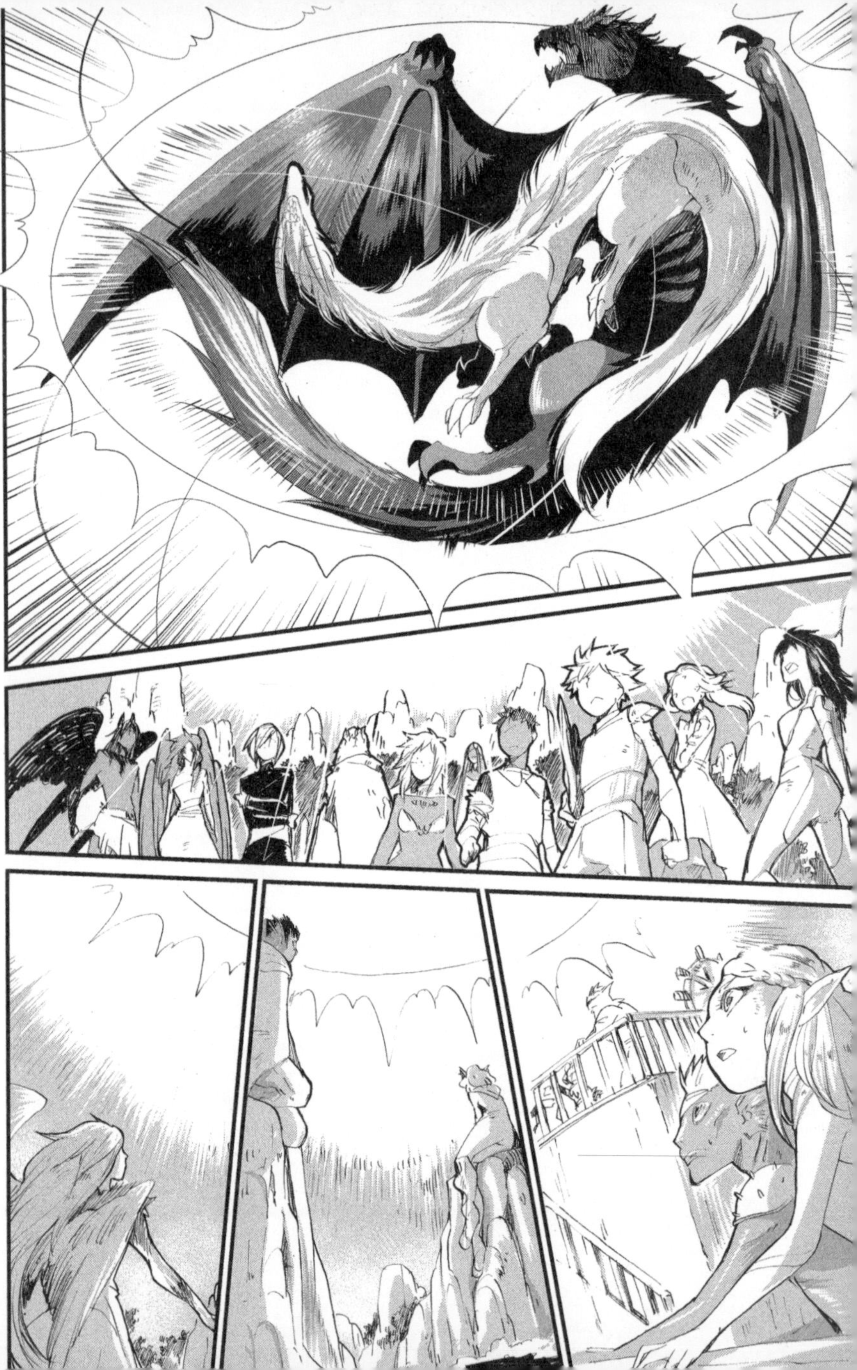

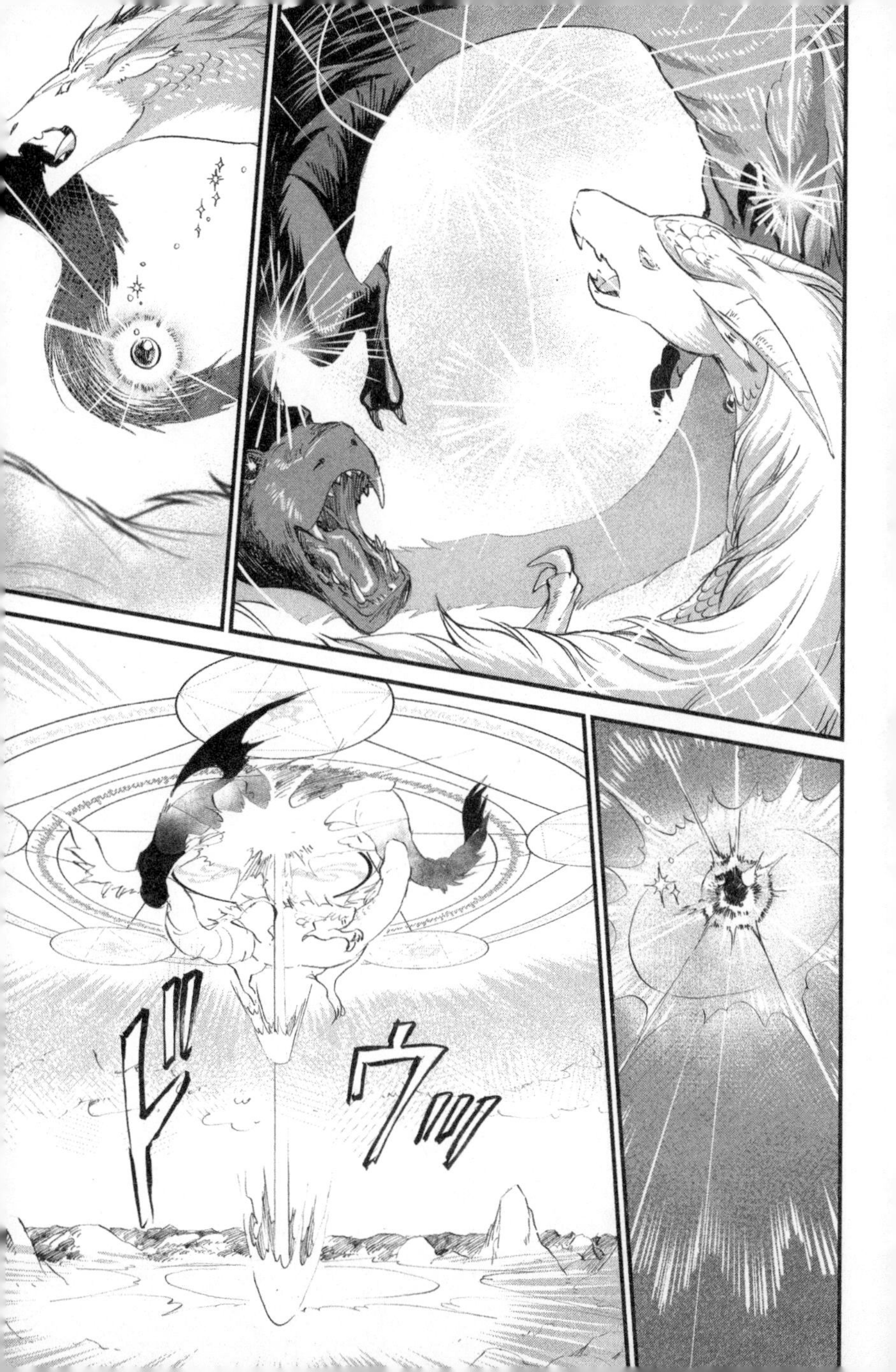
ドウッ

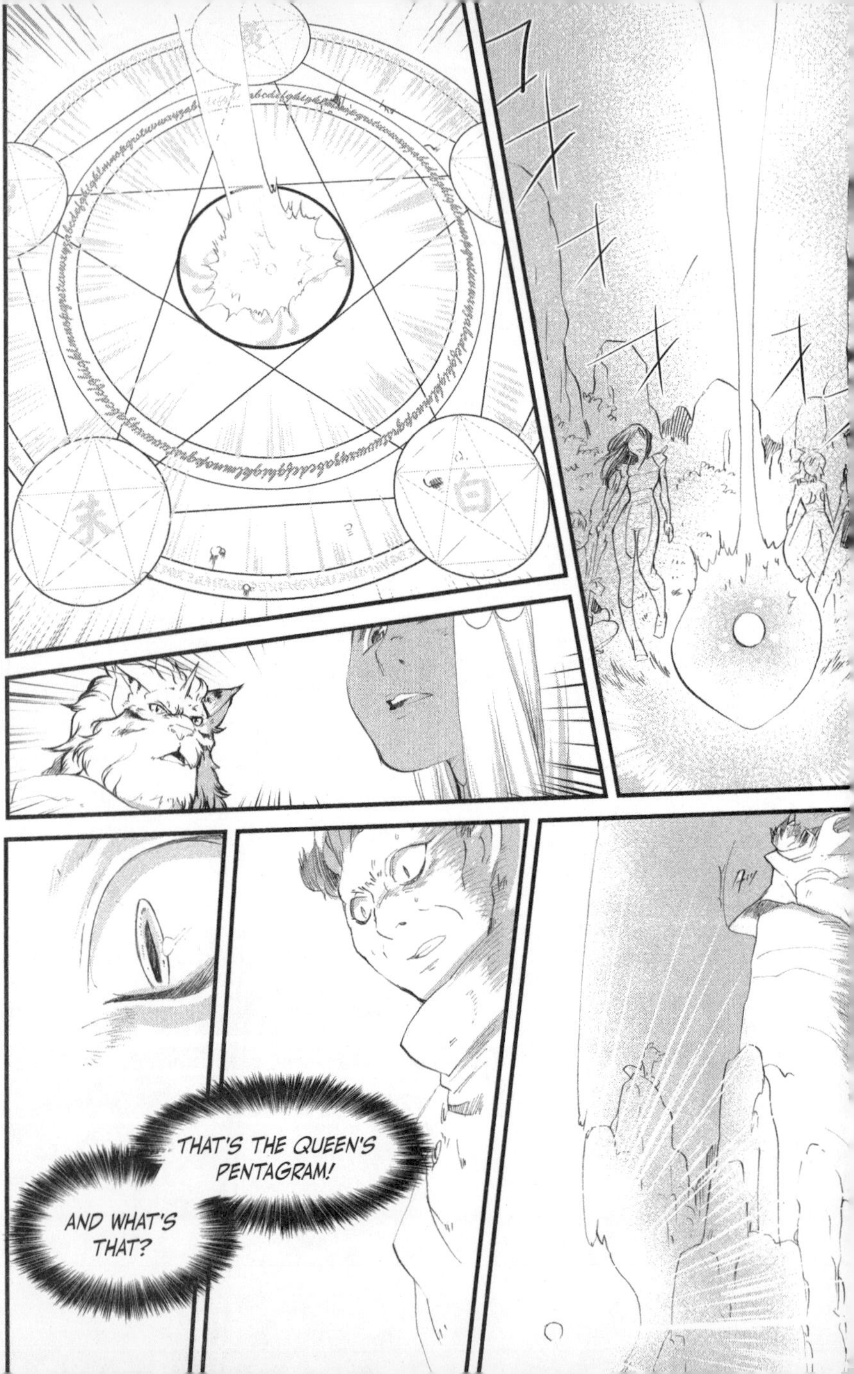
THAT'S THE QUEEN'S PENTAGRAM!
AND WHAT'S THAT?

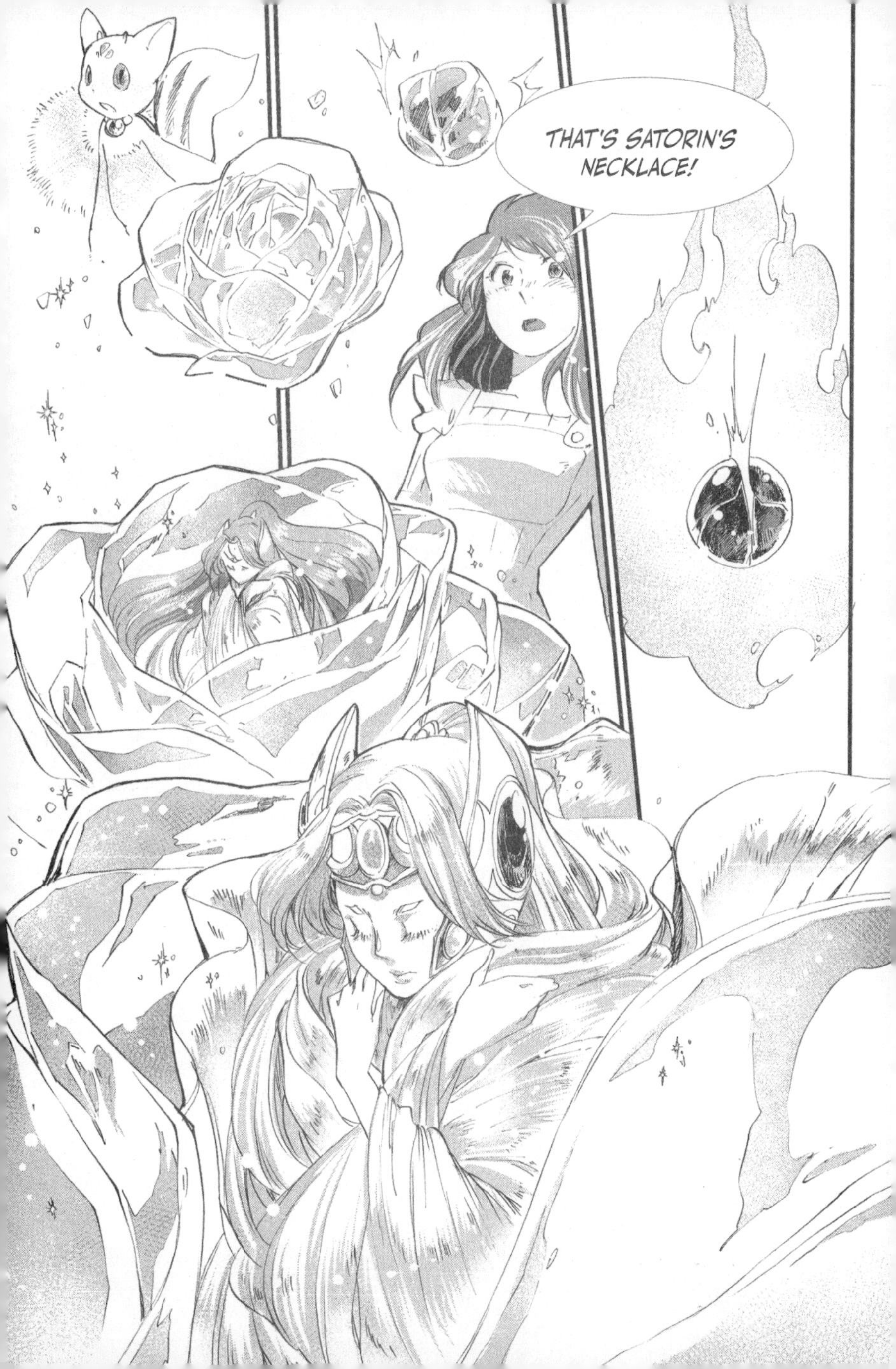
THAT'S SATORIN'S NECKLACE!

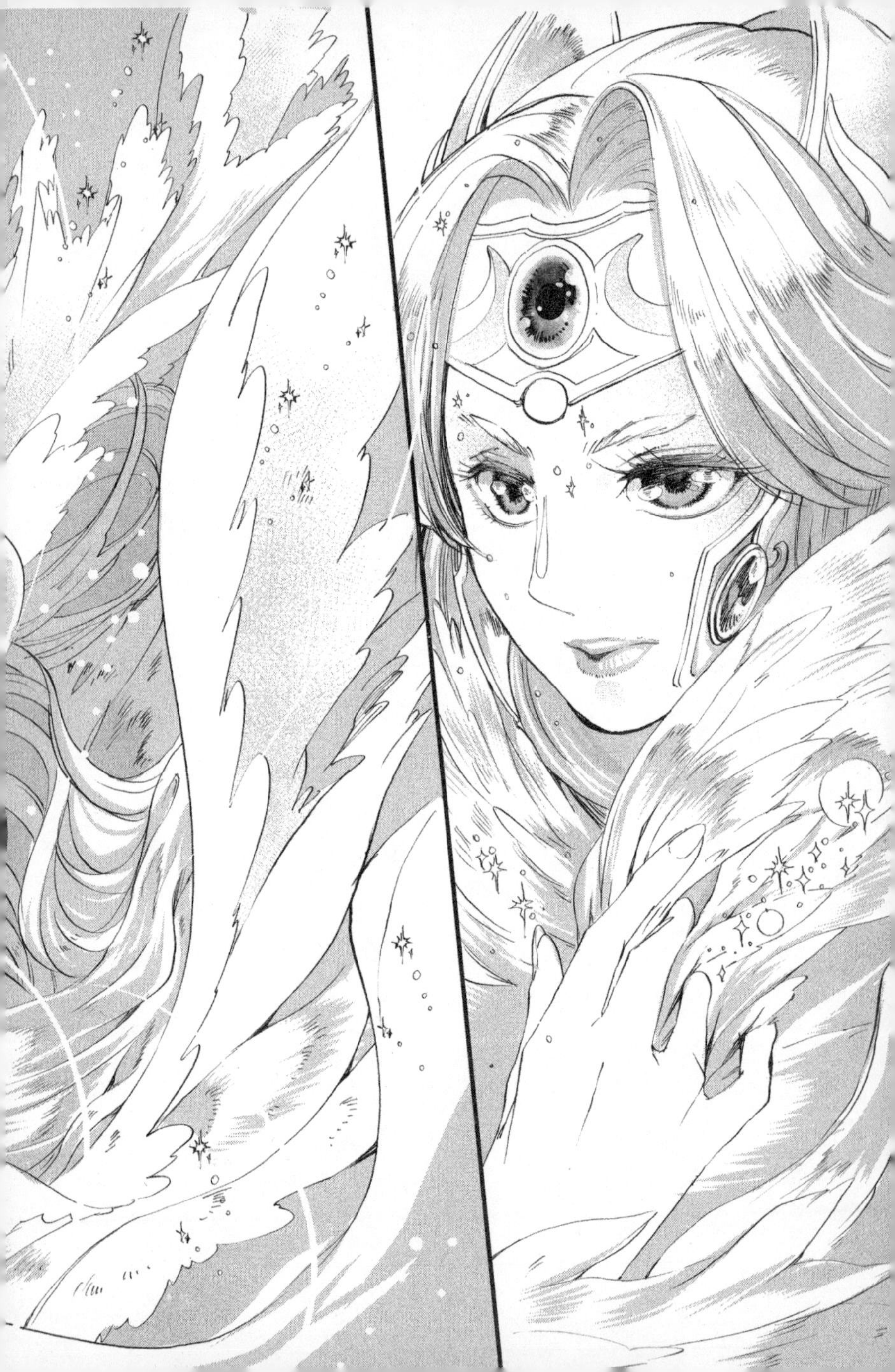

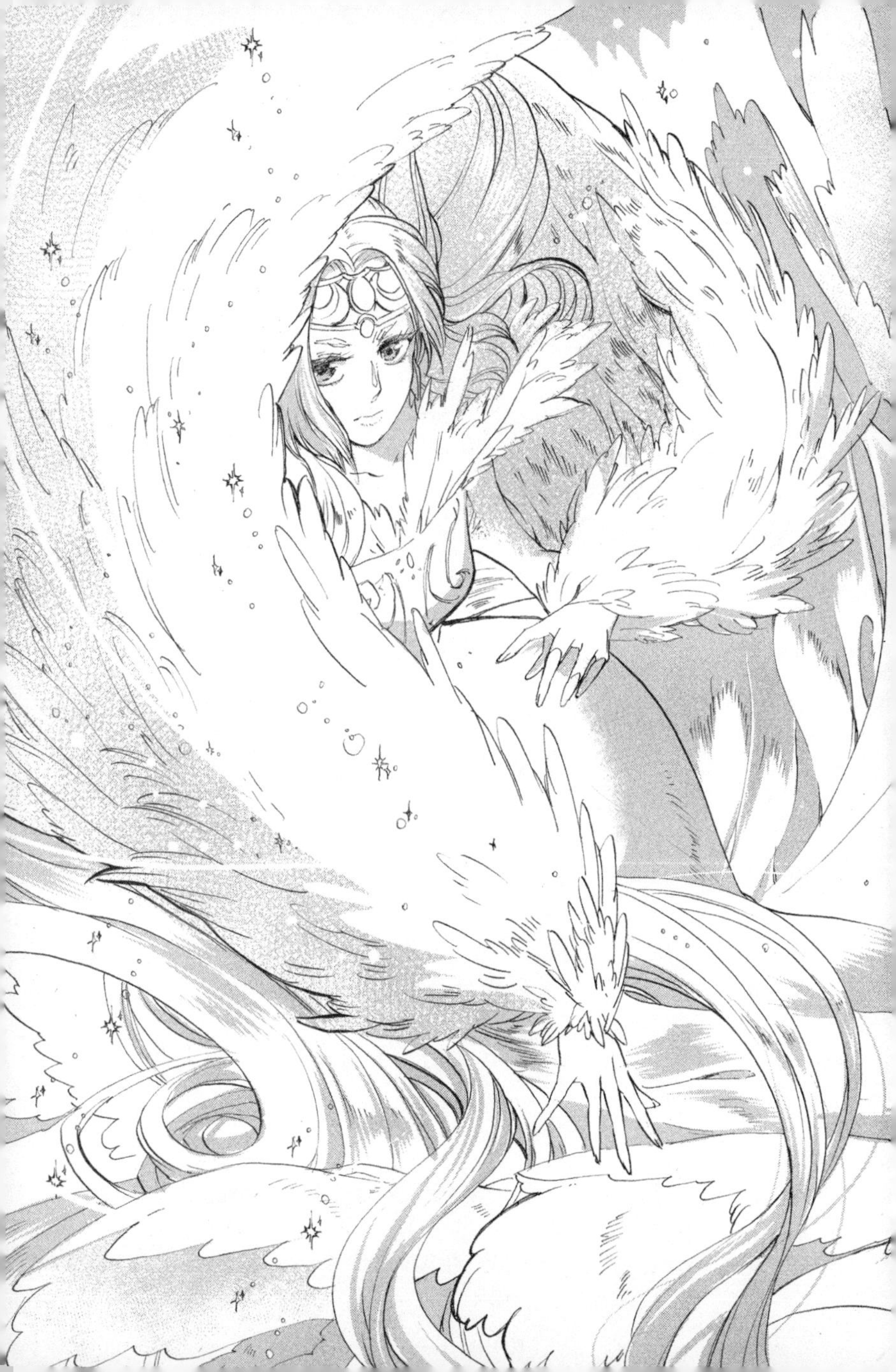

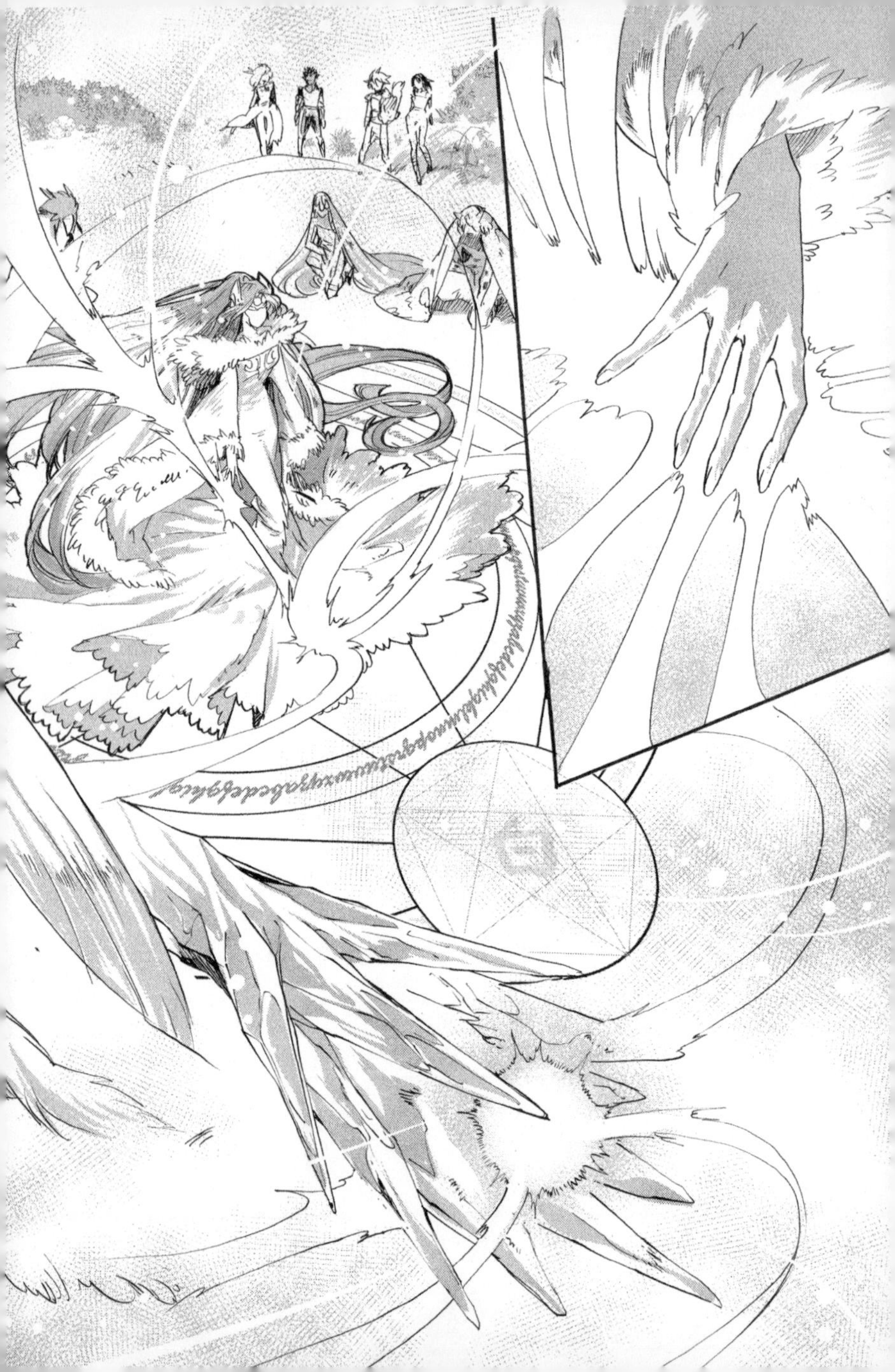

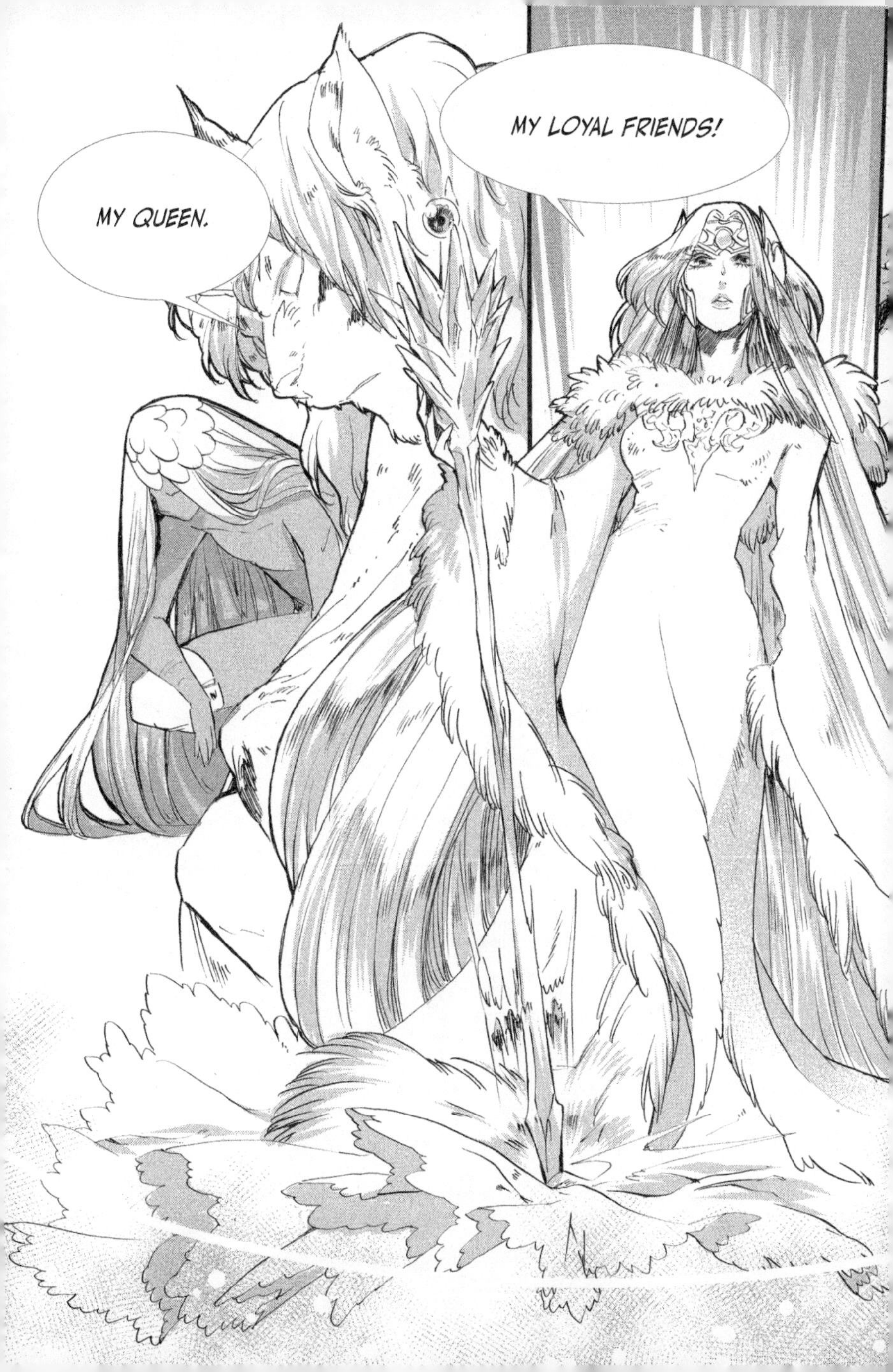
MY LOYAL FRIENDS!
MY QUEEN.

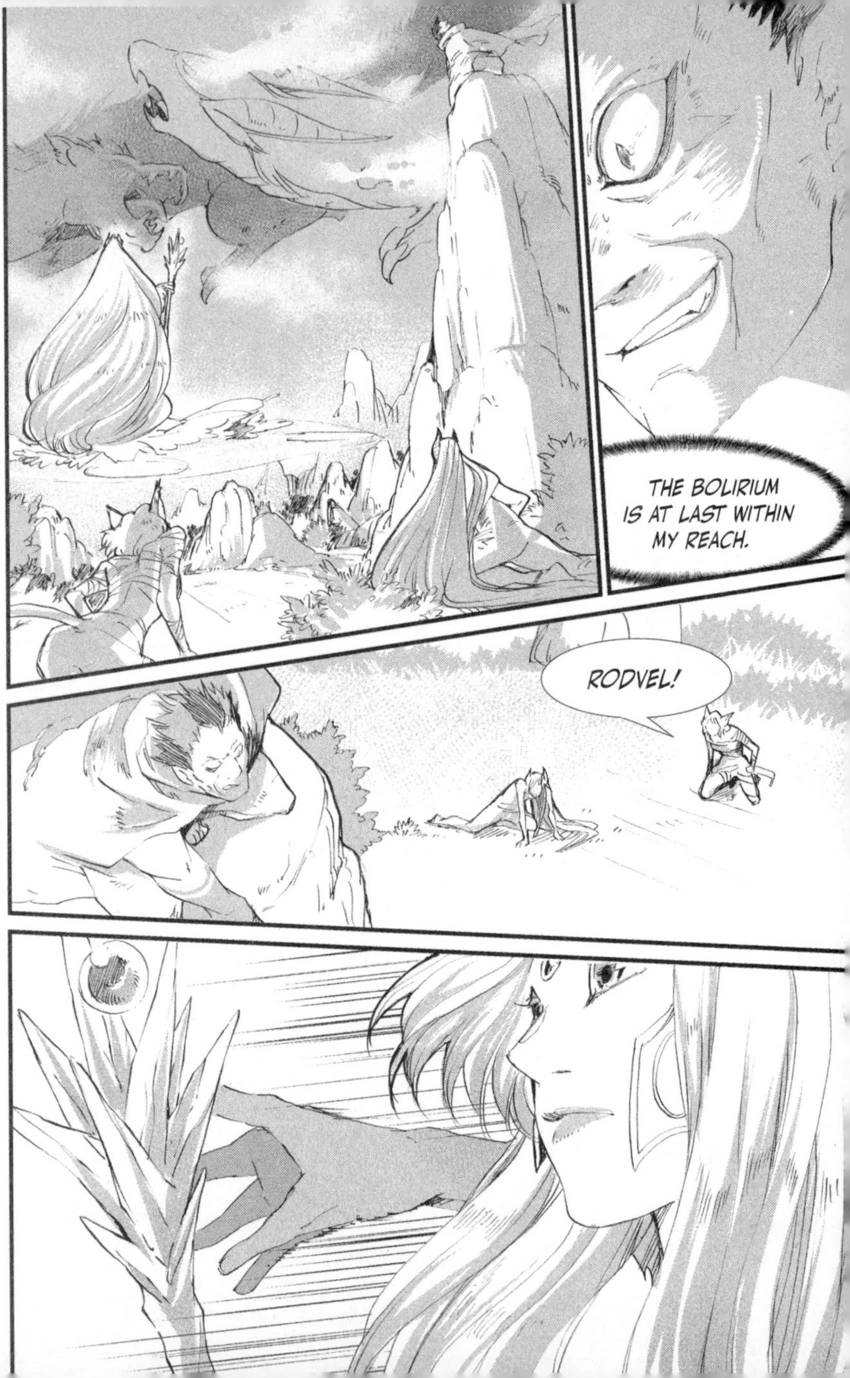
THE BOLIRIUM IS AT LAST WITHIN MY REACH.
RODVEL!

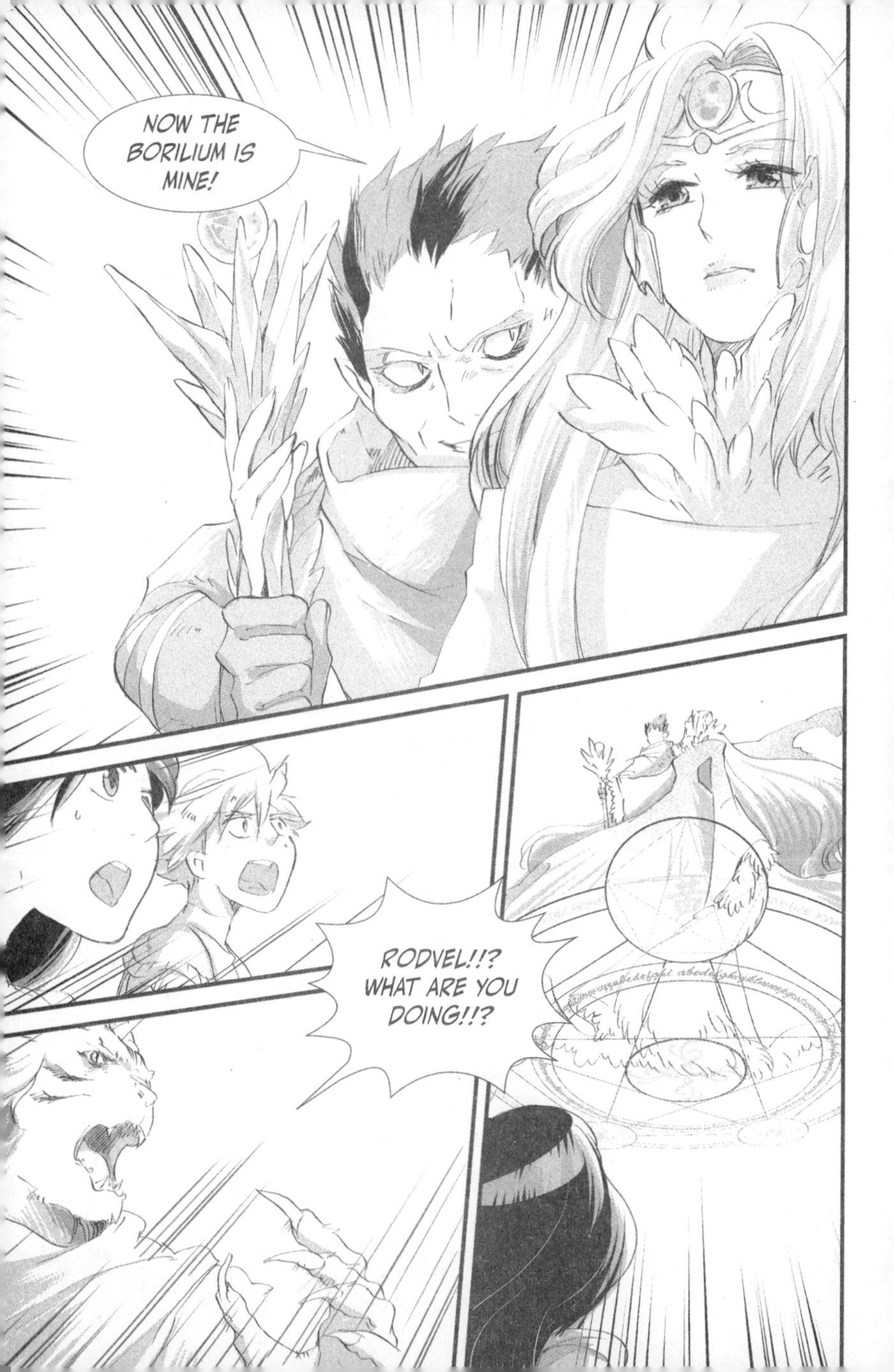
NOW THE BORILIUM IS MINE!
RODVEL!!? WHAT ARE YOU DOING!!?

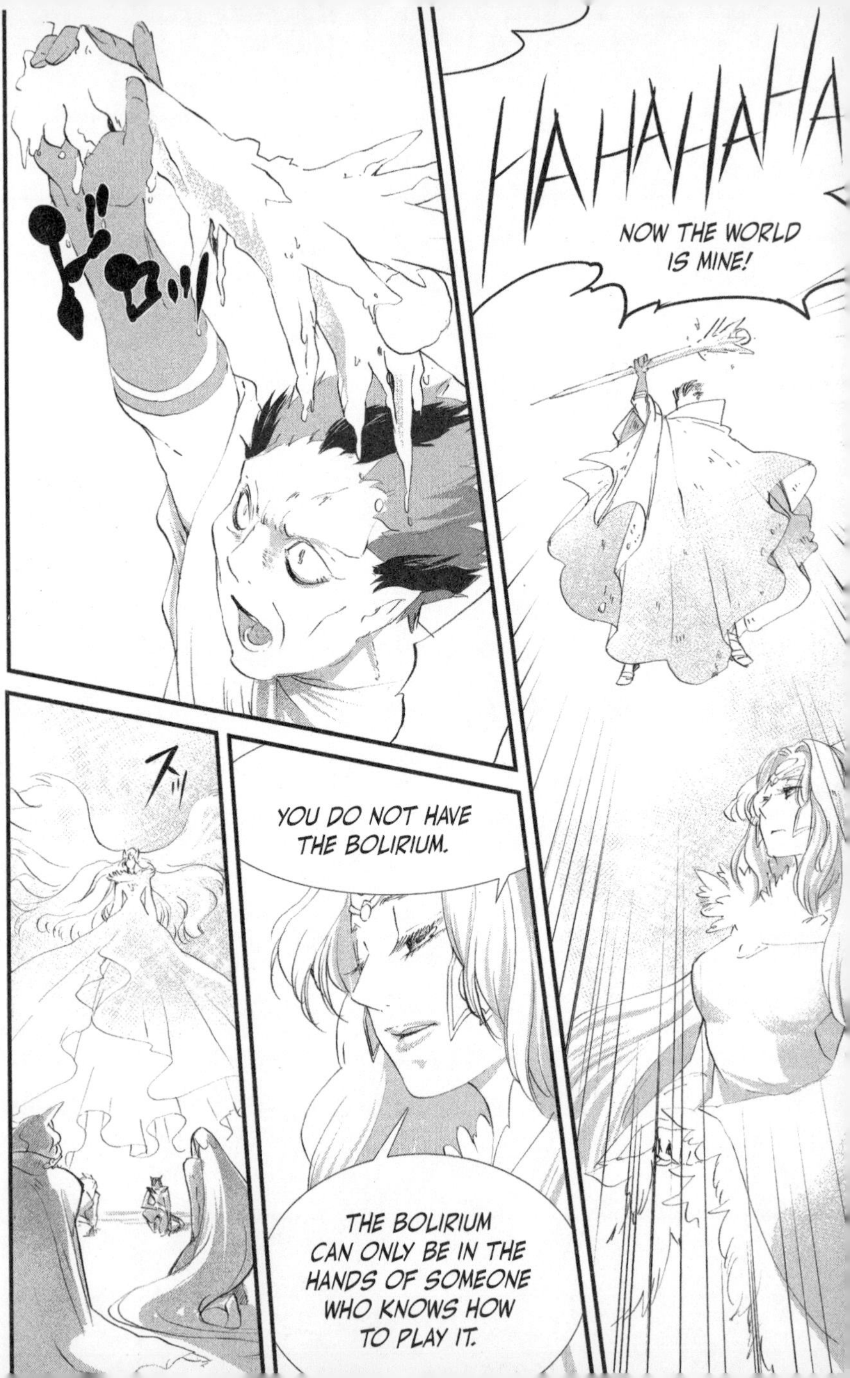
HAHAHAHA
NOW THE WORLD IS MINE!
ドロッ
YOU DO NOT HAVE THE BOLIRIUM.
THE BOLIRIUM CAN ONLY BE IN THE HANDS OF SOMEONE WHO KNOWS HOW TO PLAY IT.
スッ

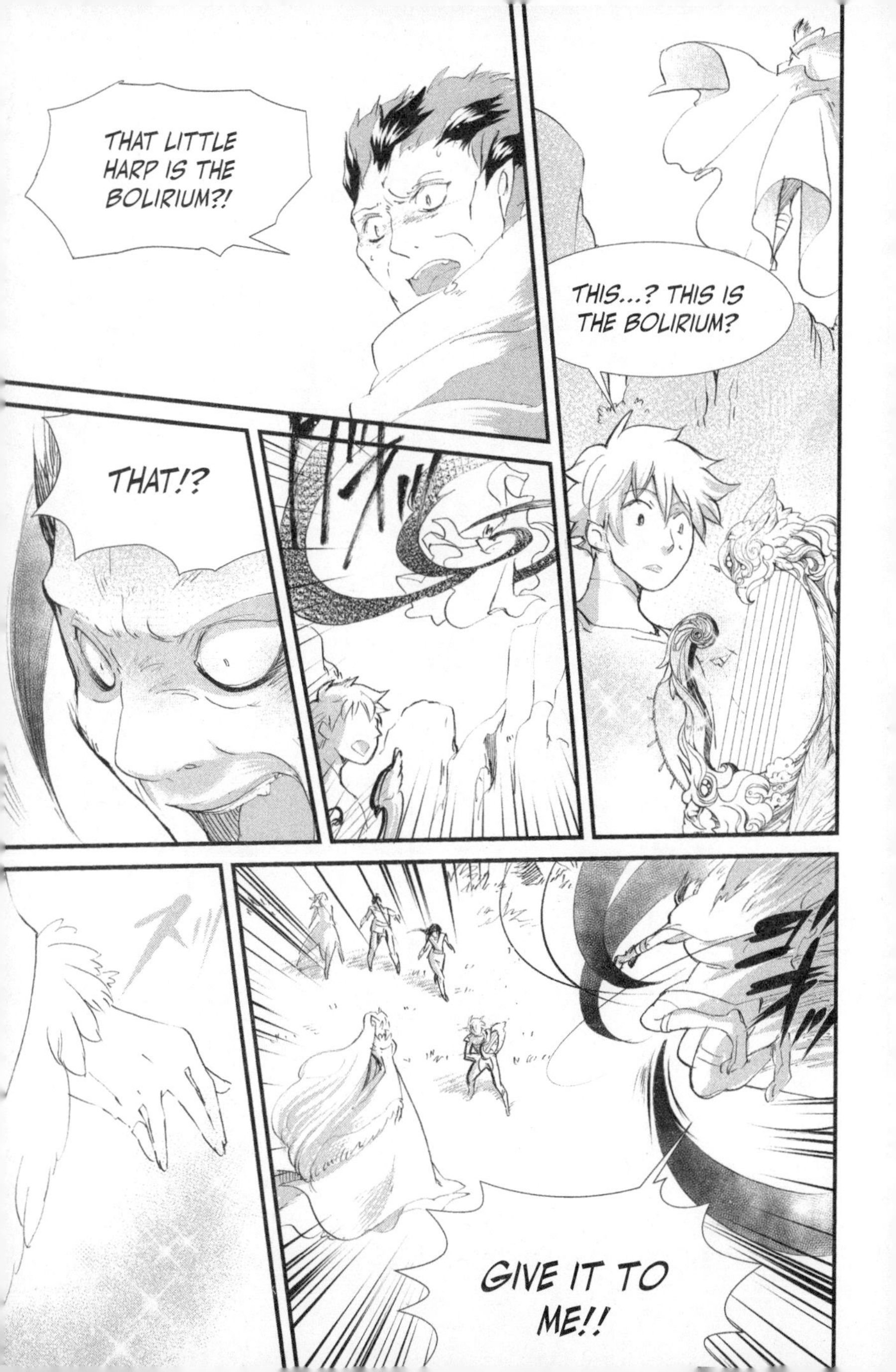
THIS...? THIS IS THE BOLIRIUM?
THAT LITTLE HARP IS THE BOLIRIUM?!
THAT!?
GIVE IT TO ME!!

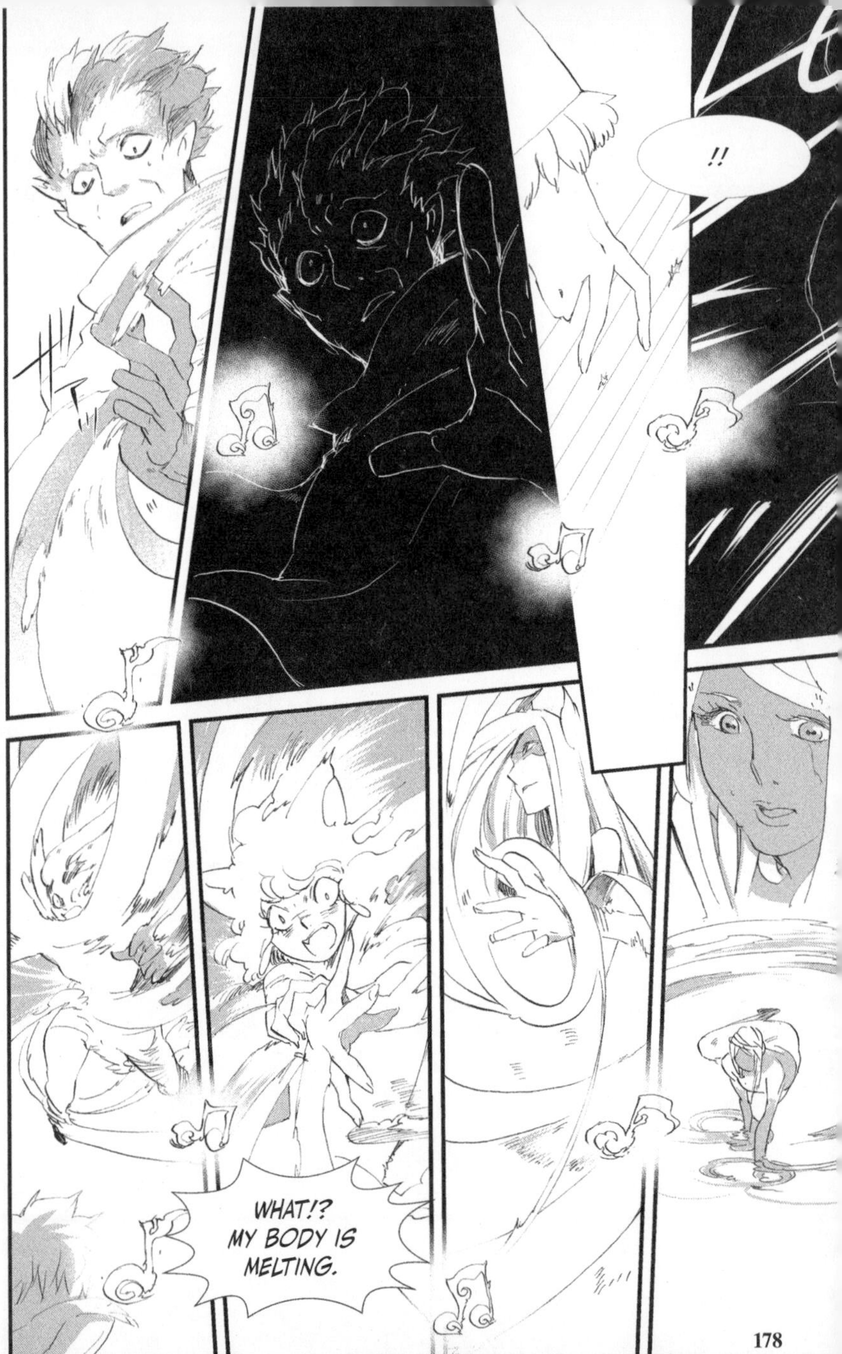
!!
WHAT!? MY BODY IS MELTING.

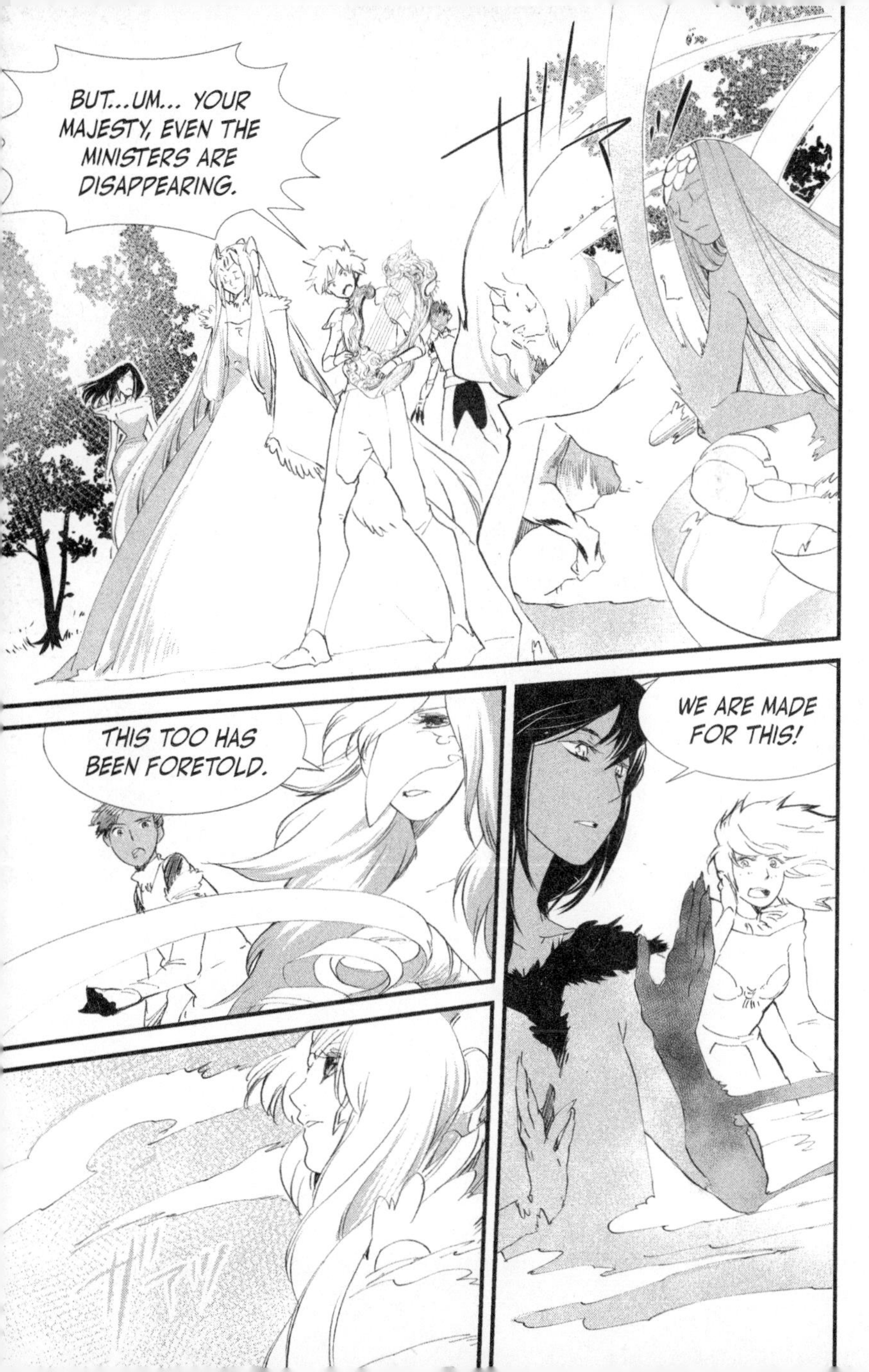
BUT...UM... YOUR MAJESTY, EVEN THE MINISTERS ARE DISAPPEARING.
WE ARE MADE FOR THIS!
THIS TOO HAS BEEN FORETOLD.

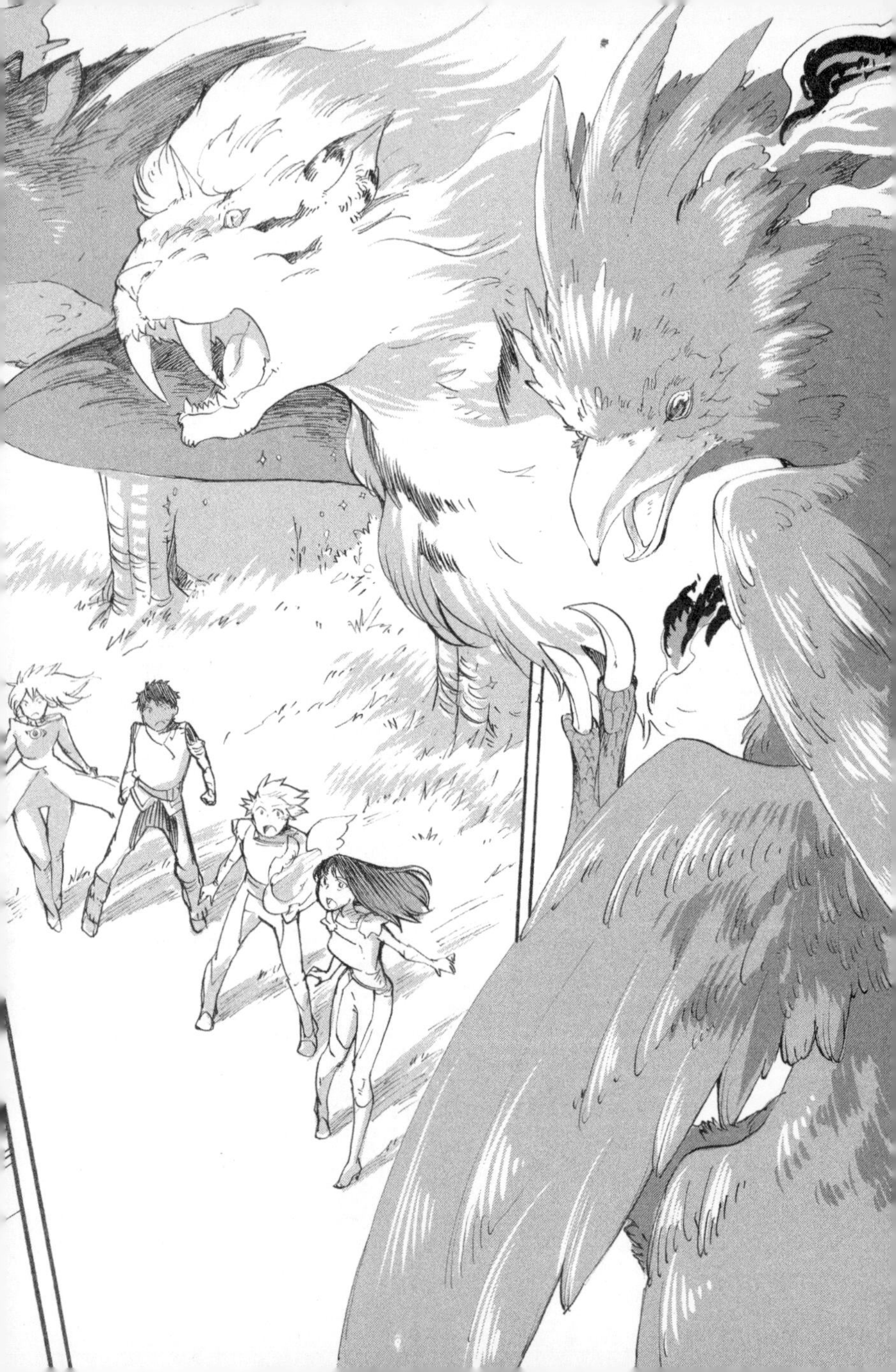

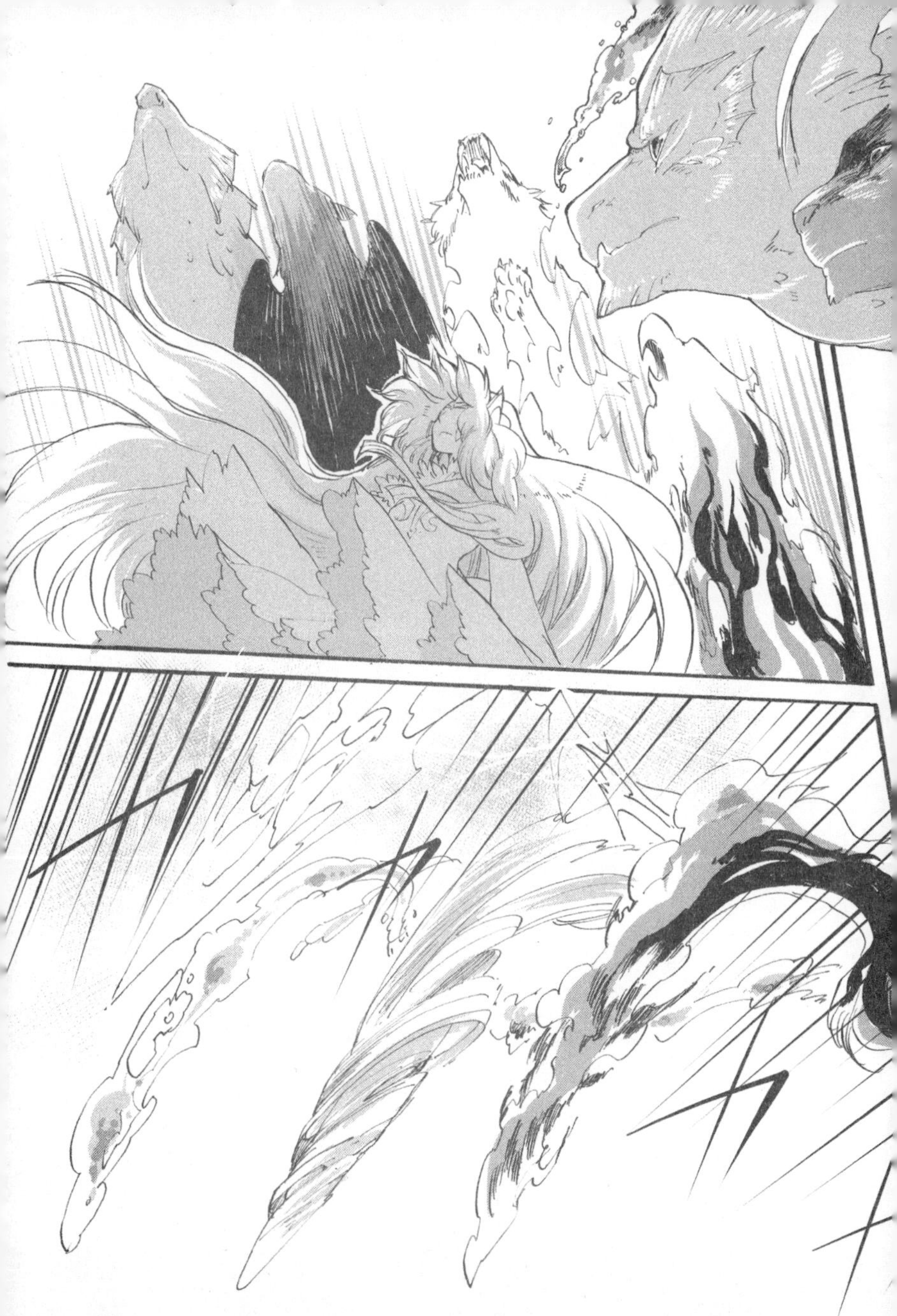

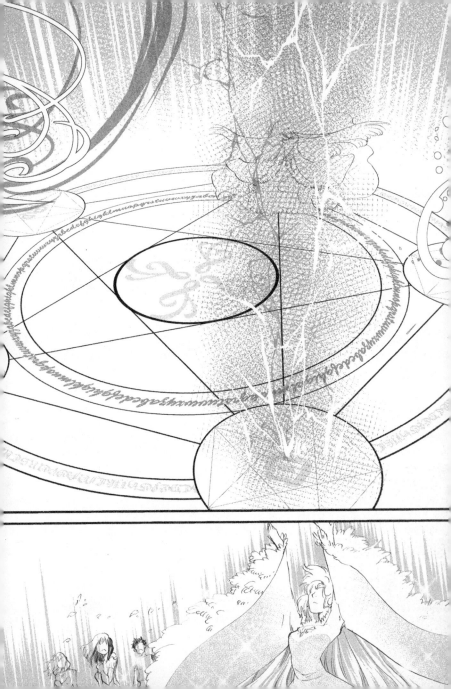

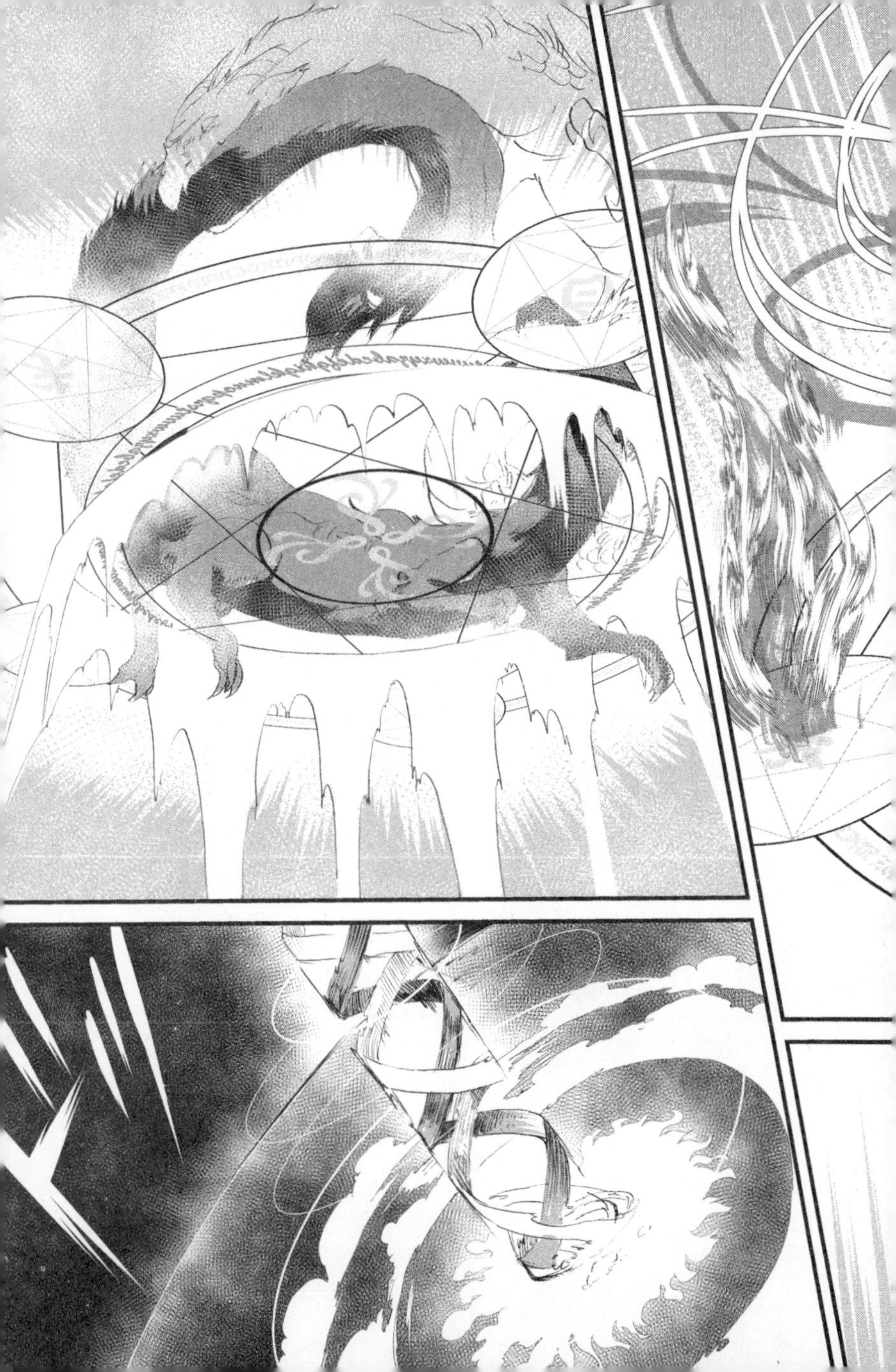

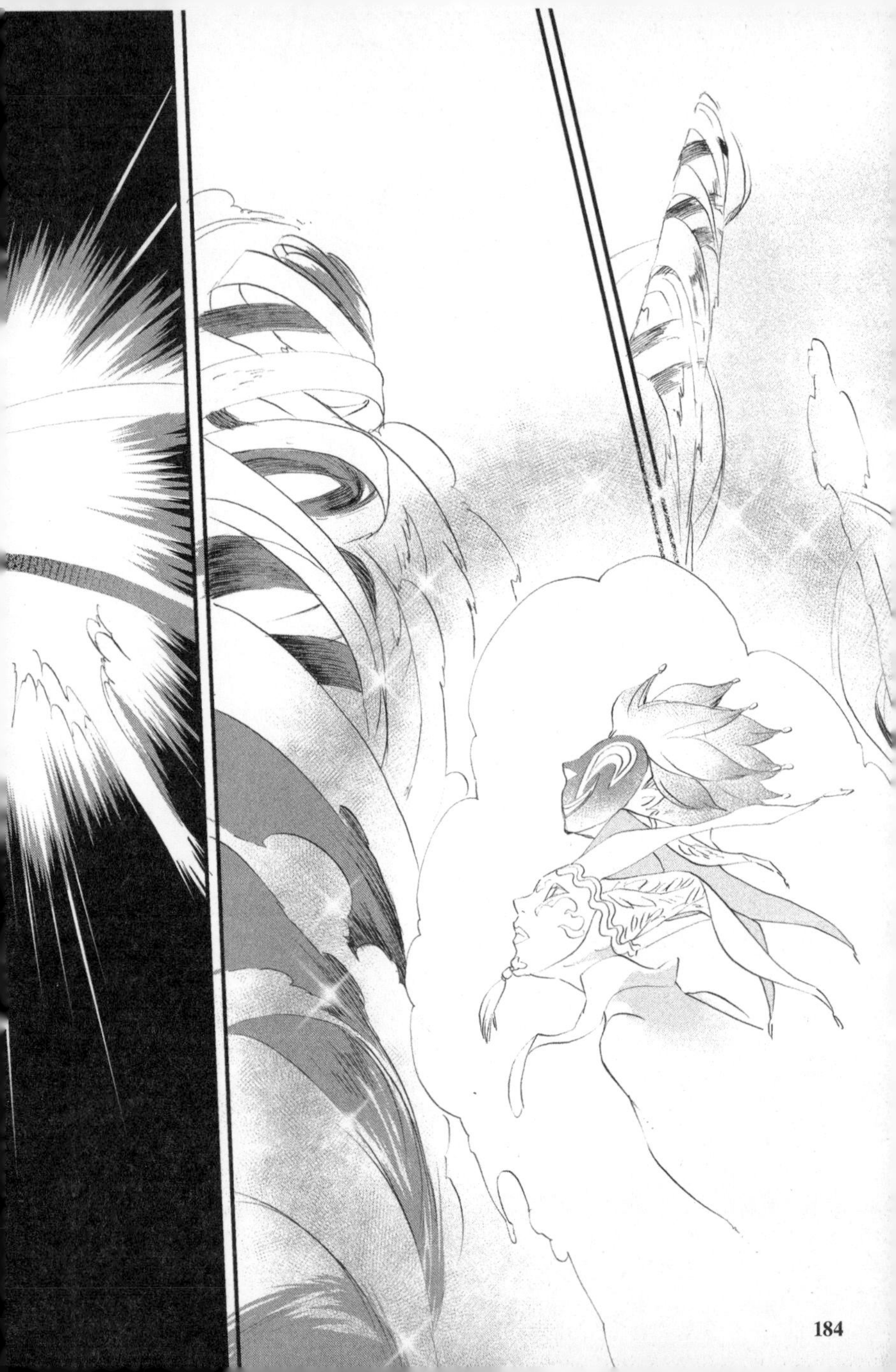

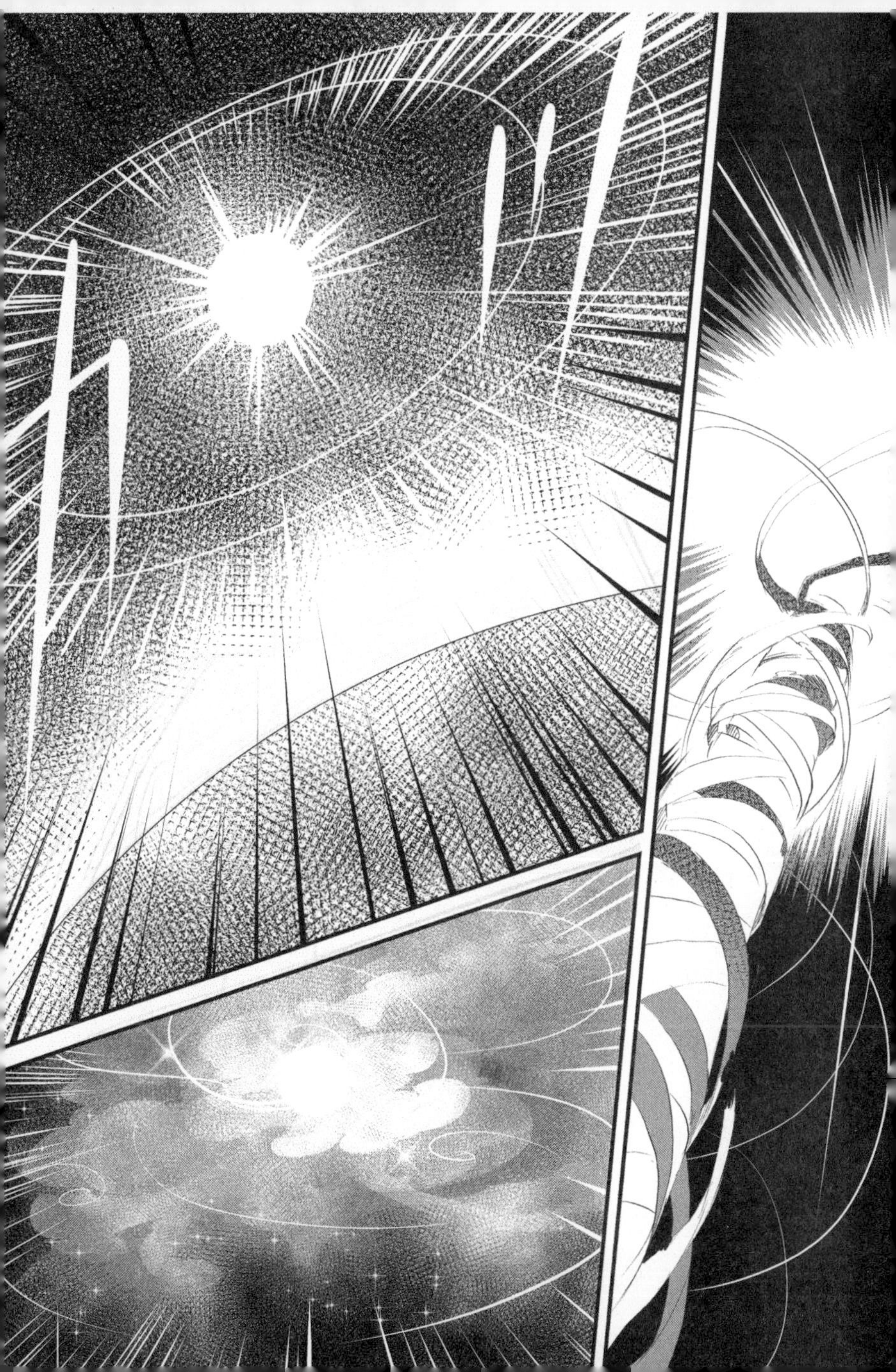

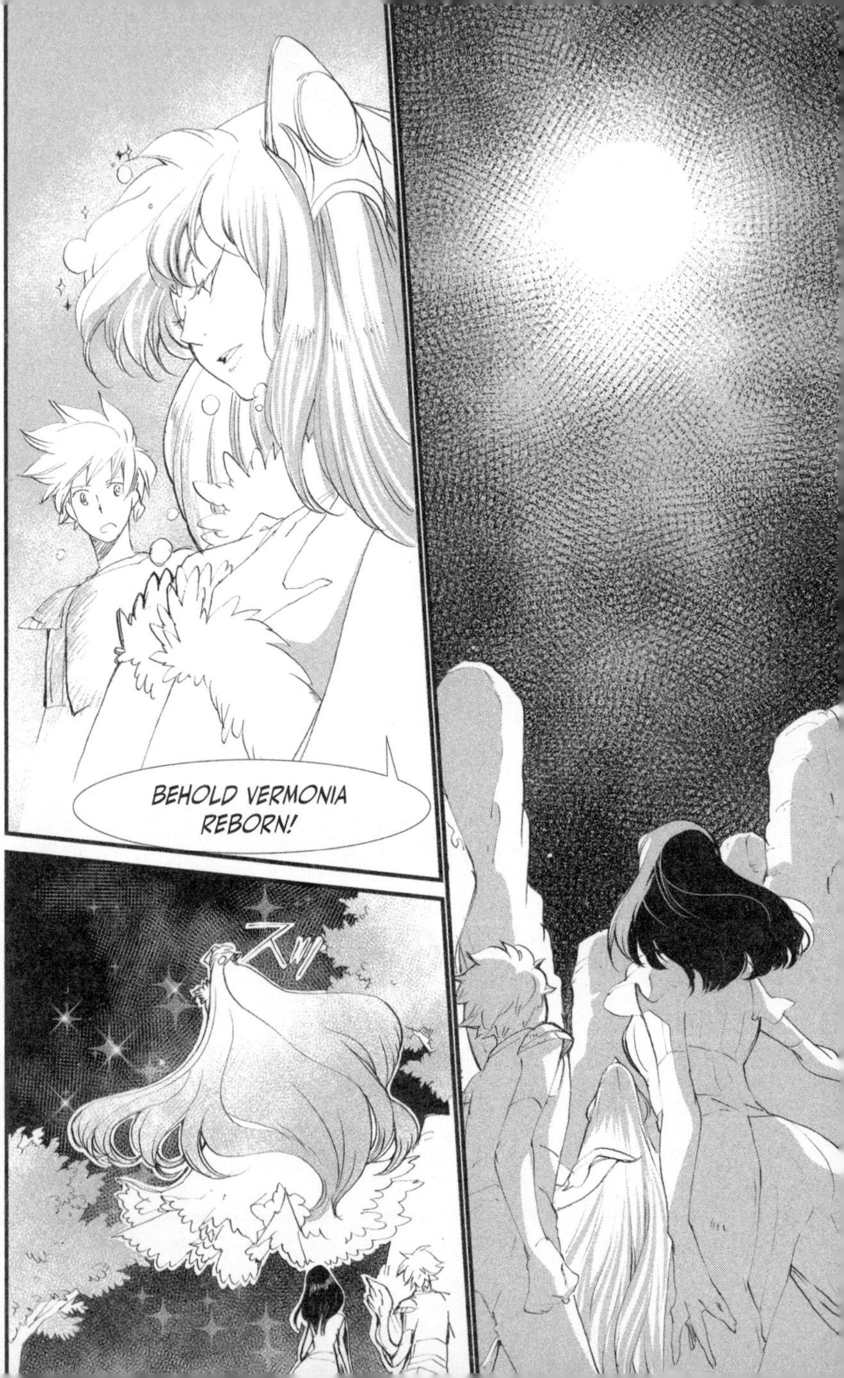
BEHOLD VERMONIA REBORN!
スッ

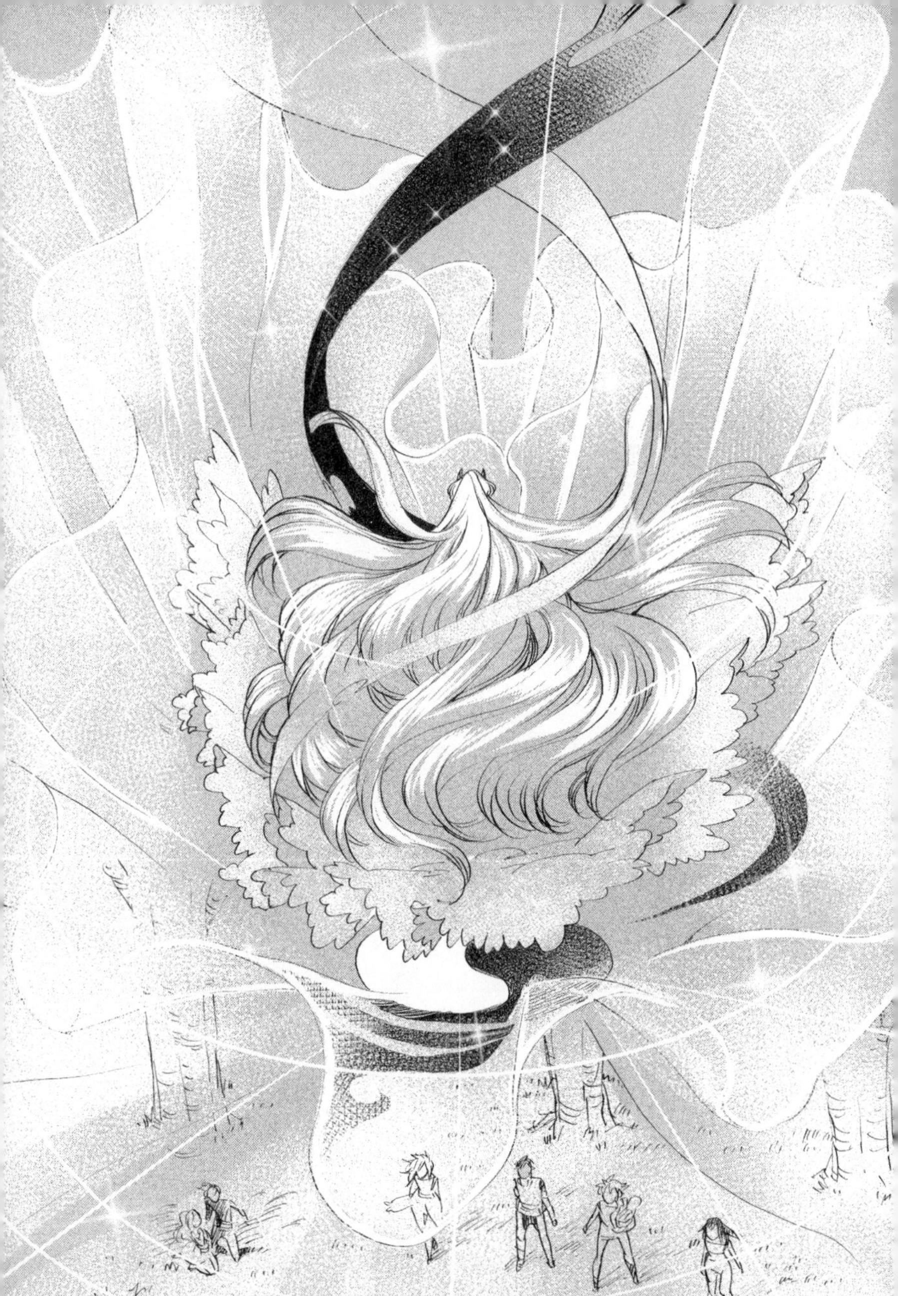

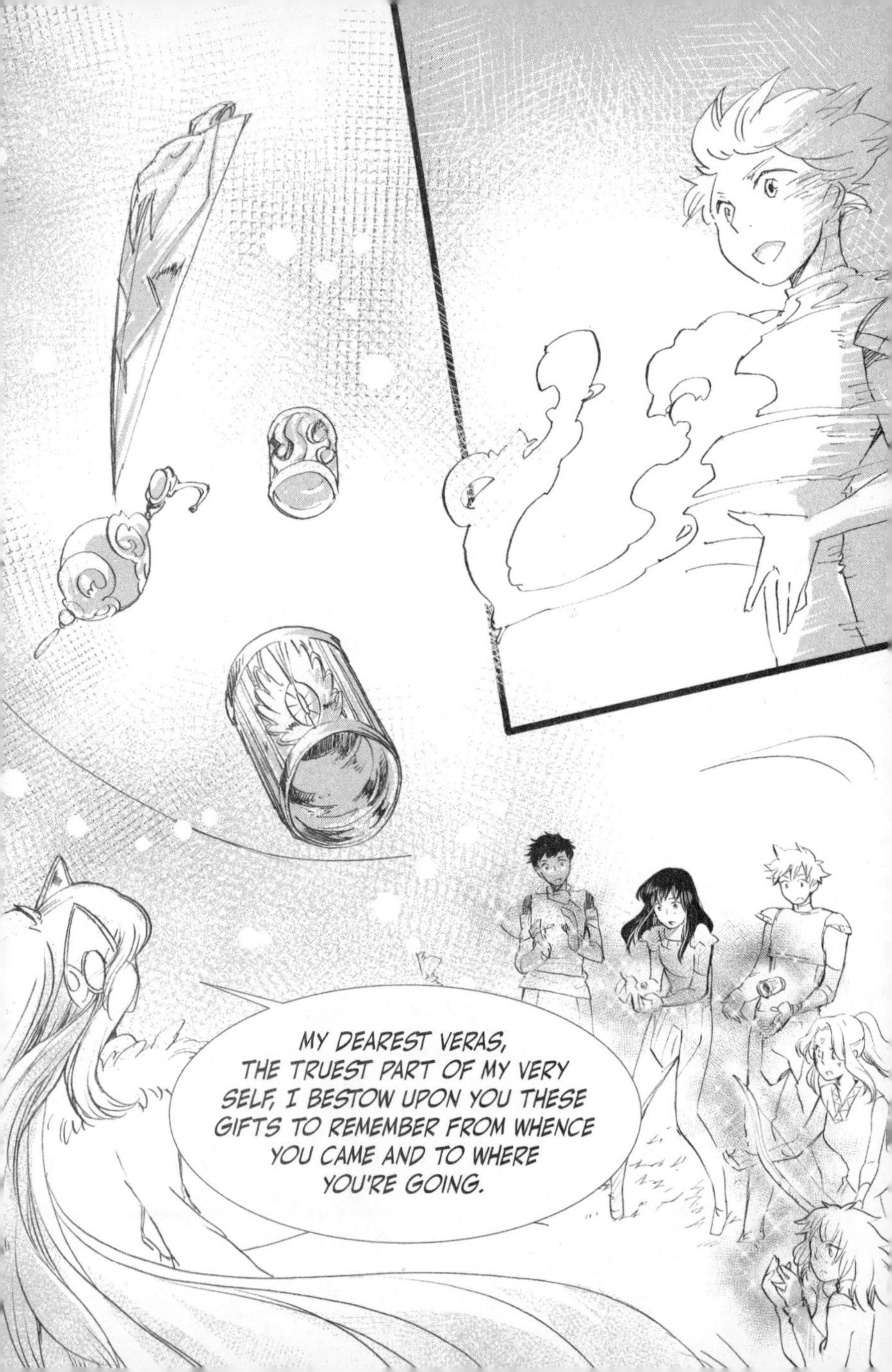
MY DEAREST VERAS, THE TRUEST PART OF MY VERY SELF, I BESTOW UPON YOU THESE GIFTS TO REMEMBER FROM WHENCE YOU CAME AND TO WHERE YOU'RE GOING.

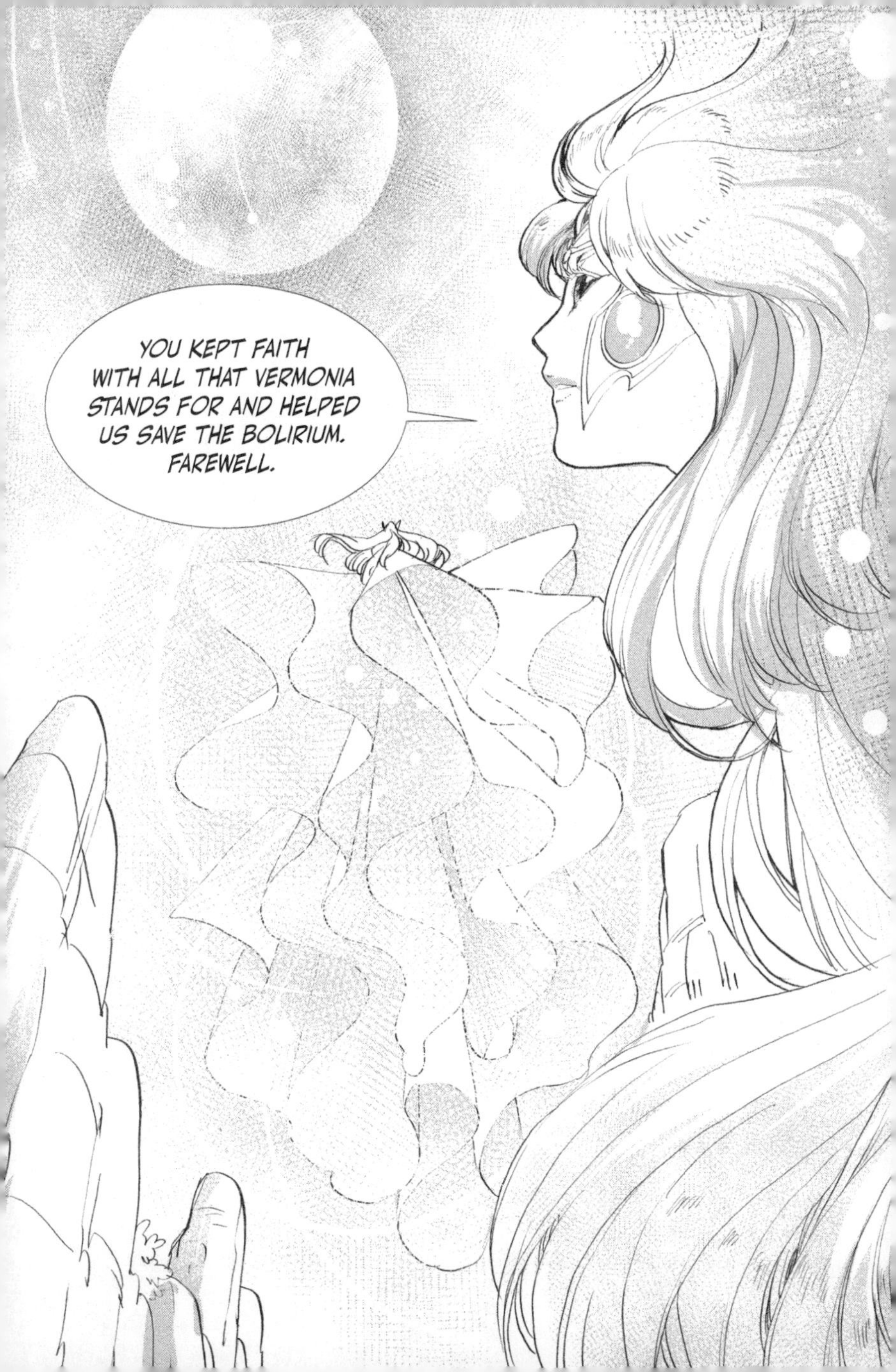
YOU KEPT FAITH WITH ALL THAT VERMONIA STANDS FOR AND HELPED US SAVE THE BOLIRIUM. FAREWELL.

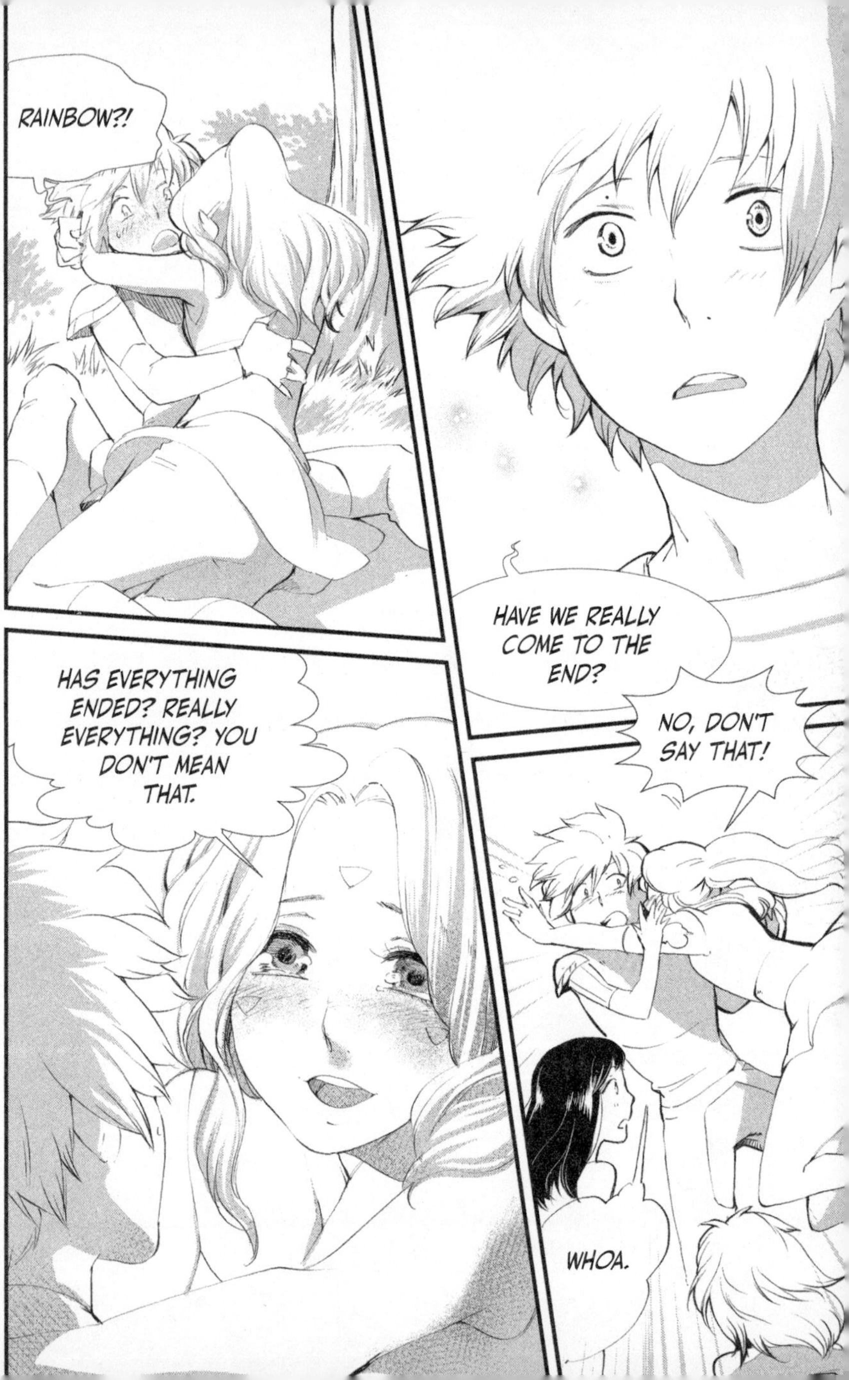
HAVE WE REALLY COME TO THE END?
RAINBOW?!
NO, DON'T SAY THAT!
WHOA.
HAS EVERYTHING ENDED? REALLY EVERYTHING? YOU DON'T MEAN THAT.

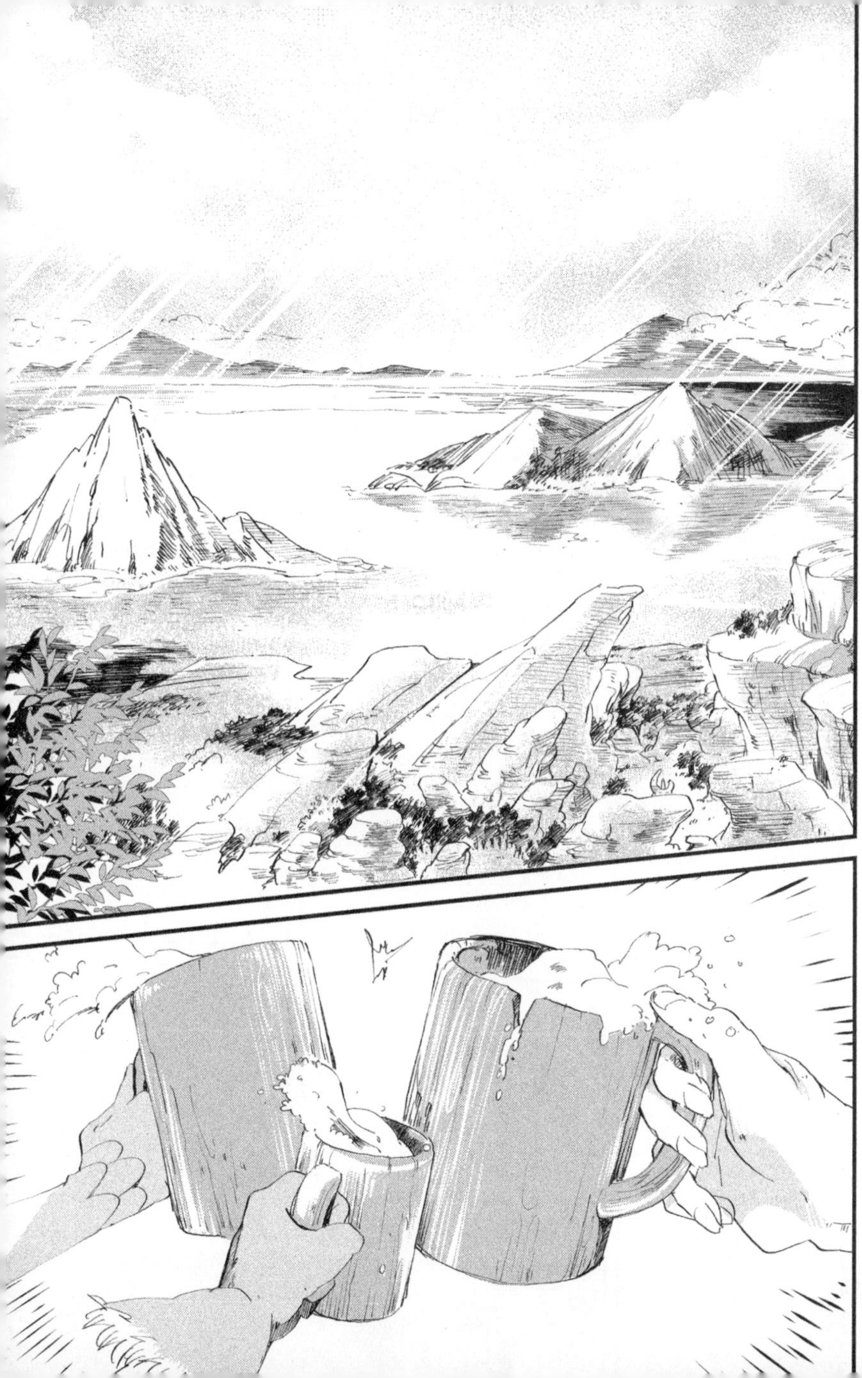

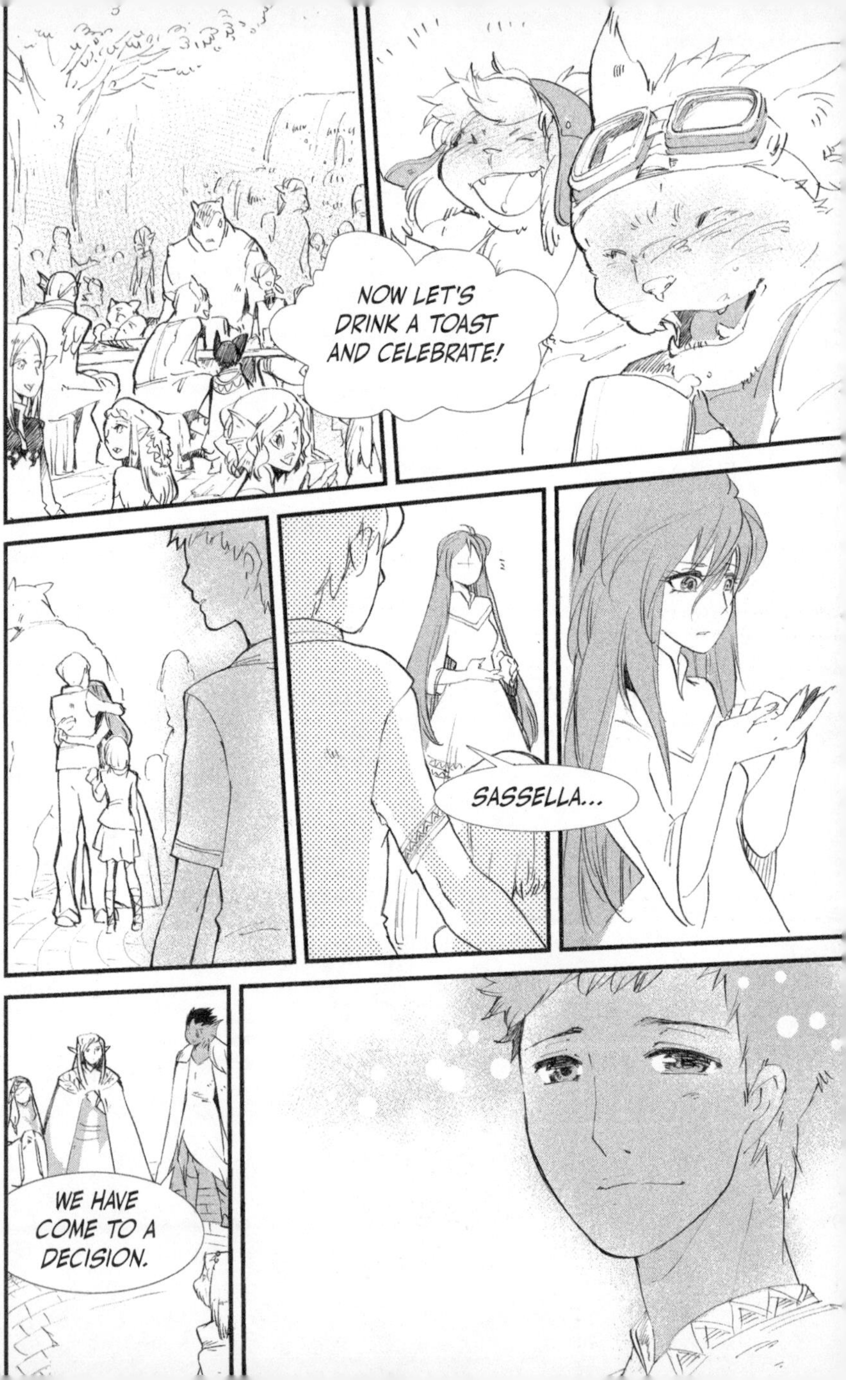
NOW LET'S DRINK A TOAST AND CELEBRATE!
SASSELLA...
WE HAVE COME TO A DECISION.

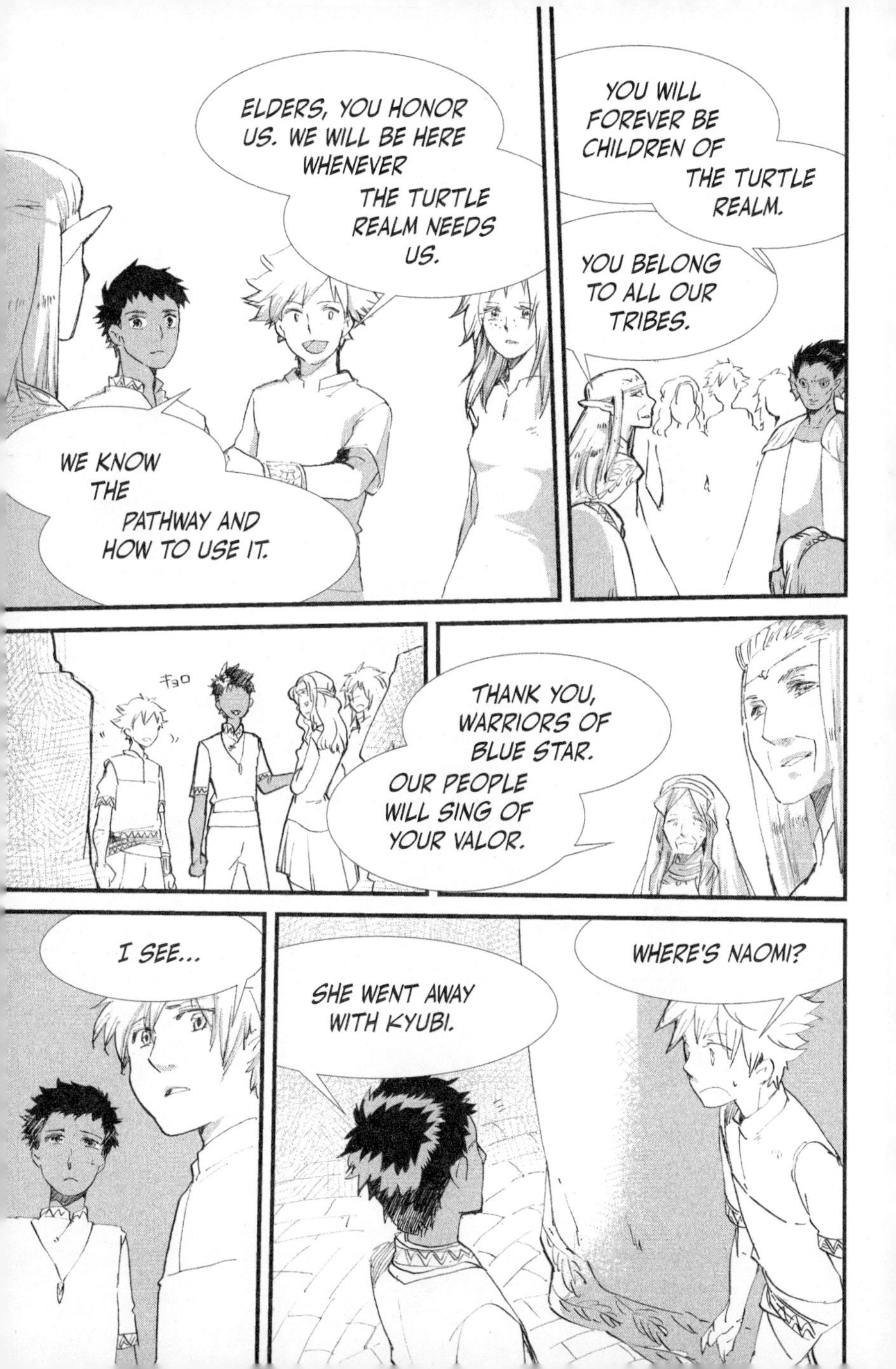
YOU WILL FOREVER BE CHILDREN OF THE TURTLE REALM.
YOU BELONG TO ALL OUR TRIBES.
ELDERS, YOU HONOR US. WE WILL BE HERE WHENEVER THE TURTLE REALM NEEDS US.
WE KNOW THE PATHWAY AND HOW TO USE IT.
THANK YOU, WARRIORS OF BLUE STAR.
OUR PEOPLE WILL SING OF YOUR VALOR.
キョロ
WHERE'S NAOMI?
SHE WENT AWAY WITH KYUBI.
I SEE...

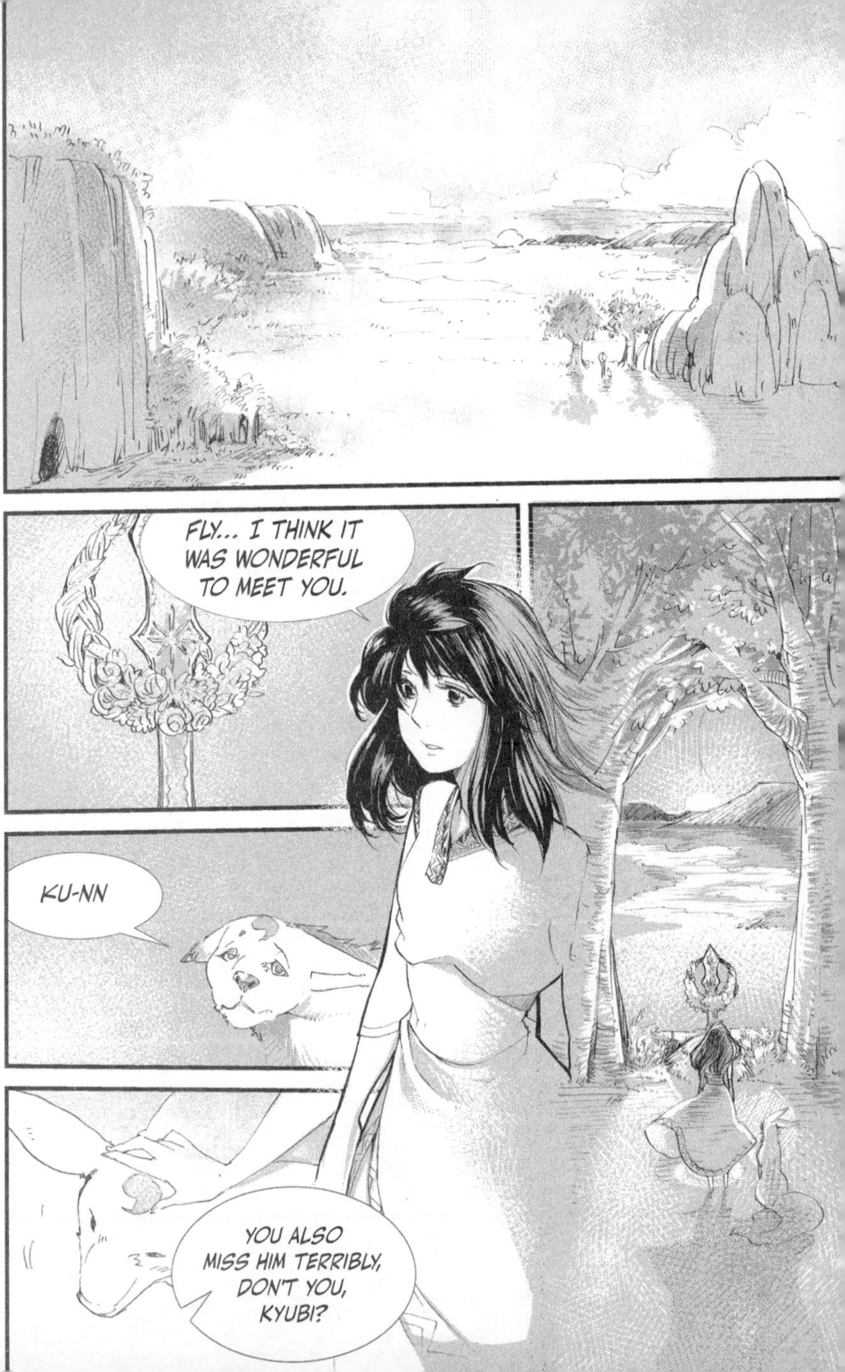
FLY... I THINK IT WAS WONDERFUL TO MEET YOU.
KU-NN
YOU ALSO MISS HIM TERRIBLY, DON'T YOU, KYUBI?

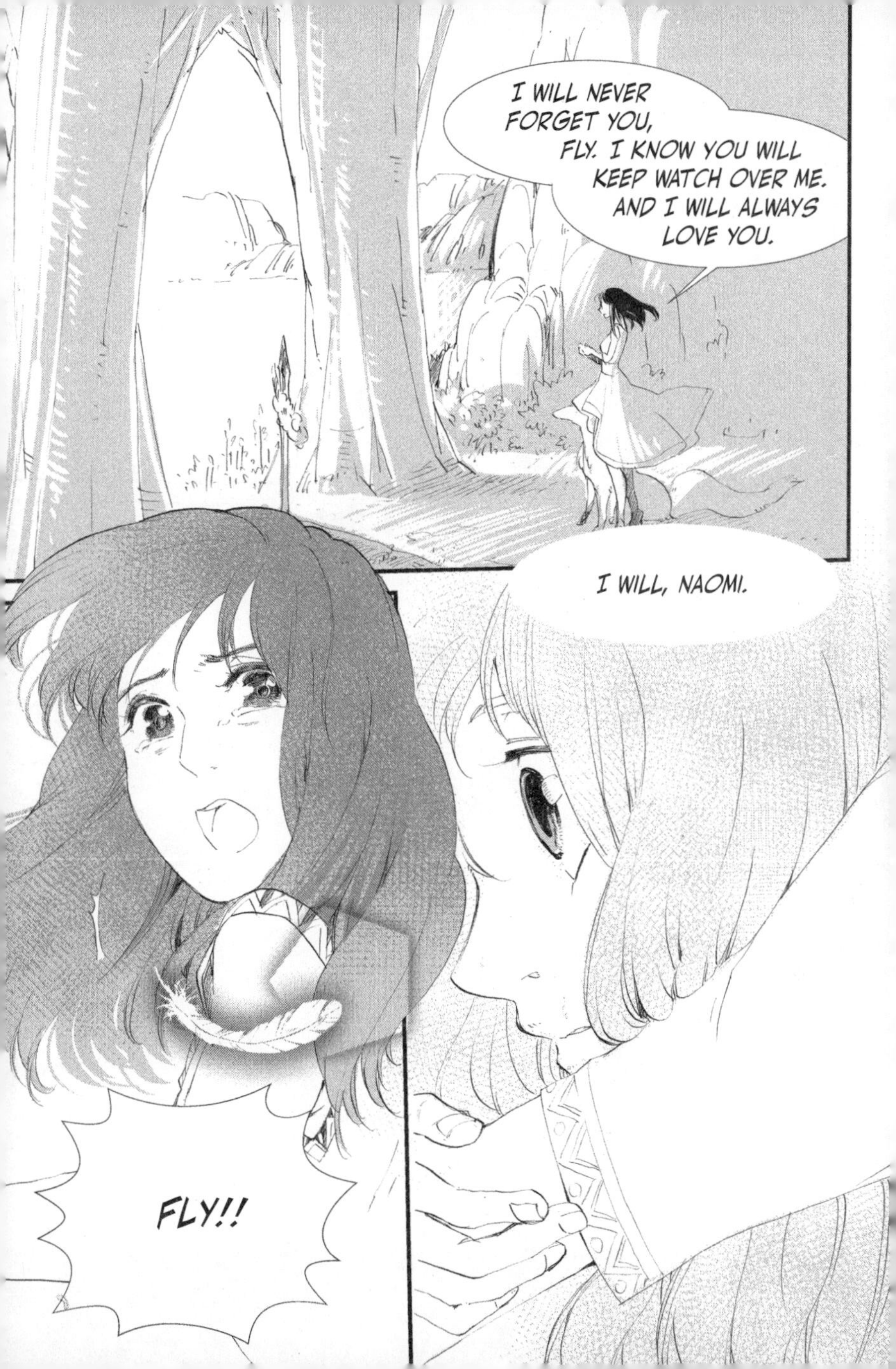
I WILL NEVER FORGET YOU, FLY. I KNOW YOU WILL KEEP WATCH OVER ME. AND I WILL ALWAYS LOVE YOU.
I WILL, NAOMI.
FLY!!

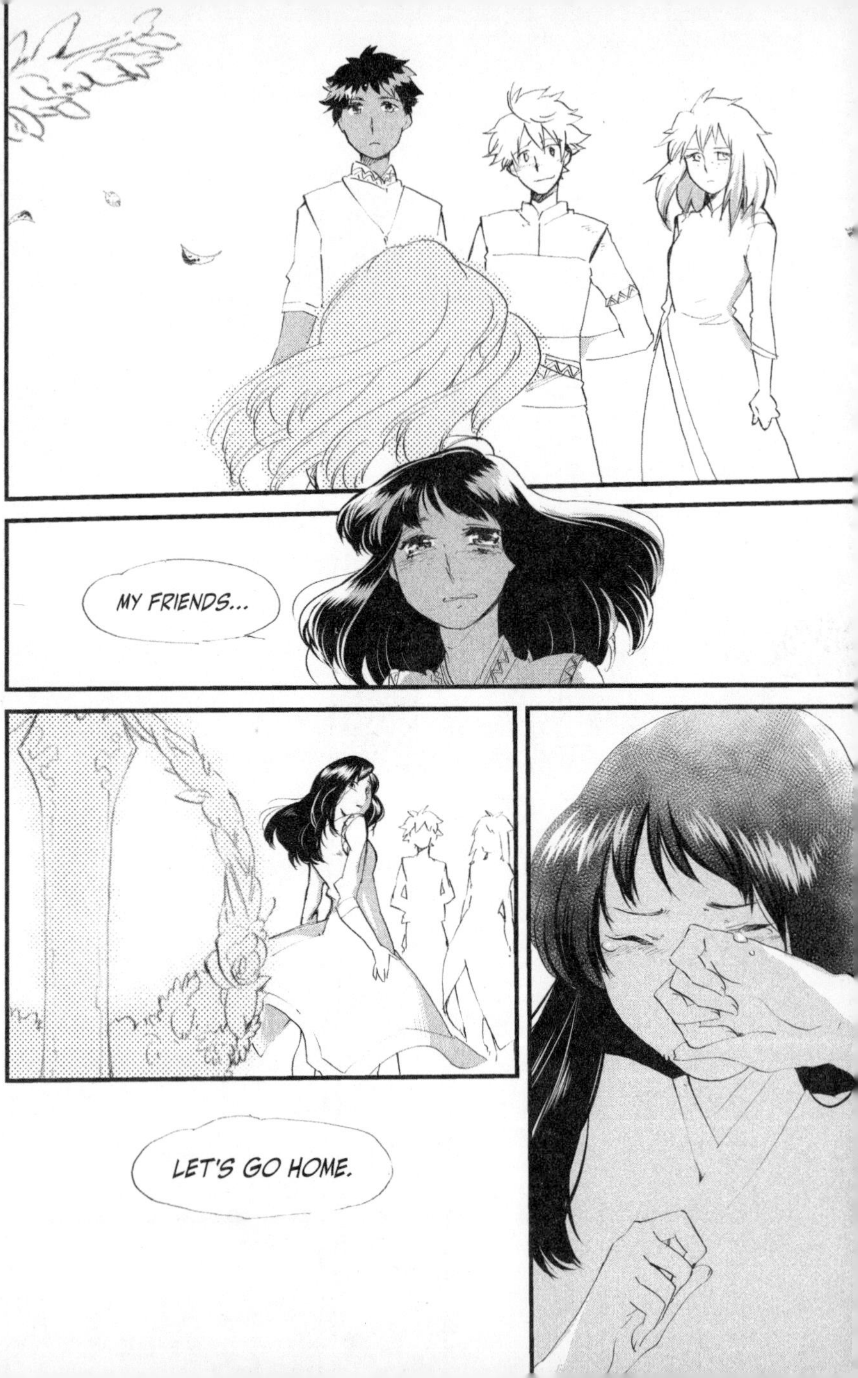
MY FRIENDS...
LET'S GO HOME.

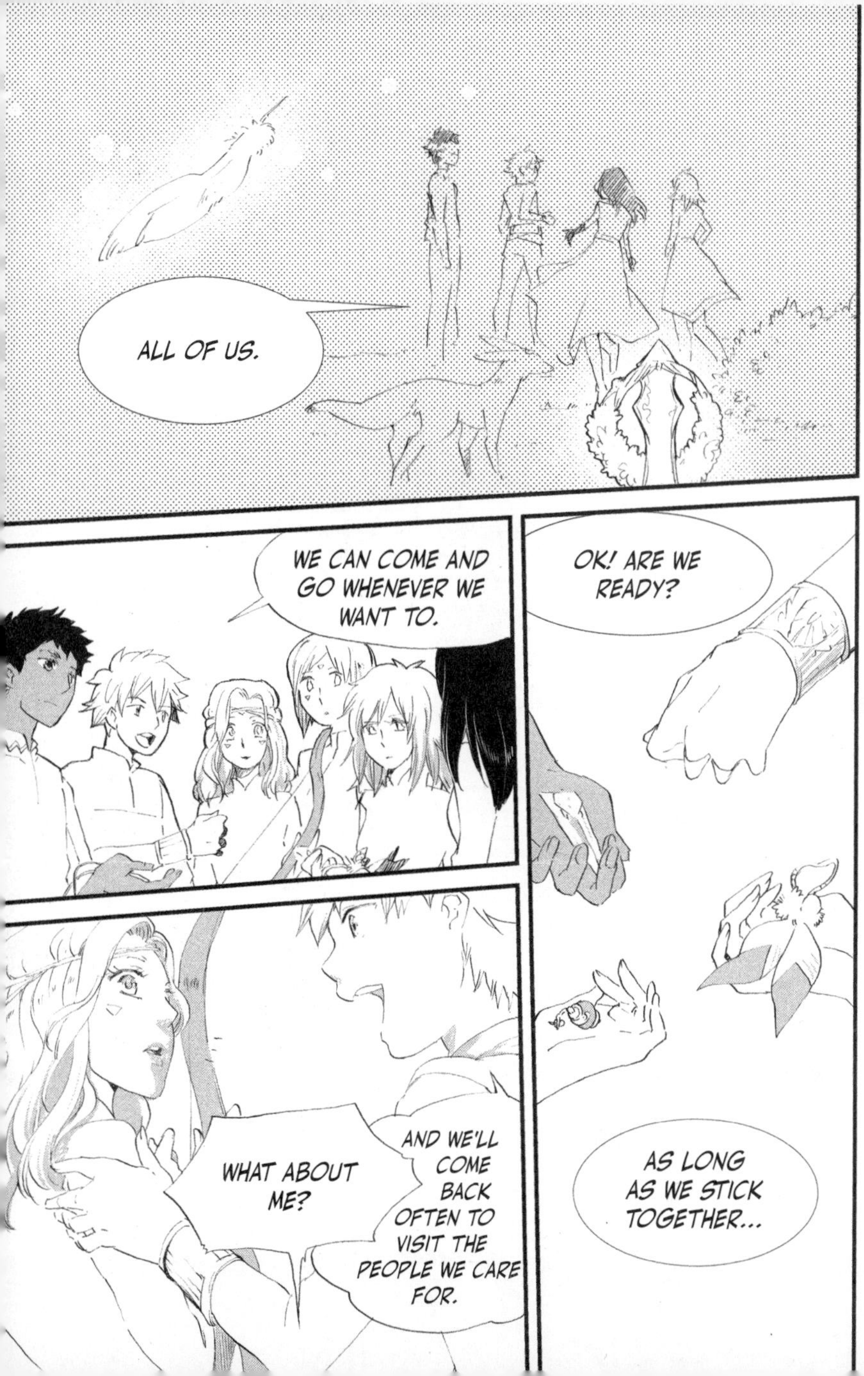
ALL OF US.
OK! ARE WE READY?
AS LONG AS WE STICK TOGETHER...
WE CAN COME AND GO WHENEVER WE WANT TO.
AND WE'LL COME BACK OFTEN TO VISIT THE PEOPLE WE CARE FOR.
WHAT ABOUT ME?

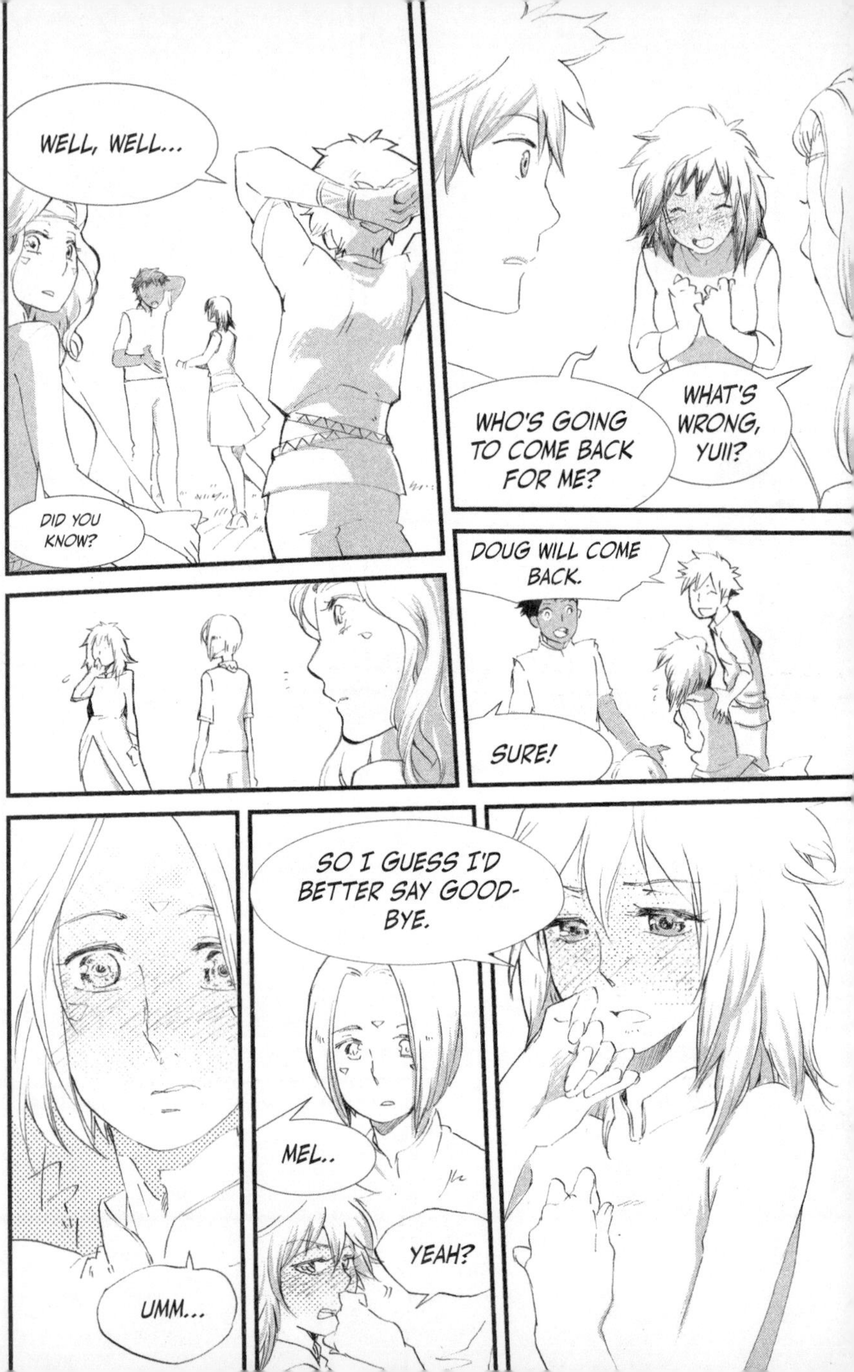
WHAT'S WRONG, YUII?
WHO'S GOING TO COME BACK FOR ME?
WELL, WELL...
DID YOU KNOW?
DOUG WILL COME BACK.
SURE!
SO I GUESS I'D BETTER SAY GOOD-BYE.
MEL..
YEAH?
UMM...

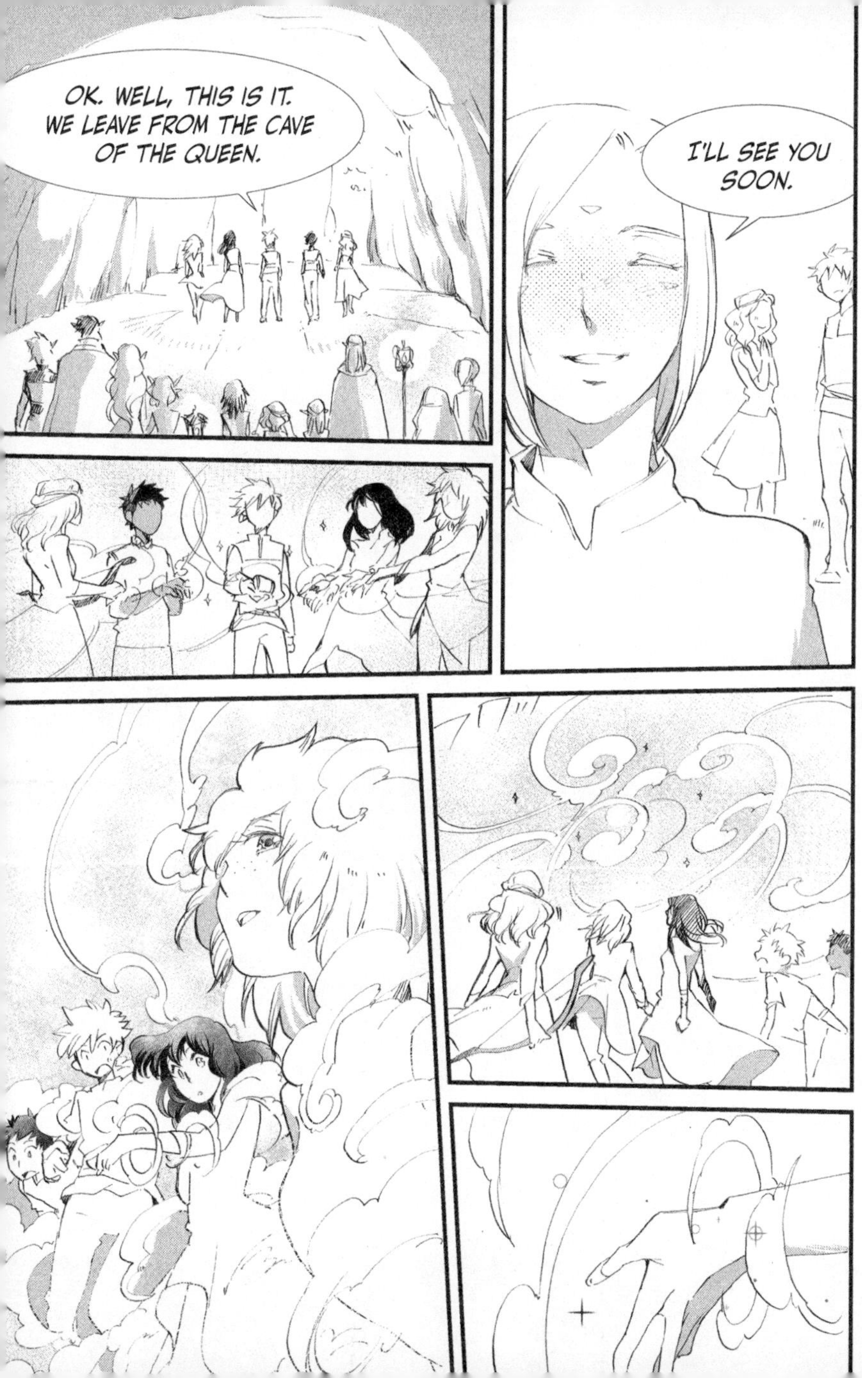
I'LL SEE YOU SOON.
OK. WELL, THIS IS IT. WE LEAVE FROM THE CAVE OF THE QUEEN.

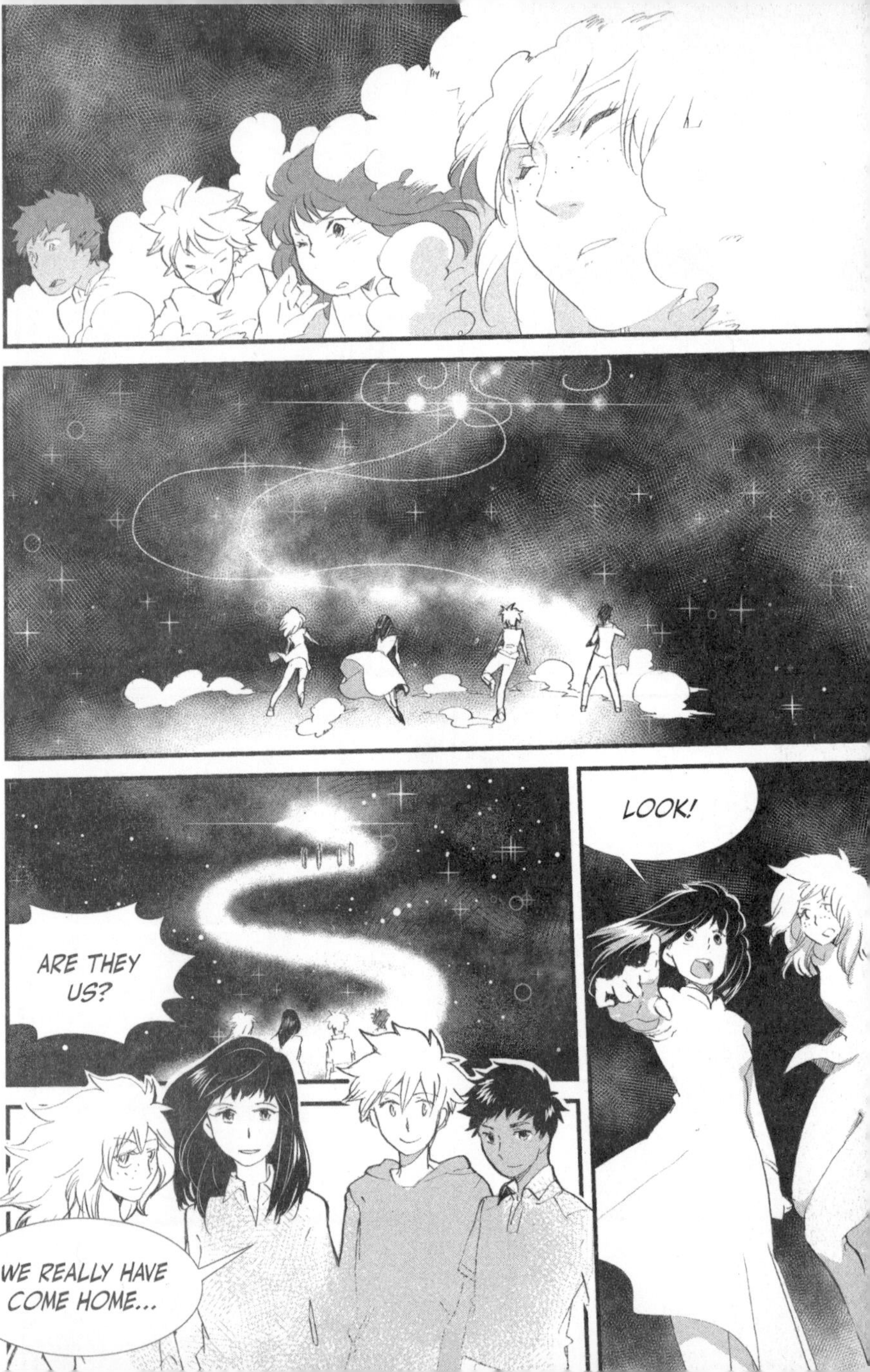
LOOK!
ARE THEY US?
WE REALLY HAVE COME HOME...

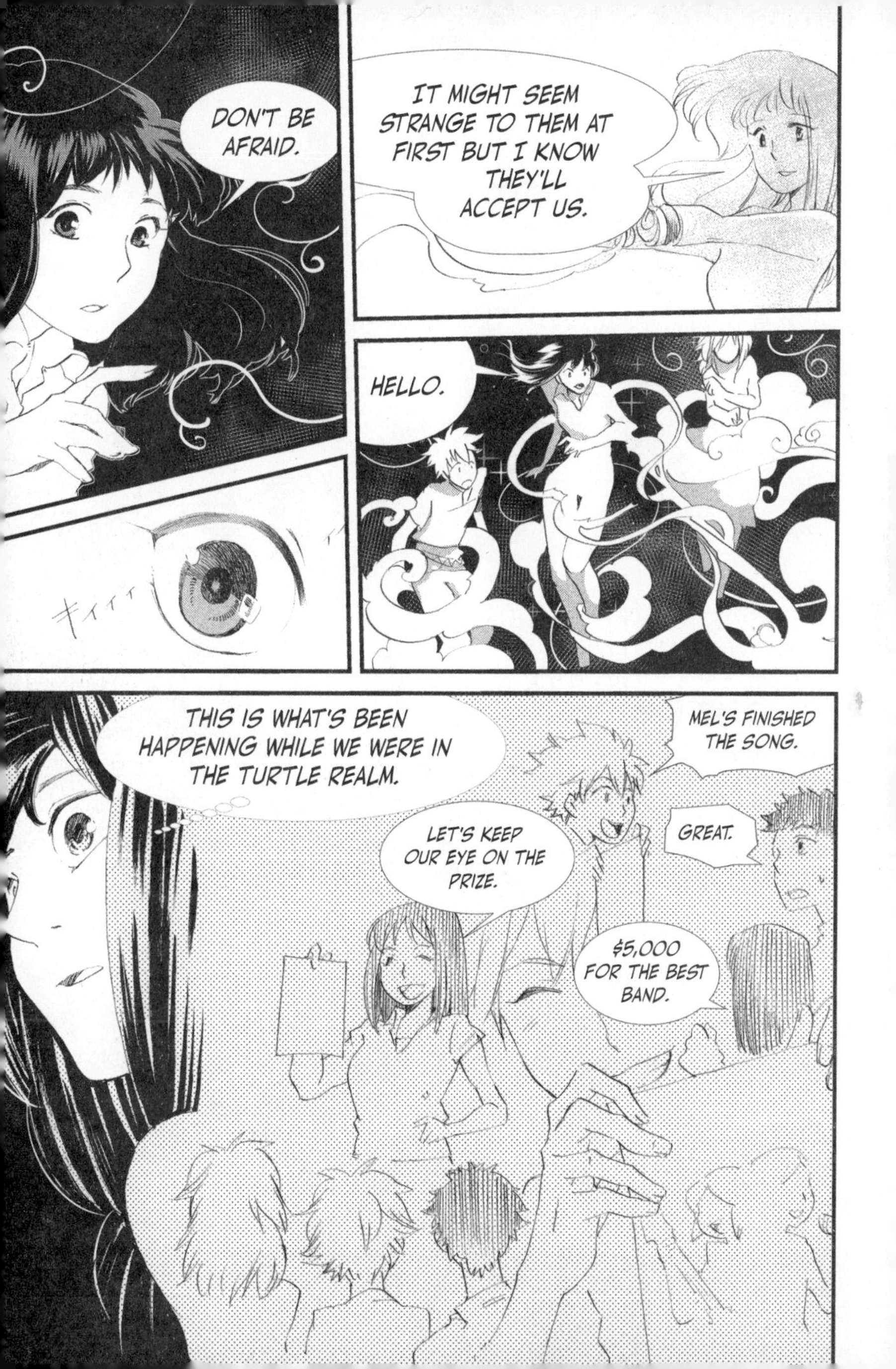

IT MIGHT SEEM STRANGE TO THEM AT FIRST BUT I KNOW THEY'LL ACCEPT US.
DON'T BE AFRAID.
HELLO.
キイイ
MEL'S FINISHED THE SONG.
THIS IS WHAT'S BEEN HAPPENING WHILE WE WERE IN THE TURTLE REALM.
GREAT.
LET'S KEEP OUR EYE ON THE PRIZE.
$5,000 FOR THE BEST BAND.

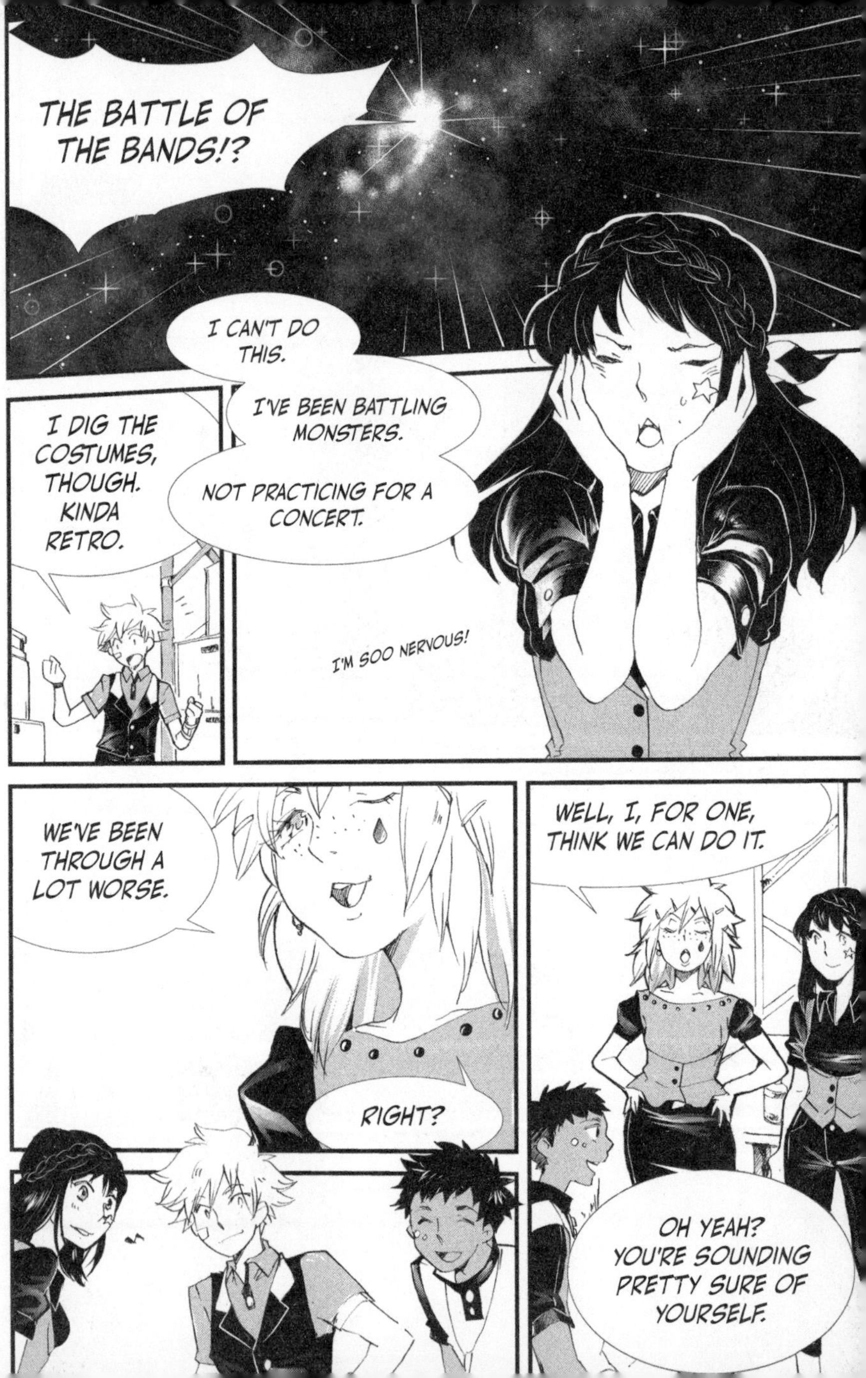
THE BATTLE OF THE BANDS!?
I CAN'T DO THIS.
I'VE BEEN BATTLING MONSTERS.
NOT PRACTICING FOR A CONCERT.
I'M SOO NERVOUS!
I DIG THE COSTUMES, THOUGH. KINDA RETRO.
WELL, I, FOR ONE, THINK WE CAN DO IT.
OH YEAH? YOU'RE SOUNDING PRETTY SURE OF YOURSELF.
WE'VE BEEN THROUGH A LOT WORSE.
RIGHT?

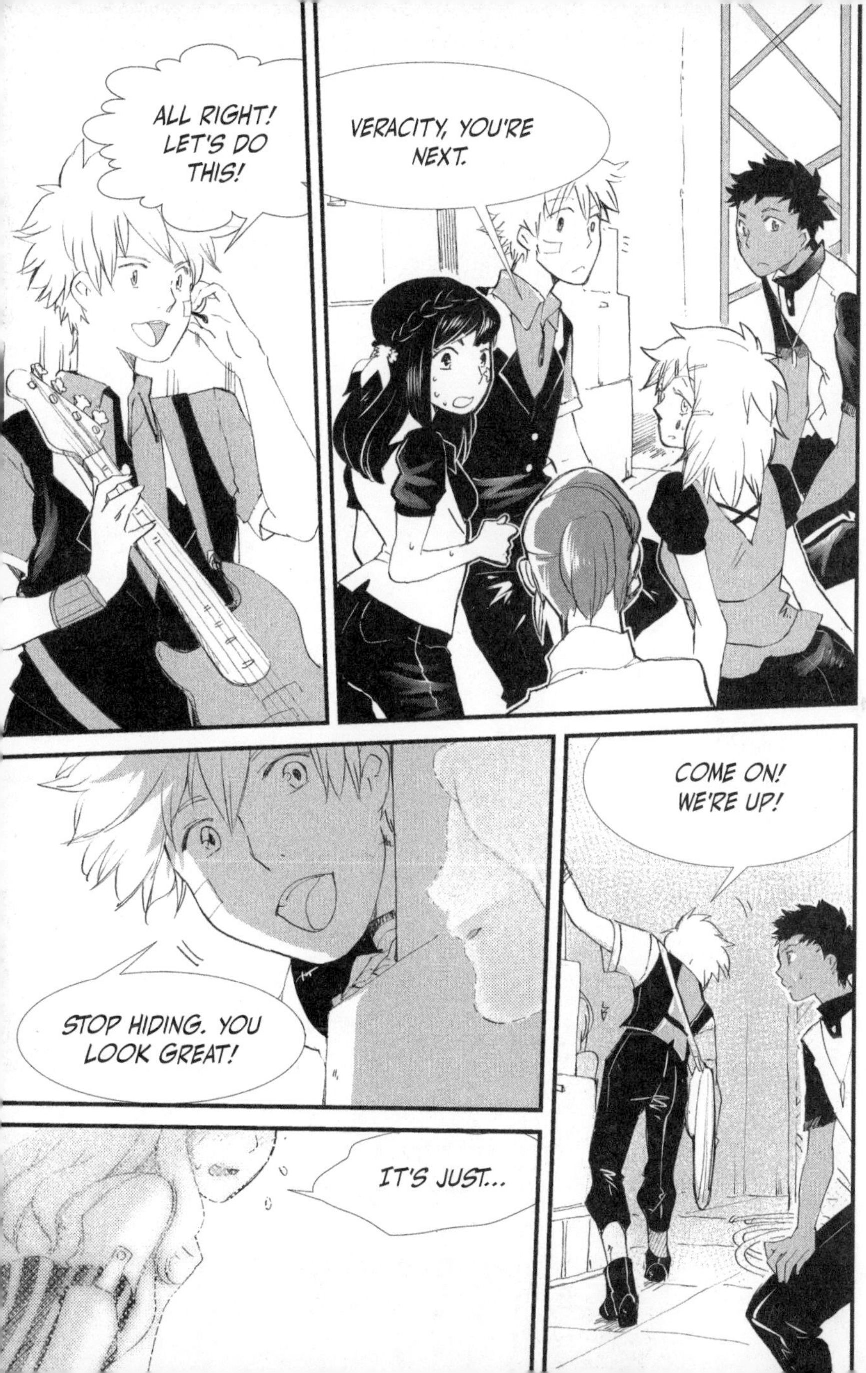
VERACITY, YOU'RE NEXT.
ALL RIGHT! LET'S DO THIS!
COME ON! WE'RE UP!
STOP HIDING. YOU LOOK GREAT!
IT'S JUST...

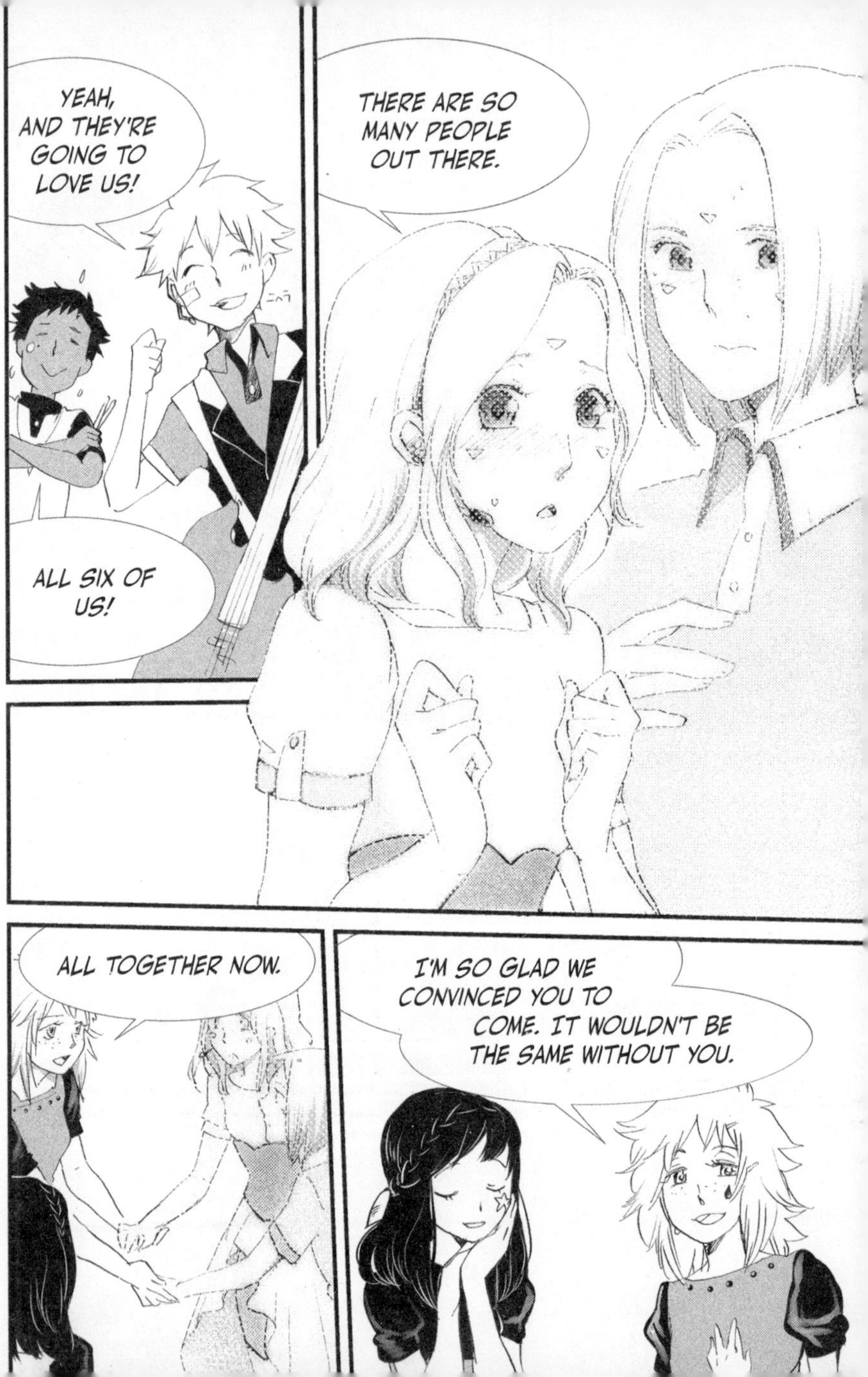
THERE ARE SO MANY PEOPLE OUT THERE.
YEAH, AND THEY'RE GOING TO LOVE US!
ALL SIX OF US!
I'M SO GLAD WE CONVINCED YOU TO COME. IT WOULDN'T BE THE SAME WITHOUT YOU.
ALL TOGETHER NOW.

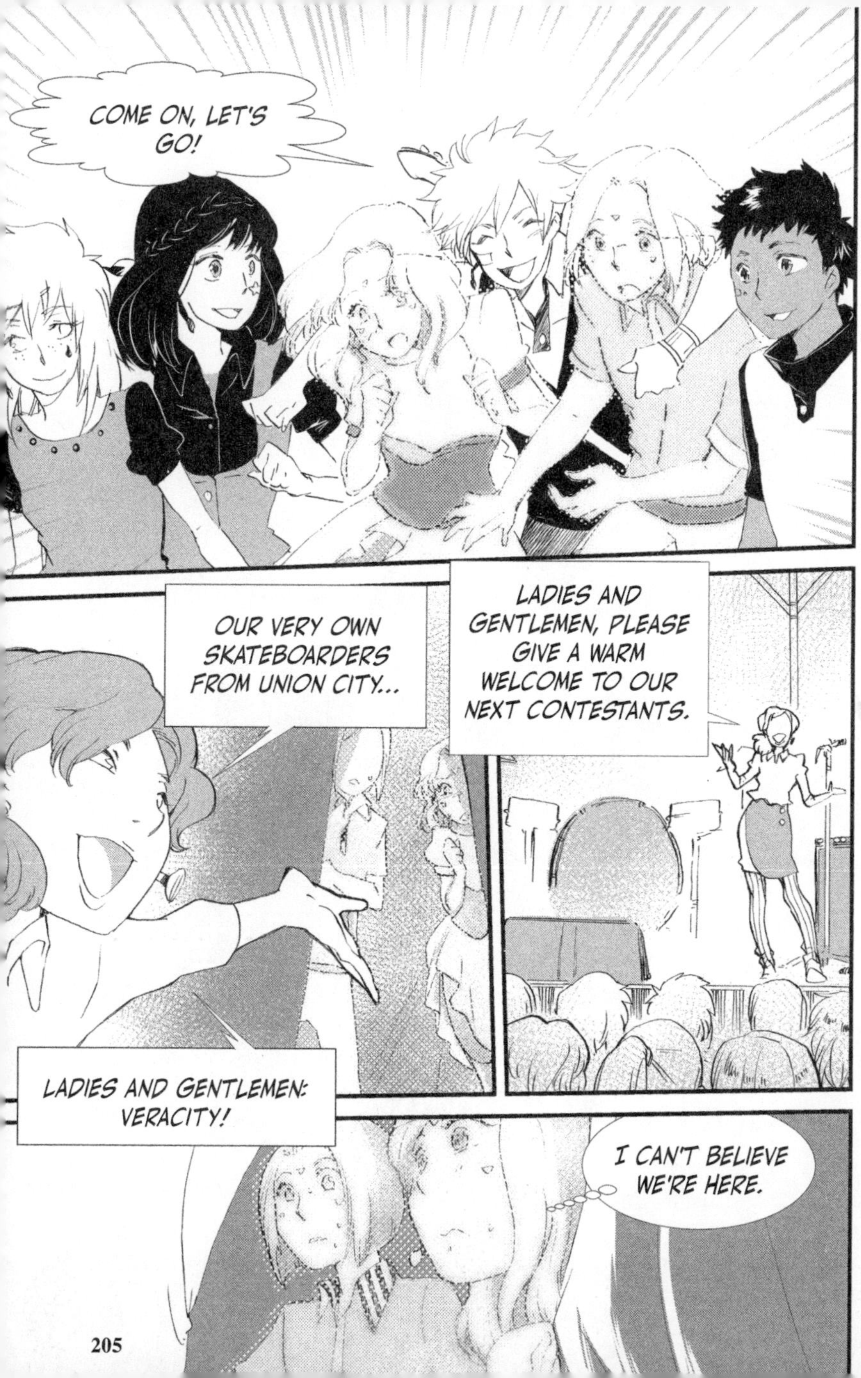

COME ON, LET'S GO!
LADIES AND GENTLEMEN, PLEASE GIVE A WARM WELCOME TO OUR NEXT CONTESTANTS.
OUR VERY OWN SKATEBOARDERS FROM UNION CITY...
LADIES AND GENTLEMEN: VERACITY!
I CAN'T BELIEVE WE'RE HERE.

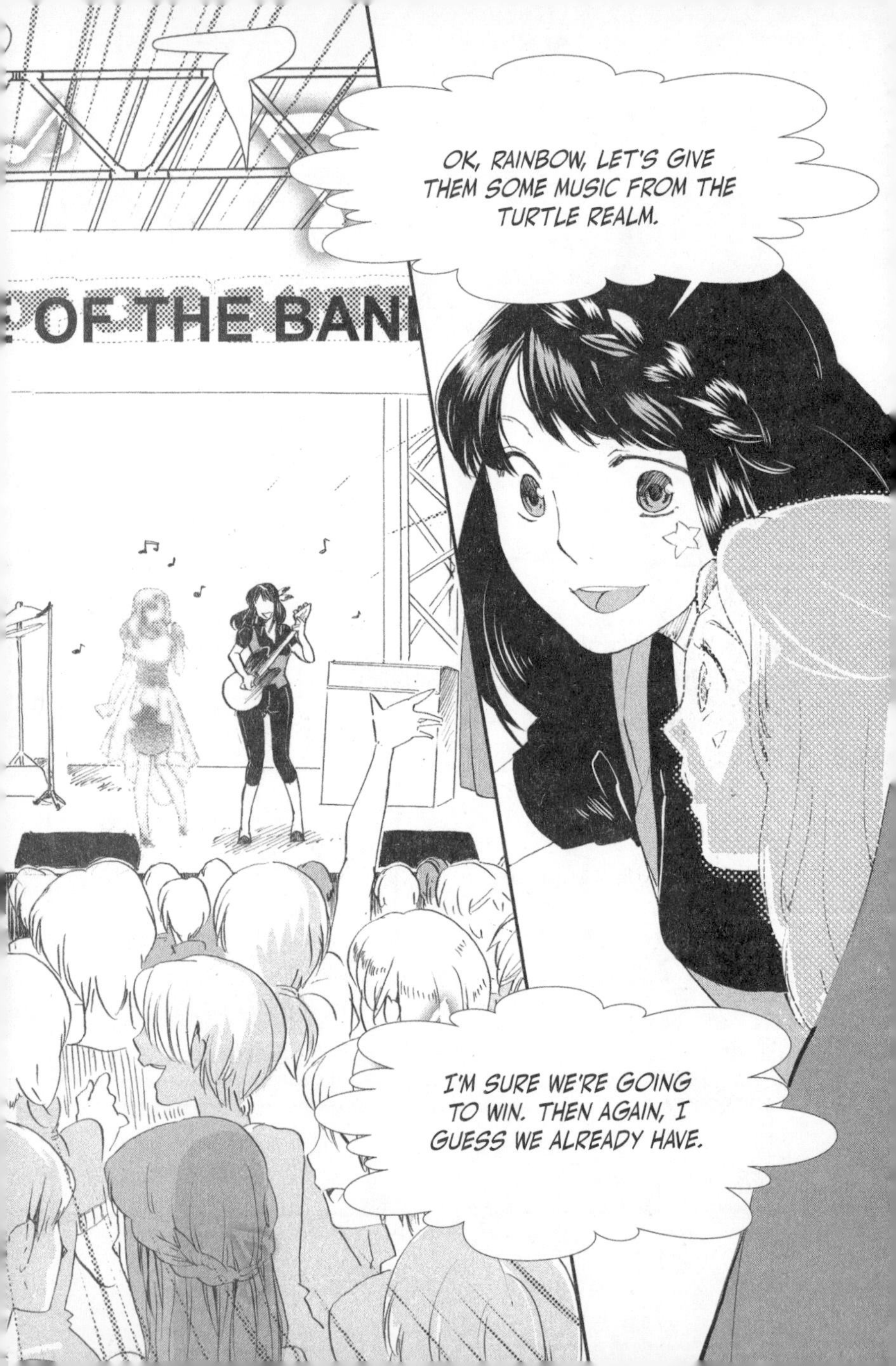
OK, RAINBOW, LET'S GIVE THEM SOME MUSIC FROM THE TURTLE REALM.
I'M SURE WE'RE GOING TO WIN. THEN AGAIN, I GUESS WE ALREADY HAVE.
OF THE BAN

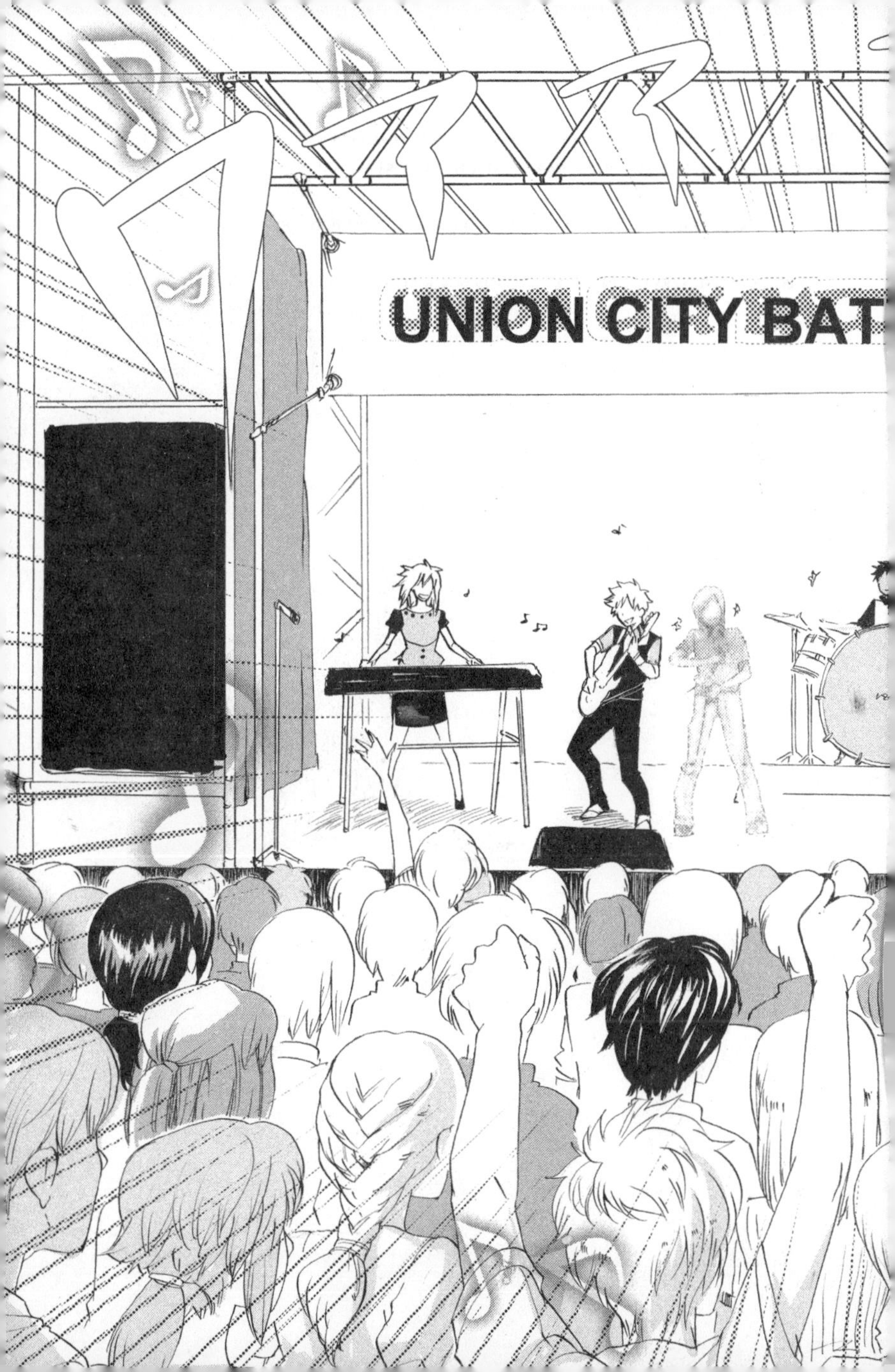
UNION CITY BAT

) INCIDENTS ARE EITHER
USED FICTITIOUSLY.

PRODUCTIONS

ODUCED, TRANSMITTED
OR STORED IN AN INFORMATION RETRIEVAL SYSTEM IN ANY FORM OR BY ANY MEANS,
GRAPHIC, ELECTRONIC, OR MECHANICAL, INCLUDING PHOTOCOPYING, TAPING, AND
RECORDING, WITHOUT PRIOR WRITTEN PERMISSION FROM THE PUBLISHER.

FIRST U.S. EDITION 2015

LIBRARY OF CONGRESS CATALOGING IN PUBLICATION DATA

YOYO
VERMONIA 8, RETURN OF THE QUEEN / BY YOYO.
P. CM. — (VERMONIA)
SUMMARY: FOUR SKATER FRIENDS FULFILL AN ANCIENT PROPHESY AS THEY DISCOVER
THEIR TRUE WARRIOR SPIRITS IN AN EPIC BATTLE TO SAVE THE PLANET OF VERMONIA.
ISBN 978-1-4777-9091-5 (PBK.)
1. PROPHECIES — COMIC BOOKS, STRIPS, ETC. 2. ADVENTURE AND ADVENTURERS —
COMIC BOOKS, STRIPS, ETC. 3. GRAPHIC NOVELS. I. YOYO (GROUP). II. TITLE.
PZ7.7 Y69 2014
741.5—DC23

THIS BOOK WAS TYPESET IN CCLADRONN ITALIC

WINDMILL BOOKS, LLC
303 PARK AVENUE SOUTH, SUITE # 1280
NEW YORK, NY 10010-3657

WWW.VERMONIA.COM